MY HIGHLAND LOVER

A SCOTTISH HISTORICAL TIME TRAVEL
ROMANCE

HIGHLAND HEARTS
BOOK 1

MAEVE GREYSON

MAEVEGREYSON.COM
Magical Romance Sizing Through Time

ALSO BY MAEVE GREYSON

HIGHLAND HEROES SERIES

The Guardian

The Warrior

The Judge

The Dreamer

The Bard

The Ghost

A Yuletide Yearning

Love's Charity

TIME TO LOVE A HIGHLANDER SERIES

Loving Her Highland Thief

Taming Her Highland Legend

Winning Her Highland Warrior

Capturing Her Highland Keeper

Saving Her Highland Traitor

Loving Her Lonely Highlander

Delighting Her Highland Devil

ONCE UPON A SCOT SERIES

A Scot of Her Own

A Scot to Have and to Hold

A Scot to Love and Protect

HIGHLAND PROTECTOR SERIES

Sadie's Highlander

Joanna's Highlander

Katie's Highlander

HIGHLAND HEARTS SERIES

My Highland Lover

My Highland Bride

My Tempting Highlander

My Seductive Highlander

THE MACKAY CLAN

Beyond A Highland Whisper

The Highlander's Fury

A Highlander In Her Past

OTHER BOOKS BY MAEVE GREYSON

Stone Guardian

Eternity's Mark

Guardian of Midnight Manor

CHAPTER 1

Kentucky
Twenty-first Century

And there he was–so heart-stoppingly close her headlights lit up his face. The bare-chested man lifted a muscular arm against the glare, then crouched low and unsheathed the biggest sword Trulie Sinclair had ever seen.

"Holy crap!" She jerked the steering wheel hard to the left.

He bared his teeth in a defensive snarl, then sprang sideways. With the daunting grace of an attacking mountain lion, he swung the massive broadsword in a lethal arc.

Trulie braced for impact. Instinct and adrenaline locked her knees as she stomped the brake to the floor. She sawed the steering wheel back and forth, slinging mud and gravel. The old truck fishtailed, bounced through twin ruts in the narrow road, then sloshed to a stop in a shallow, water-filled ditch.

She clutched the steering wheel until her knuckles ached. Where in blue blazes had that guy come from? And that sword? The high-pitched yowl of an irritated cat and a hissed *"Dammit!"* drowned out the jackhammer pounding of her heart.

Granny and Kismet.

"Are you all right?" Trulie flipped on the interior light, clawed the seatbelt out of the way, and scooted toward the tiny, gray-haired woman clutching the spitting black cat against her chest.

"You know . . ." Granny blinked a few times, then peered over the rims of her cockeyed spectacles. One sparse silver brow ratcheted a notch higher as she resettled back into the dip of the worn seat and straightened her glasses. "You know, Trulie," she started again, pausing to smooth a blue-veined hand down the insulted feline's puffed-up hackles. "If ye wouldna drive like a bat out of hell, ye might dodge things a bit easier."

Trulie blew out a relieved breath. Thank goodness. If her grandmother could still deliver a smart-ass remark, then she was okay. Of course, slipping into her seldom-heard Scottish brogue was a telltale sign that the wild ride hadn't been enjoyed. Granny only reverted to the lilting roll of her *r*'s under duress.

Trulie squirmed around in the confines of the truck and squinted out the back window. Her frazzled reflection stared back at her. "Where did he go?" She flipped off the interior light, then looked out the window again.

Nothing moved but the silhouettes of the treetops swaying beneath a star-spattered sky. The sparsely graveled road reflected silvery gray in the moonlight. No sword-brandishing warrior of muscle was anywhere to be seen. "That guy came out of nowhere. Did you see that freaking sword?" And the package of testosterone swinging it? She kept that part to herself. No sense giving her grandmother any fodder for another lecture.

Using the sleeve of her denim jacket, Trulie wiped away the moisture fogging the window. Damn it all. She couldn't see a thing from inside the truck. "Could you tell if I hit him?" she asked while still staring out the window. "The truck bounced so hard, I don't know if I missed him or not."

Granny didn't answer, just tucked her head closer to the now purring cat and murmured something unintelligible, as though the two sat back home in front of the fire instead of in a ditch out in the middle of the Kentucky woods.

Trulie ground her teeth to keep from cursing as she fumbled around in the floorboard for the flashlight shoved under the edge of the seat. She was in no mood for this crap, and now was not the time for Granny to go silent. She would bet her best batch of homemade soaps that her grandmother knew more about that half-naked mystery than she was letting on.

Granny snuggled closer to the cat and chuckled softly into its shining black fur.

Trulie snorted. That cinched it. The conniving old soul was at it again. Trulie whacked the flashlight against the back of the seat, shook it hard, then shot the beam out the back window.

Of all things to come across in the middle of the night. She knelt in the seat and squinted harder. "I don't see him anywhere. Surely I didn't knock him clear across the road into the other ditch."

She clicked off the flashlight and sat back on her heels. There was no getting around it. Sword or no sword, she was going to have to go look for him. She couldn't live with herself if she didn't find out whether or not the man was okay. She shot a sideways glance at the silver-haired elder still muttering to the cat. "And I wasn't driving that fast and you know it."

Her grandmother didn't look up, just rested back against her travel pillow and grinned.

"What do you think, Kismet?" Granny wrinkled her nose at the cat as she scratched under its chin. The purring feline sat with eyes closed to golden slits and the tip of its tail softly flipping. "Reckon we would be in this ditch with all our inventory busted in the back if our gal had been going a bit slower?"

The old woman lifted her gaze from the cat. Her smile curled to one side as she continued in a more soothing voice directed at Trulie. "And no. You didn't hit him. You just got his attention real good."

Trulie yanked the rusty door handle upward and bounced the door open. Somehow, that backhanded reassurance didn't make her feel any better. An eerie feeling skittered up her spine. What if the man was one of them? She rolled away the uneasiness with a tensed twitch of her shoulders. No. He couldn't be. Rule number one of the time runner's rede: time runners were always female. She silently ticked off the other tenets of the ancient folklore inherited by the Sinclairs:

Bloodline holds the gift to dance across the ages.

From mother to daughter the gift shall pass.

The eldest daughter of each generation shall control the most power.

A loyal familiar, a guardian, shall join the eldest daughter at birth and never leave her side.

Males shall only travel the web when chosen or sent forth by a runner.

That last tenet struck a chord. Trulie turned and glared at Granny. What the hell had the aged prankster done this time?

Granny ignored Trulie, just shook her head at the contented black cat and bent closer to whisper something in its ear. The feline looked over at Trulie, flipped its tail harder, and somehow seemed to snicker.

"Don't start with me, Kismet." Trulie hopped out of the truck and landed knee deep in mud and wet leaves. Cold water rushed in over the tops of her rubber boots and soaked into her socks. She bit the inside of her cheek to keep from damning everything in sight. "Granny, would you please stop plotting with Kismet and tell me what you know about this? You've got that look that always means trouble."

"Why, Trulie. I can't believe you would say such a thing." Granny snorted an insulted huff and straightened in the seat. Her voice echoed with authority as she lowered the much calmer cat onto the seat beside her. "Trust me. You have nothing to worry about. I know those colors. He comes from a fine, upstanding clan. You won't find a force on earth capable of striking fear into a MacKenna."

A fine upstanding clan. A MacKenna. That was all the proof Trulie needed. No wonder Granny wasn't upset. Her grandmother had orchestrated the entire thing. How many times had she begged Granny to stop meddling?

"And that's another thing—" Trulie cursed under her breath as one rubber boot decided to stay behind in the muck when she took a step forward.

"Watch your mouth." Granny shook a warning finger as though Trulie were still a child. "I did not raise you to talk like that."

Trulie gripped the side of the truck, shoved her foot back down into the wet boot, and twisted it free of the sucking mire. The next run to the barn to fetch the cured oils, either Kenna or one of the twins was coming with her. Granny was hereby banned from all visits to the backwoods no matter how much the girls complained. And Kismet could stay home and watch over the girls instead of Karma. She'd had it with that cat. Trulie sloshed forward and bit back another curse word as she whacked her knee on the bent running board of the truck. This night just kept getting better by the minute. "Where do you think I learned those words, Granny?" Trulie doubled over and massaged her throbbing knee.

A louder snort was Granny's only response.

Trulie hoisted herself up into the bed of the truck and yanked open the back window. She wasn't going to allow Granny to avoid the real issue here so easily. A sword-wielding man—one scantily clad in a plaid no less—in the backwoods of Kentucky was not an everyday occurrence. "Would you like to tell me what you know about Mr. Deer-in-the-headlights, or am I going to have to get the truth from him?"

If she could find him. The nagging voice in the back of her mind became louder, insisting she acknowledge the truth: the mysterious man was more than likely one of Granny's better illusions. The old woman had tried for years to teach Trulie how to pluck an individual's consciousness from the past or the future and stitch it so tightly into the present that it appeared as though they were physically there. Trulie had never been quite able to pull it off. Granny, on the other hand, was quite adept at that particular time-runner gift.

"Stay here, Kismet. Our girl's being hardheaded again." Granny pushed open the door and deftly hopped out of the truck. The black cat blinked one glowing eye as though winking in response.

"Granny, please get back in the truck. I don't want you to fall." Trulie straightened and rubbed the corners of her tired, gritty eyes. She was in no mood to go through this again. Granny had shifted into plotting overdrive lately to convince Trulie to accompany her back to the past. Trulie wouldn't mind a brief jaunt back to the thirteenth century, but Granny wanted to pull up stakes and relocate. The stubborn old soul was sick of using the twenty-first century as home. She wanted to return to their roots—permanently. Granny's determined scowl was a dead giveaway. The Sinclair matriarch, prime source of all the stubbornness in their family's DNA, had gone one step further in her plan to travel to thirteenth-century Scotland. She had gone to the extreme of pulling some poor unsuspecting Scot's consciousness out of his own reality and plopped him right in the truck's path.

Trulie eased down into the jumbled truck bed, gingerly stepping through the mess. Wasn't this just lovely? Exactly what she had planned on doing tonight. Tiptoe through shattered glass and slide across a truck bed coated in ruined essential oils. The farther she slogged through broken bottles and overturned cardboard boxes, the lower her spirits sank. Eye-burning fumes filled the night air. The back of the pickup reeked with eucalyptus, peppermint, and patchouli concoctions. A month's work gone in seconds. Just because Granny was determined to permanently relocate them to the past.

A cloud skittered past the swollen moon, bathing the peaceful backwoods in blue-white light and shadow. The thick, dark wood hedging in the river across the way seemed to swallow up the path. Trulie squinted at the sides of the truck, unsure what was shadow and what was new dents. She should've brought the flashlight to see if there was any damage. An irritated huff escaped her. She was in no mood to plow back through the ruined inventory, and Granny needed to get back in the cab until Trulie figured out what to do next. "Granny! Please get back in the truck."

Granny didn't grace her with a response. Head bowed and

focused on her footing, the elder supported herself with a hand on the side of the truck as she picked her way through the ditch.

Trulie resettled her ball cap farther back on her head and looked up and down the deserted stretch of roadway. Nothing out of the ordinary. Just the usual muddy path, with a hump of new spring grass greening up between a pair of pothole-riddled ruts. She tilted her head to one side and strained to hear any out-of-the-ordinary sounds.

The singsong chirrup of spring peepers *cree-creeked* up from the riverbank, echoing through the night. A light breeze whispered through the fluttering tops of newly leafed-out trees, and in the distance, an owl hooted the age old *who-cooks-for-you* call for a mate.

"I told you, you did not hit him, if that's what you're worried about." Granny shook a finger again as she slogged through the water-filled ditch. "One day you will learn to listen to me, gal." The old woman picked up speed as she cleared the muddy water and made her way up the embankment. After dusting both hands across the seat of her baggy jeans, she fisted them atop her narrow hips. "That man was a shadow, Trulie Elizabeth, and you know the truth of it. Have you forgotten everything I've taught you?"

Trulie rubbed the heels of her hands against her temples. She was too tired to be lectured tonight. Granny needed to let up. "No. I have not forgotten a single word you have drilled into me for the past twenty-seven years. But right now, keeping a roof over our heads and food in our bellies is kind of my primary concern."

Her grandmother shot back a glare of disapproval. "Don't you dare take that tone with me, little girl. You know better." Waving toward the spot in the road where the battle-ready man had just been, Granny continued. "It is time we returned to where we began. Listen to me, Trulie Elizabeth Sinclair. We have tarried here long enough, and I am sick to death of arguing with ye about it."

Great. The full name treatment. And a *"ye"* thrown in for good measure. Granny had really worked herself into a snit. Trulie hopped off the tailgate. She scrambled up the slippery bank of wet leaves and tangled honeysuckle vines, stomping globs of wet muck off her boots as she stepped into the road. "We have had this conversation more times than I really want to go over right now. You know my answer. Now call Kismet. We're going to have to walk the rest of the way home. I'll call William in the morning to pull the truck out of the ditch."

"I refuse to believe my own granddaughter would deny my dying wish." Granny's face puckered into a tighter scowl as she glanced back toward the truck. Kismet immediately wiggled through the sliding back window, nimbly danced along the side of the truck bed, and with two graceful leaps joined them on the road.

Trulie sucked in a deep breath and stared up at the winking stars peeping through the tops of the trees. Her grandmother had to be the most stubborn force on earth. She yanked off her cap and raked her fingers through her tangled hair as she repeated the argument she had chanted to Granny for the past six months. "First: you are not dying."

Trulie shivered. Her cold, soaked feet squished with every step. "And next: our roots, both mine and the girls, are here in this century." She spun a finger in an all-encompassing circle. "This is the only place and time any of us really consider home base. I kind of like it here and I think they do too . . . most days." Well . . . she liked it here when her feet were dry, her truck wasn't in a ditch, and her latest batch of inventory was in clean sparkling bottles lined up on a shelf at the shop.

Kismet trotted regally between them, her long, black tail held high, the end crooked into a question mark. The cat glanced up at Trulie and flicked an ear as though dismissing her words as pure nonsense.

From now on, the cat stayed home. Karma didn't have a judgy bone in his body. Kismet could use some how-to-play-nice lessons from the sweet-natured dog.

Granny strode along with her thin arms swinging. Her brisk pace belied the fact the tiny woman was on the downhill side of her seventies. Maybe. The chronological age of an elder Sinclair time runner was always pretty much a wild guess. If a runner skated between centuries often enough, they could cheat death for quite a while. A curt sideways glance confirmed that Granny agreed with the cat.

The senior huffed out a frustrated growl and quickened her stomping pace. Glancing down at the cat skipping along beside her, she flipped both hands upward. "She just doesn't get it, does she, Kismet? Our gal is never going to learn all the ways 'cause neither of us will live long enough to teach her."

The cat aimed another disdainful smirk at Trulie.

"Keep it up, Kismet." Trulie walked faster to catch up with her grandmother and the feline. "As soon as we get home, I am going to tell Karma where you hide your treats."

The sleek cat flattened her ears against her dark head. Her golden eyes narrowed and she whipped her tail, clearly telling Trulie to kiss her ass.

"We must return to the past." Granny exploded with short, impatient huffs as she clumped through a puddle. "It is very . . . important and we must do it soon."

Trulie drew in a deep breath of the crisp night air and forced herself to remain calm and keep the frustration out of her voice. She loved and respected Granny with all her heart, but this incessant badgering was getting old. She came to a halt, pulled her denim jacket tighter around her, and waited for Granny to realize Kismet was the only one still walking beside her.

It didn't take long. Granny stopped, spun around, and glared back at Trulie. "Well? Now what?" The senior's tone had taken on the color of a full-blown scolding.

Trulie widened her stance and tried to ignore the sudden feeling that she and Granny were facing off like a couple of gunfighters in the Old West. "You know how much I love you. I understand you miss the old Scotland, but we belong here. We belong in this century. We're pretty much settled, and life isn't too bad when our home remedies aren't sloshing around in the back of the truck."

Trulie waited, then took a step toward Granny. "Please forget about relocating. I don't want to uproot us again. We are settled. Home base for all of our trips through time is right here."

She decided to aim dead square at Granny's conscience. "And you know you can't time-jump alone anymore. And you're not able to maneuver the web as point beacon and keep all of us connected to you like you could when you were younger."

Trulie scuffed the toe of her boot in the mud. She hated pointing out anyone's weaknesses, especially Granny's. "I haven't jumped as beacon enough to connect with more than one or two travelers. If I try any more than that, I'm afraid I'll scatter the lot of us across a string of centuries. If I ran beacon to take you back, we would have to leave Kenna and the girls in this time. Alone. Would you feel good about deserting the rest of your grandchildren? Do you really think they would be okay without us?" There. That should stall out this round. Trulie forced herself not to back down. She hated using guilt on Granny, but it was the most effective ammunition she had.

Granny's shoulders sagged and her gaze sank to the patch of road between them. Her voice fell to just above a whisper as she stared at the ground. "I do not want you permanently anchored in this time, Trulie. Your babies are not meant to come from this disturbing patch of history. This place is temporary. A place of trial to help us grow and strengthen." Granny bent and ran a slightly shaking hand across Kismet's arched back. "Kenna and the twins will be fine if we have to leave them here for a bit. Kenna's grown and the girls aren't far behind. Don't think I haven't got plans for them. I mean to see all my girls properly settled before I move on."

Trulie released the breath she had held. So that was it. Granny was afraid Trulie was about to settle down and sink her roots even deeper into the current century with a man Granny didn't like. Trulie's relationship with Dan had always irritated the older woman. For what reason, Trulie wasn't quite sure. Dan was . . . okay. Most of the time. "Dan is a good man, Granny. He will take good care of me. Of all of us."

Granny stormed forward. She locked her spindly legs into sparring stance and raised a shaking fist. "Do ye really love him, Trulie? Does yer love for him make yer throat ache with tears if ye canna be near him? Do ye pine to hear the rumble of his deep voice whispering yer name in the darkness?"

Granny stomped another step closer. Her accent thickened and her voice became shriller with every word. "Say it, Trulie. Tell me the truth. If ye thought ye would never see Dan again, would ye rather die than live a day without him? Tell me. Tell me Dan is the other half of yer soul and I will never talk about jumping back again."

Granny's tone hit a low, ominous knell as she pointed a knobby finger at Trulie's heart. "But don't ye dare lie to me, gal. Because if ye do, ye willna be lying to me, ye will just be lying to yerself."

Granny's sharp brogue, paired with the fire in her eyes, shoved Trulie back a step. Apparently, it wasn't Dan that Granny had a problem with; it was whether the relationship was strong enough to satisfy Granny's standards.

Trulie swallowed hard. Did she really love Dan? She tried to conjure up tingly, I-can't-live-without-him thoughts of Dan—tall, gangly, always-preoccupied Dan. And she failed. She couldn't muster anything more than a vague, foggy feeling of *meh*. Why couldn't she bring his long, narrow face and soft, brown eyes into focus and feel . . . something? At least she thought his eyes were brown. Weren't they?

Instead, she saw eyes fierce with rage. Strange-colored eyes, an unusual shade she had never seen. They were blue. Sort of. They reminded her of a night sky exploding with tendrils of brilliant-white lightning.

Instead of Dan's lanky, underfed form, Trulie remembered corded, muscular arms bulging like banded whisky barrels as they wielded a sword as long as she was tall.

She started to speak, but then closed her mouth again. Dan was safe. Dan was security. But no, Dan was not her love, and Granny already knew the truth of it. Granny had always told Trulie never to settle, and here she was about to do that very thing. Trulie shook away the thought. No. She was not settling. She was just making sure they were all taken care of. What the devil was wrong with that? "Dan will take good care of us, Granny. Don't worry. It will be all right."

"It will not be all right!" Granny stomped her tiny boot hard against the muddy ground. "I will be damned if I allow ye to break my oath to yer mother. Ye will not settle for safe old Dan. Yer true future, the future waiting to set your soul on fire, can only be found in the past."

~

SCOTLAND

The Highlands—Thirteenth Century

GRAY MACKENNA JERKED free of the hypnotic depths of the roiling orange embers. A cold sweat peppered his body. He couldn't stop his hand from shaking as he wiped the moisture from his face. Damnation. Had it been real or just a vision? "What the hell are ye playing at, Tamhas? I bade ye show me the traitor and instead ye throw me in the path of some unearthly beast?"

Tamhas didn't look up from the worktable. His gnarled hands patiently twisted the worn stone pestle into the mixture of herbs and oils in the chipped mortar. The only sound breaking the silence of the room was the rhythmic thump and grind of stone against stone and the crackling flames consuming the wood in the hearth.

Gray shuddered. He hated the sound of fire. "Have ye gone deaf or have ye decided to ignore yer chieftain?"

The stooped old man brought the herbal concoction closer to his nose. He squinted down into the bowl, barely shook his head, then leaned once again into the grinding motion. When Tamhas still failed to respond, Gray strode to the door of the cramped dwelling and threw it open wide to the cold, clear night. He needed air. Fresh, clean air to chase away the disturbing vision wrought by Tamhas's strange incense and the smoke-filled chamber.

"Return to the bench, m'chieftain, so I might treat yer wounds."

The old man's words reawakened the throbbing pain burning down one side of Gray's back. "Uncover the window first. I canna stomach more of yer wicked smoke." Gray remained rooted to the threshold of the open door. The muted greens and grays of the night-shrouded Highlands rolled out before him.

He glanced back at the old man still standing behind the bench. Perhaps he should have sought his answers from the only thing soothing his soul of late. His beloved Highlands would have come far closer to revealing the fiend seeking the end of his clan than the damned old man with his magic and strange smoke. "I need clean air, old man. Either throw open the shutter or step outside to treat my wounds. Yer wretched cave seeks to smother me."

"As ye wish," Tamhas said. A muffled thud was followed by a beam of golden light pouring from the small round portal carved into the hillside.

"Come now, my chieftain," the old one called again. "Once the poultice draws the pain from yer burns, the smoke will no longer offend ye."

Gray slowly turned back into the room. The low ceiling of the domesticated cave nearly brushed the top of his head. The hovel was so small that if he swung his sword in a circle, the tip of the blade would surely carve a line across each of the walls. A shiver burned through the blistered skin covering more than half his back and spreading down one side. Gray flinched. The pain of raw, stinging flesh didn't bother him nearly as much as the sensation of walking into a tomb. How could Tamhas endure such a place?

As he straddled the bench in front of the hearth, Gray turned to one side, keeping his face away from the fire. Never again did he desire to see that strange monster lurking among those coals. He leaned forward and gripped the rough-hewn edges of the large wooden bench and scanned the contents of the room. "Why do ye stay in this cave when I swore ye could have yer choice of towers in the keep?"

Tamhas hugged the oversized mortar to his chest, still stirring the oily substance as he hitched his way across the cluttered room. "I told ye I have no desire to live in an infested keep." The old man squinted down into the bowl, frowned, then rapped the pestle hard against one side of the mortar. He raised it again, then nodded at the contents. "Once ye rid the place of its vermin, I shall be honored to claim a tower."

What the hell was the man talking about? There were no vermin in the keep. Gray shook his head. "Ye are daft, old man. I admit there might be a wee mousie or two but ye can hardly claim the place infested."

"Aye. Well . . ." Tamhas scooped up a handful of the muddy brown mixture and worked the concoction between his arthritic fingers. "Once ye rid the place of the wicked Aileas, I shall deem the infestation under control." Tamhas motioned toward the length of the bench in front of Gray. "Stretch forward, my chieftain so I might heal ye."

Aileas again. Gray clenched his teeth as he leaned over the bench. Gripping the thickness of the plank tighter, he locked his elbows. Aileas's cold, haughty face appeared as soon as he closed his eyes. What the hell had Father ever seen in that vile woman?

"A plump dowry overflowing with cattle, land, and coin." Tamhas splatted a cold slimy hand onto the center of Gray's back. His bemused chuckling filled the room as he glopped another handful of the muck down Gray's side. "Yet and still . . . yer father had to be one hell of a man or blind with drink to bed the likes of that woman." He poured more of the slime across Gray's shoulder.

"Dammit, man!" Gray stiffened and dug his nails into the wooden plank. A shiver burned deeper through his wounds as gooseflesh rippled across his skin. "Why the hell did ye not warn me the dung would be so cold?"

"Ye nay asked."

Gray sucked in a deep breath and blew it out slowly. "And how many times must I tell ye to stay out of my mind? When I seek yer counsel, I shall speak it. Aloud."

"Forgive me, my chieftain." Another chilly handful of sliminess across his ribs followed the apology.

Gray closed his eyes and bowed his head, forcing himself to relax. Unfortunately, Tamhas spoke the truth. His father's marriage to

Aileas had filled their coffers and stables, and increased the lands of the clan quite nicely. That had to be the only reason his sire would take such an unpleasant woman to wife. Well . . . the massive dowry and the fact Aileas's father had been overly persistent to gain an alliance with Clan MacKenna. The man's messengers had plied the keep weekly for his father's decision regarding a union.

"If ye had a daughter such as Aileas, would ye not pay dearly to be rid of her?"

Tamhas made a valid point. "Ye canna resist traipsing through my thoughts, can ye, old man?" Gray relaxed across the length of the bench and allowed his arms to dangle free on either side. He had no idea what was in the nasty mess smeared across his flesh, but once the initial shock of the chill wore off, it felt damn good. The pain of the burns disappeared.

Tamhas shuffled back to the worktable and set the mortar down. "I hear yer thoughts as clear as my own because we share a blood-line." Tamhas paused. His voice softened as he fingered a faded bit of braided hair looped around his neck. "Ye have truly done my sister proud."

Gray swallowed hard against the sudden aching lump threatening to choke off his air. "I wouldha rather saved her life than done her proud." Gray shifted on the bench and turned his face to the wall. "Pray dinna put more wood on the fire until I leave. I canna stomach the roar of the flames. They hold the sound of *Máthair*'s screams."

"Aye, my chieftain." Tamhas's voice held a hollow ring; he cleared his throat with an uneasy cough.

"Show me the traitor, Tamhas. I want the one who set the fire that took my mother's life. I want the one who lured my father to his death. I shall not rest until I hold the traitor's neck between my hands." Gray pushed himself up from the bench and swung around to a seated position. "Ye showed me a monster. A roaring beast with great glowing eyes. Why would ye do such a thing when ye kent that I seek to avenge the death of yer sister and the chieftain ye loved enough to call brother?"

Tamhas stood taller, stroking his gnarled fingers through the thickness of his graying beard. Eyes narrowed, his face darkened into a scowl. "I showed ye the key. Ye need nothing more to find the answers ye seek."

"Ye showed me nothing. Ye showed me some unholy vision ye might use to scare trespassers away from yer cave!"

Tamhas slammed the stone mortar atop the table. His words rumbled out in a deep, throaty growl, echoing with barely controlled rage. "I showed ye the only answer ye are prepared to see at this time! I would never lead ye astray." Every bowl, crucible, and pot in the small room rattled on the shelves. Candle flames danced and shivered atop their dripping tapers as though frightened by the power in the old man's voice.

Gray lunged up from the bench and yanked his plaid off the wooden peg beside the door. "No more of this foolishness." He had been a damn fool to come here. He should have known Tamhas would be of no help. How many times had *Máthair* told him her brother had long ago been addled by his unnatural gifts and the loss of the one woman he had ever dared love?

Reaching into his sporran, Gray pulled out a pouch heavy with coin. He hefted the small leather bag in one hand and returned the old man's scowl. "I thank ye for the poultice for the burns, but know this, Uncle. Never again will I make the mistake of seeking yer counsel." He tossed the bag onto the table between Tamhas's fists and turned to leave.

"She will be here soon," Tamhas said in a low, ominous tone.

"Who will be here soon?"

"The one ye need. Yer answer."

Gray shook his head and yanked open the door. "Enough, old man. No. More. Riddles."

Tamhas shrugged and turned away to stoke the fire. "As ye wish, my chieftain."

CHAPTER 2

Hostility. Prejudice. Loathing. Negative energy flashed an unpleasant tingle across Trulie's senses. She didn't bother turning from the shelves of multicolored bottles, beeswax candles, and neatly labeled paper bundles of herbs and soaps. Dark emotions so strongly transmitted before the shop door even opened could only belong to one person: the hateful Mrs. Hagerty.

A low-pitched growl rumbled from the enormous black dog standing beside Trulie. The warning confirmed her suspicion. Karma, her faithful guardian, liked Mrs. Hagerty even less than she did.

The tiny brass bell hanging atop the shop door jingled out a cheery alarm that Mrs. Hagerty had invaded the fragrant confines of Trulie's homeopathic store. The sour-faced woman slammed the door hard and glared around the brightly lit shop. Her nose lifted slightly, as did her dark, painted brows. She short-stepped forward with angry, clicking steps to ensure all in the room properly noticed her arrival.

"Good morning, Mrs. Hagerty. How are you today?" Trulie pasted a welcoming smile on her face and braced herself. The woman looked more unpleasant than usual.

"I do not have time for your fake attitude, Miss Sinclair." Mrs. Hagerty curled her heavily painted lips into a sneer that revealed her large teeth were smeared with the same crimson. Any time the woman spoke, she looked as though she smelled a stink. "Where is your grandmother? I demand to see her this very instant. I have a bone to pick with that vile woman."

Trulie's cheeks ached with the polite smile. She would be damned straight to hell before she gave Mrs. Hagerty the satisfaction of a reaction. "My grandmother isn't in the shop today. Is there something I could help you with? A soothing tea for your nerves, perhaps? Some lavender oil to help you relax?"

Mrs. Hagerty stomped closer to the counter. She slapped a plump hand down on top of the glass. "How dare you mock me." She slowly swayed back and forth like an overfed cobra about to strike. "I know about your family." The woman paused long enough to rake a gaze of disgust from the tips of Trulie's brightly painted toenails to the top of her ponytailed head." I know what the lot of you really are, and I will not rest until I cleanse this town of you and your trash."

Hackles raised, Karma edged closer to Trulie and sounded a guttural warning growl.

"You better keep that beast away from me!" Mrs. Hagerty jabbed a gaudy painted nail toward the dog's shining black nose.

"Karma is harmless," Trulie replied. She rested a staying hand on Karma's broad head. He really didn't need to bite the woman. The old cow was probably poisonous.

Mrs. Hagerty pressed her round body tighter against the counter and struggled to peer over it at the growling dog. "Is that one of those pit bulls? Or a Rottweiler? You know I convinced the council to pass an ordinance against those monstrosities. I don't think you should keep him in a place of business. I think I shall have animal control come over immediately and check his papers. That will put an end to his nonsense." She excitedly drummed the tip of one manicured nail on the glass case and smirked at Karma. "One shot in your wicked heart and you will never growl again, mutt."

Enough. It was bad enough the woman hated Granny, but

nobody threatened sweet, lovable Karma. Trulie pulled the dog closer, leaning against his reassuring weight as she returned Mrs. Hagerty's hateful glare. "Animals are not born evil or mean. Humans torture them into that disposition. And if you don't have any business here other than insulting my grandmother or threatening my dog, I suggest you relieve us of your unwanted company."

Mrs. Hagerty's eyes widened behind the rhinestone spectacles perched on the end of her hooked nose. "I have never been so insulted in all my life. I don't have to stand here and listen to such."

"You're right. You don't." An effortless, wicked smile felt quite pleasant as Trulie nodded toward the exit. "Don't let the doorknob hit you where the good Lord split you."

The few customers perusing the shelves tittered and snorted behind their hands. Mrs. Hagerty puffed up even further, stomped back across the room and slammed the door so hard upon her exit that everything on the shelves rattled and swayed.

"Bitch," Trulie muttered.

"Trulie! Such language." Granny playfully shook a finger as she emerged from the back room. Kismet trotted in beside her, greeting everyone with a trilling, happy *pprrtt*.

"How long have you been back there?" Trulie's mood lightened as Kismet's loud purring vibrated through the shop. The cat rubbed against the still-irritated dog while weaving in and out between his front legs. The bright mood faded as every customer quickly filed out without buying a thing. As the last person closed the door, the soft jingling of the bell confirmed Trulie's assumption. Everyone feared the backlash of Mrs. Hagerty's wrath. No one would go against the woman.

"I heard every word the old crow cawed." Granny took an apron off the hook behind the counter and tied it around her waist. A solemn look replaced her grin as she stepped behind the counter and laid a soft hand atop Trulie's. "You know she won't rest until you and I are ruined and gone. Since her money has never brought her happiness, she uses it to spread misery and make everyone around her hate life as much as she does. It's time we resettled to another time. I know in my heart if you and I left, things would be much easier here for Kenna and the girls until it's their time to join us in the past." Granny softly chuckled and shook her head. "For some unfathomable reason that woman steers clear of Kenna."

"Kenna has dirt on her. She caught Hagerty's housekeeper buying some of our blackberry elixir. The woman fessed up that Hagerty's a closet drinker. Poor thing lost her job once Hagerty found out she had told Kenna she likes her elixir spiked with whisky." Surely Granny wasn't using old Hagerty as an excuse to retreat to the past. "Since when do you let somebody like Hagerty run you off? I thought you enjoyed one-upping people like her. And now you want to leave Kenna and the girls here? Alone to fight their own battles?"

"We wouldn't be alone. Granny showed us how to use the fire portal. It's easier to get a hold of you and Granny with that than if we use a cell phone. You don't have to worry about a crappy signal or a dead battery with the fire portal." A curvy brunette in tight-fitting jeans bounced out of the back room. She was followed by two auburn-haired girls still too young to have many curves, but old enough that their physiques promised beautiful things to come.

"Yeah, Trulie." One of the green-eyed twins agreed. "Half the time your phone is dead and Granny won't use one. She thinks they're part of a conspiracy for the government to track down time runners and harness our powers for warmongering."

The other twin skipped over and nudged Trulie's shoulder with an affectionate punch. "And who do you think helps Granny with her 'pester Hagerty' campaign? We're not as innocent and helpless as we look."

Granny looped an arm around the shoulders of the oldest girl and hugged her with a shake and a wink. "See? Kenna, Lilia, and Mairi would be just fine. If they need us, they know how to reach us. All they need is a roaring fire with plenty of red-hot coals." Granny nodded to Kenna and hugged her tighter with a gentle shake. "Actually, any source of heat will do, but coals give the best reception in the portal."

Granny's smile faded as she gave the four girls a meaningful look, then strode across the room. "I need to see the lot of you settled." She pointed a finger at Trulie. "And you're the first, young lady. You don't belong here, and if you search your heart, you'll see the truth of it." Granny opened the cash register drawer and pawed through the plentiful receipts, dollars and coinage. "The shop is doing well in spite of not being endorsed by Hagerty the Horrible." Granny paused, winked at Mairi, and nodded once toward Lilia. "Kenna's twenty years old. Old enough to manage her sisters. All the girls will be just fine. They know every remedy and recipe for our twenty-first-century snake oil that keeps folks coming back for more."

"Homeopathic remedies and aromatherapy oils." Trulie struggled not to rise to Granny's bait. Granny was wearing her down and she damn well knew it. "The recipes are yours. You know the stuff really works."

Granny turned and gave Trulie a look she knew all too well. As she handed Kenna the oversized wad of credit card receipts, Granny added the final barb. "Your precious Dan won't protect you against the likes of Hagerty either. I've seen how he fawns all over that snobby woman and her connections. When she convinces him you are nothing better than the doormat she wipes her shoes on, what do you think he will do? No granddaughter of mine would ever accept being treated like dirt."

Kenna, Lilia, and Mairi collectively eased away to the far side of the room and pretended to dust and straighten items on the perfectly clean glass shelves.

Cowards. Trulie glared at her three sisters. She'd had enough of Granny's nettling. It was time to clear the air. "I want the truth once and for all. What the hell is going on? You can't be that concerned about me hooking up with Dan."

Karma and Kismet laid back their ears and trotted across the shop to hide behind the safety of the girls' legs. Trulie rounded the counter. She was on a roll. One way or another, they were going to settle this. Today. "You have always talked about someday resettling to the past but in the past six months you have shifted your nagging into overdrive. I want the truth. Plain and simple. What is the deal?

Why now? You're gnawing on me worse than a dog worrying an old bone and I am tired of it."

Trulie crossed the room, flipped the Open sign on the door to the Closed side, and yanked down the shade. "What is it with you? Just tell me the truth instead of all this maneuvering. Why are you so adamant about permanently moving back to the past? Why does it have to be now?" She couldn't understand it. What was this burning need Granny suddenly seemed to have to see Trulie settled in the past? It was almost as though she were afraid of something, and that just didn't make sense. Granny feared nothing.

Hadn't the tough-as-nails woman jumped to an unknown future with two little girls and an unhealthy set of newborn twins to honor her only daughter's dying wish? Trulie remembered the family's first jump through time better than any of the other jumps Granny had led. Before that initial jump, memories of the first twelve years of her life were faded and patchy at best. Granny had filled in the blanks about those early years, and from all Trulie learned, Granny was an unwavering force.

How many times had Granny told her how Mother had died bringing Lilia and Mairi into the world back in the thirteenth century? How Father had been so despondent over the loss of Mother, he had pressed the unhealthy, blue-tinged babies into Granny's arms and begged her to do whatever it took to save his children? How many times had Granny told her how her parents' bond had been so strong, Father had climbed down into the grave beside Mother and ordered his men to bury them both?

Trulie shivered and rubbed at a tiny scar at the base of her throat that always ached whenever she thought about the past. Granny had saved her life too, by bringing them all to a future where a child's underdeveloped heart could be repaired with a simple surgery. How could the woman who had endured so much be afraid of something as insignificant Mrs. Hagerty and her whining lackey?

"I fear nothing for myself, Trulie." Granny twirled the white stick hanging from the curtain rod between her bent fingers. Her frown deepened as the window blinds slowly closed. "But for all of you, I fear much once I am gone and there are none like us left in this particular patch of time to protect and teach you."

Trulie caught Kenna's eye and nodded toward Lilia and Mairi. "We won't forget the old ways, Granny. I promise we'll be all right." Trulie wrapped an arm around Granny's shoulders, noticing for the first time how thin and frail the old woman seemed.

"You don't belong here, Trulie. None of us really do. This troubling patch of time is good for nothing but a training ground." A heavy sigh shuddered through Granny, shaking her against Trulie. "But you, Trulie, especially right now, must travel back. 'Tis time to put the wheel in motion. If you stay, you will suffer. We all will. Greatly." Granny gently slid out from under Trulie's arm and bent to scoop Kismet up against her chest. "Look into your heart, Trulie. Look hard and you'll understand exactly what I mean."

Hugging the cat, Granny slowly walked across the room. A troubled look darkened her face when she reached the back-room door and turned back to face them. "One last thing I want you to know before you give me your final refusal. The time grows near for my last leap, and I will be damned if I make that crossing alone out of this godforsaken century."

CHAPTER 3

"Fearghal wishes to see his brother. Let us pass. 'Tis our right to see the chieftain."

Gray closed his eyes against the nasal voice shattering the pleasant comradery of the great hall. As much as he wished to bar the owner of the voice from his presence, his conscience refused to grant him leave to do so.

"Allow Lady Aileas entry, Colum!" His shout echoed the length of the high-ceilinged room and rang out into the bailey. All the better. At least those who might escape Aileas's presence had now received ample warning.

"May the gods strike the woman mute or have mercy and strike me deaf." The hounds sprawled at Gray's feet lifted their heads as though nodding in complete agreement. Gray dug his thumbs hard into his throbbing temples. He was in no mood for another bout of petty complaints from Lady Aileas and her simpering son.

The dried rushes spread about the stone floors hissed out whispered warnings with every sweep of Aileas's drab, heavy skirts. The great, hairy dogs lying on either side of Gray's ornate chieftain's chair perked their heads higher, then groaned with a unified whine when Aileas passed the final column and neared the center of the room.

Gray dropped a hand to the nearest dog's head and buried his fingers in the thick, wiry fur. "I feel the same way, lad. But we must be tolerant of the past chieftain's wife."

The hound disagreed with a low, rumbling growl.

Both dogs lumbered to their feet and retreated to the passage connecting the meeting hall to the outer kitchens.

Cowards. Gray glared at the retreating beasts, all the while wishing he could join them. Ever since the *dearbh fhine* had named him *Tànaiste* to the chieftainship rather than Fearghal, his father's only legitimate son, Aileas had seen fit to test his patience, along with his leadership, at every opportunity.

The bitter woman had never publicly denounced him as the bastard son of her dead husband's leman, but sources reported she had shared this opinion privately on more than one occasion.

A sad smile pinched the corner of Gray's mouth as he straightened in the chair. Damned if he wouldn't wager his best warhorse that his parents had reunited on the other side and stood together at this very moment . . . laughing because he had been left behind to deal with the unpleasant Aileas.

The tall, gangly woman lumbered forward. She kept one oversized hand locked in the crooked arm of the puny young man stumbling along beside her. Aileas's wispy hair had escaped its combs, fluttering about her perspiring face and wide shoulders like a veil of mud-brown cobwebs. The exertion of dragging her clumsy son the length of the hall had reddened the broken capillaries covering her bulbous nose and her sallow, pockmarked cheeks.

When the woman came to a halt in front of the main table, she yanked her ill-fitting dress back into place across her sturdy, big-boned frame.

As he had more times than he cared to remember, Gray wondered how his father could have ever bedded such a woman and managed to seed a son. There was not enough whisky in all the Highlands to blind a man to the undeniable truth that the Lady Aileas more closely resembled a surly blacksmith than a comely chieftain's wife.

"My chieftain." Aileas coughed out the word "chieftain" as though it had lodged crossways in her throat and she was trying to hack it loose. "Fearghal is greatly distressed over the treatment he received this verra morning at the stables."

Gray shifted his gaze to the nervous man twitching at Aileas's side. Gray almost felt sorry for the poor excuse for a Scot. Almost. Fearghal might be a sniveling wimp, but he also possessed a cruel streak Gray had witnessed on several occasions. Fearghal's preferred method of bolstering his own confidence was to torment those less fortunate than himself. Fearghal was a bully. In the worst possible ways, the unpleasant oaf mirrored the cruelties of his hateful mother. Gray rolled his shoulders against the wave of disgust Fearghal and Aileas always triggered. It could not be that he and Fearghal shared the same father.

"What distressed ye this time, Fearghal?" Gray struggled to keep the contempt out of his tone as he straightened in the chair and feigned interest in Fearghal's plight. His father's words rang in his ears: a chieftain is known by his actions as well as his word.

"They . . ." Fearghal's annoying voice stalled out. He swallowed so hard his Adam's apple skittered up and down his long narrow neck like a mouse scurrying beneath the bedclothes. His wide-set eyes darted nervously to the right of the room where several of Gray's men were seated. "Yer guard would not grant my wish to ride one of the horses that best suits my station. The man dared suggest I take one of the children's training mares."

Fearghal's pompous statement soured Gray's mood further. What arrogance. Gray did not doubt Fearghal's claim. The last time the dunce had been given a decent horse, Fearghal had returned on foot and the valuable horse had never been seen again.

By this time, Colum, Clan MacKenna's chief man-at-arms, had assumed his usual position beside Gray's chair. With one hand resting atop the pommel of his sword, Colum stepped forward and joined the conversation in a tone leaving no doubt as to how little he thought of Fearghal. "Our clan's stables can nay afford to turn our stock of best-bred horses free into the Highlands. Too many thieves lay in wait to claim them for their own." Colum jerked his chin toward Aileas's scowling face. "Perhaps yer mother might grant ye access to her decrepit mount or mayhap even her closed wagon. Yer arse might stay seated atop a wagon's board better than it stays planted in a saddle."

Gray appreciated Colum saying what he could not. He shifted in his seat and cleared his throat. "That'll do, Colum. Thank ye."

The tips of Fearghal's huge ears darkened to a deep red. Gray would not be surprised if the fool's head burst into flames.

Aileas growled and surged forward, squaring her stout body in front of Fearghal like a lioness defending her young. Her meaty fists trembled against the dark folds of her skirts. "Will ye just sit there then? Will ye not demand respect toward my Fearghal? Toward yer own brother—the chieftain's *true* son, no less?" Aileas's mouth snapped shut and her eyes widened as she realized what she had just said.

"Take care, Stepmother," Gray warned in a low voice. "I am chosen chief to Clan MacKenna." He had always defended Aileas and her worthless son to the elders, insisting his father's widow and her son be treated with honor and respect. But if Aileas decided to publicly challenge him, the two would be stripped of his protection immediately.

"Give the order," Colum hissed. The slightest wave of his hand caused every warrior seated across the room to rise and step forward. "Give the order, my chieftain," Colum repeated. "And we shall relieve your presence of this offensiveness. Permanently."

Aileas's trembling jowls and watery eyes resurrected what little compassion Gray still possessed for the two. He raised a hand and spoke to the men without taking his unblinking gaze from his step-mother's face. "Nay." He barely shook his head. "I feel sure the Lady Aileas realizes the rashness of her words. I am certain she claims a mother's concern for her child as the reason she forgets herself."

"Aye." Aileas bobbed her head and stood taller while her cold, proud gaze swept across those standing in the room. "I dare say any of ye would not do any less if yer child's honor had been so sullied."

Gray slowly rose from his seat. For some strange reason, the tender healing flesh of the burns across his shoulders had suddenly begun to tingle. A warning, perhaps? Gray shrugged away the feeling and motioned toward Fearghal where he stood trembling behind his mother. "No more horses, Fearghal. If ye must travel, ye will go by wagon until ye learn to better stay astride."

Aileas emitted a strained groaning noise from deep within her throat.

"Ye would say something, Lady Aileas?" Gray waited. It was Aileas's move. He would not have his authority questioned further.

"Nay," Aileas snapped.

"Nay?" Gray repeated sharply.

"Nay." Aileas's voice softened and she respectfully lowered her gaze in as humble a bow as she could manage. "I would say nothing more, *my chieftain.*"

～

"I DON'T UNDERSTAND why you don't want to go. You've always loved time-jumping and enjoy exploring different centuries even more. How many history books did old Mr. Brown make you copy to the blackboard because you argued they were wrong? Granny taught us more in all our jumps than Mr. Brown could ever imagine." An impatient *tappity-tap-tap* bounced against the loose plank flooring of the outside shed attached to the old barn.

Kenna. Even if the girl hadn't spoken, Trulie would know it was her from the rabbit-kicking thump against the wood floor. Whenever Kenna didn't or couldn't control the outcome of a situation, the tapping and jiggling of her right foot transmitted her frustration better than Morse code. Trulie didn't bother turning around. Instead, she slid on the heavy gloves, clicked the striker, and lit the propane torch. Maybe if she ignored Kenna, her sister would go away.

"I am not going away. You know better." Rusted springs squeaking in protest told Trulie that Kenna had just planted herself in the lean-to's only chair.

Trulie settled the safety glasses more comfortably on her nose, touched the solder to the joint of copper tubing, and carefully applied the heat of the torch. "I'm busy, Kenna. I'm behind a full month in orders since I lost that truckload of oils and I won't be able to restock the shelves in the store if I fill all the website orders first. If you're not going to help me get this second distiller going, then go check the drying racks and see if they're ready to be rotated. I don't have time for idle chatter. Either make yourself useful or go away."

The worn springs of the chair groaned again and the old wood comprising the frame of it crackled and popped as though about to disintegrate. Trulie gritted her teeth and leaned in closer to the expensive coils of copper pipe. If Kenna would get off Granny's meddling team and help, they could get this second distiller built in no time and replace the lost stock. Trulie clicked off the torch, pushed the safety glasses to the top of her head, and scrutinized her work. Not too shabby. This one would be producing essential oils in no time. Now, if she could just resolve the uneasiness gnawing at the back of her mind just as smoothly. A growing restlessness, a sense of opportunities slipping away, stirred deep inside her. She felt like she was perched on a rickety footbridge over a bottomless pit. One wrong move in either direction and it would all be over. What the devil should she do?

"I am still here. You ready to talk or do you still think this is all just going to go away?" Now both of Kenna's feet thumped an impatient tap-tapping against the floor.

Trulie rolled from her knees to her heels and carefully rose from the corner where the metallic monster promising to double production stood. Edging sideways out from behind it, she returned the torch to the work crate along with her gloves and safety glasses. "I am ignoring you. Now go away." She flexed and stretched, working out the kinks that had knotted her muscles during the overlong squat.

Kenna snorted and drummed her fingers on the weathered frame of the chair. She shifted to sit with her legs crossed, her right foot still bouncing. "Be honest, Trulie. Don't you really think it's past time"— Kenna winked and folded her hands into a fidgeting knot in her lap —"you gave Granny the benefit of the doubt and took her up on an extended visit to the past? What's a few months—give or take a year or two—to a time runner?" Kenna jiggled her foot faster and grinned. "Think of it as a vacation. You've never had a real vacation."

Trulie ignored Kenna's flippant attitude. Thirteenth-century Scotland was not at the top of her list of perfect vacation spots. "Since when do you side with Granny? You two usually mix like oil and water." Kneading the small of her back, Trulie made her way to the open end of the three-sided shed and looked out into the trees. Great. She smelled rain. The muddy ruts of the road were never going to dry out if the spring rains didn't let up.

"Why are you so determined not to give an inch this time? Aren't you ready for a change? Just the other day you were complaining about how life had gotten so predictable." Kenna rose from the chair and joined Trulie. She wrinkled her nose as she squinted up into the treetops. "The leaves are blowing inside out. It's fixin' to storm."

"Yeah, it is. In more ways than one." Trulie trudged across the springy moss of the clearing and yanked open the truck door. She was so sick of this conversation. As soon as she cranked one turn of the window crank, the corroded piece of metal fell off in her hand. A fat raindrop plopped into her palm beside the broken window handle. The drop of water was soon joined by another and another. Trulie glared up into the clouds as the gently pattering droplets increased to a pouring deluge.

She tossed the broken bit of metal to the ground. Everything was falling apart all at once. Nothing seemed to be going right. Maybe she did need a break from this time. "Are you trying to tell me something?" She scowled at the stormy sky, squinting at the raindrops.

Kenna swooped toward her with a tattered quilt held over her head. "Get in the truck. I know you've got enough sense to know when to come in out of the rain."

Trulie slid beneath the steering wheel and scooted over to the passenger side. Kenna could drive. With her run of bad luck, she trusted Kenna's driving better than her own.

Kenna shoved the quilt between them and slammed the truck door shut. Grabbing the edge of the lowered window, she jiggled and cursed at the piece of glass until it finally inched upward. Glancing back over her shoulder, Kenna feigned a stern expression. "If I break a nail, Trulie Elizabeth, you are paying for my next manicure."

Trulie rolled her eyes as she grabbed the quilt and wrapped it around her shoulders. "Take it out of the money you owe me. I think you've built up a pretty good-sized tab over the past few years."

"Then what better time to jump back in time and start all over again?" Kenna grinned as she settled back in the seat. "Just think. You'll be going back to before you loaned me so much money. I will be paid in full and you'll be ahead. Am I smart or what?"

Or what. Trulie bit back the words before they escaped her mouth. Kenna was such an optimist she was borderline infuriating. Always upbeat and glass half-full—Kenna was the Sinclair family's ray of sunshine. Trulie wasn't in the mood for sunshine right now. She needed her sister to butt out, and she needed Granny to get off her back.

Snuggling deeper into the warmth of the damp quilt, Trulie stared at the droplets of rain skittering down the cracked windshield of the truck. Jump back in time and start over—at least give the past a chance. Granny had hinted at the prospect for months now—especially every time Trulie voiced a thought about switching towns because even after fifteen years, they were still outsiders in the small town of Masonville, Kentucky. Everyone pretty much gave them a wide berth unless they needed a remedy from the shop. The Sinclair women had always been the town's oddities—some gossip even named them witches.

Trulie glanced over at quietly humming Kenna. Drops of rain glistened in her sister's dark curls as she carefully examined each trimmed cuticle and carefully painted nail tip.

"You know Granny wants to leave you and the girls here. Alone. In this time. For a few months—maybe even a year or so until I get back. You do realize you will have the sole responsibility of running the business and holding the family together until then? That means keeping two teenage girls out of all the trouble the puberty years bring." Trulie watched Kenna closely. How committed was happy little sister to becoming the one in charge? Could free-spirited, didn't-have-a-care-in-the-world Kenna really lay down the law when the twins tested the limits?

Kenna shrugged as she extended one hand and compared the nail tips in the fading light of the rainy afternoon. "I can handle it. The girls won't be that bad."

"Granny threatened to lock us up in barrels until we turned twenty for some of the stuff we pulled. What makes you so sure the twins won't be so bad?" Had Kenna forgotten some of the tearful shouting matches they'd had while struggling through the growing pains of puberty? Teenage years were difficult enough for normal kids. But raging hormones coupled with the strain of keeping the family's unusual abilities hidden had made maturing a royal pain in the ass for the Sinclair girls.

"I am not the empty-headed ninny you think I am." Kenna dropped both hands to her lap and turned sideways in the seat, staring Trulie down. "And who cares if half the town thinks we're poor white trash and the other half thinks we're witches? They all flock to the shop, and their money is still good no matter what they think about us." Kenna's voice lowered as did her gaze. "Besides . . . Granny says she has plans for all of us. You need to find out just what those plans are and cash in." Kenna's hands tightened into fists until her knuckles turned white. Her voice became even softer. "She sacrificed everything for us, Trulie. I can't let her down when she has done so much for us."

And there it was. The troubled look on Kenna's face twisted Trulie's heart. Her sister had voiced the nagging thought demonizing her own emotions. Granny had given up everything. Left everything she had ever known and loved to keep her word to her dying daughter and make sure her grandbabies were raised right and healthy in the future.

Maybe little sister wasn't the perennial sunshine spewer after all. Trulie blew out a deep, despondent sigh. Dammit. She had tried so hard to help Granny set them all up with normal lives, but it looked like she had failed miserably. There was no denying the Sinclair heritage, or what the Fates might have in mind. Some things were just meant to be. Trulie drew in another deep breath and curled her legs up tighter beneath her.

Reaching across the seat, she lightly trailed a fingertip across the top of Kenna's hand. "I won't know how to act if you're not around. Who will I talk to when I've gotten in over my head?" Trulie struggled to keep her voice from breaking, struggled to keep all the dark uncertainties at bay. "Granny easily blended us into the ways of this era. Jumping back for an extended amount of time will be more difficult. If I'm not careful to completely blend in, I'll get stuck on a rotisserie at the next village barbecue."

Kenna yanked her hand away and rubbed it against her jeans. "Cut it out. That tickles."

"I'm serious, Kenna." Trulie grabbed Kenna's hand. She had to make the girl understand the danger of what they were about to do ... if she actually decided to go through with it.

"I know you're serious." Kenna's smile quivered a bit as she winked a sparkling green eye. "I'm smiling 'cause I just won the bet with the twins. They didn't think I could convince you to do it. And judging by the look in your eye, you have finally decided to give the past a try. Now let's head home and get you and Granny packed."

CHAPTER 4

"What are you going to do about clothes?" Lilia edged around the table in front of the couch and dumped another huge armload of assorted clothing into the recliner. Kismet dove into the pile, nosing and burrowing until the only thing visible was the tip of her softly flipping tail. Lilia plucked a shirt from the pile and held it up to her chest. A black paw darted out from under a towel, swatting at the shifting clothes. "If you're not taking all of these, can I have this one?"

"Tamhas will see to it that Trulie and I have proper attire for the era. Of course, we might take a few of our more favorite things to . . . uhm . . . help get us started." Granny pawed through the pile of clothing, plucked out a hooded sweatshirt and slipped it on. "Nice and toasty." She made a sound that greatly resembled Kismet's purring as she hugged it around her and rubbed a hand up and down one sleeve. "And we'll also store some items in our cache. You girls don't need all of our things. Some things must be set aside for *just in case.* You know that." Granny patted a folded pile of towels as she nodded at Trulie. "If you ever have to pass through this time again, just remember to get up to the north side of the bluff and you'll find the sealed cache in the cave just above the pond." Granny wagged a finger at each of the girls. "Always remember, you never ever leave a wrinkle in time without stashing away necessities in case you have to return. Your survival could depend on it."

Nodding at her small pile of clothing on the couch, Trulie snapped her fingers at Lilia. "No. You can't have any of my clothes. I am coming back—remember?" She extricated a couple of matching socks, balled them together and tossed them next to the pile of already folded clothes sitting on the table. She had heard the rat-hole-your-necessities lecture every time they had visited a different century. She could recite it in her sleep. Time to get Granny off that tirade before she got wound up. "Who exactly is Tamhas?" Tamhas was a name she hadn't heard before. In Granny's excitement over their trip preparations, she had apparently let down her guard and allowed the name to slip.

Granny hummed under her breath as she fished a worn T-shirt out of the load and held it up for inspection. "I always loved this shirt, but I fear it's seen better days. I guess I'll go ahead and part with it, as much as I hate to leave it behind."

"Granny—"

"And be certain to take some of those thick socks you love so much, Trulie. You'll not be able to find those supersoft fuzzy socks in the Highlands of 1247." Granny pulled a pair of fluffy, hot-pink socks from the back of the pile and tossed them over to Trulie.

"Granny!"

Granny straightened from the pile of clothes and faced Trulie. Her brow puckered into a rare expression of impatient annoyance. "What?"

"Stop ignoring me and answer the question. Who is Tamhas?" Trulie stepped around the table and positioned herself between Granny and the clean clothes. No more babbling about laundry. It was time Granny fessed up about Tamhas.

The lines around Granny's pursed lips twitched and she quickly looked away. That confirmed it. Tamhas must be someone important, because Granny was never the first to break eye contact when it came to a stare down.

"Wow." Kenna nudged into Trulie with another load of clothes. "Reckon Tamhas is Granny's boyfriend?"

"He must be," Trulie said, happy to join the teasing. "That explains the voices I've been hearing over by the hearth after everyone's gone to bed. Have you been carrying on a long-distance love affair through the fire portal, Granny? Is Tamhas the real reason you want to go back to the past?"

"I have heard enough." Granny snapped her fingers within an inch of Trulie's nose, then yanked the sweatshirt off over her head, balled it up, and threw it on the couch. "I didn't raise any of you to treat me with such disrespect." Head tipped to a haughty angle, Granny marched to the bar of cabinets separating the kitchen from the living area and perched on one of the stools. With a sharp flip of one hand, she nodded at the disorder filling the room. "I advise you all to get busy. I will not have us jumping the web before we've properly set everything in order and I know all is ready."

The elder lifted her chin a notch higher and motioned toward a rolltop desk in the corner. "Kenna, you'll find the papers granting you guardianship and power of attorney in the lockbox in the bottom drawer. If anyone gives you any trouble over their legitimacy, one quick shout through the fire portal will bring Trulie and I home before the coals even cool."

Trulie shared a meaningful look with her sisters, added a pair of folded jeans to the pile, and stepped over a softly snoring Karma as she headed toward the kitchen. Grabbing the teakettle off the back of the stove, she went to the sink and filled the pot. "You know we mean no disrespect, Granny." She settled the kettle on the stove and lit the burner. Leaning against the counter beside the old woman, Trulie gently nudged her. "Now who is Tamhas? Spill it. You know we only want you happy."

Granny pulled in a slow, deep breath and ran a fingernail along a scratch that ran the length of the cutting-board countertop. "Tamhas was the man I intended to marry. Seems like an eternity ago."

Marry? Trulie straightened without speaking and quickly double-checked the height of the flame underneath the already sputtering teakettle. Confusion successfully clipped her tongue and muddled her ability to think. Granny had never mentioned leaving behind a man she had intended to marry. Glancing across the counter into the living room, her three sisters had frozen in place, their eyes rounded as wide as their open mouths.

"Is Tamhas our grandfather?" Trulie shrugged behind Granny's back when Kenna gave her the I-can't-believe-you-just-asked-that look.

"Your mother was not born illegitimate." Granny rolled her eyes and shook her head. "My husband—your grandfather—died while out hunting with the chieftain. Wild boars are very dangerous creatures."

Trulie waited. Maybe Granny would go ahead and spill the beans if she wasn't interrupted. Catching Kenna looking as though she were about to speak, Trulie made the "zip it" motion across her mouth.

Kenna snapped her mouth shut and folded her hands in her lap.

"Tamhas was your grandfather's closest friend. He became my protector after I was widowed. The protection grew to love . . . and it was returned." Granny's voice softened as though she were talking more to herself than to them. She swallowed hard and straightened her back as though struggling to contain her emotions. She looked up and smiled at Lilia and Mairi. "Tamhas and I were to be married the summer you two were born."

Trulie's heart fell and she turned away. Leaning against the sink, she stared out the kitchen window at the treetops swaying in the breeze. The summer Lilia and Mairi were born was when all their lives had drastically changed. Their parents had died and Granny had brought them all to a future filled with the promise of life through the miracles of modern medicine. Granny had made an oath and she had more than kept it. Not only had she saved her grand-daughters' lives, she had raised them at the cost of losing the man she loved.

Granny pressed a trembling hand on Trulie's shoulder. Her voice hitched with unshed tears as she leaned in close. "I will not have you or your sisters feeling bad. I would make the same choice if I had to do it all over again. You four are my dear sweet babies. You all are the lifeblood that keeps my old heart beating."

Trulie's throat ached with unshed tears. All that Granny had lost weighed heavy on her heart. Sniffing against the threat of losing control, Trulie coughed and cleared her throat. "You sacrificed so much. Why didn't you tell us all this sooner? We could have jumped back to Tamhas before now."

Granny patted the corners of her glistening eyes and shook her head. She swallowed hard, sniffed in a deep breath, and squared her shoulders again. "The time was not right. I had to make sure you were all properly trained. You especially, Trulie."

A sense of uneasiness sprouted deep in Trulie's core. Maybe she would have been better off if she had just allowed Granny to keep her secrets to herself.

Granny turned to her, took her hands in hers, and clasped them tightly. Her calloused thumbs rubbed across the tops of Trulie's knuckles as she stared down at their joined hands. "You know the time runner legacy—our folklore. Of all the time runner bloodlines I have ever known, our line is by far the most gifted."

She paused and glanced around the room, smiling at each of the girls. "You each have been blessed with powerful gifts, along with the ability to walk across time. Reading auras and sensing energy have been child's play to all of you since you were born. And you . . ." Granny paused again, bounced their clasped hands up and down, then peered into Trulie's face with a shaking smile. "You, my dear, are just like me. You are the eldest daughter. Therefore, your talents include those of your sisters as well as many other blessings."

Granny gently squeezed her hands again. "As the eldest daughters of our respective generations, we can snip out bits of any timeline and weave them into delightful illusions in the present. If need be, we're also capable of showing the future or the past to those who need to see it most. With greater focus, we can glimpse down any number of possible futures depending on the choices made. These gifts all demand greater responsibility."

Trulie swallowed hard. She didn't want to hear this. She knew the responsibility of a time runner. Granny had also made it quite clear on several occasions the dire risks involved if any of them succumbed to the temptations their gifts created. The Sinclair legacy was sometimes a heavy yoke—and often more a curse than a blessing.

Granny released her hands and pressed her own tightly against her middle. Trulie clenched her teeth. She could tell by Granny's faraway look that her litany of the Sinclair heritage wasn't over.

With a deep breath, Granny's unblinking gaze locked on Trulie. "You are just as able to heal when the Fates allow it as Mairi when she lays hands on someone in need." Granny's smile faltered a bit more as her gaze shifted to focus on something only she could see. "If only the Fates had seen fit to allow my healing of your mother . . . and of you and your sisters."

Granny cleared her throat, took another deep breath, and straightened her shoulders as though shrugging against the weight of the painful memories. "Visions come to you, just as they do to Lilia when she happens to meet a person chosen by the Fates to be warned."

Trulie eased a step away from Granny. She didn't want or need an itemized review of the gifts and idiosyncrasies of the eldest time runner daughters. Not now. "We are all special, Granny. We understand that." Regular responsibilities were enough to worry about. Trulie should know. She had been saddled with them ever since she was old enough to help Granny take care of the rest of the girls. She would rather not dwell on the additional responsibilities she had inherited through birth order.

"The burden is yours, Trulie. As it is mine." Granny's voice held a hint of sadness. "Life is always more difficult for those of us who feel other people's true souls and read their auras." Granny opened the cabinet, pulled down five cups and dropped a teabag in each of them. "But you should be thankful you also have Kenna's gift. You can wipe a person's mind clean of painful memories. Sometimes folks just need a fresh start."

Trulie accepted the steaming hot cup of tea and leaned back against the counter. She had done her best to ignore Granny's private tutoring on the multitude of abilities given to an eldest time runner. She had kept the knowledge to herself. Hadn't even shared it with Kenna. She had convinced herself the other girls would catch up when they reached a certain age. Lord knows they were all odd. She didn't want to be the oddest of them all. "When did you know I would be saddled with all the extra . . . stuff?" A bitter huff escaped her. She sounded like a deluxe model with extra attachments.

"Since before you were born," Granny replied as she softly blew across the top of her steaming tea. Her voice took on a chiding tone as she peered across her cup. "You know that, gal. How many times have I had you recite our rede and name off your abilities?"

Kenna, Lilia, and Mairi lined up along the other side of the counter like magpies on a fence line. Kenna reached across the counter and playfully poked Trulie's arm. "We always knew you were the weirdest one of us."

"Nice." Trulie jerked away and dumped what was left of her tea in the sink. A nagging sense of impatience swelled within her. As she turned the cup upside down in the rack, she couldn't help but feel Granny's current sense of victory. The sly old woman. Granny had successfully steered them all down Mysticism Lane to get the conversation off Tamhas and her cross-century affair.

Turning back to face them all, Trulie crossed her arms and leaned back against the counter. "So tell us, Granny. Once we get back to Tamhas's time, are you two going to . . ." Trulie cocked an eyebrow and twirled one finger in the air.

Granny stood as tall as her tiny four-foot-ten frame allowed and stuck her chin in the air. "That, young lady, is none of your business."

CHAPTER 5

Clothes were sorted. Bags packed. Everything was ready. Tomorrow, they would leave. Trulie nudged the porch swing into motion. She needed to hear the soothing lullaby of the creaking chains as the swing softly swayed. Tomorrow brought a lot of uncertainty. She hoped with all her heart and soul that she was doing the right thing.

Mairi slipped out the screen door, stepped over Karma sprawled on the porch, and plopped down in the swing beside her. "You going to say bye to anyone besides Dan? Did he really believe you when you told him that lie about moving to Scotland for a few months?"

"It wasn't a lie." Trulie scooted over and looped her arm around the chain suspending it from the roof of the porch. She replayed the memory of the emotionless conversation with Dan. He had been so absorbed in his stock-trading reports that he had barely acknowledged she was even in the room.

A smile came to her as she realized it hadn't even bothered her. In fact, truth be told, she felt a bit . . . what? Freer, maybe? Less tense? She pulled in a deep breath and released it. Relaxed. That was the word. She felt more relaxed with the knowledge that her days of tiptoeing on eggshells with good old Dan were over.

"It wasn't a lie," she repeated. "I am moving to Scotland for a while. It just happens to be in a different century." She restarted the gentle rhythm of the swing Mairi had disrupted with her entry. "Aren't you supposed to be in bed?"

The young girl tucked her legs up under the folds of the oversized terry bathrobe and hugged her knees against her chest. "I can't sleep." The bright-pink bunny ears on her worn slippers flopped in time with the movement of the swing. "It's going to be so strange here without you and Granny." She sniffed and rubbed the end of her nose.

Trulie nudged the floor with one toe to keep the old swing in motion. She blinked hard against the sting of unshed tears. Mairi was right. It was going to be strange for the family to be split. They had never separated before. Even during Granny's lessons on managing the time web, they always jumped together. "We will be fine," Trulie reassured. "I know Granny is up to something. I don't know exactly what, but she always has a good reason for everything she does. She wouldn't have suggested we separate without good reason."

Mairi sat silent with her small chin propped on her knees. The only sound interrupting the night was the rhythmic squeaking whine of the porch swing and the cricket song echoing through the darkness.

"Mairi?" Trulie gently nudged the girl's arm. "I know it's not going to be easy, but I promise we will talk all the time through the fire portal. We can even see each other if the coals are hot enough. We have to trust that Granny knows best." She curled an arm around her sister and leaned her cheek against the top of Mairi's head. "What are you thinking? I promise to keep it just between us."

Mairi's shoulders hitched up and down in a hurried shrug as the girl wiped her cheek with her sleeve. "I know we can visit through the fire portal. But . . ." Her halting whisper barely rose above the sound of the rusty chains. "This is the only real place Lilia and I have ever lived. It's not like jumping and visiting history. This place has always been the home we have come back to. You and Kenna came from back there. You lived there for a while. When Granny decides she wants us to leave this time . . . I don't think I want to do it."

So that was it. The child was afraid she was next—and probably with good reason. Trulie stroked her fingers through Mairi's curls and chose her words carefully. She understood Mairi's fears but the child needed to embrace Granny's number one rule about life: it was meant to be lived to the fullest . . . not just endured.

"I was only twelve years old when we relocated our home to this time. It's not like I'm an expert on the thirteenth century." Trulie tapped Mairi on the head. "I'll have a lot to learn once we get back there, but I know I can adapt." She gave a playfully tugged one of Mairi's curls. "We Sinclairs are pretty smart, you know? We're survivors."

Trulie tried not to think about the harsh challenges of the past. No good ever came from dwelling on the negative. Most scenes of her early childhood seemed disjointed and foggy, as if someone had taken a poor-quality video and accidentally deleted some of the scenes. Trulie felt sure Granny and Kenna had wiped away some of the more unpleasant memories. Try as she might, even after all these years, she still couldn't visualize her parents' funeral or the time right before they had all jumped to the future. All that came back to her was an overwhelming sense of despair.

"Will folks back then think we are weird too?" Mairi lowered her feet, stopped the motion of the swing, and stared at Trulie, her eyes wide with fear. "Won't they try to hurt us if they find out we're . . . special? Have you read about what they did to people they didn't understand back then?"

Trulie's heart hitched at the worry in her sister's voice. Granny had never shielded them from what could happen if their heritage wasn't kept a secret, but any time they had skipped back to the past, Granny had always chosen a fairly safe era to visit. Unfortunately, Mairi voiced valid concerns that couldn't be ignored. Patting the child's back, Trulie forced a smile. "We are going to be all right. We'll hide each other's secrets like we always do. I promise. We will be all right."

"I hope so." Mairi rose from the swing and went back inside the house.

"I do too," Trulie whispered to the peepers singing in the trees.

FREEZING rain pelted down from the dreary blanket of clouds. The droplets stung against Gray's flesh as he kicked a charred beam sticking out of the muddy ground. He squinted up into the sky. Lore a'mighty, he hated this time of year. Nature could not decide whether to punish the land with more of the harshness of winter or give hope of the longed-for spring with a warm gentle breeze.

He bent back to his work with a harsh snort. The place still reeked of death and sorrow. The acridness of burned wood, seared stone, and now, rotting debris hung heavy in the damp air. He shifted against the weight of the wool mantle resting across his shoulders. The tender scars of his newly healed burns twitched with every move. The sensitive flesh nagged him with the memory of his failed attempt to reach his parents through the wall of roaring flames.

He bowed his head and swallowed hard against the crushing weight of failure throbbing in his chest. "Forgive me, *Máthair*," he whispered.

No reply came but the cold wind moaning through the ruins.

He stomped deeper into the gutted frame of the once-ornate tower where his father had housed the only woman who had ever won his heart. Gray smiled as he ducked beneath a collapsed beam. His father had never attempted to hide the fact he adored his leman and barely tolerated his petty, obnoxious wife. Gray frowned and kicked at the debris. He knew in his heart those very feelings had surely led to his father's death.

The distinctive crunch of horse's hooves on the frozen ground echoed from beyond the blackened walls. Gray ignored it and moved deeper into the belly of the silent monument of betrayal. It had to be Colum approaching. No one else had the courage or stupidity to interrupt him while he searched through the debris for what seemed like the hundredth time. The answer had to be here. There had to be an overlooked sign that would point him to his parent's murderer. All he had to do was find it and find it he damn well would.

"Come out, Gray. Ye ken as well as I ye've tramped through those ashes too many times already. If the answer lay hidden within those walls, ye wouldha found it well before now." The slow, steady sound of the horse picking through the ruins halted beyond the collapsed wall to Gray's right.

Gray pushed aside a blackened beam and squinted at the patch of ground where it had rested. "My mood will not bear yer lectures today, Colum. I advise ye leave off and tend to other business."

Colum's horse snorted and scraped a hoof against the ground, moving back and forth as though the scent of the place made the beast uneasy. "Steady, lad," Colum said as he urged the horse closer to the dismantled wall. "Come out, Gray. Even Rua knows ye waste yer time."

Gray rested both hands atop the cold, jagged blocks of crumbled stone and leaned against the wall. The scorch marks were darker here. The fire must have burned longer on this side.

Colum's horse drew closer, fogging the air with a huff of warm, moist breath mere inches from Gray's face. The mount shook its head, grumbled a low nervous whinny, then sneezed a burst of sliminess across the tops of Gray's freezing hands.

"And how long did it take ye to teach yer horse to snot on command?" Gray flung the mess to the ground, then dried his hands on his clothes.

Colum chuckled. "Rua always knows the remedy for any situation."

Gray ignored the urge to knock Colum's grinning arse out of the saddle. It would be unseemly for a chieftain to behave so. Plowing back through the debris, Gray stepped through the broken archway and emerged from the ruins. He held his hands out to the freezing mist still drizzling down from the clouds. Might as well make use of the damnable rain to wash the soot and horse snot from his hands. "Did ye come up here for a reason, or have ye no better use for your time?" Perhaps he needed to assign more responsibilities to the worrisome man-at-arms.

Colum's face darkened. His gaze lowered and he stared at the knotted reins draped across his thighs. "I come here because of Tamhas."

"Tamhas?" Gray straightened and took a step forward. "What of him?"

Colum cleared his throat and urged his horse back several steps. "I fear the old man is unwell, or perhaps dead. No smoke comes from his dwelling and ye know how he hates bone-chilling days such as this. He would surely have a fire."

Tamhas never allowed his fires to die, not even during the hottest days of summer. But if Colum was so concerned about the old conjurer, why had he not checked on the man himself? Gray shook away the freezing rain and shrugged deeper into his plaid. "Did ye call out to the man or pound upon his door?"

Colum's face blanched a shade lighter 'neath the reddish stubble of his day's growth of beard. He quickly shook his head, staring at Gray as though he had sprouted a second head. "Och, no. Ye think me a fool just begging to be cursed?"

"Fool? Nay." Gray chuckled low, then jabbed a finger at the center of Colum's chest. "Coward? Perhaps."

Colum's eyes narrowed and his chin lifted as he turned the horse aside. "Aye, well . . . I dinna think it cowardly to give a man who is so powerful in the old magic the privacy and respect he deserves."

"But ye think I should darken his door just because ye've not seen any sign of life from his cave?" Gray studied Colum closer. The man was lying. What plot had he and the old demon conjured? Why else would Colum refuse to look him in the eye?

Colum shrugged and nosed his horse toward the bare, hard-packed earth leading away from the clearing. "Do as ye will, my chieftain. I only thought ye might have a bit of concern for yer only uncle."

Hell fire, Colum would have to voice that. Gray swiped the rain from his face then worried a hand through his soaked hair. Mother had made him swear to always watch out for Tamhas. She knew the dangers the old man faced from those outside Clan MacKenna. Not everyone in this part of the Highlands was so accepting of the old man's strange ways.

"Colum!"

The horse stopped and Colum turned in the saddle. "Aye?"

"Did ye happen to bring me a mount or do ye plan for yer chieftain to walk to the old devil's lair?"

Colum grinned and nodded down the hillside toward a large outcropping of boulders. The moss-covered stones sprouted like jagged teeth around a bubbling trickle of water. A monstrous horse that dwarfed many of its breed stood patiently waiting beside the crooked stream. "Yon stands yer Cythraul. 'Twas as close as I could get him to the ruins."

Gray pressed his thumb and pinky finger against the corners of his mouth and pierced the oppressive stillness of the hillside with a sharp whistle.

Cythraul turned with ears perked forward, then violently shook his shaggy black head and took a step back.

Colum laughed. "Now do ye believe me?"

"Aye, well . . ." Gray dropped his hand to his side and shook his head. "Ye canna blame the poor beast. The night of the fire is still too fresh in his memory." He felt the warhorse's uneasiness. The animal was not the only one still troubled by that night.

"'Tis all right lad," he called down to the horse. If not for the loyal Cythraul, Gray would have died that night as well. He worried his thumb across the tips of his fingers. His hand still tingled with the memory of the reins nearly cutting his flesh as Cythraul dragged him out from under the blazing collapsed beam.

With one last glance back at the ruins, Gray motioned Colum forward as he started down the hill. "Come. Let us check on dear uncle and see what mess the old devil has conjured this time."

"Aye, m'chieftain." Colum grinned and as he headed his horse down the hillside.

∾

"So, we're all good then?" Trulie looked up and down the line of troubled faces, then forced her reassuring smile more firmly in place. She had to be brave. She wouldn't leave her sisters with a parting memory of her losing the battle with her insecurities. Thunder rumbled in the distance, interrupting the high-pitched cadence of crickets and katydids chirping in the darkness.

"You're using the pond instead of the wading pool? Seriously?" Lilia tiptoed, stretching to eye the shimmering expanse of water. She reminded Trulie of a chipmunk perched on its hindquarters. Her eyes flared wider as the ring of fire blazing around the pond popped and threw orange sparks up into the darkness.

Granny nodded at the small pond reflecting the glow of the crackling flames. The dry tinder stacked around the water's edge roared and sizzled. Long fingers of orange, yellow, and white clawed at the night. "The wading pool is cracked. Won't hold water long enough. Remember what I taught you. Never rely on just the strength of the moonlight to open the web. Fire and water increase your accuracy for the day you wish to hit."

"I have seen snakes . . . and worse in that pond." Kenna wrinkled her nose as she nodded at the surface undulating inside the circle of fire. "And now you're telling me you're going to jump into that nasty water?"

Trulie took a deep breath. She had known this wasn't going to be easy. All her emotions knotted into a lump in her throat, trying to choke her. Together, they had all jumped centuries dozens of times, but this was the first time they had ever separated. Her heart ached as she remembered that very first jump for them all. The twins had been infants swaddled against Granny's chest, and five-year-old Kenna had buried her face in Trulie's embrace. She wondered how poor Granny had felt about dragging them all to the future. Trulie straightened her shoulders and cleared her throat. Granny feared nothing. It was time she did the same. "I know it's been a while since our last jump together." She forced a brave smile she didn't really feel. "You know you don't touch the water or the flames. It's like the turnstile to enter a ride at the amusement park. Kind of like waiting to ride a cosmic roller coaster."

"I hate roller coasters and you know it. They always make me puke." Kenna scowled at the flames and squeezed Trulie's fingers so hard they started to go numb.

And Kenna would puke again when it came time for her next jump. Poor thing. Traveling across the web always made her sick. Trulie chose not to voice that thought. No sense in talking Kenna into feeling queasy. The time web would take care of that. Skating through the centuries was not for the faint of heart. She leaned forward and looked down the line at Mairi. The young girl had gone quite pale. "Mairi, you are awfully quiet. Do you have any more questions before we go? Are you good until we can light the fire porthole and let you know we're settled?"

Mairi caught her bottom lip between her teeth and nodded with a single sharp dip.

"She's terrified," Lilia said. "She's so scared for you and Granny she can't even speak."

"Karma." Trulie nudged the big, black dog sitting to her right. "Stay with Mairi. I think she is going to need you more than I will. Keep her company until I get back."

Karma protested with a soft whine, but his thick, black tail slowly wagged that he would obey. Ears sagging, his head drooped as he lumbered his way down the line. With a disgruntled huff, he plopped down between Mairi and Lilia and leaned against the young girl's leg.

Not to be outdone, Granny looked down at the black cat sitting between her feet. "Kismet. Watch after Lilia. She's putting on a brave face, but I know she will feel better if you stay here with her."

Kismet flattened her ears and settled more solidly between Granny's feet. Her golden eyes narrowed to slits and she glared into the fire. The cat was obviously not going to move.

"Kismet!" Granny nudged her toe under the cat's behind and gently lifted.

Kismet replied with an insulted *rowrr*, glared at Granny with a pointed look, and switched her tail.

"Do as you're told." Granny fixed the cat with a threatening glare only Granny could pull off.

Kismet hissed an ugly reply and slunk around to the spot between Lilia's feet. Once there, she sat as stiff and erect as a statue, her disgruntled glare fixed on the flames.

"All right." Trulie exhaled and tried to relax the tensed muscles knotting in her gut. "I guess we are all set." She glanced up and noted the position of the moon. She couldn't remember a time Granny had done a jump this size as a follower. She silently prayed the strong-willed woman would be able to assume the role and remain focused.

Granny nodded her encouragement, smiled over at the girls huddled close together, then turned back to Trulie. "Go ahead, gal."

Trulie curled her bare toes deeper into the cool, damp earth and sucked in a deep cleansing breath. She cleared her mind of everything except a vision of a mist-covered land of deep green, bordered by the blue-gray mountains she remembered from her dreams. As she relaxed and focused, the cool softness of the rich, black soil beneath her feet pulsed with an ancient energy and sent warmth running up her legs. With every breath, the warm tingling grew stronger, until Trulie's entire body hummed.

The energy surge strengthened. The power of the primeval force roared in Trulie's ears. Her heartbeat slowed to a strong, dull thud filling her with anticipation. It seemed an eternity between heartbeats. As she lifted her hands into the air, the flames encircling the small, dark pond rose higher, matching their swaying rhythm to the slow, steady pounding threatening to burst from her chest.

She focused on the center of the pond's now gently swirling waters. The dark ripples circled faster in a counterclockwise motion. The undulating waves gained momentum in their spin. The edges of the pool frothed and bubbled. A haze misted up into the swaying stalks of cattails growing along the banks. The pool swelled, then solidified into a glowing ebony mirror. Its smooth surface sparkled and danced with the orange-white light of the tall, roaring flames.

With one last look at her family, Trulie sang out the time

command. Her throat burned as she raised her voice to shout over the high-pitched whine of the rising wind.

"Web of time,

Veil of space,

Carry us to our chosen place.

Borne of water,

Trialed by fire,

Our blood bespeaks our rightful power.

For the good of all,

With harm to none,

So as it is spoken,

So let it be done."

The fire around the pool immediately solidified, frozen in place. The long orange-and-white tongues of the curling flames sprouted and stretched up around the portal like an eerie circle of sculpted glass.

Trulie crouched, nodded affirmation to Granny, then launched forward. The final command ripped from her lungs in a high-pitched shout into the roaring void. "So mote it be!"

She shivered with the surge of energy as her feet shattered the surface of the pond into thousands of sparkling shards. Her fingers trailed through the jagged pieces as they spun away in slow motion, scattering out into the star-filled darkness of the time tunnel. Anticipation spiked with a heady dose of excitement jolted through her. Mercy on her soul, she had missed the exhilaration of the ancient energy.

"Yes!" Trulie shivered with giddiness as she kicked harder and dove forward. She couldn't help it. The icy wind of time whooshing across her skin was intoxicating.

"Trulie Elizabeth!" Kenna's shout echoed from far away and repeated a thousand times across the endless void.

"I love you all! We will be together again before you know it," Trulie called back to her. An excited giggle bubbled up from her core. She loved swimming through time and had to admit she didn't mind handing over the responsibility of raising her younger sisters to

Kenna. Her fingers tingled as she somersaulted through the air. How could she have forgotten the rush of traveling across the web?

"We love you too." Kenna's sounded fainter. "And your stubborn dog is coming with you."

A deep bark reverberated through the shifting cosmos, followed by an irritated hissing yowl. Apparently, Kismet was coming too.

CHAPTER 6

"Tamhas?" Gray scanned the area as he slid off of Cythraul's broad back. With one hand resting on the beast's warm, shaggy neck, he leaned forward and listened. Nothing but silence. Not even the sound of the wind stirring through the trees. Gray tensed as he looked around. Even the drizzling rain had disappeared. Such stillness was unnatural. No good could come of this.

"Tamhas?" he repeated, louder this time. Where the devil was the old man? An eerie foreboding knotted his gut.

"Still no smoke or sign of life." Colum edged his horse up beside Gray. "I have never known the old one to leave his cave unattended for more than a few hours. The sly fox keeps close to his burrow. Do ye think he may be dead?"

Gray eased closer to the battered wooden door built into the side of the mountain. He searched for the small, thatched hole that drew the smoke from the hearth out of the confines of the cave. There. Right there, centered in a roll of the hill a bit higher up the side of the rocky embankment. The frosty wetness dripping from the loose bundles of grass piled around the opening told Gray no heat had risen from the hearth in a while. Gray moved to the shuttered window cut just a few feet to the left of the doorway. The gaps between the thick, lashed-together boards revealed nothing but darkness within.

Gray risked a hesitant sniff, held in the breath, then exhaled. Thank the gods he nay detected the smell of death or spilled blood. "If Tamhas is dead, his body isna here."

Both horses let out low, nervous whinnies, and skittered a few paces back from the clearing. They shook their heads and pawed at the ground, clearly ready to be done with the place.

"Easy now, lads," Colum reassured them. He dismounted and took a firmer hold of the reins of both mounts. "I dinna care for this overly much, myself."

Gray backed up a few steps. Something was not right. Even the air had a strange feel to it. He scrubbed a hand up and down his forearm. A strange tension stung his flesh, making every hair stand on end.

A rumbling groan rose from deep below Gray's feet. The sound deepened and then gained momentum, as though the very earth itself was about to wrench open its ancient maw. He staggered sideways, struggling to remain standing on the shaking ground. What evil awakened? The land was alive like a great beast trying to buck him from its back.

The horses screamed and reared away from the heaving earth. Colum gave them the length of their reins, their sharp, flailing hooves.

A sudden shifting in the darkness of the sky forced Gray's attention upward. "What the devil. . ." He stumbled back from the black stain swirling in an ominous circle above the mountain's clearing.

The air exploded with a deafening rush of wind and flying debris. The blast whirled through the clearing with a piercing screech so loud the howl echoed across the land. The horses shied, bucking and pawing against the unseen.

Gray shielded his face against the battering wind just as a solid force hit him square in the chest and knocked him to the ground. All went silent. The air went dead. Even the horses ceased their thrashing.

A violent updraft rattled the land. The force whooshed up from the ground, creating a choking, dirt-filled cloud. Gray turned his face from the stinging blackness, blinking hard against the swirling dust. What devilry had the gods rained down upon them? Coughing and wheezing, he struggled to see and shift aside the clinging weight draped across his chest.

"Lore a'mighty," Colum shouted from the other side of the clearing. "Ye are not going to believe this. The clouds are raining women!"

Gray rubbed his eyes and blinked hard against the silt clouding his vision. "I canna see a feckin' thing, Colum. What say ye?"

What had the man said about women? Gray swiped a hand across his face while pushing up on his elbow. The dead weight draped across his chest emitted a soft, groan. Gray froze. Such a delicate moan could only come from a female. He blinked hard one last time and scrubbed the final blurriness from his vision.

Dark hair soft as silk and smelling of a beguiling sweetness tickled against his chin. Gray inhaled another deep breath of the alluring fragrance and sent up a silent prayer that he had not gone mad. Had the gods truly dropped a woman from the sky? He blinked down at the tangled mass of curls scattered across his chest.

The woman shifted. He steadied her with one hand and moved a bit to one side to keep her from rolling away. The softness of her curves sank into him in all the right places. He leaned back and lightly stroked a finger down her arm. She was real. And her sweet warmth melting into him was quite pleasant. In fact, perhaps this gift from the heavens was not so bad after all.

He tilted his head to better examine the intriguing present Fate had seen fit to drop onto his chest. What the devil was that strange pouch strapped to her back? Odd bits of metal fashioned into the tiniest teeth ran along several of the bundle's seams. Knotted hanks of the silkiest rope Gray had ever seen dangled from various spots in bright, multicolored bits. Her oddly clothed—albeit very nice, from all he had seen thus far—body rumbled against his chest with another moan as she shifted positions again. Gray grabbed her by the shoulders and eased her to one side before her bent knee succeeded in squashing the part of him welcoming her with ever-hardening interest.

The woman slowly lifted her head. She blinked up at him through a tangle of curls hanging across her eyes. Green eyes looked through him, blindly staring past him as if he weren't there. Such an unusual shade of green. The fresh, deep hue of an angry sea when it crashed into the shallows. Dark pupils fluctuated as though unable to adjust to the light. Her dark-fringed eyes crinkled at the corners as she squinted through her hair. Her nose twitched. Her tiny nostrils flared as though she were a huntress scenting her prey. A split second later, she sprang away and stumbled across the rough ground until she was several feet away.

"Granny?" the girl cried out, growing frantic as she looked all around, her head whipping from side to side. "Granny! Karma! Kismet! Where are you?" Her voice hit a higher note of hysteria with every name she called out.

"Lass, calm down." Gray shushed her quietly in the tone he used to gentle horses. The woman would surely harm herself if she continued staggering about. He reached out and tried to catch her flailing hands. "Tell me who ye are and where ye are from?" Heaven help the poor beauty. She looked to be blind. Gray sidestepped a wild kick and grabbed at the strange pack strapped to her back. She moved with amazing agility for one who could not see. Gently, he forced her to be still, then slowly turned her to face. "There now. Much better. Easy now, lass. 'Twill be all right."

She yanked her arm away and stumbled backward. "Don't you touch me. I am not as helpless as I look."

"Easy now. I merely mean to help ye." He caught hold of her arm again, hopping sideways when she jerked out of his grasp and kicked wildly once more. Perhaps, the poor woman was mad too.

A deep warning growl rumbled behind him. The chilling sound transmitted such raw fury the hairs raised on the back of Gray's neck. Without taking his eyes off the wild-eyed woman, he eased to one side until he could see the animal out of the corner of his eye.

Damnation. That huge black beast with its teeth bared dwarfed any hound he had ever seen.

"Karma! Karma come to me. I can't see." The frantic woman crouched and held out her arms.

The black dog leaped across the clearing and pressed against his mistress's side. The woman dropped to her knees, wrapped her arms around the brute's neck, and pressed a cheek against his broad head. "Karma. Thank goodness. Please stay with me."

Gray studied the pair. The softly mumbling lass twisted him inside, made him want to protect her. The helpless beauty obviously loved and trusted the animal with all her heart—and the hound returned her love and devotion. Guilt left a bad taste in his mouth as his hand fell away from the dagger strapped to his leg. Thank the gods he had not caused the beast harm.

"Trulie?" a weak voice called out from higher up the hillside.

The girl lifted her head, turning her face toward the sound. "Granny? Granny is that you?"

So the lass's name was Trulie. Odd name for a woman. Gray moved a step closer, coming to a quick halt when the dog snarled another warning. "Lass—Mistress—call off yer beast. I mean ye no harm."

Trulie leaned closer to the great, black brute and hugged him against her side. "It's okay, Karma. Don't bite him. Just watch and be ready . . . just in case."

Karma stood taller, ears perked and focus locked on Gray. Fearlessness shone in the dog's eyes as he showed his teeth even more, daring Gray to make a wrong move.

The rattle of tumbling rocks echoed around the edge of the hill. A soft thud, followed by a faint grunt, came from behind a cluster of saplings. The young trees gently shook as more rocks bounced down the hillside around them.

"Crap on crackers, that was a rough ride." An old woman covered in dust hitched her way out from the center of the bushes, clapping the dirt from her hands. "How many times have I told you not to bust through flat-footed, Trulie? You have to work on your reentry, young lady."

"Granny, I can't see!" Trulie hitched sideways toward the old woman; her hands held out in a feeble attempt to feel her way.

Granny shook a finger at Gray as she rubbed her hip and gimped over to Trulie. *Stay there*, she mouthed to him, then pointed at the ground in front of his feet.

His mouth dropped open. Did that old woman just tell him to stay put as though he were a lad due a scolding? "Woman, ye best be telling me who ye are. I will have ye know ye are standing on my land."

Granny pointed at the spot where he stood and hiked a brow like a mother daring a child to disobey. She gave him one last, irritated scowl as she wrapped an arm around Trulie's shoulders. "It's all right, gal. You know it sometimes takes your sight a while to adjust. Especially when you are the beacon." Granny stretched on tiptoe and peered into Trulie's red-rimmed eyes. She rubbed a wrinkled thumb across the girl's reddened cheek in a gentle caress. "You dove through head first with your eyes open, didn't you?"

Gray eased closer. The two women were obviously kin. Mother and daughter? Nay. The old one was too long in the tooth to have a child the age of the young woman. The girl had called the old woman "Granny." Aye, the old one was the lass's grandmother.

Trulie sniffed and ducked her head away from Granny's touch. A mumbled "Yes" floated from behind her shirt sleeve as she dragged her arm across her face.

"You know better, Trulie," Granny gently scolded as she stepped away. "Your sight will take a few days to return. Until then, Karma will have to be your eyes."

Gray cleared his throat. He was tired of being ignored. "Who are ye?" He did his best not to bite out the words, but damn, this situation was getting stranger by the minute. "And where the devil did ye from?"

"I am Nia Sinclair," Granny said as she pulled off her spectacles and cleaned them with her shirttail. "And this"—she tipped her head toward Trulie—"is my granddaughter, Trulie Elizabeth Sinclair." She leaned to one side and looked around Gray, her gaze searching around the clearing. "And somewhere close by is my cat, Kismet. You haven't by chance seen a very opinionated black cat around here, have you?"

"Witches." Gray released the word with a strained breath. Just what he needed. Could this day get any worse?

"We are not witches." Granny hiked her chin to a haughty angle and widened her stance. "We are time runners with a few extra abilities tossed in for good measure." She settled the wire-rimmed spectacles back on her nose and planted her fists on her narrow hips. "And since when does a MacKenna fear witches? I believe quite a few of them come from your line."

"Get off me, ye wretched beast! Off, I say." Colum's enraged roar rang out from just beyond a pile of stones stacked against the hillside.

"Now what?" Gray whirled around just as Colum rounded the pile at a swift hop while trying to kick free the yowling feline wrapped around his calf.

The man at arms danced back and forth, narrow rivulets of blood streaming down his leg. Every time he grabbed the cat by the scruff of its neck, Kismet sank her fangs and claws deeper into his leg.

"Don't you hurt my cat," Granny warned while shaking her fist.

"If I ever get this wee demon off my leg, its feckin' pelt will be my next sporran." Colum hopped over to the stone trough beside the door. He lifted his leg over the side and plunged it down into the murky water.

Kismet released her hold just before hitting the water. The hissing feline raced up Colum's thigh, launched to his chest, and swiped her unsheathed claws across his cheek as a parting gift before leaping over his shoulder.

Colum gingerly palmed his crotch as he wiped the blood from his face. With a deadly look around the clearing, he unsheathed his sword. "That little bastard nearly split my bollocks in two. That wee demon is mine."

"You are not going to harm my cat." Granny stomped across the clearing and jabbed a bony finger into the center of his wide chest. "If you hadn't startled her, she wouldn't have felt the need to deball you. Now stop acting like such a bully."

Gray took this opportunity to move to Trulie's side, taking care to give the growling black dog a wide berth. "Where did ye . . . " Gray paused and glanced toward Granny, still telling Colum in no uncertain terms how she did not appreciate his behavior. "How did ye and yer grandmother get here?"

"They are the ones we have waited for. Their time has finally arrived." The door to Tamhas's cave slammed open with a thud and bounced against the wall. The old man stood with both hands folded atop the polished knob of a twisted cane that stood nearly to his shoulders. A quivering smile split his grizzled beard as he looked past Gray's shoulder. "My Nia," he tenderly crooned. "I feared I would not live to see yer lovely face in this time ever again."

Granny pressed a hand to the base of her throat and softly sobbed. A tear trailed down her wrinkled cheeks as she stood in place shaking her head. "My Tamhas," she finally choked out with a trembling smile.

"Ye know these women?" Gray struggled to keep his voice tempered to a low roar. He turned his back to the irritated huff from Trulie. He did not relish the role of fool, and from where he stood, he was being well-fitted with that title. He wanted to know what the devil was going on and he wanted to know now. "Explain. Now."

"Well, aren't you the little moment killer?" Trulie's vacant gaze snapped toward Gray. Her scowl reinforced her reprimanding tone as she groped for Karma's collar. "I am freakin' blind and I could tell they needed a private minute or two to reconnect. Would it have killed you to keep your mouth shut that long?" She finally latched onto the worn leather strap around Karma's neck and leaned toward the dog. "Take me to Granny. I don't like this guy."

Gray promptly forgot all questions for Tamhas as he watched Trulie cross the clearing. He did not know where the woman had come from and at this very moment, he didn't truly care. The way those trews molded themselves to the sightless beauty's fine round arse chased all reason from his head. He widened his stance to accommodate the hardening ache in his crotch.

Tamhas's quiet chuckle brought him back to reality.

Gray spun around and faced the grinning old man. "Explain this. Now." He forced the words through his gritted teeth to keep from roaring them across the hillside. He did not appreciate the amusement dancing in the old man's eyes. Tamhas had never been this happy. It was not natural.

Tamhas stepped out of the doorway with a graceful swing of his walking stick. He pointed a gnarled finger at a small stone cairn as he smiled tenderly at Granny. "The marker worked, me fine lass, just as ye said it would." Then he tucked his chin and playfully waggled a finger. "Ye surprised me, love. Ye said she would come alone."

Gray grabbed hold of Tamhas's staff, stopping the old man in his tracks. "Do not err by continuing to ignore me, old demon."

Tamhas faced Gray and bowed his head. "Forgive me, my chieftain. The excitement of reuniting with my love from so long ago has muddled my brain." He tipped his head toward the pair of women standing behind the great black dog and the growling cat. "The answer to yer problems lies with that one there." He aimed his staff at Trulie. "I assure ye, I hadna dared hope my love would join us at this time." Tamhas's smile widened and his beard trembled as a soft chuckle underscored his words. "But then again, who can predict all that Destiny has planned?"

Destiny. The word sent a chill down Gray's spine, especially when Tamhas used it. He motioned to Colum. "Fetch the wagon to carry our guests to the keep. I prefer the safety of my own walls to learn of this *destiny*."

CHAPTER 7

Trulie kept her fingers buried in the depths of Karma's thick ruff. The sweet dog's presence comforted her. Helped her keep a firm grip on her wits. How could she have been so stupid? She knew better than to dive across the web with her eyes wide open. But the glowing stars streaming by like rivers of white lava always tempted her. Usually, she settled for a few quick peeks as they leaped across time. This time, she had watched the entire trip. She blew out a disgusted snort. Temporary blindness was her punishment for being greedy. She rubbed her cheek against Karma's velvety ears. The dog leaned against her and responded with a sympathetic grumble.

After a heavy sigh, she straightened and ran her hand down the canine's broad back. Granny might have sucked them into one of her biggest schemes of all times, but Trulie had to admit she had never heard so much emotion jammed in one word than when Granny had said, "Tamhas." Years had fallen away from her grandmother's voice. She had sounded like a young woman again. A young woman totally consumed by love.

Trulie shifted on the bench and leaned back against the cold stone wall. What kind of love lasted over so many years of separation?

She counted backward. Almost fifteen years, to be exact. She trailed her hand across the wooden bench, taking in its texture. How could a love last across centuries? A twinge of jealousy nipped at her. She had never known a love like that.

A shuffling sound across the room pulled Trulie from her thoughts. "Who is there?" She squinted all around but saw nothing but a flannel-like mist. Holding her breath, she strained to pick up on every sound. She didn't like this place. It smelled odd and there was too much of . . . something . . . permeating the very atmosphere. She shifted on the bench and smoothed her clammy palms up and down the gooseflesh prickling her arms.

As soon as they had helped her from the wagon and led her up the stone steps, an off the charts sizzling had filled her senses with— some. Hatred, maybe. Or betrayal. Definitely some jealousy. There was so much negative energy, she couldn't nail all the emotions down. The place reeked with it.

She ran her fingers along the wall at her back. Stone. Rough chiseled edges fitted together with no discernible mortar. She curled her toes into the carpet. It felt...furry. A sense of revulsion filled her. This room's decorator liked killing things and spreading their pelts on the floor.

A throat cleared.

She jumped and turned toward the sound. "It's rude to sneak up on someone who can't see." Reaching for Karma, she rose from the bench and lifted her chin. Never. Show. Fear. Even when your innards felt like jelly.

"Ye have nothing to fear from me, young one. I would never cause ye harm."

Tamhas. She relaxed somewhat and scanned the room until she found the bright cloud of undulating colors. There he was. The old man had the strangest aura she had ever seen. She wasn't quite sure about him just yet. But if Granny trusted him, he had to be safe. She just wished her sight would hurry and return. She could always tell a person's true spirit by reading their eyes. "Why aren't you with

Granny and Kismet? I thought you were going to help her get settled. I am sure a lot has changed after fifteen years."

A calloused hand pressed up into hers. He led her gently across the room and settled her on a cushioned seat. This part of the room seemed warmer. She must be closer to the fire.

"Ye know yer grandmother, lass." His chuckle filled the room, sounding like the deep ring of large brass wind chimes. "That woman needs aid from no one when her mind is set. She only needs my love." A rough palm lightly patted the top of Trulie's hand. "And this place is not so unknown to her. The fire portal has been her window to this world through the years."

Trulie relaxed even more, allowing herself to trust him. It sounded like the man knew Granny to a tee. "Where are we? Or maybe I should say 'when' are we?"

"Ye dinna ken?" He sounded surprised.

"Well . . ." She swept her hair back from her face and edged closer to the warmth coming from her right. That had to be the hearth. She wouldn't mind getting closer to the fire. A damp chill filled the room. "I know where I was aiming, but I just wanted to make sure I hit the right year. I have never led a leap across so many centuries."

"The twentieth of February in the year 1247." Tamhas patted her hand again. "And I dare say the earthquake ye caused was felt from shore to shore and will be recorded by every monk possessing a quill."

"Sorry." She reached toward the heat of the fire, rose from the cushions, and edged closer. Stone floor now. And it was warmer. "For some reason, I have never been able to control my entry like Granny does." She turned and backed up until the blaze warmed her nicely through her jeans. "I think it's because she rarely lets me jump as the beacon." In fact, she could count on one hand the times Granny had allowed her to lead any leaps across the continuum's web.

"Hmm," was Tamhas's only reply.

"Who was that surly man I landed on?" She frowned as her body flushed from heat not caused by the fire toasting her rear. The man had been muscular and solid as a boulder—quite nice if you liked the herculean alpha type. She swallowed hard and cleared her throat. Why had her mouth suddenly gotten so dry? Maybe because she had never sprawled on top of a breathing mountain before . . . and enjoy it.

Tamhas chuckled from across the room.

For some reason, the man's amusement grated on her nerves. She wished she could see his face and get a read on him. "I really don't see the humor in that question," she said while tapping her toes on the rough floor. She needed to find her backpack and slip on some shoes. The feeling was just now coming back to her toes after nearly freezing them off in the chill of a Scottish February.

"The fine man who caught ye when the time cloud spat ye forth was Chieftain Gray MacKenna. Ye should ask yer grandmother of that action's significance." Tamhas's sparkling aura bobbed slowly across the room. The old man was on the move. "And Chieftain MacKenna needs the assistance that only ye can give him. Never forget that." Hinges creaked and then came the sound of a door thudding closed.

Trulie shivered. That sounded like a door that weighed a ton. Images of thick oak doors sealing off dank medieval dungeons came to mind, speeding up the already fast pounding of her heart until she became almost breathless. She sucked in a deep breath and shook away the feeling. "What do you mean he needs my assistance?"

Nothing but silence filled the room.

"Tamhas?" She searched for his sparkling aura of indescribable colors. Gone. The old man had just left without saying another word. She almost growled as she rubbed her hands up and down her now toasty backside.

"Karma?"

A soft woof made her feel slightly better. At least she wasn't alone.

The hinges of the door creaked again, followed by Karma's low, clicking growl. That warning tone could only mean one thing. She stood taller and widened her stance on the hearth. "Did Tamhas send you in here?"

"So, yer sight has returned to ye?" Gray's rich, deep voice flowed through the room like a seductive melody.

She blinked harder, wishing that it had. All she could make out were fuzzy shapes of light against dark. Her ability to see auras seemed to be healing faster than her normal eyesight. The circle of light standing across the room was a brilliant royal blue. The light shimmered when the chieftain spoke. Blue? Trulie blinked again. Loyalty. Intelligence. Honor. Maybe her first impression that Gray MacKenna was an insensitive ass had been a bit premature.

The intense aura moved closer. "Can ye see me, lass?"

"Sort of." She rubbed her hands together. What was it about this man that made her palms—and a few other places she refused to acknowledge right now—go all warm and tingly?

"Sort . . . of?" Gray repeated.

"It's hard to explain." She shrugged, aiming her focus at the regal indigo aura. No need to spill all the beans about her abilities just yet. In the thirteenth century, one never knew for sure which side of the "witch issue" someone might be on. She had already revealed enough when they entered this time to send them all to a witch burning. "Tamhas said you needed my help. What is it you need me to do?"

A chair scraped against the floor and the blur of shimmering cerulean folded in the middle. He must have taken a seat. The sound of liquid gurgling into a container reminded her of just how dry her mouth currently felt.

"Can you . . . um." Merciful heavens, she hated to ask for help, but who knew if there was another chair over there? Irritation flashed through her. Wouldn't a gentleman ask if she wanted to sit or would like a drink before he took care of himself?

A large warm hand cupped her elbow. She squeaked and jumped away from the touch.

"Forgive me, lass." His deep voice rumbled. "I only mean to lead ye to the table. I thought ye might like to sit and have a drink. Would ye care to?"

"But I saw you sitting over there." She turned toward the spot where she had last seen the blue cloud. It was gone. Now Gray's aura shimmered right beside her.

"I nay sat." He sounded confused and just a little bit insulted. "I pulled out the chair to better lead ye to it. And I thought ye said ye couldna see me?"

"I told you, it's rather complicated." She swallowed a groan and rubbed the hot gritty corners of her eyes. Irritation filled her. The color of his aura paired with his current behavior completely overrode his bullish attitude back at Tamhas and Granny's reunion. She felt like a complete idiot, having badly misjudged him.

"Thank you," she said as she reached toward the shimmering patch of blue. Confusion, irritation, and pride stuck crossways in her throat. She hated being wrong. And hated admitting it even more. "I really do appreciate your help."

Gray didn't respond. Just slid his calloused palm up into her hand and waited.

She chewed on the corner of her bottom lip as her hands sank into the soothing blue light. The pulsating tingle in both of them shifted into high gear and rippled through her body. A sly voice in the back of her mind whispered, "*Wonder how hard the rest of him would make us tingle?*"

The memory of lying across the muscled expanse of the man's chest sucked every last drop of moisture from her already dry mouth. The *rest* of him had felt very nice. Very nice, indeed.

He gently pulled her forward. "Your grandmother is resting comfortably farther down the way." He cleared his throat and his tone changed. "And that cat is with her as well."

Trulie couldn't resist a smile. When Gray said, "that cat," his voice took on a resigned tone, as though he despised the feline but didn't want her to know it. "Kismet takes some getting used to. She thinks she's the center of the universe and everything revolves around her."

"Kismet?"

Trulie nodded as he carefully placed her hand onto the smooth arm of a large wooden chair. "Granny's cat."

"Aye. Well . . ." His voice seemed softer as the blue aura eased a few steps away and another heavy chair scraped against the stone floor. "If ye ask me, cats belong down in the pantries keeping the rodents at bay."

Trulie smoothed her palms across what felt to be a large wood table. A shiver rippled across her as she folded both hands in front of her. She missed the warmth of the fire. Maybe. Or could be nerves making her insides feel as though she were on the verge of a monster case of caffeine jitters. She eased in another deep breath, catching the same scent of mouthwatering spice she had detected when she first realized she was sprawled across a very large man.

The tantalizing aroma became stronger as the blue aura leaned toward her, took her hand, and wrapped it around a cool metal container. Her nose twitched, and before she caught herself, her thoughts tumbled out of her mouth. "You smell very good."

Gray chuckled. "Thank ye, lass." His tone was textured with a seductive echo. "Ye smell verra fine yourself."

She pressed her cold fingers onto her now very warm cheeks. "I meant . . . " She patted around to relocate the glass Gray had placed in front of her. "It seems like I remember this era smelling really bad the last time I was here." Mercy, did she really just say that? She lifted the glass and sipped the water. Maybe if she shoved something in her mouth, she would stop babbling like an idiot.

"I see," Gray said, his tone strained.

She lowered the glass back to the table and closed her eyes. What the devil was wrong with her? She never babbled. Babbling was for . . . well, she just didn't babble. "Please forgive me. I didn't mean that everything stunk. It's just that . . ." Oh holy hell, the more she talked the farther she shoved her foot in her mouth. At the rate she was going, she would soon have her leg inserted clear to the hip.

His rumbling laugh filled the room. "I canna say I understand a word yer saying, but I will say ye definitely have me intrigued."

Intrigued was good. Maybe. She settled the glass back on the table and slid it farther away. "Tamhas said you needed my help. What exactly did he mean by that?"

The atmosphere of the room immediately shifted. A tense silence filled it. Karma's toenails clicked across the stone flooring, then faded into muffled thumps. A grumbling huff told Trulie the dog had found a spot on the pelt-covered portion of the room and settled down. Apparently, Karma had decided Gray MacKenna wasn't a threat. That made her feel better . . . somewhat.

"Mr. MacKenna? Did you hear me?" Trulie settled more comfortably against the curved back of the chair.

"Mister?" Gray spit out the word as though it tasted bad. "Ye may call me Gray, or the MacKenna. If ye wish, ye may call me chieftain. But I canna say I take to the word 'mister.' Sounds like lowlander speech to me."

"It is meant as a word of respect." Trulie tightened her hands into fists. He didn't like the word 'mister'? Had the word originally held a different connotation? "Granny always taught me to respect my elders."

"Elders?" Gray now clearly sounded insulted. "I dare say I am not an elder to ye. How old do ye think I am?"

An irritated huff escaped her as she raked her fingers through her tousled hair. Could she not keep her foot out of her mouth for five minutes? Now she had insulted the man by insinuating he was old. She tucked her stubborn curls behind her ears. "I do not think you are old. I have no idea how old you are, and I really don't care. You said you were the chieftain so I figured you were probably very . . . mature." Well, that sounded lame. Somebody just needed to hand her a shovel so she could bury herself in the hole she had just dug herself into.

"I have not led my clan verra long. My father died a short time ago."

"Oh. I am so sorry." Her heart dropped with a painful thud. Poor man. No wonder he was so intense. Not only had he just lost his father, but he hadn't been a leader to his people very long.

She felt more than heard the heaviness of his sigh.

After a few more minutes of uncomfortable silence, she leaned toward the blue cloud sitting across the table. Maybe the third time would be the charm. She had to find out what Tamhas meant about

helping this man. There was just something about this whole situation that filled her with an almost uncomfortable anticipation. She
had to help Gray to get it out of her system. Was this why Granny had
been so adamant about hurrying back to the past? "How can I help
you, Chieftain MacKenna? What did Tamhas mean about your
needing my help?"

The vibrant deep blue of Gray's aura shifted to a dark, disturbing
misty gray.

She scooted back. She had definitely upset him this time.

"Gray," he said.

Trulie folded her hands in her lap and nodded. "Yes. Your aura
has turned gray. Please forgive me. I did not mean to upset you."

"No," he said a bit louder. "I would rather ye call me Gray—if ye
dinna mind."

"Oh." She caught her bottom lip between her teeth. Never had
she had so much trouble communicating with another human being
in her entire life. What the devil was wrong with her? It had to be
because she had to rely solely on her extra senses. That had to be it.
She took another sip of water, trying to deny that the zero comfort
level of this conversation had anything to do with the fluttery feeling
in her stomach every time Gray MacKenna rolled his *r*'s in her
direction.

She batted a tickling curl away from her forehead and leaned
forward again. "Okay, Gray. What was Tamhas talking about? He said
I was the only one who could help you. So, I am asking . . . how can I
help you?"

The loud scraping of a chair hurriedly pushed aside, accompanied by the elongation of the murky aura told her that Gray now
stood. The cloud of color receded, then bounced back and forth with
a jerking rhythm. She blinked hard and tried to focus, wishing she
could see the man. It was hard to concentrate on a bouncing blob of
shifting mist.

"My parents were murdered," he finally said. "Burned to death in
the north tower. I believe the fire was no accident." The pacing
stopped as Gray's aura darkened even more. "I intend to find and pass

judgment on the killer. Tamhas said ye would know exactly how to make that come to pass. He said ye had the sight."

She leaned back and swallowed hard. Murdered? Burned to death? A violent shudder shook through her. What a horrible way to die. And that explained a lot about the eerie feeling of this place.

"I . . ." She opened her mouth, then closed it, uncertain how to respond.

"Once ye find the bastard . . . or bastards who started the fire, I will handle the rest."

His tone growled with emotion. Raw anger and a thirst for vengeance dripped from every syllable.

"So Tamhas told you I can read people?" Trulie knotted her hands into fists and pressed them against her stomach. The thought of trying to solve the murder filled her with gut-wrenching uneasiness. Had Granny known about all this when she had insisted on returning to this time? Had Granny really wanted to land in the middle of all this conflict? Trulie's inner voice—the voice that always added commentary where Granny was concerned—responded with a loud *What do you think?*

"Aye." Gray's terse one-word response spoke volumes. "He said ye had the sight."

Trulie took a deep breath and ignored the uncomfortable queasiness burning in the back of her throat. "Well. I think I need to explain it a bit more. I can read people and get a very accurate sense of what type of person they are, but I can't always see everything in their minds." Well. She really *could* see into peoples' minds. But sorting through a person's thoughts and memories always made her uneasy. She rarely used that particular gift. It drained her physically, and if she happened across someone's more disturbing memories, the darkness haunted her for days. There were just some things she never wanted to know. "Uhm. I guess if you already have someone in mind, I could talk to them and see what I could find out. Do you have any idea who might have done it?"

She needed to stop babbling now. With a shaky pat of her hand, she found her glass and brought it to her lips. The cool springwater made the stomach-clenching nervousness even worse.

Calm down. Her oversensitive sense of self-preservation blared a loud and clear warning. Could Gray really be trusted? Was it safe to share the truth about her abilities—all her gifts? How many times had Granny told her keeping quiet about the Sinclair *talents* was key to the family's survival?

"All I ask is that ye help find the one who set the fire. Help me find the one who bolted my mother's doors and blocked the stairwell leading down from her private rooms. Help me find the cur who warned my father of the danger to his woman. The bastard lured my sire there before the fire was set. I want the one who barred the tower entrance from the outside and trapped my parents inside that fiery hell. I want their neck between my hands."

The room pulsated with Gray's anger. His rage battered against her senses like missiles exploding on impact. She closed her eyes and pressed her palms against her temples. His heartbreak and bleak sense of complete loss crashed into her. She flinched and shied away. Yes. This man could be trusted. All he wanted was to avenge his family.

"Are ye unwell, lass? Should I send for yer grandmother?" His was warm and reassuring on her shoulders. His aura surrounded her, then lowered to the floor. The man must be on his knees.

She pressed the back of her hand to her mouth. Here he was, racked by such pain, and yet he knelt at her feet out of concern for her. Her stomach somersaulted and her heart double-thumped a fluttering sigh. Fingers shaking, she smoothed them across her cheeks and blinked against the sting of unshed tears. With a sniff, she straightened in the chair and forced a smile. He is just polite. Don't read anything into it. "Forgive me. I didn't mean to break down like that. I'm fine. I'll be . . . just fine."

"Perhaps yer weariness has overly taxed ye."

The vibrant blue aura rose as he stood and moved away. The warmth of Gray's touch slid away from her shoulders, triggering an immediate shiver. *Come back*, all her senses cried out. She rubbed her hands up and down her arms, shaking the feeling away. Breathe. Just breathe.

"I shall have yer grandmother sent to ye." His voice now came from behind her. He was back at the door.

The slow creaking hinges and the soft thud confirmed it. Just that quick, he was gone.

She sagged forward and held her head. Why did alone suddenly seem . . . lonely? A cold wet nose snuffled against her. Karma grumbled a low, soothing whine and bumped his silky head up beneath her arm.

"I love you too, Karma." She buried her face in his wooly ruff and rubbed his velvety ears. A metallic clatter and the rasping whisper of a moving door straightened her in the chair. "Who's there?"

"It's only me, gal." A trilling *prrrpp* announced Kismet accompanied Granny. Soft footsteps echoed across the room, then the gentle weight of Granny's hand rested on her shoulder. "Gray said you weren't well." A familiar, gnarled finger lifted her chin. "What's ailin' you, gal?"

"Other than my eyes, I'm fine," Trulie lied. She patted the table until she found her cup. A rough tongue rasped across the back of her hand, then water splashed across her fingers. "Kismet. That was my water."

A lapping sound echoed, then the rough tongue swiped her hand again. Trulie sagged back in the chair. "You're welcome."

Granny squeezed her shoulders. "Come on. Get up."

"Where are we going now?" She really preferred staying put until her sight returned.

"Coira's waiting for you in your room. She will get you fed and settled in." Granny gave her shoulders another impatient shake. "Come on, now. Time's a wastin'."

"Who is Coira?" Without her sight, she felt like she needed a scorecard to keep up with all the players in this twisted game of thirteenth-century Name That Scot. Trulie held out her hands and slowly rose from the chair before Granny could shake her again. Patience was not one of Granny's virtues.

Granny steered her clear of the chair, then tucked her hand in the crook of her arm. "She is our maidservant. I have spoken to her. She'll help get you acclimated."

"So, she knows about us?" Trulie lifted her face as a waft of cool air brushed past her and the door groaned shut behind them.

"She knows enough." Granny patted Trulie's hand and turned her down the hallway.

CHAPTER 8

"Dinna fret now, Mistress Trulie. Coira will have ye all unpacked and settled in yer rooms in no time at all." The bright-pink aura jabbering away in third person buzzed around the room in such a frenzy it made Trulie's head spin. Coira must have been a hummingbird in a past life.

"Thank you, Coira." Trulie moved carefully through the unknown space with both hands extended. Karma's firm weight against her leg helped keep her on course. "And it's just Trulie. Remember?"

"Ah now, mistress. Ye will have Steward and Cook switching me arse with a stick if I dinna show ye proper respect." The fuchsia cloud ping-ponged back to Trulie and took hold of both her hands. "Here now. Allow me to lead ye to the settee. Ye must sit and enjoy Cook's fine biscuits and mead whilst I undo yer strange wee bag."

Trulie eased down, expecting another hard bench, but was pleasantly surprised by the softness of a plush cushion. She ran her fingertips across the seat. A knobby weave. Smooth silkiness interlaced with rough knotted threads. The cushions reminded her of Granny's needlepoint and tapestry pillows.

"Hold out yer hands, m'lady, and I shall hand ye the cup." Coira's cotton-candy-pink aura hovered patiently in front of Trulie.

"I will make you a deal." Trulie held up both hands. "When it is just you and me in the room, call me Trulie." Having a personal servant didn't feel quite right, but Trulie gladly welcomed a friend and confidante to help her adapt to this strange new world.

"Make . . . a . . . deal." Coira repeated the phrase as though not entirely sure of its meaning. "Is that the same sort of thing as an agreement . . . or perhaps a pact?"

"Yes." Trulie nodded as Coira placed a heavy metal cup between her hands. "We will make a pact that whenever we are alone, you have permission to call me Trulie. You can do that and not get into any trouble with the rest of the household—right?"

"Aye, m'lady . . . er, Trulie." Coira's aura bounced down, then up again in what had to have been a curtsy.

The cloud of pink floated a bit to the right as Trulie hesitantly sipped what smelled like cloyingly sweet wine. She held the liquid on her tongue and slowly breathed in, savoring the unusual flavor. The drink wasn't like any wine she had ever had before, and if she remembered Granny's tales of the past correctly, the unusual twang deepening the flavor of the fermented, fruity liquid had to be honey. Trulie swallowed and quietly smacked her lips. She had no tolerance for alcohol, but this didn't taste strong at all. Not bad.

An amused snort reminded Trulie that Coira was still very much in the room.

"What?"

"Ye look like Cook when she tastes the soup to see if more salt is needed. Have ye never tasted mead afore?" Coira chuckled and flitted around the room with soft thuds and pats that told Trulie that the maid was still busily setting everything in order while they talked.

"No. I think this is my first taste of honey wine." Trulie took another sip, savoring the light alcoholic warmth trickling down her throat. The sound of nylon cloth being frantically handled, then a dull thud followed by a word hissed out in a language Trulie didn't understand, pulled her attention away from the mead. "Do you need some help with that zipper? Sometimes it sticks if you don't hold it straight while you're trying to undo it."

Coira's hot-pink aura had deepened to a fiery red. "I am afraid I dinna ken what ye mean, m'lady." Coira's voice was strained, as though she was ready to spit nails.

Trulie carefully rose from the bench. Red aura and strained voice. Apparently, the sticky zipper had won this round with Coira. Trulie held out the cup of mead with one hand and reached with the other. "Here. Take this and I'll open the bag. I'm used to it being ornery."

"Where are ye from, mistress? Yer grandmother didna see fit to tell me, and for the life of me, I barely understand what ye are saying half the time. I ken I am not a dull-witted lass, but lore a mercy, I wonder at the emptiness of me own head whenever ye speak."

There was that word *mistress* again. Apparently, Coira's manners were so deeply ingrained that it was going to take a bit to overcome them. She decided to let it pass.

"Uhm . . ." Trulie patted the bag until she found the silk rope attached to the pull of the main zipper. She stretched it taut between her hands and yanked with no success. Crap on a cracker. The silly thing was really stuck this time. She pulled it closed and jerked again as a suitably vague answer to Coira's question finally came to her. "I am from a land quite far from here. Really far. Kind of off to the southwest." Coira seemed genuinely nice, but best ease her into the complicated world of the Sinclair family until Trulie knew her better.

"I see," Coira replied in a tone that clearly said she didn't see at all.

With a successful *whirrup* of the heavy zipper, Trulie pulled open the backpack. Before she could pull free any of the contents, Coira gently pushed her aside. "Nay, m'lady. 'Tis my job to set yer things in order."

At Trulie's exasperated huff, Coira giggled and carefully turned Trulie, then helped her sit on the edge of the bed. "What I meant to say is, nay, Trulie. 'Tis my duty to stick my wee nose through all yer things so I can see all yer treasures."

Trulie relaxed, scooted back on the bed, and assumed her favorite cross-legged position. Maybe there was hope for a friendship with Coira, after all.

"Oh . . . my . . . heavens." Coira's tone echoed with wonder.

"What?" Damning her lost sight, Trulie sat taller. All she could see was another flashing shade shift in the color of Coira's aura.

"What . . ." Coira's voice stalled out as though the girl had suddenly forgotten how to speak. Finally, she took Trulie's hand up and pressed a wadded jumble of silk and lace into it. "What is . . . where . . . how exactly do ye wear . . . *these.*"

Trulie fingered through the bundle. Lace. Silk. Ribbon. Recognition finally registered. Trulie grinned. She held between her hands what she affectionately called her power package. Be it by intention or by chance, whenever she wore this particular set of black thong panties and show-off-the-girls bra, her confidence soared and she succeeded at whatever she tried. They always brought her good karma. "It is my favorite set of bra and panties. There is more lingerie stuffed in those outside pockets, but this set and the red set I am wearing are my favorites. They bring me luck."

The satiny articles were slowly pulled out of her hands. Trulie heard a sharp intake of breath and something muttered so low that she leaned forward to try to hear it. "What did you say, Coira?"

The maid cleared her throat with a nervous cough. "These bits of lace and ribbon will bring ye a great deal more than luck if the chieftain sees ye wearin' them."

Trulie did her best to ignore the rising heat of her cheeks. Why would Coira say such a thing? "I am not exactly going to be parading around the keep in my underwear. I'm sure Chieftain MacKenna won't get a viewing of my power package. He is much too busy running the clan to be troubled by a couple of new houseguests . . . and my favorite underwear."

"Hmm," was Coira's only response.

"What is that supposed to mean?" Trulie scooted to the edge of the bed and carefully lowered her feet to the floor. Coira's "Hmmm" spoke volumes, presenting all sorts of possibilities that effectively released an oversized horde of fluttering butterflies in Trulie's stomach.

"Well . . ." Coira made an odd chirping noise like a hen about to lay an egg. "All I know is how the MacKenna looked at ye when ye walked in front of him in those tight-fittin' trews ye are a wearin'." Coira giggled out a bubbling chortle as she rattled around in the backpack. "If he caught sight of ye in yer wee bit of black lace, the man's plaid would surely stand out stiff as a banner hung across a pole."

So, the honey-voiced chieftain liked the rear view of her jeans? Trulie pressed both hands to her flaming cheeks again but couldn't resist joining Coira's infectious giggling. Maybe this short visit to the thirteenth century wouldn't be so bad after all.

"HOLY SHIT, THAT IS COLD!" Trulie crossed her arms tighter over her bare breasts as the icy water sluiced down her body and splashed into the tub at her feet.

"Aye, mistress." Coira scrubbed her back with a rough cloth. "Fresh water from the loch gets the humors a movin' first thing in the morn."

"Give me that rag. I can wash myself." Trulie jerked her hand toward the bright pink aura. "D-d-dammit, I can barely talk. My teeth are chattering from hypothermia."

"I shall stoke the fire. Hurry and wash, m'lady. I have a nice hot bowl of parritch for ye over by the fire.

"Is there any soap?" Trulie gingerly dipped the rag in the cold water around her feet and scrubbed up and down her legs. Damnation. The more she scrubbed, the colder the water seemed. "And what is parritch?" She was in an ill mood this morning and ice water dumped over her head didn't improve it. She was still sightless, had a crick in her neck and a stuffy nose from the down pillows, and was just pretty much angry at the world.

"Oats, mistress," Coira answered in a wounded tone. "Hold out yer wee rag and I will guide ye to the bowl of soap."

Trulie held out the square of linen. She really shouldn't snap at Coira. It wasn't the girl's fault indoor plumbing and foam pillows had yet to be invented. The cool rim of a stoneware bowl pushed up against her hand. She dipped the cloth in the slimy substance and brought it to her nose. Whew. That should burn the hair off her legs. She soused the cloth in the water, shook it free of the acrid-smelling soap, then finished scrubbing her body.

"Here, mistress. Hold fast to my shoulder and step free of the tub. I'll lead ye to the fire and rub ye down. Ye will feel refreshed in no time."

Trulie very much doubted that, but what other choice did she have? Giving up on her last shred of modesty, she extended her arms and slowly turned in front of the fire while Coira dried her off. She felt like a rotisserie chicken getting ready for the spit.

"There now. All dry and smelling sweet as a spring breeze." Coira shoved a garment over her head, pulled her arms through the sleeves, and shook it down her body.

Trulie smoothed her hands down the nubby weave. Must be some sort of linen. She shoved the sleeves up to her elbows and pushed her wet curls behind her ears. "I'm sorry I snapped at you. I have never been a morning person."

"Never ye mind," Coira said soothingly, as she led Trulie to a chair. "Sit ye down and eat. A warm full belly will lift yer mood."

Gingerly patting her hands in front of her, Trulie found the bowl and the handle of a wooden spoon. She leaned forward and inhaled deeply. Yuck. Oatmeal. She pushed it away and folded her hands in her lap. "I am really not hungry this morning. If I could just have a nice hot cup of tea, that would be awesome." Coffee would be even better, but she knew that was an impossibility.

Coira took hold of her hand and wrapped her fingers around a warm cup. "Yer grandmother told me of yer druthers. I dinna ken what tea is but this here is a fine warmed wine. There is a nice hot bannock here for ye too. Fresh from Cook's fire." Coira guided her other hand and rested it atop what felt like a toasty square biscuit.

"Thank you." Her frame of mind improved considerably with every sip of the wine. The warm bannock melted in her mouth, rich and oaty, in a good way.

Coira's pink aura bounced around the room, banging furniture and fluffing cloth as Trulie ate. "Mother Sinclair says Master Tamhas has a fine poultice that will hurry the healin' of yer eyes. Once ye are dressed, the wagon is a waitin' in the bailey to carry ye to his croft."

Trulie popped the last of the bannock in her mouth and washed it down with a gulp of the hot wine. If Coira had told her that in the first place, she would have been a lot more cooperative. She was sick and tired of being sightless. She patted the table and stood. "I am ready. Let's go."

"Nay, mistress." Coira carefully walked her around the table and moved her closer to the fire. "Ye must finish dressing first. Ye have nothin' on but yer shift."

Trulie fluffed the loose-fitting garment around her legs. "I am ready whenever you are."

"First yer stockings." Coira gently pushed her down and to one side. "Sit on the wee bench so ye dinna fall."

Trulie propped herself on the edge of the cushion and lifted a foot. Coira smoothed what felt like a thick wool sock up to her thigh and secured it with a tightening tug and pull of some sort of string. Trulie patted her fingers atop the strange stock and the ribbon knotted around her thigh.

Coira batted away her hands. "Dinna untie the ribbons or yer hose will be down around yer ankles."

Flexing her toes in the soft wooly weave, Trulie latched onto the edge of the stool as Coira yanked a soft leather shoe onto her foot and tied it around her ankle.

"Too tight. My toes will turn blue." Trulie bent to loosen the shoe only to have her hands batted away again.

"Quit yer havering and lift yer other foot. The ties will ease as ye walk. The laces are leather and dinna need loosening."

Coira was turning out to be bossier than Granny. Trulie stuck her bare foot in the air, drumming her fingers on the cushions as Coira secured the other stocking and shoe. "Hurry up."

"Hush now. Up wi' ye then." Coira pulled on her hands and led her across the room. "Up with yer arms. All we have left is yer overdress and belt. Then it's down to the bailey and off to Master Tamhas's croft."

Thank goodness. Trulie rolled her shoulders and smoothed the heavy wool down around her waist. Who knew getting dressed could be such an ordeal? "Now are we ready?"

"Aye, Mistress," Coira snorted out in an exasperated huff. "Ye are ready at last."

"ONCE I WIPE yer eyes with this poultice, the rest of yer sight should return." Tamhas pressed a cool cloth, sticky with some sort of unimaginable glop, against her closed eyelids.

Ick. Trulie forced herself not to recoil. If the nastiness hastened the full return of her sight, she would tolerate a little slimy grossness. "Granny, you didn't answer me. Did you know about what happened to Gray's parents before we came here?"

The bench made of woven twine creaked with Granny's slight weight as she settled down beside Trulie. "Somewhat," Granny finally said. Her voice sounded cautious . . . and guilty.

"Either you knew or you didn't. There is no such thing as *somewhat* in a yes or no question. Is that why you brought me back here? To help solve the murder?"

Granny chuckled and replied with a vague "Perhaps."

"Coira, are you still here?" Trulie wrapped her hands around the rough stick forming the frame of the flimsy bench and currently biting into the backs of her knees. "Coira, do not be a tease. You know I won't be blind forever. Speak up."

"Aye, m'lady. I am over here in the corner beside the worktable." Coira's voice sounded a bit strained.

Coira used the official m'lady. Who else was in Tamhas's room? The only auras she had seen before her eyes were covered with slime belonged to Granny and Tamhas, and they cared little about servant versus mistress protocol. An uncomfortable twinge of foreboding plucked at her senses.

Trulie gripped the edge of the seat tighter, fighting against the urge to fling the tickling cold mess off her face and scan the room again. "Have you been able to find out anything? Did you have any luck with the questions I wanted you to ask around the keep?" She very much doubted Coira had discovered anything. Even without her eyesight, she had noticed how the other servants in the household had distanced themselves from Coira. They knew the girl was close to the Sinclairs and feared the advantage it gave her.

"Well . . ." Coira's voice trailed off. Rushes scattered across the dirt floor shuffled with the dry crunching rustle. The maid's nervous cough interrupted the whisper of the dried grass. That nailed it. Coira had discovered something.

"Well, what?" Trulie waited. If she turned and faced Coira long enough, the girl would eventually spill all that was on her mind. Trulie could sense it.

"I am not so sure 'tis wise to repeat all I learned, m'lady. 'Tis about yer chieftain's half-brother, Fearghal."

"Well for one thing, he is not *my* chieftain. He belongs to Clan MacKenna." Why would Coira say such a thing? Was Granny planting little plotting seeds again, even though she knew Trulie planned on returning to the future?

"Beggin' yer pardon, m'lady." The tone of Coira's rapid-fire apology missed hitting true sincerity by just a hair. Trulie didn't miss the note of tensed irritation in the pitch of Coira's voice.

Trulie took a deep breath. Getting information out of the maid was like picking up a boulder with a pair of tweezers. Why was she acting so leery? "Please, Coira. Share what you heard about Fearghal."

"Cook's lad said the man is a cruel arse." Coira's hesitant voice bounced from all around the room. Apparently, she was either pacing or exploring as she spoke. Coira was as inquisitive as a cat.

"Dinna touch that!" Tamhas barked.

The sound of pottery breaking and a pungent odor told Trulie that Tamhas's order came a second too late.

Coira coughed and gagged. "What was in that jar, master?"

"Fermented marsh salamander, if ye must know. Ye just ruined a month's work. Stupid, clumsy girl." Tamhas huffed out a muttered curse as he smeared another layer of ooze across Trulie's eyelids. Globs of chilly sliminess snaked down one of her temples and dripped entirely too close to her ear.

Trulie cringed and batted Tamhas's hand away. Blind or not, she did not want rotten lizard entrails smeared across her face. "No more and wash those nasty lizard guts off me right now, please."

"Fermented marsh salamander doesna cure blindness. At least this spotted variety has never been found to have any effect." Tamhas's insulted tone conveyed quite clearly that he did not appreciate Trulie's assumptions. "Have ye taught the lass nothing, Nia?"

Granny grabbed Trulie by the wrists and kept her from touching her face. "It's herbs on your face, gal. Nothing more than simple herbs mixed with mud from the loch's edge to speed along the clearing of your sight."

Trulie relaxed back onto the woven bench. She wasn't too sure about the mud part, and the goop still felt nasty, but she guessed she might as well go with it. "So, Gray has a half-brother who is an ass. Is he a lot older than Gray, or what? And why did no one tell me Gray's father had been married more than once? That could have something to do with the murders. If Fearghal is the oldest son, shouldn't he have inherited the job of chieftain instead of Gray?" Trulie mentally added Fearghal to the potential suspect list, along with a woman named Aileas. In the short time they had been at the keep, Trulie had already picked up on the fact that the servant girls loathed the woman and did their best to avoid her.

"Gray's father loved only one woman in his life, and that was Gray's mother." Tamhas underscored this observation with a disgusted snort. "Unfortunately for all concerned, Gray's mother, Isabeau, was never his father's wife."

Trulie understood completely now. Gray's mother must have been the old chieftain's mistress. She had read how some high-ranking men in this time provided for women who were not their wives. What was it they called them? Wiggling her nose against the slime trickling down one cheek, Trulie turned toward Tamhas. "Then how could Gray become chieftain if he was illegitimate?"

"MacKenna blood flows through Gray's veins, and he carries his ancestry well. He was chosen to be chief." Tamhas grumbled something unintelligible again as he turned away. "The son born of the chieftain's legal union shouldha been drowned at birth."

The bench creaked with a new weight. Coira's familiar scent of lye soap and dried heather announced her presence. The hushed loathing in the girl's tone conveyed her feelings clearly. "All of us agree with Master Tamhas. The wicked Fearghal is much younger than the MacKenna and greatly resembles one of Master Tamhas's dried-up toads that he keeps in his wee jars."

Trulie mulled over this newest bit of information. "Surely you don't think Fearghal should've been drowned at birth just because he's a dried-up little pipsqueak?" That didn't seem in character for anyone she had met at MacKenna keep.

"Nay . . ." Coira drew out the word as though keeping her emotions in check was becoming an unbearable strain. "But he is wicked. I know this firsthand. One of the newest girls, a meek young lass, and newly orphaned afore she came to the keep, was one of the poor serving girls unfortunate enough to catch the evil Fearghal's eye. When she walked by him one evening with a tray full of trenchers, he kicked her feet out from under her and laughed when all she carried crashed to the floor. Then the cur told her he would see to it that his brother banished her from the keep for being so clumsy and wasting food. The MacKenna doesna tolerate waste when so many over the years have died the slow death of starvation."

"What an ass." Anger flashed hot through Trulie. She hated a bully. No wonder Granny had been in such a hurry to get back to the past and set things right.

"Aye. And that was not the worst part." Caught up in her story, Coira squirmed in place until the entire bench shook. "When the poor lass started crying, he told her that if she didna . . ." Coira shuddered, shaking the bench even more. "He told the lass to service him or he would turn her over to the MacKenna for not only being a clumsy wench but a thief."

"That is a complete load of crap." Trulie couldn't stand it any longer. She scraped the hardening mud from her eyes and groped the air in front of her for water or a towel. "Help me get this mess cleaned off. It sounds like we have been brought here to clean house and we will start with that obnoxious little jerk." Trulie nodded as a particularly wicked idea dawned. "Maybe I'll let Karma neuter him. That'll convince him to keep his man parts to himself."

A shallow wooden bowl filled with cool water rose up beneath her hands and barely touched her fingers. Trulie leaned over the basin, splashed her face until it felt goop-free, and then batted blindly for a towel. She blinked away the moisture into the folds of the rough cloth and dried the residue off her face. Tossing the rag to the bench beside her, she slowly opened her eyes, then gasped.

Electrifying eyes—those ice-blue irises resembling a lightning-filled sky—stared back at her. The man she had nearly taken out with the truck crouched at her feet. Granny's primary reason for returning to the past suddenly became very clear.

"You!" Trulie scrambled sideways and sprang up from the bench. A firm knowing settled within her as she remembered Granny's words from that night: *Besides—I know those colors. He comes from a fine, upstanding clan. You won't find a force on earth able to strike fear into a MacKenna.*

Gray MacKenna didn't say a word. Eyes narrowed and rugged jaw set to a defiant angle, he slowly rose and slid the bowl of water over to the table.

Trulie whirled on Granny, her entire body trembling. "Out with it, Granny. No more games. You're the only one who could've hidden his aura so I wouldn't know he was here. No more lies about dying wishes or solving murders. I want the truth and I want it now. You hinted at seeing me settled. You said you had a plan for all your granddaughters." Trulie jerked her head toward Gray. "I suppose you think if I fall for him, I will stay in the past forever?"

Granny's eyes widened. Her mouth opened and then pressed tightly closed as if she thought better of what she was about to say.

Dammit. Trulie was sick and tired of everyone else's choices controlling her entire life. She was an adult now. It was time she lived or died by her own decisions. Getting angrier by the minute, she shook a finger at Tamhas. "And what part did you have in all this? I know you have been contacting Granny through the fire portal. But I thought you two were just carrying on an over-the-eras relationship until you could be reunited. Are you in on this matchmaking garbage too?"

With another angry toss of her head in Gray's direction, she took another step toward the old man frowning down at the greasy bowl clenched between his hands. "Does that poor man over there even know who or what we are? Does he have any idea how you are attempting to complicate his life?"

"Poor man?" Gray's tensed expression grew darker than a storm cloud. "Do I look like a *poor* man to ye?"

Trulie spun, then jerked to a stop. The tip of her nose almost touched Gray's breastbone. Gritting her teeth, she thumped the center of his chest, then shook her finger just inches from the end of his nose. "One stubborn persona at a time. Get in line and wait your turn."

His eyes flared wide. He looked as though he was about to bare his teeth and snarl.

"And don't give me that insulted-chief look," she warned before turning back to Tamhas. "Answer me. Did you set him in the middle of my road that night or did Granny do it?"

"Both," Granny snapped as she stepped between Trulie and Tamhas. "You refused to listen. We had to do something drastic."

"I wouldn't listen?" Trulie could not believe what she had just heard. Granny had completely betrayed her. If they hadn't lost that truckload of inventory and had to suspend their internet sales, she would've never entertained the thought of leaving the shop in her sisters' care while she took Granny back to the past. But the ruined truckload, the ongoing war with Mrs. Hagerty, and the realization that her personal life sucked finally convinced her to take a little time off from the twenty-first century.

A cold feeling of certainty settled in her bones. They were here because of Granny's grand plan. "How far were you willing to go to get me back to this century, Granny? What are you capable of doing to get your own way and carry out your plans?"

Granny didn't answer—just stared at the ground.

Trulie turned to the wide-eyed girl sitting on the bench. Coira was a mere slip of a girl. Her tiny appearance somehow didn't fit the robust belly laugh and larger-than-life sense of humor Trulie had come to know. "Coira, you have never seemed very surprised by anything I've ever told you. Did they suck you into their scheming too?"

Coira's reddish-blonde curls trembled as she stared down at her freckle-dusted hands clasped tightly in her lap. "Nay, mistress. I swear to ye I know of no plot. I only know I was meant to serve ye."

"What about the girls back home?" Trulie asked.

Granny shook her head. "No. Your sisters only know what you were told. They think we came back here to get me set for my final leap with Tamhas and that you would then return to them back in the future. They all figured you would never be happy here in this time, so you'd return as soon as I was settled."

Gray pushed forward, wrapped a strong hand around Trulie's upper arm, and turned her back toward him. "Ye spoke of a strange night. A dark road. That unholy thing was of yer doing?" Gray grabbed her by the shoulders and pulled her closer still. "Ye controlled the monster with the glowing eyes. Ye tried to kill me?"

Trulie squirmed out of his grasp. "I did not try to kill you. Granny and your sorcerer over there plopped you in the middle of the road just as I drove through. If you want to be angry at someone, be angry at them. I know I am."

"And . . . and . . . as for you two," Trulie sputtered. Dammit! Now was not the time for her emotionally triggered stutter to return. She had finally gotten that irritating trait under control when she'd escaped the stress of high school. She took a deep breath and pointed a finger at Tamhas while at the same time staring down Granny. "It will be a cold d-day in hell before I ever believe a single word out of either of you again. Dammit, Granny! How could you?"

Stomping across the room, Trulie yanked open the door. Without looking back, she squared her shoulders and growled back to the room. "Come on, Karma. We have a trip back to the future to plan."

The dog rose, trotted past Trulie, then turned and waited. Trulie glared back into the room one last time then stomped out and slammed the door behind her.

CHAPTER 9

"Never have I heard a woman speak in such a manner." Gray stared at the closed door. Trulie's angry stream of stuttering profanity gradually faded as she stomped away.

"Stuttering is a good indicator that Trulie is royally irritated." Granny's shoulders sagged as she blew out a dismal sigh. "That's what she does when she feels like she has lost control. And if you make her really mad, she cries. You best take cover if she ever cries, because hell hath no fury compared to Trulie on an angry rampage."

Gray mulled over Trulie's tirade, more certain than ever that those words should not come out of a woman's mouth. He stared at the door, remembering her rage and how it had only accentuated her delicate features. God help him. What fire that woman possessed. He scrubbed his fingers across his jaw and turned back toward Tamhas and Granny. "So ye tricked the woman to bring her here. Why?"

Tamhas flashed a toothy grin. "Are ye blind then, man?" The old sorcerer tossed the soiled bowl back into the midst of the worktable's clutter. "That fiery lass is the perfect match for ye. The children the two of ye sire will be fine and bonnie—perfect descendants to perpetuate this powerful clan."

"Of course, you will have to woo her." Granny beamed up at him with a knowing smile and a pat on his arm. "Trulie tends to get a bit out of sorts when she feels she's been maneuvered. It might take you a bit to get through to her, but don't give up. I feel sure you can wear her down and convince her the charade was all for the best."

"I am not the one who lied to the woman." Gray backed up a step and thumped himself on the chest. "And who said I wanted such a fiery-tongued woman to wife?"

"I will wait until after the two of you are married to tell Trulie you said that." Granny winked and primly folded her hands in front of her waist. The old woman looked smug and pleased with herself. She greatly resembled her wicked cat after Cook discovered the cream pans licked clean.

He had to get out of here. He felt trapped, both by the tiny confines of Tamhas's abode and by the sudden plot to get him wed. All he had asked of the old man was the identity of the culprit who had murdered his parents. How the hell had the old demon turned that into a matchmaking request? Gray moved toward the door and stomped squarely on Kismet's tail.

The enraged cat exploded into a black ball of fury and embedded its claws in his leg.

"Off me, wicked beast." Gray bent, latched onto Kismet's scruff, and flinched as two paws of barbs tore free of his flesh. Tiny rivulets of warm blood trickled down his stinging calf.

Kismet exploded again with furious hissing. A high-pitched yowl vibrated into Gray's hand as the cat twisted in his grasp. Her puffed tail whipped back and forth as the feline threw another swipe at Gray.

"I will thank ye to keep this menace away from me if ye dinna wish to see yer wee cat skinned." Gray bent and dropped the spitting fur ball into Granny's arms.

"You are definitely a dog person," Granny observed. She cuddled the enraged Kismet close and whispered soothing words to the feline. "That's a good thing. I think Trulie prefers dogs too."

Gray held up a hand to silence them all and yanked open the

door. "Nary another word about yer damnable matchmaking. When I find Mistress Trulie, I intend to leave her with no doubt about my intentions."

"Which are?" Granny prompted as Coira knocked over another stack of bowls and sidestepped the resulting crash.

"By hell's fiends," Tamhas cursed as he shooed the maid away from his cluttered storage shelves. "Take this one with ye afore she destroys everything I own. Be gone, girl. I do my own housekeeping."

Coira dropped a polite curtsy, scurried across the room, and flitted out the door ahead of Gray. "Come, my chieftain. Mistress Trulie is already well ahead of us. The lady walks quite fast when she is angry. Shall I run to fetch her for ye?"

"Nay!" Gray pointed back to the bench inside the croft. "Ye shall wait here. I dinna give a damn what Master Tamhas wishes." How the devil had he lost control of this situation? "I am chieftain here. Ye shall stay and assist Master Tamhas in the long overdue clearing out of this hellhole."

Coira's eyes rounded and her pale brows arched nearly to her hairline. She bobbed another quick curtsy, skittered back inside the croft, and set to gathering the soiled wooden bowls scattered across the floor.

Gray turned back to Tamhas, fighting against the urge to demand a burning out of his cluttered burrow. He could almost hear his mother's voice pleading for her brother's case. *Ye know yer uncle is nay quite right. He is too gifted wi' the ways. Ye must be patient wi' him, son, for his heart and soul are pure.*

Gray clenched his teeth, struggling to rein in his temper. "I may lose control and kill ye for this yet, old man." He snatched hold of the rope handle of the door and slammed it hard behind him.

TRULIE SLOWED, then came to a complete stop. Her rage evaporated, loosening the band of tension squeezing her chest. Scotland. So beautiful she could hardly bear it.

And it was so much more than that one word could describe. The rugged land spread out before her, patient and waiting for her to appreciate it for what it truly was. A sky the vibrant clear blue of Scotland's flag. Clouds so wispy and white that they resembled water-color brush strokes. Thickets of pines, blue-green in their scattered clusters, softened the jagged edges of stony hillsides and cliffs forming the ridge of a valley leading down to the ocean.

Her gaze traveled past the thickest line of gnarled trees hemming in the bit of land leading down to the sea. Tall fierce crags, topped with the brown grasses of winter, jutted out into the bay like fingers of a great hand dipping down into the water. Atop the highest one, majestic and proud against the sky, stood what had to be MacKenna keep.

Four tall stone towers connected with great walls of weathered block stood almost silver against the skyline. The grounds surrounding the outer wall gently sloped a few feet away from the fortress, then sheared off into the waves. The keep itself had been built on the thickest part of the peninsula jutting into the bay. Either the battering sea or the determined Highland weather had eroded away enough of the land to partially disconnect the keep from the mainland. Trulie stood on tiptoe and shaded her eyes. As near as she could tell, the only access to the keep was by crossing the wide stone bridge connecting the two pieces of land.

The steady pounding of footsteps behind her pulled her attention away from the newly discovered splendor. A subtle tingle surged through her. Not unpleasant. More like an exciting shiver of anticipation. Her senses recognized the only man who had ever succeeded in triggering such a reaction.

"Ye should never travel alone in the Highlands," Gray said. "'Tis unsafe."

Hackles raised and teeth bared, Karma leaned against Trulie's leg and rumbled a warning growl. She pulled the heavy arisaid tighter around her body and hugged her arms across her chest. Shooting a dismissive glance back over one shoulder, she hurried to bite her lip to keep from laughing. Chieftain MacKenna looked as if he had a royal case of the red arse.

"I am never alone." She nodded down at the dog. "I believe you've met Karma."

"Aye." Gray scowled at the dog and risked a step closer.

Karma's clicking growl shifted into a faster gear as he hunkered down and prepared to spring.

Gray backed up a step. "I agree ye are quite safe with that great beast watching over ye." Gray widened his stance. "But nonetheless, I shall see to it that ye travel safely back to the keep."

Trulie rested a hand on Karma's velvety head and dug her fingers into his hackles. "That's enough, Karma. You know Chieftain MacKenna means us no harm." And he didn't. The poor man was as much a pawn in Granny's scheme as she was.

"I would hope ye both know I would never harm ye." Gray spared a disgruntled scowl at Karma. "Either of ye."

Something in Gray's tone triggered an even warmer flash of tingles. Trulie loosened the wool wrap a bit. "I know you're a victim here too. And I'm sorry I yelled at you back there." She took a step closer and held out her hand. She really did owe him an apology. "I am mad at Granny and Tamhas for their manipulative little game. I am not mad at you."

Gray looked down at her hand long enough to make Trulie wonder if he was going to shake hands and play nice or not. She kept it extended and lifted it a bit higher. "Friends?"

The hint of a smile played across his mouth as he took her hand, lifted it to his mouth, and pressed a gentle kiss to the inside of her wrist. She swallowed hard as a delicious surge shifted all her senses into a breathless fury. Well, dammit then.

His watchful gaze gave her the urge to squirm as he stepped to her side and tucked her arm through his. "I would be more than honored to claim ye as friend."

Claim ye. There was something about the way he said those two words that made her look forward to his claiming whatever he wanted. She blinked free of the sensuous spell and motioned toward the keep. This erotic spiral needed to be slowed. "Karma and I were headed back to the keep to have a chat with Mr. Fearghal. Would you like to walk with us?"

Gray scanned the land, then nodded at the keep. "'Tis a bit farther then ye ken. That is why Tamhas had the lot of ye brought up here in the wagon. Are ye certain ye wish to walk?"

Trulie eyed the sprawling land. It was a pretty good distance. "We have to walk. We can't leave them without a wagon."

"Nay, lass. We dinna have to walk." Gray grinned, then split the air with a sharp whistle.

Karma perked his ears and turned toward a dirt path disappearing around a swell of scrub and stone. The ground trembled as the biggest horse Trulie had ever seen thundered up the path. Black as coal from the tips of his ears to the shaggy feathers skirting each foot, the monstrous beast miniaturized everything around him.

"Cythraul will carry us to the keep."

Trulie backed up a step. The horse was huge. "Uhm. All right." She couldn't very well refuse on the grounds that heights terrified her. It was either ride the four-story horse to the keep or wait and travel with Granny and Tamhas. She was not in the mood to ride with them.

Amusement and something not quite readable sparkled in Gray's eyes as he held out his hand. "M'lady?"

If she didn't know better, she would swear Gray was waiting to see if she was going to accept the challenge or turn tail and run. She stepped forward and grabbed his hand. She didn't run from anything.

He turned her, set his hands around her waist, and lifted her up into the saddle as though she weighed no more than a whisper. She locked onto the lip of the saddle with both hands and concentrated on the thick tuft of mane directly in front of her knuckles. As long as she didn't look down at the ground, she would be fine. Hopefully. A high-pitched squeak escaped her as Gray swung himself up into the saddle behind her.

"Something wrong, lass?"

"No." Her voice cracked. Trulie cleared her throat and tried again.

"Nothing." It broke again. She sounded like a schoolboy whose voice was changing. "Nothing is wrong." There. That sounded much better. She had to admit, the wall of muscle at her back and the safety harness of Gray's arms on either side of her did make her feel a lot better.

His warm breath brushed her cheek as he leaned forward, scooped up the reins in one hand, and wrapped his other arm around her waist. "I willna let ye fall."

Trulie shivered and couldn't resist melting back into his warmth. At this point in time, falling from the horse was the least of her worries.

Cythraul lurched forward into a rolling gallop thundering down the hillside. Trulie shut her eyes, tucked her chin to her chest, and dug her fingers into Grays' arm. *Shit. Shit. Shit.*

His deep chuckle rumbled against her back as he held her tighter. "Rest easy, lass. I will slow the beastie down."

She barely opened one eye and peeped out from the folds of her wrap, which she clutched over her face. They were moving much slower now. Gray had reined in Cythraul to a peaceful trot. "Thank you." She loosened her grip on his arm, horrified as four half-moon slits cut into his forearm beaded up with blood.

"Oh good heavens, I am so sorry." Trulie worked a square of linen free of her tightly laced kirtle and dabbed at the cuts. Thank goodness Coira had insisted she tuck the handkerchief into the cleft of her bosom *just in case.* "I am so so sorry. I didn't mean to dig my fingernails into you."

He flexed his arm tighter around her waist. "'Tis nothing, lass. Dinna fash yerself over some wee scratches that I didna feel." His deep voice rumbled against her cheek as he leaned in closer. "I take it ye are not well acquainted with riding?"

"No. Not really." A wave of nausea washed across her and she clutched his arm again. "I need you to stop and let me down. Please." She held her breath, praying she could stop herself from throwing up her bannock.

Cythraul immediately stopped. Gray folded the reins across the great horse's neck and leaned around. Concern and worry filled his face. "What have I done to offend ye?"

Trulie pointed at the bridge in front of them. The wide stone bridge spanned a sheer breathless drop into a jagged stretch of what looked like razor-sharp stones surrounded with angry, roiling seawater. "I can't be up this high and ride across that."

Gray looked at the bridge, then returned his focus to Trulie. His expression clearly relayed that he didn't understand. But without another word, he slid down from the horse's back and held up his hands to her. "Come, m'lady. We will walk the rest of the way."

Her heart double-thumped a hard, breathless beat. He could've cajoled her into riding across the bridge or made fun of her for being afraid. But he hadn't. He had accepted her fears for what they were and tried to ease them without hesitation. Gray was the real deal. The living definition of chivalry. She swallowed hard. She had never met a man quite like him.

She leaned forward into his arms, holding her breath as he slowly pulled her from the saddle and lowered her to the ground. Her mouth went dry as she stood there, her arms resting on his, looking up into his face.

His gaze locked on her mouth. The tip of his tongue raced across his bottom lip as though anxious for the taste of her. She found herself wetting her own lips. What would she do if he tried to kiss her? Easy. Kiss him back. Trulie waited for him to make the first move.

With the barest flicker of a smile, Gray dipped his head, took a step back, and proffered his arm like a true gentleman. "Come, m'lady. 'Twould be my pleasure to show ye MacKenna keep now that ye can see."

Well, dammit. Disappointed but determined to hide it, she forced a smile and hooked her arm through his. The chilling height of the structure spanning the ravine could no longer be blamed for the tingling dizziness spinning across her senses. Fear of heights was nothing compared to this subtle emotional dance with a heart-stopping Highlander.

CHAPTER 10

The busy community housed inside the protective skirting walls of the MacKenna holdings filled Trulie with amazement. The fortress was a small village. To the left, a split rail fence hemmed in a training paddock connected to a stable. Two young boys, looking to be in their teens, led a skittish horse in a circle under the watchful eye of a barrel-chested man in a tattered plaid. He leaned against the fence, calling out instructions to the lads.

Against the farthest wall to the right, a smithy, covered in sweat and grime, held a glowing horseshoe with long-handled tongs against the curve of his blackened angle. Sparks showered from the red-hot metal as the iron sang out with every strike of his hammer.

Wariness pulled her closer to Gray as a cluster of women weaving baskets openly gawked at her with curious stares. She relaxed a bit when Karma pushed his wet nose into her palm, reassuring her that he was still close.

Stone dragons, weathered to a weary gray, flanked either side of the wide stone steps leading up to the main entrance of the keep. Gray led her up them and through the huge oak double doors leading to the main hall. Trulie came to a halt. The grandeur of the massive room was too impressive to take in with a simple glance.

Banners of plaid framed crossed broadswords and the clan crest hanging behind the raised stone dais bearing the chieftain's chair. Long wooden tables and their benches had been pushed against the walls. A pair of serving maids swept aside soil and discarded scraps even the hounds had refused. Grimy-cheeked lads scurried around the room replacing spent torches with those freshly pitched.

Trulie lifted her gaze to the ornate gallery bordering the second floor of the room. The MacKenna colors hung from the dark wood banisters running along the balcony. The high ceilings caught her eye. The intricate masonry was astounding. The weathered stones arched overhead created a breathtaking mosaic of cobbled stones framed with ancient timbers blackened from years of smoke.

Gray motioned to a young man hoisting a log into the massive hearth that took up one side of the long room. "Bread and cheese, lad. In my solar." Gray tipped his head toward Karma. "And a fine meaty knuckle for Mistress Trulie's fine lad here."

"Aye, MacKenna." The boy bobbed his head, then took off through an arch at a quick trot.

"I thought 'twould be best if we had a bit to eat before meeting with my stepmother and Fearghal." With a slight bow, Gray motioned Trulie toward a narrow alcove between two ornate tapestries suspended from silky braided ropes secured to dragon sconce embedded in the walls. One weave depicted a gnarled tree of Celtic knots filled with all manner of birds. The other was a colorful scene of a successful hunt.

Before Trulie could respond, men shouting and the squeals of an angry horse rang out from the courtyard. Karma pressed against Trulie, lowered his head, and growled.

"What the hell—" Gray bounded for the door, coming to a halt as a scrawny wild-eyed man shot into the narrow entryway walled off from the main room. Colum followed close behind, his teeth bared in an angry snarl. "That feckin' idiot grabbed Cythraul's reins. Put him on the demon's back, my chieftain. I beg ye. Let the mighty Cythraul teach the foolish bastard a thing or two."

Waves of loathing hit Trulie's senses as the sniveling man jerked what could only be an obscene gesture at Colum. She blinked and focused harder on the man. She couldn't tell if she was picking up his emotions or if Colum's palpable hatred was fouling her reading.

Karma lowered his head and unleashed a deep rumbling growl. Trulie took a step closer. "It's all right, Karma," she whispered. "I have to get closer and get a better read." She aimed her senses at the unpleasant man and forced herself not to recoil. She had never encountered such pure, unadulterated hatred in one person.

"Ye are drunk, Fearghal. Ye reek of it." Gray moved to the door and glared outside.

The ruckus in the courtyard appeared to be dying down. All Trulie could hear now was the previous level of activity.

"Ye're damn lucky Cythraul spared yer arse. I doubt verra much if yer mother wouldha been pleased to find ye stomped to death in the bailey." Gray motioned Colum out of the room.

"I tire of bein' treated like I am the bastard son." Fearghal narrowed his red-rimmed eyes at Gray, his scowl deepening as he crossed his arms over his scrawny chest.

"Fearghal!"

A warning tingled across the back of Trulie's neck. She turned and forced herself not to back away from the waves of negativity emanating from the unpleasant woman. This had to be the infamous Aileas.

The scowling matron stormed forward, her heavy black skirts sweeping aside the dried rushes scattered across the floor. She waved a meaty hand toward a narrow archway to the left of the hall. "Not another word from ye. Hie to yer room. Now."

A range of emotions flashed across Fearghal's face, twisting his sneer into several variations before he finally turned and staggered from the room. He paused when he reached the doorway, turned, and opened his mouth.

"I said not another word!" Aileas fisted both hands and lunged a few steps toward him as though coming after him.

Fearghal's eyes flared wide. His mouth snapped shut, and he staggered out of sight.

Aileas turned and settled her scowl on Trulie. "So, yer sight's returned to ye." Aileas didn't say it like a question. She said it with the irritation of a child who had just received a lump of coal from Santa.

Trulie stepped forward. If Aileas wanted a fight, so be it. "Yes. My eyes are fully healed, thank you. Now, I am able to enjoy all the beauty of MacKenna keep." She swept a meaningful glance up and down Aileas, then glanced toward the hallway where Fearghal had disappeared. "And the not so beautiful," she added. Might as well lay out the ground rules now. She refused to take any abuse from Aileas.

Gray's soft chuckle from close behind her sent a warm ripple through her. Good. It pleased her to know he agreed.

Aileas clenched her hands in front of her thick waist. She jutted her chin and took a step forward. Her narrow-eyed glare shifted to Gray, then returned to Trulie. "Ye will find a great deal of unpleasantness in this hall. Ye would do well to make yer visit brief."

Gray stepped around Trulie and stood in front of her like a shield. "Dare ye threaten my guest?"

The matron's mouth tightened as though straining to keep from spouting the wrong words. After a tense moment, she jerked her head from side to side. "Nay, my chieftain. No threat. Just a warning. Ye ken yerself the unknown evil in this place."

Trulie rested a hand on Gray's tensed forearm, eased out from behind him, and stood at his side. "Thank you for the warning, Lady Aileas." She patted Gray's arm and fixed the arrogant woman with a glaring look she would have no danger of misinterpreting. "Your warning is noted." Then she turned her warmest smile on Gray. "I'm hungry. Did you not promise me a treat of bread and cheese in the solar?"

"Aye. That I did." Without another word to Aileas, Gray hugged Trulie closer to his side and turned them toward the stair.

"Ye vile bastard. I shall have ye skinned!"

Trulie turned just in time to catch Karma lowering his leg and calmly trotting away from Lady Aileas. The dark streak of wetness splattering her wool skirts attested to the precision of his aim. Trulie struggled not to smile as she snapped her fingers and called him to her side. "Karma! Shame on you."

"Leave the lad alone, lass," Gray whispered against her cheek. Then he raised his voice and shouted to the boy bearing a platter of food from the kitchen. "Hie back to the kitchen, Rabbie. Master Karma warrants Cook's best meats along with his bone."

Aileas exploded with an enraged roar and stormed from the room.

Gray gave her a look that warmed her heart as he tucked her arm back into his. "'Tis a verra fine dog, indeed. Now, mistress. On to the meal I promised ye."

Trulie held tight to him as they wound their way up the spiraling stairs. The stone steps were steep and narrow. One misplaced step and a nasty fall would follow. She breathed easier when they reached the much wider landing. "I guess it was rude of me to poke the bear. I hope I didn't cause you any problems."

Gray pushed open the wide oak door and waited for her to enter the room. "Poke the bear?"

She almost groaned aloud, scolding herself for using slang from her time. "I should not have been rude to Aileas," she said. "I'm sorry." She wasn't sorry, but she didn't want to make matters worse for Gray.

Rabbie and Karma trotted around them, hurrying deeper into the room. The young boy balanced the edge of the tray on the small round table in front of the hearth. He transferred plates of cheeses, meats, and breads onto the table, and plunked a heavy pitcher into the midst of the food. "Here, lad." He pulled two huge, meaty bones from the woven sack hung across his chest and set them on the floor in front of Karma. Karma wasted no time in settling down to gnawing the meat from the bones.

Gray led Trulie to one of the chairs at the table and held it for her as she sat. "I did not notice any rudeness directed at Aileas. I am sure ye are quite mistaken." He filled a metal goblet with a ruby liquid and offered it with a knowing smile.

"Thank you." Trulie took the glass, her fingers gently touching his for a long, breathless moment. Was the room spinning or was it her imagination?

"Ye are most welcome, mistress." He gave her a polite nod, then took his seat.

She gladly sipped the cool wine. The comfortable room furnished with cushioned benches scattered throughout the sprawling space was overly warm and it had nothing to do with the fire in the hearth. She drained the glass.

Gray quickly refilled it.

Cracking bones and a contented grumbling broke the silence. Gray chuckled as he turned and nodded at the dog. "Set well into the bones, lad. Ye earned them."

"I can't believe he peed on her." Trulie pinched off a crumbling nugget of cheese and popped it into her mouth. Creamy and tart. Perfect with the wine and hopefully it would help her control the effects of the alcohol. "I promise he has never done that before." She treated herself to another deep drink of the fruity liquid, then eyed the ruby tastiness. Surely it couldn't be that strong. She should be okay.

Gray topped off her glass again. "The lad only did what the rest of us have wanted to do for ages."

She giggled and struggled to keep from snorting out loud with laughter. The mental image of Gray and Colum peeing on Aileas was almost more than she could bear. "Well, I'm sure Karma doesn't mind you living vicariously through him." She returned her empty cup to the table.

"Yer glass is empty. Allow me to fill it." Gray smiled and nodded toward her cup.

Trulie wrinkled her nose at the seemingly bottomless pitcher of wine. She had no tolerance for alcohol and already had quite the buzzy feeling going on. She wasn't sure if it was solely from wine on an almost empty stomach, or whether the lovely privacy of Gray's solar was to blame. All she knew for certain was she liked it. Why shouldn't she enjoy it? After all, it had been a rough couple of days. She held out her cup. "Maybe just a little bit more."

Gray nodded. "Aye. A wee bit more." The lovely burgundy liquid gurgled into her cup.

She took another deep sip, eyeing Gray over the rim. "Damn, I love the way you talk."

One of his dark brows arched higher and his lopsided smile widened.

Dammit. Had she said that out loud? She set the glass in the center of the table. "I think I have had enough." She attempted to stand and bumped into the table. Dammit. The nice buzzy feeling was fouling her balance.

"Easy now, lass." Gray caught hold of her and steadied her against his side.

"This is so embarrassing." She rubbed the tip of her nose. Bad sign. Numb itchy nose. She had discovered that sign back in Kentucky. When her nose got all numb and itchy, it was time to curl up somewhere until the alcohol wore off. She swallowed hard. "How far is my room from here? I really need to rest for a bit." The longer she stared up at Gray, the more she teetered to one side.

"I dinna think ye can make it that far." He turned her slowly toward a wide bench lined with pillows.

She stumbled, clutched at his arm, then tried another step. "I am so sorry. I can't believe a few glasses of wine . . ." She swerved off balance and landed hard against his chest.

Gray didn't speak, just held her steady against him, his gaze locked on her mouth.

Trulie slowly licked her lips, then swallowed hard. She needed to lie down all right. With him. "Uhm . . ."

He swept her up, carried her to the bench, then gently lowered her into the pillows. Kneeling at her side for the longest time, he stared down at her. Finally, he slowly rose, pulled a plaid from the back of the bench, and spread it over her. "Rest well, lass. I will leave ye to yer dreams."

Before she realized what he was doing, he had left the room and closed the door softly behind him. She stared at the door for the longest moment, then huffed out an irritated, "Well damn." She dropped one foot to the floor to stop its spinning and covered her eyes with her arm. Just her luck. She had gotten all tingly with wine with a sexy Highlander and he had turned out to be a gentleman.

"Ye are certain ye dinna wish to ride in the wagon?" Gray watched it rattle up the hillside and disappear into the trees, then turned back to Trulie. "'Tis not more than a wee stretch of the legs for myself. But for ye . . ." Suddenly, all words left him.

The high color on the lass's cheeks only enhanced her beauty, but it was very clear she was a bit under the weather from yesterday's wine and most definitely out of breath. He turned aside and rubbed the back of his hand across his mouth to hide his smile.

Trulie huffed to a stop. "The only reason I am so out of breath is because this hill is a lot steeper than it looks." She leaned to one side and massaged her ribcage. "And my legs are a lot shorter than yours. I take four steps to one of yours."

Aye, well. He would give her that. Although he readily admitted he enjoyed the way her lovely bosoms bounced as she hurried to keep up. He supposed he should be ashamed, but it would only be a lie to say that he was. "I shall walk a bit slower. Forgive me."

Karma bounded past them, nose to the ground and tail in the air. He snuffled through the dried heather and sedge covering the hillside in thick clusters. Trulie smiled and pointed at the happy dog. "That is why I wanted to walk to Tamhas's croft. Karma is a big dog. He's sort of hemmed in at the keep."

Gray watched the great beast zigzagging his way up the hillside. He well understood how the dog felt. Oft times, he felt the same. He offered his hand to Trulie. His heart lightened as she took it without hesitation and fell in step beside him. How could a woman he had only known so briefly make him feel as though he had known her a lifetime?

He stole a glance down at her, quietly chuckling as she batted her curls out of her face. Those silky tresses had escaped their ribbons again, the dark tendrils dancing in the wind. The creamy whiteness of her throat made him long to brush his lips across her softness. He sucked in a deep breath of the chilly air and walked slower, eyeing the tempting mounds of her bosoms rounding nicely above her tightly laced kirtle. The loose weave of her shawl gathered around her did nothing to hide her bounty.

Aye. At this rate, he needed a cold blast of wind up his plaid to keep his cock at bay. The memory of the perfect weight of her on top of him came unbidden, the sweet soft feel of her curves when she had first fallen from the sky. Aye, and now that he knew her, understood more about her, the wanting of her gnawed within him like a deep hunger.

"How many more wagonloads do you think it will take to move Tamhas down to the keep? Granny said he has already filled the top level of the north tower." Trulie gathered her skirts higher and climbed atop a rock shelf jutting out of the embankment. She shielded her eyes with one hand and squinted farther up the mountain. "Karma! Don't get so far ahead of us. Come back here. Now."

"I told the old one this is the final trip we will make. He best gather and pack only what he canna live without. He shouldha moved down to the keep ages ago, but apparently, the wishes of his chieftain fail to carry the weight of the wishes of his woman." Gray motioned toward the edge of the woods. "There be yer great beast."

The tip of Karma's tail wagged a few inches above the thick tangle of grass adjoining the line of trees. Occasionally, the black tail would pause in its traveling wag above the dried grasses and quiver.

Trulie hopped down from the rock, gathered her skirts higher, and waded into the grass. "He needs to stay closer. It worries me when I can't see him."

"The lad will be fine." Gray held out his hand. "Come. Stay to the path. This part of the land can be treacherous to those who dinna ken it."

"That is exactly what I'm talking about." She pointed at the edge of the trees. "Karma doesn't know this place. He needs to stay with me." She turned back toward the wood. "Karma! Come here."

"Why do ye worry so? The lad will be fine."

Her voice quivered as she stopped wallowing through the tall grass and faced him. "You don't understand. I am the eldest. Karma is more than just a dog." She cast another worried glance up the hillside before turning back to Gray. "Karma has been with me ever since I can remember. He will be with me until my soul travels on. He is a part of me. My guardian. My familiar. The eldest daughter of every time runner generation is gifted with an animal spirit guide." She hitched in a deep breath, gathered up her skirts, and started toward the woods. "I can't lose him, Gray. I have to keep him safe."

The emotions in her voice stirred his heart even more than the eeriness of her words. *Guardian. Familiar.* A worried knowing filled his gut. The Sinclair women needed to stay well within the MacKenna lands. Superstition and belief in the old ways had long been held sacred by the MacKenna clan. The old magic was still considered holy. But in other parts of Scotland, the Sinclair women would not be so safe.

"Come." Gray waved her toward him. "We will follow the path to Tamhas's dwelling. I feel certain that is where the lad is headed. Ye ken he has always gone ahead of us before and been waiting there when we arrived."

An excited bark echoed from the woods, followed by a deep baying howl. The sound traveled across the hillside, gradually growing fainter by the minute.

"Karma!" Trulie shouted and took off in that direction.

"Lass!" Gray loped up the hillside, dodging and leaping over tangled clumps of matted heather. How the hell could the woman move so fast? This was not the place for her to wander alone. Gray crashed through a tangle of saplings and fought deeper into the woods.

"D-dammit!" A cursing shriek followed by splashing water came from just up ahead. Karma's steady bark echoed through the woods as though he were shouting instructions to his mistress.

Even before he had shoved his way through the thick under-brush, Gray knew exactly what had happened. He had hunted these hills many a time and cooled his body in the spring-fed pool just up ahead. An unwary traveler could easily be deceived by the grade and lay of the land. If they did not keep to the steep side of the path and carefully set each step, the unknowing discovered too late how the loose shale paving the slight walkway would throw them. The unseen trap would quickly shift and send them tumbling into the deepest end of the pool.

Louder splashing and curse words hurried Gray farther down the path. If he remembered correctly, an overhang of stone should be just up ahead. Depending on how high the level of the pool had risen from the most recent storms and snow melt, he should be able to reach the lass from there.

"Karma! Get help!" Trulie's gasps for breath spiked her words with panic.

Gray pushed through a tangled mass of carpet willows and came to an abrupt halt.

The huge black bear of a dog sat at the edge of the wide plate of limestone. The stone shelf hung several feet above the rippling surface of the pool. Ears perked, head cocked to one side, the great beast's enormous tail swept slowly back and forth atop the rock as he stared down at the water.

"Karma, please! Go get Gray or Granny or somebody. I am freezing my assets off and can't make it up the bank. The rocks are too steep and I can't get past all that brush on the shallow end."

Gray couldn't help but chuckle. Her assets. Aye. He had admired them every time Mistress Trulie walked away from him. More splashing sounded, followed by a very feminine growl of frustra-tion. He halted at the edge of the stone as Karma turned and faced him.

"Easy, lad." He kept his voice low as he moved up beside the dog.

"I mean yer mistress no harm. I only mean to pull her from the water."

Karma's long pink tongue lolled out one side of his mouth, between several large, sharp-looking teeth. If Gray didn't know better, he would swear the beast was actually smiling. He nodded to the dog and lowered himself to his hands and knees.

Trulie's pale face bobbed just above the black surface of the pool. Her wide eyes flickered with growing panic. With fingers outspread, the pallor of her hands reflected beneath the spreading ripples like shining fish skimming near the surface. Her long, dark hair shimmered like polished ebony, slicked down against the sides of her face and floating across the top of the water like rich, black ribbons.

Gray stretched out his hand and motioned her forward. "Here, lass. Come. Take my hand."

The top of the pool bubbled and foamed as Trulie flailed closer to the rock shelf. She grunted and lunged upward for Gray's hand.

"Get lower. I can't reach you." She sputtered and gasped as she sank back into the water. "You're going to have to get down on your belly and hang farther over the water." Her blue-tinged lips trembled and her teeth started to chatter.

He flopped down on his stomach and stretched out over the pool. He had to get the woman out of the water fast. The cold was beginning to take its toll. She would surely drown if he didn't rescue her soon. Locking the toes of his boots into the dips and bumps in the rock, he held out both hands. "Now, lass. Take my hands."

She took in a deep breath and lunged upward, missing Gray's fingertips by a whisper. When she fell back into the water this time, she submerged completely.

Karma stood at attention. He dug and pawed at the front of the stone while barking down at the water. Ears perked forward toward the spot where his mistress had disappeared, his tail no longer wagged.

"Enough of this." Gray jumped to his feet, stripped off his great plaid, and peeled off his knee-length léine. The cold Highland air against his flesh strengthened his resolve. He would be damned if he allowed the lass to drown and saddle him with her grandmother. He dove headfirst into the freezing water. Opening his eyes to liquid blackness, his fingers brushed against Trulie as she struggled to rise to the surface. He rose up behind her, hooked an arm around her torso and pulled her back against his chest. No wonder the lass could hardly stay afloat. Her heavy layers of clothing made an effective anchor.

He pushed them both back up to the blessed air. "I have ye now," he said against her chilled cheek as her head fell back against his shoulder.

She coughed and closed her eyes. Her arms floated limp on the water. "Good. Because I am entirely too tired to swim anymore."

"Open yer damn eyes!" He shook her. Now was not the time for the woman to give up. Not when he nearly had her saved.

Her dark lashes fluttered against her pale cheeks, then her eyes slowly opened. In a breathless voice, weak and rasping, she nodded toward the rock ledge looming up ahead. "If you're going to save me from drowning or freezing to death, I wish you would hurry up and do it. I am really tired of being cold and I have never liked swimming."

"Aye, lass. I will warm ye." Those firm breasts of hers currently caught beneath his arm deserved his undivided attention. A violent shiver shook her in his arms, triggering immediate remorse. What the hell was wrong with him? The woman was about to freeze to death and he had bed play on his mind?

"I is now or never, Gray," she whispered, then went limp against him.

"As ye wish, my headstrong woman." He sucked in a deep breath, then ducked beneath the surface. With his shoulder settled nicely under her fine round arse, he pushed off from a submerged boulder and launched himself upward. The force of his thrust shot her up out of the water and toward Karma.

She flopped across the rock with a heavy splat. Her top half landed well up on the stone but her rear and legs still dangled off the edge. Gray lunged upward, hooked the ledge under his arms, and shouted at the dog standing at Trulie's head. "Grab her, lad. Help me get her up the rest of the way."

Karma crouched over her upper body, buried his muzzle in the depths of her tangled hair and bit into her clothes. Gray cupped Trulie's bottom in his palm and nodded toward the waiting canine. "Now, lad."

In one great yanking lunge by both man and beast, Trulie shifted to the middle portion of the ledge.

Gray hung on to the side of the rock, adrenalin pounding through every fiber. His flesh hummed with energy. The worst was done. Now all he had to do was get her dry and warm. In one great push, he heaved himself up the rest of the way and landed on the rock beside her.

"Good job, MacKenna," she said softly as her head fell to the side. Her face was too pale. Her skin too blue. Gray pushed the soaked curls away from her clammy face. He had to get her out of those clothes. If he didn't get her dry and warm, Trulie Sinclair would never jump through time again.

He reached for the pile of clothing he had shed before diving into the water. He sorted through the items until his fingers closed around the bone handle of his dirk. Crouching beside her, he ignored the freezing wind stinging his bare arse.

Shoving her wet hair to the side, he hooked the blade under the back collar of her dress and split the garment down to the hem. With shaking hands, he peeled away the heavy layers of cold, soaked clothing. Heaven help him, her skin was white and smooth as finely polished ivory. He swallowed hard, then barely touched her glistening back. So very soft and so very cold. He shook himself free of the trance, rolled her out of her clothes, and curled her against his chest. Bless her soul, 'twas like cradling silky ice.

Gray held her tight and roughly rubbed up and down her back. Thank the heavens for the frigid air. He would play hell controlling his man parts if not for the freezing cold. The icy softness of her curves burned into his flesh as though he embraced molten steel.

Struggling to hold her limp form upright, he managed to work his thick woven lèine over her head and down around her body. He held his breath and barely stroked the back of his hand along the smoothness of her jaw. "Ye must live," he whispered. Lore, he would give anything if she would just open her eyes.

She slumped against him. Gray pressed an ear to her chest, searching for a heartbeat. *There.* It was faint and rapid, but at least the spark of life remained. He bundled the length of his plaid around her. The heavy wool of his colors would shield her from the bitter wind.

Her head rolled against his shoulder as he stood with her in his arms. "Ye must live," he gently ordered, then closed his eyes and sent up a prayer. *Dinna let her die.*

"Come, beast. We must get her to a fire." He shoved through the tangle of willows and overgrown sedge. Carefully, setting one soggy boot at a time on the treacherous shale, he made his way to the safety of the higher path. Karma shot past him, a dark streak racing up the trail toward the clearing. Gray prayed the dog would somehow raise the alarm.

As he shoved through the brush, he turned sideways and held her closer. Perhaps he should have left the shoes on her wee feet to protect them from the branches' claws. Karma's baying bark echoed back to him, hurrying him along.

"Quickly. We have stoked the fire." Granny stood at the head of the path, waving him forward. As he pushed out into the open, the old woman tiptoed beside him, one hand lightly patting Trulie's bundled form. "She will be just fine. I shall not consider otherwise."

Gray hoped the crone was right. Trulie's heartbeat barely tickled against his chest. "Have Tamhas spread a pallet as close to the fire as possible."

"It is already done," Granny said. "And I have sent Coira to the keep to alert yer men until we know . . ."

Gray did not care for the way the woman's voice trailed off. "Until we know what? Ye just said ye would not consider anything for yer granddaughter other than a full recovery."

The white-haired matron's mouth flattened into a determined

line and she bowed her head. She went silent as she hobbled ahead of him and threw the door open wide.

"Come, my chieftain. Place her right there." Tamhas hurried Gray forward, pointing to the thick mat of blankets spread before the hearth.

The heat of the room hit Gray full on as soon as he stepped through the door. And he welcomed it. His own flesh had already gone numb. Flames raged in the hearth. The inferno roared up into the mudded flue.

He eased Trulie down onto the pallet, then gently slid his arms from around her. She looked so tiny, almost colorless. He cursed his shaking hands as he pulled away the folds of his damp frozen mantle and exposed her to the heat.

Granny knelt beside him, shooing him away. She bent lower, pressed an ear to her granddaughter's chest and closed her eyes. "Her heart still beats," the old woman whispered. Her voice trembled with emotion. Straightening, she bunched the wet folds of Gray's plaid in both hands and tugged. "Lift her up so I can get rid of this wet cloth. She has to be dry and warm."

Gray held his breath as he slid both arms under Trulie's naked form and took her back into his arms. Lore a'mighty, the room suddenly seemed stifling.

"There now." Granny patted a blue-veined hand atop the dry blankets. "Now you can settle her back."

He closed his eyes and sucked in a deep breath. She smelled of honey, warm spice, an indescribable sweetness that he craved. He cradled her closer, reveling as Trulie's warming flesh melted against his.

"Gray!"

He jolted, rocked back on his heels, and held Trulie tighter. "What?" he snapped.

"I said," Granny repeated quietly with a nod at the pallet, "you can put her down now. I removed all the wet cloth."

What if he didn't wish to relieve himself of his sweet burden? He glared at the old woman, resenting the amusement flickering in her eyes. Plotting old crone. He could see mischief growing in her mind.

With a reluctant huff, he rested Trulie back on the mat. He gently arranged her arm across her side and swept her hair away from her face. "Rest well, lass. Find strength in yer dreams."

CHAPTER 11

A deep rumbling snore beside Trulie's head tugged her into wakefulness. She curled into a tighter ball and pulled the blanket higher around her shoulders. "Roll over, Karma. You're snoring."

The toasty warmth beneath the blanket sent her back into the arms of delicious drowsiness. She snuggled deeper and yawned. The softly crackling fire lulled her the rest of the way into the warm, velvety darkness.

A louder snort shattered the peacefulness and jerked her back awake.

"Karma! I said roll over." She didn't bother opening her eyes, just reached above her head to nudge the dog.

Instead of fur, she touched warm, smooth skin. Skin? Her eyes popped open and she lifted her head. The warm, yellow light of the dancing flames poured across the source of the deep, rumbling snores. Flat on his back, with hands folded across his taut stomach, Gray was stretched across one end of the pallet, the end closest to her head.

She blinked hard, then rubbed the corners of her eyes, trying to remember how exactly this situation had come to pass. A quick scan of the dimly lit room revealed this was Tamhas's place. Elongated shadows danced across the low-ceilinged dirt walls. The light of the hearth bounced off the mess left behind by the old man when he moved down to the keep.

She pushed herself upright, then realized she was naked. What happened to her clothes? Grabbing the pile of blankets pooled around her waist, she yanked them up to her throat.

Gray remained motionless except for the subtle rise and fall of his chest.

And what a chest. She couldn't help but stare. Clutching the rough blankets tight, she inched closer. Was he naked too? A corner of the blanket draped across his middle did little to hide the fact that he was.

She scrubbed her face with one hand. What was she doing naked in Tamhas's cottage—and why was she here with Gray? A shiver tickled up her spine into her damp hair.

Damp hair. Water. Numbing cold. Darkness. Memories tumbled over themselves as though her mind had suddenly thawed. She kept her gaze locked on the sleeping man, her heart swelling with a warm rush of emotion as everything became clear. Gray had saved her. Something clicked inside her. Like the last piece of a puzzle popped into place. She released a soft sigh. Yes. She and Gray *fit* each other.

The firelight flickered across the ridges of his muscled form. She relaxed her stranglehold on the blankets and barely kept them covering her chest. Those powerful arms had cradled her against that broad chest. Her body hummed with the memory; the tingling sensation fully imprinted in her flesh.

"Go back to sleep, lass," he said after a deep yawn.

She fumbled the blankets back up under her chin. "I thought you were asleep."

He settled his folded hands lower across his flat stomach and smiled without opening his eyes. "I was."

Tucking the blanket close, she locked it tight with her arms. "Care to tell me why we are *both* sleeping here . . . uhm . . . naked?"

He drew in a deep breath. The delicious plane of his broad chest expanded even more. His jaw-cracking yawn popped through the darkness as he settled deeper into the mat. "Our clothes were soaked. Stripping down is the best way to get warm and dry." The bit of blanket tossed just below his stomach appeared to be rising into a very impressive tent.

Merciful heavens, she scooted to the edge of the pallet farthest from the fire. The heat of the room suddenly seemed almost smothering. "Do you think we could open those shutters? It's kind of hot in here."

Gray rolled over onto his side and propped his head in his hand. The impressive blanket tent shifted to a pile of teasing folds just below his waist. "Aye," he rumbled softly. "'Tis verra warm in here."

Her fingers itched to trace the lines of those strong arms that had held her close. The glow of the fire turned his skin to a burnished copper. He stared at her, unblinking.

She parted her lips and drew in a shallow breath. *Do it*, her inner voice dared. Should she? Really? *What are you waiting for?* the wicked voice prodded again. She took another deep breath and allowed her blanket to fall away.

Gray's stare never wavered. Raw hunger blazed in his eyes. Slowly, he reached for her. "Come to me," he whispered.

She sat there hypnotized, her heart rate turning into an excited pounding.

"Come to me," Gray repeated, a hair's breadth louder than before. His deep voice stroked her like a lover's caress. He didn't move an inch toward her, just waited, with his hand outstretched.

She rose up on her knees and leaned across the pallet. Moving toward him on all fours, her body burned hotter, matching the inferno in his eyes. When she reached him, she barely rested her fingertips in his warm, calloused palm. A sense of completeness tingled through her. Yes. This was meant to be. And it wasn't alcohol talking this time.

Slow and steady, he gently pulled her closer, then slid his hand to the swell of her hip and cupped her behind. "I want ye," he rasped as he leaned up and brushed her lips with his.

She closed her eyes and gave herself to the sensations exploding across her senses. Yes, she needed this so very badly. The teasing of his lips . . . so insistent. The taste of him . . . warm and rich, flavored with the intoxicating spirits she vaguely remembered sipping as he supported her head. She opened wider to his kiss and melted into his embrace, molding herself against him.

He rolled her to her back without breaking their bond. He traced his fingertips along her jawline as he deepened the claiming and hungrily took more.

She welcomed the taking, knotting her fingers in his still-damp hair and arching into his touch. She ached with need, hardening into tight buttons as he licked a circle around her breast, then pulled her nipple deep into his mouth. She shuddered and rocked harder against him as waves of pleasure swept through her. Paradise. At last.

She smoothed her hands down his back, pulsating with the pleasure of touching him. She urged him closer, wrapping her legs around him as he shifted between her thighs.

He rumbled out a soft chuckle as he rose from nibbling a fiery trail down the center of her stomach. "Och, now. Patience, my love. Such a joining should never be rushed." He cradled her in the crook of his arm as he traced a teasing touch down her curves, then slid a finger deep into her wetness.

She bucked into the heel of his hand as he deftly massaged her mound faster and harder, then slid a second finger inside with the first. Waves of ecstasy built within her as he swallowed her cries with a hungry kiss.

As the delicious spasms slowly abated, he kept his fingers deep inside and ever so slowly worked his thumb back and forth across her still throbbing nub. With every stroke of his masterful hand, the urge to flip him onto his back and ride him hard grew.

"More," she panted against his mouth while wrapping her leg around his flank and arching against him. "I need you. Now." A groan escaped her as she slid, wet and eager against the length of his hardness and his talented fingers.

Every nerve ending threatened to explode as he took his cock and teased it against her opening. He swirled and rubbed the swollen head against the heat she longed to wrap around him. She shuddered, aching with excruciating pleasure. This was torture. She needed him inside her. All the way. Now. "Take me now!" She slid her hand down between them, grabbed his cock and aligned it for immediate entry.

"As ye will it, mistress," he said in a rasping whisper. He slid both arms beneath her and settled down hard between her thighs. "As ye will it," he groaned as he shoved deeper into her heat.

She bucked with the joining. A gasping moan escaped her as the melding crashed wave after wave of almost unbearable pleasure through her. She met him thrust for thrust, until the night shattered and her senses exploded with pure bliss. Gray's thunderous growl echoed her cries as his body tensed beneath her hands then hammered into her with primal urgency.

As the aftershocks crashed through her, he collapsed and tightened his arms around her. She closed her eyes and molded herself against him. What better way to stay warm at night than with your very own Highlander?

Gray rumbled with what sounded like a deep satisfied purr as he kissed the tender spot behind her ear and nuzzled a hungry trail down to her collarbone. He slid his hand down to the curve of her hip and rocked into her with his already returning hardness. He lifted his head and lightly kissed the tip of her nose. "I fear there shall be no more sleeping tonight, *mo chridhe*," he whispered with a wicked grin.

"As you will it," she said as she wrapped her legs around him and squeezed.

"Are you warm enough, gal?" Granny draped another wrap across her legs and tucked the ends snug inside the chair. "You haven't said two words since Gray brought you down from Tamhas's mountain."

Trulie wiggled her toes in the luxury of a pan of hot water and breathed in the herb-scented steam wafting up around her. "I am fine, Granny."

Sort of. Truth be told, she was a muddled mess of confusing emotions. What the devil was she going to do now? She had fully planned on returning to the future. But now? How could she leave now?

Granny studied her, peering over the top of her spectacles, perched on their usual spot at the end of her nose. "Coira will be here soon with a nice breakfast that will stick to your ribs and warm you from the inside out."

Trulie stared at the fire. The soft, glow of the red-orange coals triggered memories of last night. The firelight had burnished their skin a coppery gold. Gray had cradled her back against his chest as they watched the fire. His husky whisper had warmed her as he had spoken Gaelic, then fully ensnared her heart when he explained the meaning of the words.

She blinked, breaking the spell of the memory. Granny had been dead on the money. She ached to hear Gray's deep voice whisper her name in the darkness. She finally understood what Granny had meant about a love that made you burn. Gray was the one.

"Trulie?" Granny pulled a stool up beside the chair. "I've got just the thing to lift your spirits. How 'bout if we check on your sisters?"

Poor Granny. She didn't understand. There was nothing wrong with her spirits. Currently, she only had two major problems: one, she had fallen—and fallen hard—for a man from the thirteenth century, and two, Granny had been right about finding love in the past. The second problem was actually the biggest problem of all. Because it wasn't beneath Granny to do the *I told you so* dance. Trulie nodded and patted Granny's hand. "Talking to the girls would be great. I couldn't see them the last time we opened the portal."

Granny pushed up from the stool, grabbed the iron poker propped against the hearth, and stirred the fire. The action awakened the flames hidden in the chunks of wood, and soon yellow-white tongues of fire danced among the coals. Granny bent and scraped up a handful of cooled ashes piled against the stones. She stood for a long moment, fully focused on the flames. Then with a barely perceptible nod, she bent and softly blew the handful of ashes into the blaze.

The coals glowed brighter and the flames crackled and popped. A hollow roaring whooshed up the flue as an inky darkness rose from the center of the coals and grew until it spread across the width of the flames.

Kenna's yawning, sleepy-eyed face flickered into view. "Seriously, Granny? You know it's two in the morning here."

Granny frowned, then silently counted by tapping a thumb across her fingertips. "Sorry, gal. I forgot the time difference was still the same, even across centuries."

Kenna yawned again, turned, and shouted back over one shoulder. "You two get up. Granny and Trulie are on the line."

Trulie's heart warmed. Little sister sounded as though she had fully embraced the job of head of household. She leaned closer to the fire. "How did the twins do on their history test? You said they were having the same problems we did about finding all the errors in the history books."

"We aced them." Lilia shouldered Kenna aside. "Kenna told us to lie and just put down the answers the teacher wanted to hear."

"Kenna!" Granny shook her finger at the girls' image wavering above the flames. "What did I tell you?"

"You and I will talk later about throwing me under the bus." Kenna pushed Lilia out of the picture. "Go get Mairi so she can say hi."

Lilia pushed back into the picture and waved. "Love you, Granny! Love you, Trulie!"

"Love you more!" Trulie waved back, her heart aching. She missed those pestering little rascals.

Mairi wavered into view, her eyes barely open. "Is something wrong?"

"No, gal." Granny motioned to Trulie. "We just wanted to check in. It's been a few days."

Mairi yawned and listed slightly to one side. Kenna grabbed her by the shoulder and pulled her back upright. "She's toast. She stayed up till just about an hour ago reading some book on medicinal herbs."

"We love you, Mairi. Go back to bed." Trulie nudged Granny's shoulder and pointed to the portal. "Look. She didn't even make it past the couch."

Granny chuckled and gently blew another fistful of ashes into the hearth. "Take care, my babies. We'll check back in a few days."

Kenna's image wavered as she smiled and waved. "Love you both bunches!"

"Love you more!" Trulie waved back, a pang of homesickness settling like a weight across her as the fire portal closed.

A soft rap on the door preceded Coira's singsong chirp. "Time for breakfast. I have a fine feast, sure to warm yer bones."

"Let me dry your feet, gal." Granny held a cloth ready as she nodded across the room at Coira. "She'll sit over at yon table, Coira."

Coira's cheerful humming filled the room as she eased a linen-covered platter and a pitcher down on the table. She fixed Trulie with a mischievous look as she uncovered the food and tucked the linen into the waistband of her skirt. "Ye know, mistress, I canna remember the day when our chieftain has ever been so happy. Cook said she heard him actually singing as he passed through the kitchens."

Trulie glared at Coira as she settled in the chair at the table, willing her to hush it. "I'm glad Chieftain MacKenna's spirits are lifted. From what I've gathered, he has had more than his share of unhappiness."

Coira snorted and bobbed with a polite curtsy. "Oh, aye. That he has. But I do believe he has finally found the cure for his unhappiness."

"I may be old but I am not stupid." Granny took a bannock, split it in two, and smeared a healthy dollop of honey over it. "Eat this first and then I want you to try and get down some of that parritch." She pushed the pewter dish with the bannock in front of Trulie. "And I am well aware of what happened last night." Granny squared her shoulders with a proud wiggle. "I told you so."

"You just couldn't wait to say that, could you?" Trulie tore off a hunk of the bannock and popped it in her mouth. The warm, chewy bread covered with honey softened Granny's *I told you so* dance just a bit.

Granny drizzled more of the honey over the steaming bowl of oats, a smug look brightening her face. "There is no shame in taking credit where credit is due." She pushed the bowl in front of Trulie. "Now eat up. Tamhas said Gray has agreed to teach you to ride."

Trulie nearly choked on the sip of water. Last night's riding lesson had been stellar, but she was pretty sure Granny was referring to riding a horse. She coughed and pushed the bowl of oats to the side. "You know I don't eat oatmeal."

Granny plopped the bowl back in front of her. "Eat it. You are going to need your strength." She added another healthy dollop of honey and stirred it in with a wooden spoon. "Once you're able to ride a horse, we're going to the gravesite to pay our respects."

The gravesite. Trulie took the spoon from Granny and plopped it upright in the gummy oats. "Do you think we can find it?" It had been over fifteen years since her parents died. Highland weather could erase a lot in fifteen years.

"We will find it." Granny gave her a soft pat on the shoulder, then leaned in close and laughed as she whispered, "Now eat your oats like a good Scottish lass. Ye have a braw bonnie man to keep happy."

Trulie shoved a spoonful of the gummy oats in her mouth and tried not to gag. What a price to pay for an unforgettable night with a Highland lover.

CHAPTER 12

"Ye never rode a horse before ye rode with me?" Gray stared at her. Disbelief tilted his head to the side. "How do ye travel in Kentucky? By wagon only? Or are ye able to walk everywhere since the land is filled with so many"—What had she called them? Metro . . . metro . . . politans? That was it—"since Kentucky is covered with metro . . . politans?"

Trulie took a step back from the docile, brown mare patiently standing in front of her. She crossed her arms over her chest and ran her gaze from the back end of the horse to its head. As she reached out and hesitantly touched the horse's neck, she glanced back at him. "You remember that monster with the glowing eyes? The one that tried to run you down?"

How the hell could he forget? He thought Tamhas had surely sent him straight to some hellish world when that roaring apparition had charged him.

"Aye." He nodded. "What of it?"

"That was a truck." She skittered closer to the patient mare as another horse moved in the stall behind her. Casting a nervous glance back, Trulie slid well out of reach of the long black nose now stretching toward her.

"Aye. Ye best watch that one there." Gray chuckled as he gently pulled Trulie over until he stood between her and the inquisitive black horse. "Cythraul likes to pull hair."

Her hand flew to the thick braid coiled at the base of her neck and patted it. She leaned sideways, peeping around Gray and eying the horse much like a timid mouse watches a sleeping cat.

He chuckled again. Lore a'mighty, but the lass lightened his heart whenever he was with her. "Ye know he willna hurt ye, lass. He just likes to tug on ye a bit until ye give him the attention he feels he deserves."

Her watchful gaze slid from the black warhorse to Gray. "I'll take your word for it."

Gray reached out to the mare. The small horse stepped forward and nuzzled his palm. "Now, Sorrel here is quite the lady." He smoothed his hand up the horse's cheek and rubbed her warm, silky neck. "She will cause ye nary a trouble. Come. I'll settle ye on her back."

Sorrel affirmed Gray's invitation with a soft whinny and toss of her head.

Trulie didn't move, just stood with her gaze locked on the horse and silent.

"Trulie." He reached out, snagged the sleeve of her dress, and gently pulled her closer to the horse. "Ye dinna have to mount her just yet. Come and get to know her. See what a wee lamb she is."

"There is nothing wee about her," Trulie said as she grudgingly allowed him to position her in front of the gentle beast. She eyed him, then nodded at Sorrel's whisker-covered nose just inches from her face. "She looks small to you because you're so big."

He couldn't resist the look on Trulie's face, a delightful combination of frustration, wonder, and maybe just a tiny bit of fear. Grasping her shoulders, he turned her toward him and pecked a quick kiss on the end of her nose.

Her soft green eyes nearly crossed as she glared up at him. "Kissing me will not make the horse any smaller."

Laughter rumbled from him as he pulled her closer. He inhaled the sweetness of her hair and nuzzled the warm silkiness just behind her ear. "Kissing ye will not make me any smaller either."

She immediately melted into his embrace and slid her hands up his back. "I can think of a better way to spend the afternoon than teaching me to ride a horse."

"Aye. So can I." If he had his way about it, Trulie would not be mounting anything but him. A groan escaped him as he found her mouth. Lore, the woman already had him aching to take her.

Leaning Trulie back in one arm, he ran a hand down the rough weave of her overdress and cradled the enticing swell of her hip. As he dove deeper into the warm welcome of her mouth, he edged them back into an empty stall. The thought of bedding down in the fresh clean hay spurred him onward. Aye. This was the perfect place for an afternoon of pleasure.

She slid her hands up around his neck and molded herself against him, returning his kiss with an urgency that nearly undid him. She wanted him as much as he wanted her. He shuddered and hungrily opened her mouth for more. Lore—the taste of her lured him like wine tempting a drunkard.

He would never get his fill of her. Couldn't imagine the keep without her. But what if she chose to leave? What if she chose another time over him? He eased back a bit, shaken by the thought.

"What's wrong?" she whispered.

"Nothing." He swept her up into his arms and laid her gently down in the hay.

"Wait a minute." She gently pushed him away.

Wait? He stopped and pulled back. "I thought . . ."

She patted him on the chest and grinned. "I'm tangled in all these clothes. I need to shed some if we're going to . . ." Her words trailed off, but the look in her eyes left no doubt as to what she meant.

Now, that sounded like a fine idea indeed. He shifted to his side and propped his head in his hand. "Aye. Rid yourself of those trappings. I promise ye, I willna let ye get cold."

The look she gave him fanned the aching burn pulsing through him. Damn, but the woman set him on fire.

She rolled to her feet and shucked the heavy overdress off over her head, then bent to gather up the next layer.

He sat up and peered closer. What the devil did the woman have on beneath her léine?

The soft, white linen of Trulie's ankle-length underdress appeared much darker from her waist down. Instead of a teasing outline of her bare legs, the tunic revealed some sort of skin-tight blue trews.

"What the devil do ye have on yer legs?" he asked.

"Leggings." She bunched up the yards of linen around her waist and danced around in a circle. "See?"

He swallowed hard. Aye. He saw all right. How could he not see the way the *leggings* molded across the perfection of her fine arse?

"But why?" He leaned back against the stall and flicked a hand toward her. "Ye should be bare beneath yer dress. Women dinna wear trews or . . . leggings. Why are ye not wearing stockings?"

Her brows arched nearly to her hairline. "It's cold outside. You might be used to the wind whistling up your bare backside, but I'm not. These keep me nice and warm on a chilly day. Stockings don't insulate anything but my legs."

"If ye keep yer skirts down where they belong, the wind cannot get beneath them." The way she filled out the strange clothing disturbed him—in both a good and bad way. Such trappings were not a part of this time. If she planned to stay here, she should set them aside. The thought of her leaving disturbed him worse than the clothing revealing entirely too much of her lovely arse.

She yanked the dress back down over her leggings with a stomp of one foot. With a threatening scowl, she jabbed a finger at the center of his chest. "If I keep my skirts down where they belong, the wind won't be the only thing that won't get underneath them."

Lore a'mighty. That most certainly was not what he had meant. His aching man parts demanded he fix this. Now. Gray stood and moved toward Trulie, grateful when she didn't move away. "Ye know I meant no disrespect. 'Tis just . . ." Words failed him as he waved a hand toward the lower half of her body. How the devil could he put it without fanning her ire?

"Be careful what you say," she said with a toss of her head. "You don't want to dig that hole you're in any deeper."

Aye. She spoke the truth of it there. He closed his mouth and scrubbed a hand down his face. His cock roared its disapproval. How the devil had they gone from love play to sparring in just the blink of an eye?

He surrendered by lifting both hands in the air. "Forgive me, *mo chridhe*. I meant no slight to ye. Please know I would never treat ye with disrespect. I swear it."

The stiff set of her shoulders softened with the apology and a forgiving smile curved her lovely mouth.

Thank the gods. Maybe there was hope for a bit of afternoon pleasure after all. He eased forward, pulled Trulie closer, and pressed his forehead against hers. "Can ye forgive a backward Scot who fails to understand yer new ways?"

Her soft giggle bubbled between them. "Yes." She leaned back and slid her hands up and cradled his face. "And I am sorry too. I should not be so quick to judge."

He bent and found her mouth. Enough talking. Time for pleasure.

She stiffened in his arms, then jerked a step away from him. "Did you hear that?"

He bit back a groan. Now what the devil had gone astray? Were the Fates determined to turn his bollocks blue? Gray tipped his head to the side and listened. Animals rustled in their stalls. A hoof occasionally stomped on the hard-packed earth. "I hear nothing, *mo luaidh*. 'Twas more than likely one of the horses . . . or mayhap Rory tending them."

She took another step back. A faraway gaze filled her eyes as she lifted her face and listened. Turning in a slow circle with her head cocked to the side, her cheeks reddened as she listened. "No. It is not the horses or your stable guard. There is someone else . . ." Her voice trailed off as she closed her eyes.

What the devil had she heard? Concern washed across him like a bucket of icy water. He had seen that look before, on Tamhas's face when the old man received a disturbing vision. He strode out of the stall and scowled up and down the dimly lit dirt aisle running the length of the stable. He saw naught amiss.

Trulie shot out of the stall, looped her arm around his, and pulled. "Come on. We have to get the horses out of here. Now!"

"What say ye?" Gray planted his feet.

The alarm flashing in her eyes flooded a rush of adrenaline through him. He reached out and steadied her. "What the hell are ye saying? What did ye hear?"

She fidgeted back and forth while nervously glancing all around. "I heard—" She jerked her head from side to side and frowned. "Never mind what I heard. There is going to be a fire. We can't waste any more time. I promise I'll explain later."

Fire. The word shot through him like fast-acting poison. Memories of the last fire twisted through his gut. Spurred to action, he shoved her toward the outer door. "Out. Now. I will tend to the animals."

She yanked free of his grip and stomped deeper into the stable. "I'm going to help you. Now, come on!"

"For once, will ye listen?" He charged forward, scooped her up, and flopped her over his shoulder. From what she said, he had no time to reason with her, and he damn sure was not going to risk losing her to a fire.

"Rory!" he roared as he plowed through the stable.

She rained punches across his back and shoulders, squirming in his grasp. "P-put me down! D-damn you, Gray. I am going to make you sorry if you don't put me down."

Gray snorted out a bitter laugh. He knew the best way to handle a hysterical woman—ignore her until she realized he was right. "Rory!" he shouted again as he stepped outside.

"Aye?" A man the size of a well-fed bear gimped forward with a rolling, uneven gait. "What say ye, my chieftain?"

"Call the lads and make haste. Turn out all the horses. Not a single animal must be left in the stalls." Gray shifted Trulie more solidly across his shoulder, grateful that she had stopped pummeling him when Rory emerged from the paddock.

The balding man didn't crack a smile, but his bushy gray brows did ratchet a few inches higher as his gaze settled on Trulie's rump nestled tight against Gray's head. His thick, stubby fingers scratched the graying stubble of his cheek as he squinted back toward the building. "Ye want the stable empty?"

"Aye." Gray nodded once. Good man. Rory was a man of few words and loyal clear to the bone. "As soon as I"—Gray swatted Trulie's arse with the flat of his hand and grinned at the resulting enraged growl—"relieve myself of this load, I shall be back to help ye."

"Aye, my chief." Rory nodded once, glanced one more time at Trulie's squirming form, then turned toward the training yards to the left of the stables. Several young boys, gangly and nothing but knees and elbows, worked in the lot tending to their duties. "Come now, lads," Rory boomed out across the way. "There's a chore to be done."

The boys scrabbled to set aside their rakes and buckets, hurrying forward at their taskmaster's request.

Gray nodded his approval, then hurried up the stone path toward the private gardens at the rear of the keep.

"Put me down! I can help you. You better listen to me." Trulie reared back and rolled sideways. She grabbed a hank of his hair and yanked hard, as though she held reins to stop him.

Enough. He plopped her down hard on the square corner post of the inner garden's low wall. "I willna have it," he roared. He set his hands on either side of her hips and got right down in her face. "Ye are a stubborn lass. I'll give ye that. But ye best learn that I am even more stubborn. When I see what I want, I claim it. And once I make that claim, I protect what is mine."

"I am not—"

"The hell ye're not!" He tangled his fingers in her loosely braided bun, yanked her forward, and kissed her hard. *Mine.* A guttural growl shook through him. *Mine* echoed through his being as he unleashed the claim into the kiss.

Gray finally jerked back. "Ye will stay here," he ordered. Then he turned and strode away. Minutes later a roaring explosion shook the ground.

B<small>ILLOWING</small> black smoke shot through with orange flames that engulfed one side of the stables. Horses' screams and frantic shouts filled the air as both animals and humans reacted to the chaos.

Trulie hopped off the fence, hiked up her skirts, and took off at a dead run. No way was she going to sit idly by and watch the madness like it was some sort of show.

Scrawny stable boys staggered through the yard, sloshing buckets of water. Men and women came running from all directions. Some stopped to soak yards of cloth in the troughs then hurried to slap the sopping wet rags against the base of the flames. Rearing horses foamed at the mouth, their eyes rolling white with terror.

Trulie dodged the dangerous hooves of a pair of roans being coaxed to safety by a boy who couldn't have been more than eight or nine years old. She ducked underneath the center rail of the wood fence that encircled the training paddock. She needed to get close and reach out with her senses. She had to find Gray.

A watering trough nudged up against a side of the building not yet overtaken in flames caught her eye. Yes. Right there. The shadowy corner called out to her like a beacon through the melee. Heart pounding, she backed up against the wall and wedged herself in the dark corner next to the trough.

Blocking out the shouts and screams, she forced herself to ignore the stench of choking smoke, muddied earth, and manure. She had to focus. Where was Gray? She had to make sure he was safe.

Earlier in the stall, just as she had blissfully lost herself in the pleasure of his kiss, her mind had filled with visions of the impending blaze. Echoing screams of terrified animals had drummed in her ears. An angry bellow had followed a deafening crash and then her senses had filled with the worst sound of all: cold, hollow laughter. Heartless laughter had blocked all else from her mind. She would never forget that sound as long she lived and she had to make sure the owner of that laugh failed at whatever evil he was attempting. She couldn't bear to hear it again.

A relieved tingle spread gooseflesh across her skin. There, Gray was right there. She shimmied under a tangle of wagons waiting to be repaired and raced around to the outer back wall of the stable. Her heart fell when she spotted the barricaded doors. Someone had worked hard to ensure an escape out the rear of the building would not be possible.

A crashing woosh thundered as the front half of the thatched roof collapsed inward. Black smoke billowed up past the orange sparks showering through the air. The barred doors of the stable shook as something solid hit them. A horse screamed and the doors shook again.

Trulie covered her ears with her hands. The terror echoing in the animal's cries broke her heart.

An angry bellow roared just behind the doors right before they rattled with another heavy impact on the other side.

Trulie knew that roar. Gray was trapped with one of the horses.

She had to get that post moved. She frantically glanced around the back lot. The clan was battling the blaze from the front of the stable. There was no time to run for help. It was all up to her. She set her shoulder against the wide oak beam butted up against the door and shoved. It didn't budge.

"Dammit!" She leaned into it again. No luck. The heavy length of lumber barely shifted with her effort. Time to change strategy. She wrapped her arms around the post and yanked upward. The thing still didn't move from its wedged position.

Tendrils of smoke escaped through cracks in the rear wall. The fire was slowly eating its way to the back of the stable.

She stepped back one more time and examined the jammed beam of wood. Maybe if she crouched under it and lifted with her legs, she could pop the thing out of the way. Leverage was her only hope.

Just as she was about to crawl under the beam, the doors shook again but they didn't move with nearly the intensity as they had the last time they'd been struck.

"Gray. Hang on. I'm going to get you out of there. Just hang on." She scrambled underneath the six-by-six wood beam, centered the solid bar of wood across her shoulders, and locked her arms against the side of the barn. With a deep breath, she shoved upward as hard as her legs could push. The beam shifted a bit to the side then wedged atop the cross latch set across the door.

"Dammit!" Staggering a few steps back, she knew she had to do it again. She had to make this work. Positioning herself on the ground underneath the pole, she inched down the beam with her feet until her bent legs were effectively wedged between her body and the wood. Feet angled against the pole, she kicked upward with the mightiest shove she could manage. Relief exploded through her as the beam popped free and tumbled down to the ground.

She jumped up and wrestled the cross latch out of the way, ignoring the rough wood splintering into her as she clawed the doors open.

Her heart nearly stopped as daylight poured into the smoke-filled stable and illuminated the back aisle. The mighty black Cythraul lay motionless, and stretched out on his side beside him, with an arm thrown across the horse's neck, was Gray.

"You are not going to die on me, Gray MacKenna." She clenched her teeth and dropped to her knees. Hungry orange flames crackled ever closer as she crawled to him.

There was no way she could physically drag the man or the horse to safety, and there wasn't time to run and get help. But if she healed them here—she sent up a silent plea to the Fates to let it be so—if she could heal them, maybe they could reach safety under their own steam.

The fire roared and growled as it ate into the walls. It seemed to laugh at her plan to steal the man and beast from its grasp.

She ignored the pulsating heat already stinging her flesh. She turned her back to the inferno and wormed her way between Gray's side and Cythraul's belly. Thank goodness she could still see the barest movement of the flesh along Gray's ribs as he struggled to breathe.

Swallowing hard, Trulie turned and rested her head against the great black horse's side and listened. She could heal, but she couldn't raise the dead. She had to make sure she wasn't too late.

A weak tap beneath her cheek filled her with hope. There was still time. She could pull this off—as long as they both responded quickly.

Trulie rubbed her fingers together. She hadn't healed nearly as many times as her sister Mairi, but she knew she could do it. She had discovered that she too was blessed with Mairi's gift when she had healed Karma after he had been hit by a car.

She flattened her palm on Gray's side and pressed the other on Cythraul's neck. Head bowed, she closed her eyes. Now all she had to do was build and release the energy. The gift of the Fates would take care of the rest.

A familiar burn exploded in the center of her chest and radiated out to her arms. The scorching energy squeezed through her veins and surged down into her hands. She kept her eyes shut and concentrated as the aching grew more intense. Healing required the most energy of all. More energy meant more pain.

She clenched her teeth, her hands shaking with the growing intensity of the power. She had to wait until the proper moment to shoot the energy into her charges. They needed the biggest surge she could propel.

Blood seeped from her hands. Crimson droplets peppered her arms, coursed down, and dripped off the tips of her fingertips. Just a little more. She bent her head, clenched her teeth, and struggled to keep from passing out.

Now. Certainty burst across her consciousness. A scream ripped from her throat as a blinding white shaft of energy exploded out of her hands.

The bodies of both man and horse rocked with the force of the impact.

She sagged forward, catching herself with her bloody hands. Forcing herself upright, she rocked back on her heels as Cythraul grumbled out an angry knicker and struggled to gain his footing. The great horse rose and staggered the few steps it took to clear the stable door, his long reins dragging in the dirt beside him. His glistening black nostrils flared as he pawed the ground and squealed out his rage.

Trulie pressed a hand to Gray's cheek. His eyes flickered open, then narrowed as he tapped a finger on her chin. "I told ye to stay in the garden. Ye're a stubborn wench who doesna listen."

"Get up." She pulled on him. "We'll talk stubbornness later. You must get up. We have to get out of here."

He struggled to his hands and knees, then fell back to the ground. Coughing and gagging, his eyes slowly closed.

"Open your damn eyes! Don't you dare give up now." She pounded on him as she stole a glance at the wall of flames steadily marching toward them. Shouts of the clansmen fighting the inferno broke through the blazing barrier. "Help us!" she screamed. But the others couldn't hear her through the roaring chaos. She had to do something. She refused to let him die.

"You're gonna burn to death if you don't open your damn eyes and help me." She held his face between her hands, willing him to listen.

He slowly rolled to his stomach and lifted his head. "The reins," he said, coughing as he weakly pointed toward the angry black horse still pawing at the ground just beyond the stable.

The reins. She staggered to her feet. Cythraul reared up, pawing at the air and shaking his great shaggy head as he screamed. She skittered sideways, eyeing the horse's sharp hooves cutting the air.

"Nice horse. Work with me here. Please." Trulie struggled to keep her voice calm. Thank goodness the beast was hemmed in. The small patch of ground behind the stables was blocked off on one side by broken-down wagons and the solid-stone skirting wall on the other.

A black streak sped past her with a warning growl. Karma barked, hopping and dancing around the angry horse. Avoiding Cythraul's pawing hooves, Karma lunged and caught one of the reins between his teeth. He clenched it tight and started backing up as though playing his favorite game of tug.

Trulie rushed forward grabbed the rein and pulled. "Calm down, Cythraul. Calm down."

With Karma growling encouragement, Trulie managed to snag the other rein. She pulled hard and inch by inch, and with Karma nipping at the horse's heels, together, they maneuvered the great beast close enough to get the reins to Gray.

"Here. Wrap them around your hands and hang on." She shoved the reins into Gray's hands. When he failed to respond, she punched his shoulder. "Gray! Do it now."

"Ye are a worrisome wench." He slowly wrapped the reins around one hand, then pressed his fingers against his mouth and blew a weak whistle.

Cythraul's ears perked, then he dug in and backed away from the fire. Gray half rolled, crawled, then finally just held on and allowed the horse to drag him across the clearing. Behind them, burning hay crackled out a warning as the remainder of the roof plummeted to the ground. Shouts echoed through the bailey as the fire roared hotter. Trulie's burning hair crackled in her ears. The cloying smell of singed hair and black smoke gagged her. She turned away and sucked in deep breaths of cold Highland air.

Wiping her bloody hands against the tattered remains of her dress, she scooted closer to Gray and pressed her hot face against the clammy coolness of his skin. As he coughed and noisily sucked in a healthy inrush of air, she wept.

He wrapped an arm around her and yanked her back against his chest. "Do ye ever do as ye are told?" he asked with a hoarse growl.

"Rarely," she said as she hugged his arm tighter around her. Without opening her eyes, she listened hard and scanned the area with her senses. Good. For the most part, the chaos was dying down as the fire destroyed what was left of the stable. They wouldn't have much time to rest before the clan picked their way around the destruction and discovered them. Better rest with what little time they had. Lordy, she was completely drained.

His chest shifted against her, as though he was about to speak. She cut him off with a sharp jab of her elbow. "Not now. I am worn out. We can talk later. Right now, I need a few minutes of peace and quiet before everyone finds us. Healing drains me."

"Woman—"

She jabbed him again. "I said hush."

"As ye wish it," he finally rumbled with a defeated sigh.

CHAPTER 13

"Aileas stirs unrest against Mistress Trulie." Colum stopped beside the head table. His hand rested atop the worn pommel of his sword as he eyed those gathered in the hall. He stepped closer and lowered his voice. "She raises questions about the fire and how ye were saved. She stirs suspicion in everyone's mind. The Sinclair women—they must take care."

This information did not surprise Gray, nor did he care for it any better now that Colum had voiced it. The familiar revulsion Aileas always triggered soured even more in his gut. He shifted in the chair and brought his attention to the small cluster of higher-ranking clanswomen gathered across the room. "Perhaps the Lady Aileas seeks to shift suspicion from herself." Gray's fists tightened atop the arms of his chair. "Or her beloved spawn."

Aileas's blotchy face was even ruddier than usual. The furious stirring of her pot of lies had no doubt set fire to her blood. She hunched forward, eyes bulging for want of air as her thin lips moved at lightning speed. Suddenly, she stopped speaking, straightened from the cluster of women, and looked all around the room. Her uneasy gaze locked with Gray's glare.

She scowled right back at him, widening her stance and squaring her shoulders as though preparing to plow across the room. With a challenging toss of her head, she smoothed back the usual web of stringy brown curls wisping around her face. A conniving sneer tightened her mouth as she motioned for the group of women to join her in a more private corner.

Gray snorted. The women hanging on Aileas's every word were the usual harpies who caused the most tension within the clan. The bitter females only found happiness when causing trouble for others. Three were widowed. One soon would be. Her frail husband had been ill for months. Gray slowly shook his head. The poor man probably prayed for death to escape his wife.

The quartet of self-proclaimed righteous women stood with their plump hands pressed against their bosoms as though they couldn't believe Aileas's latest revelations. And they shouldn't believe a word from her lips. The woman was a lying bitch.

"Have ye warned Granny and bade Coira to make certain that Trulie kens the danger?" Gray turned back to Colum as he shifted in the chair and forced himself to maintain the controlled air befitting a Highland chieftain.

Colum's ears flushed a deep red and he fidgeted in place. "When I spoke to Granny Sinclair, the old woman gave me a hard look up and down and asked how I felt about marriage."

"Did she now?" Gray cast another sideways glance at Colum and chuckled. So Colum was to be Granny Nia's next target, perhaps? Good. Being chosen by Granny Sinclair was not so bad—after all, had she not matched him to a green-eyed beauty well fitted to his heart and soul? Aye, she would do Colum justice as well. "And pray tell, how did ye respond?"

Colum huffed in a deep breath then released it with a groan. "I told her I was a man of the sword. I had no time for a wife."

"And her response?"

Colum shuffled uncomfortably in place while his gaze darted about the room. "She laughed."

"I see." Gray did his best not to smile. Poor Colum. The man was no match for Granny Sinclair. He might as well place his sword at her feet and beg for a merciful decision.

"Aye." Colum bobbed his head faster as if affirming every word. "And then she added that Aileas was . . . " Colum paused and scrubbed a hand down his face as though trying to choose his carefully. "She said Aileas better not tangle with them because they had trapped worse sore-tailed bears than her."

Sore-tailed bears? Gray turned and fully faced Colum. "What the hell is that supposed to mean?"

Colum shrugged and shook his head. "I canna say. Half of what either of those women say makes no sense to me."

Gray chuckled. Poor Colum. He had to admit he felt the same. He knew the clan was curious about the Sinclair women's words as well, adding weight to Aileas's accusations.

His amusement disappeared as the four troublesome shrews and Aileas went silent. They turned as one and trained haughty stares on Trulie as she entered the room with Coira at her side.

Trulie paused and stared them all down until they turned away.

Admiration filled Gray as he rose from his seat. Such strength. Trulie was fearless. Tamhas and Granny had not been so far off the mark with their wee matchmaking game.

"And how do ye fare this fine, frosty morning, Mistress Trulie?" Gray knew exactly how she fared this morning. She had been smiling and flushed pink with pleasure when he had risen from her bed after properly thanking her yet again for saving him from the stable fire.

"I am quite well, thank you." She flashed a meaningful smile back at Gray, which was fully understood. "Colum said we might be of some help to you today."

Grudgingly, Gray pushed the memory of her sprawled across piles of pillows to the back of his mind. He nodded toward the gaggle of scowling women gathered across the room. "Aye. Today, the hall is open for the airing of grievances. I would like ye to be present while I hear them. I would know yer thoughts about each person once they have spoken. Perhaps ye can discover who set fire to the stable."

"Perhaps a murderer might be found as well," Colum said as

he scowled first at Aileas and then swiveled his glare to the other side of the room. The long plank tables had been pulled to the side nearest the kitchens. Several men sat scattered among the benches, their weapons laid atop the table beside their tankards as they quietly talked. Sitting alone at the table closest to the corner, Fearghal slumped forward clutching a chipped mug with both hands as though he feared it was about to escape him.

Trulie gasped, her eyes went wide, and her face paled. She latched onto Coira's arm for balance as she bowed her head.

Gray rushed to gather her hands in his. His alarm deepened at the unnatural iciness of her flesh. "What troubles ye? What has made ye unwell?"

She coughed as though about to choke, then opened her eyes. As she leaned in close, she weakly squeezed his hands. "I saw . . ." She stared off into space, her lips barely parted.

"Ye saw what?" He gently pulled her closer. "Tell me, love. What did ye see?"

"We can prevent it," she assured him with a firm nod, slowly blinking as though she had just awakened.

"What?" He did his best not to raise his voice. It was obvious the woman was deeply troubled. What the devil had she seen? The last incident she had foretold—the stable fire—had nearly ended him. If there was ill afoot, he needed to know what it was and he needed to know it now.

She wet her lips, took a deep breath, and smoothed her hands back across the sleek darkness of her upswept hair. After a quick glance around the room, she directed Coira to the wide stone archway leading to the kitchens. "Could you please wait for me in the kitchens? We need to look . . ." Her voice faltered and she stopped speaking.

"We need to look for what, mistress?" Coira glanced back and forth between Trulie and Gray.

"Aye, I would hear yer thoughts as well." He moved closer and set a hand on Trulie's waist.

"I will explain everything once I am done here." She gave him and Coira a trembling smile and nodded once again toward the archway.

Tension burned through him as he watched Coira duck her head and scurry from the room. Pulling Trulie closer, he whispered into her hair, "What the hell was that about? What did ye see?"

"Nothing I want to tell you about right now." She took a step back and clasped her hands in front of her. Coldness emanated from the grim look on her face, but at least her color had returned.

Gray scowled at the archway Coira had just passed through, then turned back to Trulie. "I need to know if aught is amiss—if trouble is about to befall."

"It is not going to fall," Trulie said in a firm voice. "I am not going to let it."

SEETHING HATRED. Jealousy. Loathing. Fear and . . . secrecy? Trulie peered closer. What kind of secret did Aileas MacKenna hide? Did she really have something to do with the most recent fire, and maybe even the murder of Gray's parents?

Trulie concentrated. She wet her lips, amped up her sensors, and braced herself against the wave of negativity battering her like a relentless demon. Lady MacKenna was an unhappy woman. Misery oozed from the woman's pores like the stench of an unhealthy sweat. It was going to take a lot of work to sort through that emotional mess. No way was Trulie going anywhere near Aileas's mind. As loudly as Aileas transmitted her foul, septic soul, her mind surely had to be a tormented level of hell.

Trulie eased down into the chair Gray had ordered placed beside his own and studied the foul woman. She hadn't missed the flush of anger staining Aileas's cheeks when she had joined Gray at the head of the great hall. And a smile at the fuming woman enraged Aileas even more. As deep a red as her face was, the woman needed to calm down before the top of her head blew off.

"I feel it unfair that the number of my serving girls has been decreased." Aileas's high-pitched voice echoed through the hall with a nerve-grating whine. She twisted her hands in front of her thick waist and swayed back and forth like an oversized pendulum. "My rooms grow shabby with neglect. 'Tis not befitting for the chieftain's widow."

"I have not decreased yer household." Gray leaned heavily to one side and nodded to the next individual waiting to speak. "If that be all, Lady Aileas—"

"That be far from all." Aileas sniffed and lifted the end of her wrinkled nose an inch higher. She stomped her oversized foot so hard that her heavy, dark skirts bounced. "If my servants have not been decreased by yer order, I demand to know who has abused such power." Aileas's scowl deepened as she swiveled her entire girth to glare at Trulie.

Trulie glared right back and smiled. Aileas reminded her a great deal of the unpleasant Mrs. Hagerty back in Kentucky, making Trulie wonder if the vile woman happened to be Hagerty's ancestor. The only difference between the two was that Mrs. Hagerty lifted the art of bitchiness to an almost admirable level. Poor Aileas floundered at the task, landing somewhere between pathetic and easily forgettable.

Sensing Gray's growing impatience, Trulie rested her hand atop his and spoke before he could respond. "Lady Aileas, my grandmother and I assumed you sent those two helpful serving maids to our rooms permanently. Please forgive us if we assumed incorrectly. After all, everyone here is well aware of the caring and generosity of the great chief's widow."

Aileas's jaw dropped and her mouth gaped open. Several rotted and missing teeth did nothing to improve her appearance. Her knuckles whitened as she strangled the bit of white linen clutched between her hands.

Trulie forced herself not to cringe. With teeth like that, Aileas's breath had to be fierce. An errant draft wafted through the hall, making Trulie blink hard against the wall of foul air it brought to her. She parted her lips and blew out short strained breaths. The rancid odor of Aileas's unwashed body poisoned the air like a noxious cloud. Heaven help them all, Aileas was ripe.

"Perhaps I spoke rashly," Aileas stammered. She slightly turned and darted a glance upward to the gallery and her cluster of friends. "Aye. Now that I think longer upon it, I do remember telling two of the girls to make certain yer rooms were suitable." The unbearable matron stood taller, seeming to grow more pleased with herself as she looked up at the head-bobbing group of women again. "But I assumed the chieftain would see them returned to me once he set ye up in yer own tower—much as his father did for his mother."

A collective gasp rippled through the crowd gathered on either side of the hall.

"Ye have overstepped yer bounds, Aileas." Gray lunged up from his seat.

Fearghal clumsily made his way out from behind the bench and table. He teetered to a stop, twisted back, and loudly cursed it. After properly denouncing the ancestry of the carpenter who had crafted the bench, Fearghal whirled back around and stumbled forward. He came to an unsteady stop beside his mother. After swiping his face with his stained sleeve, he threw out his chest and took a staggering step toward Gray. "I shall not allow ye to speak to the Lady Aileas in such a manner when ye have the likes of that one standing at yer side." He fixed Trulie with a bleary-eyed glare, then punctuated the challenge with a gurgling belch.

"Ye are drunk again, Fearghal. How else would ye find the courage to speak?" Gray slowly pulled Trulie closer. "Forgive me, *mo luaidh*," he said softly. "Pray ignore the drunken fool and his mother."

Fearghal tucked his chin and belched louder. Stumbling a bit to one side, he drew his dirk and waved it in the air. "What kind of chieftain has his leman sit beside him in great hall? What kind of chief takes council from a whore?"

Gray drew his blade and surged forward. Trulie snagged his sleeve and yanked back. "Gray—no!" He didn't need to kill a drunken fool on her account.

Red-faced, Fearghal spat and sputtered profanity as he struggled to free himself from his mother's hold. Even Aileas realized her son had gone too far and was attempting to drag him from the room.

Trulie planted herself in front of Gray. He pushed around her.

"Stop." Trulie rounded Gray again and flattened both hands against his chest. "Gray. Please don't."

He grabbed her by the shoulders and set her aside as though she hadn't said a word.

"Gray, you must stop. Now." She pushed back into his arms and held his face between her hands. "Let it pass," she pleaded, searching his eyes for the slightest flicker of reason. Rage simmered in their depths. Thirst for blood turned them an even colder blue. "You are better than them. Besides, I need to hear everything to gather information. I need to read the room—including them. Please."

"I command respect in my hall. Nothing less."

His jaw tensed beneath her hands. His muscles rippled with barely controlled rage. She swore she heard his clenched teeth crack with the pressure. Poor Gray. He just didn't understand. She had been singled out and ostracized by the best of them because of her family's strange ways. Fearghal and his mother were amateurs when it came to trying to make her feel uneasy.

"They don't bother me," she said, soothingly. With one hand still resting on his hard-muscled arm, Trulie turned away and focused on Fearghal and Aileas. Time to get a quick read of Mr. Personality and his mama.

Whore. Bits of muddled conversation colored with emotion raced through Trulie's consciousness. *Half brother. Unwanted stepmother. Murder. The whore's tower. Jealousy. Loathing. Fear.* All the dark energy emanating from the pathetic duo standing in front of her suddenly made complete sense—all except the odd reading of some sort of secrecy. One or both of them was definitely afraid of something being discovered. They weren't afraid of physical harm. Trulie focused harder. They feared being found out. Perhaps about the murder? But which one was it, and was the murder the secret they didn't want revealed? Bless her, she needed to read their minds, but she just couldn't force herself to go there. As sloppy as these two were, surely, she could figure them out without having to wade through the nastiness of their inner selves.

She clicked off the facts in cold, analytical order. Gray's mother was the chieftain's leman, the favored mistress the old man had dearly loved. Aileas was the political marriage, the wife who loathed her unfeeling husband even more than she loathed herself. Trulie almost felt sorry for Aileas. Almost. The ballsy woman had as much as come out and called Trulie a slut in front of Gray's clan. And then her son had actually done it.

And Fearghal—the man could hardly stand upright. He leaned heavily against his mother. His balding head bobbed up and down. His red-rimmed eyes insisted on slamming shut as he struggled to gain his balance. How could such a pitiful creature share a bloodline with Gray? She stepped closer and peered harder at Fearghal.

A sudden flood of emotions battered so hard against her that it knocked her a few steps back. Never had she felt such a wave of deep hatred. It had to be eating Fearghal and Aileas alive. But wait—she focused harder. The disturbing hum of hatred wasn't coming from either Aileas or her son.

Aileas yanked the staggering Fearghal back toward the archway. The woman obviously feared her son was about to say too much. Trulie felt sure of it. Perhaps they would rise to properly tendered bait. Yes. She had to do it. Surely that would loosen their tongues and stir the strange hate enough that she could hone in on its source without having to visit the dark recesses of anyone's mind.

Holding her breath against Aileas's stench, Trulie closed the distance between herself and the scowling woman. Adrenaline pounded through her. Surely all present could hear the hammer of her heart echoing across the deathly silent hall. Jaw set, Trulie pointed a finger at Aileas's heart. "Do not make the mistake of challenging me again. I know your secret and won't hesitate to reveal it."

Aileas flinched as though she had been struck. She plucked at Fearghal's sleeve as though trying to position the drunken fool between herself and Trulie. Her thin lips opened and closed, but no sound came forth.

Spinning around, Trulie gave Aileas her back and took her time walking regally back to the front of the room. That ought to push the woman over the edge and loosen her tongue. Trulie smiled and arched a brow at Gray.

Gray's expression was stone-cold hatred. He didn't even blink. Trulie struggled to keep her smile from slipping. Gray's rage and hatred troubled her. Such poisonous negativity always caused more harm to the bearer than the target. Aileas and Fearghal were not a threat. She had to make him see that.

Trulie glanced back over one shoulder at Aileas and Fearghal. Still no outburst from the pair?

Fearghal hitched to one side and Aileas's jowls waggled as her scowl deepened.

Well, that hadn't worked out as she had hoped.

A prickling sensation tingled up the back of Trulie's neck, pulling her attention to the far side of the room. Two massive tapestries hung from the first level of supporting beams jutting out from the stone wall. She wasn't sure, but she thought the vibrant scenes of successful hunts weren't hanging flat against a stone wall. Trulie concentrated harder on the two wall coverings and saw them gently moving, as though stirred by something behind them. Shifting to one side, she ran her gaze along the floor beneath the tasseled ends of the weavings. *Yes.* The darkness running the width of both hangings indicated some sort of hidden alcove behind them.

The prickling sensation disappeared. Trulie shrugged away the disturbing feeling that she had just missed discovering something very important.

Fearghal shook the hall with another wet belch, one that sounded as though it had come dangerously close to emptying his stomach. Trulie shivered with disgust. She couldn't handle the sound of puking. Time to end this happy little family gathering.

She walked over and smoothed a hand up the center of Gray's chest. She needed to soothe her enraged Highlander before he did something he might regret. Speaking low so no one else could hear, she leaned close until the heat of his rage radiated against her. "Let her go, Gray. I don't care what she calls me. She's just a miserable old woman who can't get over the fact that she has never been wanted."

Low murmurings stirred through the crowd like the droning of angry bees.

Gray bared his teeth as though he were about to sprout a set of fangs and roar. With one glance to the back of the room, he shouted over one shoulder to his man-at-arms. "Colum, clear this hall. I can no longer stomach the stench of it."

"I be glad Father lies dead," Fearghal squeaked as a muscular guard slammed a large hand atop one of his shoulders and pulled him backward. "I be glad his whore lies dead too," Fearghal said, choking and coughing as the guard cursed and wrapped a hand around his throat.

The chilling clatter of drawn steel echoed to the rafters.

"Fearghal, enough!" Aileas hissed as she shoved her wadded bit of linen deep into her son's mouth. Then she bowed her head once in Gray's direction and attempted a rough curtsy. "Forgive," she croaked as she continuously bobbed up and down humbly as they backed their way out of the hall.

TENSION HUNG heavy in the air of the now-silent hall—empty of everyone except Gray and Trulie. Even the fires glowing in the two hearths danced across the wood without a single pop or hiss. The MacKenna colors barely fluttered against the faded stones of the keep's walls.

Gray tensed against the eerie feel of the air. He felt no draft. No stirring of a breeze. Perhaps the souls of those already crossed over moved among them. Perhaps they stood witness to the trials of their descendants.

He pulled his gaze from the fluttering banners of tartan and scrubbed the heels of his hands across his eyes. If his ancestor's spirits were in the room, he wished to hell the wise ones would tell him what he should do.

"Gray." Trulie's soft touch slid up his arm. The scent of her sweetness embraced him, instantly bringing him comfort. The woman rendered him powerless yet completed his very soul at the same time. He dropped his hands and opened his eyes.

"Forgive me, *mo chridhe*." He pulled her close. "I should have known better than to have ye join me in great hall. Not only was I dishonored, but they shamed ye as well. I should have never put ye through it."

She hugged him tighter, patting his back as though consoling a child. Her silky curls tickled underneath his jaw. "I told you not to let those two bother you. Trust me"—She leaned back and grinned up into his face—"I have dealt with much worse."

"I will not have ye treated in such a way. Fearghal and Aileas were not the only ones that showed us disrespect." He set her aside and turned away, refusing to put her through the years of loneliness and pain his mother had endured. *Máthair* had never complained about the life she had chosen, but Gray had seen her suffering. He could still see the wistful look in his mother's eyes as she watched the other women laughing and chatting among themselves. Few women of the clan took it upon themselves to befriend the chieftain's mistress. A leman, especially one as fair as *Máthair*, always stood alone.

Gray swiped a hand across his face and turned back to Trulie. He knew what he must do. There was only one way to ensure his clan treated Trulie with the respect she deserved. "We will marry before the next full moon. I shall order the preparations started immediately."

Her mouth dropped open and her sleek brows nearly disappeared into the dark curls framing her face. "What?"

"Aye." He nodded. The decision eased the band of tension around his chest. Why hadn't he thought of this earlier? "A fortnight should be enough for Cook to put together a fine feast." He rubbed his hands together. "Colum will see to it the day is properly announced across our lands. All the clan will attend."

His spirits lifted. Aye. Marriage was the perfect answer. A pleasant rush of anticipation tightened his groin. Then he would have an even better excuse to keep his lady love in his bed. After all, as soon as they married, they needed to set about the business of producing heirs. "'Tis the perfect answer. All MacKennas will then treat ye with the respect ye deserve."

"But I'm not ready to get married. At least not yet. And not when you put it like that."

The uneasiness pinching her tone troubled him even more than her refusal.

"Don't look at me like that, Gray. Granny and I j-just got here. And I don't even know if I am staying."

She didn't know if she would stay? And she was stuttering? Now? She hadn't stuttered a single time while under attack in the great hall, but now she couldn't smoothly speak her mind? He sucked in a deep breath, tensing against the return of the frustration closing in like a tempest. While he realized they had not been together more than a few weeks, he already recognized a revealing trait about the woman. She only stuttered whenever she felt so strongly about something that her emotions tangled her tongue. In fact, she had confirmed this flaw late one evening when they took their leisure along the path around the bailey.

Trulie flicked both hands into the air. Her lower lip quivered when she opened her mouth, but no words came out. She finally blew out a frustrated huff, stamped her foot, and snapped her mouth shut.

Gray waited, a sense of dread taking root in his gut. What the hell was she struggling to say?

She took another step toward him, clutching her hands in front of her. "I admit I feel very . . ." She paused, caught her bottom lip between her teeth, and stared down at the floor.

"Ye feel what? By the grace of the Almighty, woman, would ye please try to say what fills yer heart?" He fought the urge to grab her by the shoulders and shake the words out of her. *Damnation.* This should not be so difficult for the lass. 'Twas just a matter of agreeing to wed her lover.

Trulie's cheeks reddened as she eased a step back. "I think . . . we are very . . . *good* together. But deciding to marry just to stop gossip is not the answer." She squared her shoulders and backed up another step. "I don't even know how long I might stay in this time. After Granny gets good and settled, I might decide to return to the future—permanently. After all, before long, I need to jump back and check on the girls anyway."

"What?" Gray lost the battle with self-control and grabbed her by the shoulders. Instead of giving her a good shake, he pulled her forward and planted her directly in front of him. Had she lost her senses? There would be no more traipsing across time. She belonged here. She belonged with him.

The soft green of her eyes darkened to the shade of a troubled sea as she averted her gaze, refusing to look him in the eye.

"Trulie." He ground his teeth against his inability to control this situation. Why was the prospect of this joining so difficult for her to accept? Did he really have to say the words aloud? He cupped her cheek and brushed his thumb across the silk of her skin. No. He should not have to say a word. She knew how he felt.

But she still didn't meet his gaze.

His heart clenched as a single tear rolled down her cheek. "Why do ye cry?" he whispered.

"Because I don't want to hurt you," she answered in a small voice.

The center of his chest burned as though she had stabbed him and twisted the blade. He forced her face upward, forced her to look him in the eyes. "I thought . . ." He fought the frustration closing off his throat. This should not be this hard. "I thought ye felt . . . make me understand why ye have no wish to wed me."

She gently pulled away. "I think we have a great beginning." She wet her lips and twitched a shrug. "But great beginnings don't guarantee a great forever. I am not going to marry a man just because he is embarrassed by the way his clan treats me."

Gray took a step back. Her words stung as sharply as a slap. "I am not embarrassed."

He only thought of her, only wished to spare her the pain his mother had endured.

"Yes, you are." Her tone strengthened. Gone was the uncertain tremor of only a moment ago. "You were the one who flew into a rage and had Fearghal and Aileas dragged out of the room when they started hurling insults at your family because of me. I understand you have to demand respect, and a healthy dose of pride is fine, but it should not be the catalyst for a marriage." She strode a few paces across the room. Suddenly, she halted as though an unseen force held her in place. She didn't turn as she spoke, just stared down at the floor. "You better worry about what your clan thinks about the way *you* behave. Not what they think about me. There is such a thing as too much pride, you know."

"I dinna care what they think!" A frustrated growl tore free of his throat as he stormed after her. "Dinna run from me, woman. And I will have ye know that I am their chieftain. I behave any way I wish."

"Then why did you suddenly decide we needed to marry?" She turned and faced him, her arms crossed over her chest. "If you'll think back to just a few minutes ago, you'll recall that you did not ask me to marry you—which is what you're supposed to do, by the way— you *told* me we were going to get married because that would solve all the problems of how your clan views me." She jabbed a finger at him as though throwing a dagger. "You explicitly stated that once we were married, all the MacKennas would treat me with respect. Do you really think that's the kind of marriage proposal a woman wants to hear?"

"I thought ye wished to be a part of my life. . . a part of my clan." He risked taking a few steps closer, ignoring the finer points of her speech. Damnation, but the woman had too good of a memory.

She released a strained groan and stared up at the ceiling. "Thanks a lot for this mess, Granny."

Irritation pricked him. He wasn't sure what Trulie meant, but he was certain that if he figured it out, it would most definitely stir his ire. "So ye refuse to wed me?" He stormed closer. "Ye refuse to see reason?"

"Getting married isn't supposed to have anything to do with

reason!" Her scowl darkened then she spun and headed toward a narrow hallway leading out of the main room.

"We are not done here, woman!" He strode after her. "I am chieftain. Ye will not leave this hall until I grant ye leave to do so."

She halted just beneath the arch, her back stiff and her shoulders squared.

Good. About time the woman realized what was best. He threw out his chest and folded his arms over it. It might take a wee bit of time to rid Trulie of her stubbornness and her strange ways of the future. He affirmed that thought with a sharp nod. But she would find he was a very patient man. His heart softened and a grin tickled the corner of his mouth. She could use her stubbornness in the raising of their many fine sons.

Trulie slowly turned and faced him.

His smile slipped at the murderous look in her eyes. By the hounds of hell, she looked as though she could kill him.

"This is now finished, Chieftain MacKenna. Completely!" She slowly lifted her hand and pointed at his crotch. "And don't you dare talk to me like that again or I will have Karma relieve you of your balls."

Gray instinctively clasped both hands atop his sporran as she turned and stomped from the room. What the hell had he done wrong? All he did was tell her to marry him.

CHAPTER 14

The more Trulie thought about it, the madder she got. *We will be married. Then the clan will respect ye.*

"Yeah, well it *will* be a cold day in hell before *I* follow a marriage edict just to win a popularity contest." She snorted and picked up the pace. The sooner they packed up and jumped back to Kentucky, the better.

Trotting along beside her, Karma acknowledged her statement with a single wag of his thick tail. He loped ahead of her as the long, narrow hallway made a sharp turn to the right.

Thank goodness Karma led the way. The flickering torches ensconced every so many feet did little to beat back the shadows of early evening. She yanked the boxy wool jacket tighter around her and shivered. The keep hadn't seemed nearly this damp and chilly before. All the more reason for them to pull up stakes and head back to a nice, humid summer in Kentucky.

Karma sat patiently waiting beside the broad oak door leading to their suite of rooms. A twinge of regret stabbed at Trulie. Gray had set them up in the nicest level of the keep. Even the serving girls had said so.

"It doesn't matter," she informed the dog.

She grabbed the iron ring bolted to the door and shoved. Karma wiggled through the doorway in front of her, touched noses with sleepy-eyed Kismet, then curled up on the rug of pelts spread in front of the hearth.

Granny and Coira sat opposite each other on a pair of cushioned benches angled in front of the low burning fire. Neither of them looked up as Trulie plowed into the room.

Trulie waited. She wasn't stupid. She knew full well Coira and Granny had nearly broken their necks racing back to the rooms ahead of her. The pair must've been standing just outside the main hall eavesdropping on the stellar marriage proposal because Coira had been extremely pale when Trulie had stomped through the kitchens and barked out the barest details of her troubling vision. She was too pissed off to go into any great detail. In her current frame of mind, the thirteenth century could go straight to hell.

Now the white bib of Coira's apron rose and fell with a rapid rhythm. Granny swallowed hard and kept pressing a hand to her chest. Both women were clearly out of breath.

As minutes passed, Coira's cheeks became a brighter scarlet. Trulie crossed her arms and tilted her head, studying Coira more closely. "If you keep trying to hold your breath, you are going to pass out."

The girl's body visibly deflated as Coira shook her head. She pulled the rough linen stretched across the wooden frame closer to her face and scowled down at the small patch of colors knotted across the cloth. "I dinna ken what ye are talking about. I'm just sitting here trying to keep this stag from looking like a Highland coo."

Granny patted a bent hand atop her jiggling knee. She stared into the hearth and didn't say a word.

"Gather your things. First thing in the morning, we are out of here." There. She had thrown down the gauntlet. Trulie glared at Granny. Let the games begin.

Granny's lips twitched into a displeased line as she leaned back against the high back of the bench. She didn't pull her gaze from the weak flames flickering among the dying coals and still didn't speak.

"Say something, Granny. I know you're dying to wade in on this." Trulie widened her stance and planted her feet. No way was this bound to be good, so they might as well get it over with.

"So, you're giving up? Acting the coward. Going to walk away from the very man that completes you. From the one man who fills you with passion and joy." Granny broke her stare at the fire and faced Trulie. "I raised you better than that, Trulie. No blood of mine ever turned tail and ran. No Sinclair is a coward."

"I am not running."

"The hell you aren't."

"So, you want me to go belly up? Just cow down to a man's orders and do whatever he says? Since when, Granny? You always taught your *blood* to rear back on our own hind legs and handle it! How many times have you told us we don't take crap from anybody?" Trulie knotted her fists in the folds of her skirts. Granny was *not* going to win this one.

Karma and Kismet raised their heads, flattened their ears, and glanced toward each other. The dog and cat rose in unison and moved to a corner across the room, as though they had telepathically agreed to get as far as possible from the dueling women.

Granny rose from the bench. Her pale-blue eyes flashed with fury behind her wire-rimmed lenses. "You know what he meant, Trulie! He's a man, for heaven's sake. They rarely say what's in their hearts. You have to listen deeper than their words. They never know how to say what they really mean."

"And ye said ye would stay and prevent yer troubling vision." Coira's voice trembled with emotion. "I dinna ken all that ye saw, but from what ye said and the pallor of yer face when the telling hit ye, I ken it canna be good."

"What is she talking about?" Granny asked. "What have you seen?

Trulie yanked off the stiff jacket and threw it across the back of one bench. The castle wasn't cold anymore. "I promised it would be okay, Coira. You should know by now that I never break my word."

"What did you see, Trulie?" Granny grew louder as she followed

Trulie across the room. "Coira. What did Trulie tell you about her vision?"

Coira clamped her lips together and shook her head.

Trulie closed her eyes, bowed her head, and pressed her knuckles against her temples. As the troubling vision replayed through her mind, it triggered a nauseating fear that went straight to her knees and weakened them. She struggled to calm her pounding heart and reached out to steady herself against the table. That damn vision. Since she was able to recall it so strongly, the Fates were still warning her against what might possibly happen and they were granting her permission to intervene. Damn it all to hell and back. Could they please just handle one crisis at a time?

"If somebody doesn't answer me, I am going to find me a switch and start heating up some tails." Granny swatted a shaking hand against her skirts and glared at Trulie. "Tell me what you saw, young lady. I have had just about enough hardheadedness for one evening."

"I saw Colum and Gray stretched out on big stone blocks. They were...lifeless. Their skin had turned an ugly gray." Trulie swallowed hard against the sickly bile burning the back of her throat. "They were dead. I know they were both dead."

Granny didn't say a word, just slowly lowered herself into a chair.

"You"—Trulie motioned toward Granny—"draped a square of gauze over Colum's face and I covered Gray. Neither one of them looked older than they do now, and the trees . . ." Trulie paused and replayed the latter half of the vision, trying to remember the tiniest details. "The trees' leaves were out in full, and so green. It has to be sometime during mid to late summer of this year."

"This is now late March," Granny observed as she folded her hands in her lap. Her scowl deepened as she stared into the fire. "Did you see how they died? Is there a way to prevent it?"

"I saw everything." Trulie nodded, then continued in a halting whisper, "They were both poisoned—and it wasn't quick or painless."

"Then we—especially you—must stay to see this evil averted." Granny broke her stare from the fire and turned to Trulie. "The Fates only give such visions when they expect something done to change them."

Trulie clenched her fists until her nails dug into her palms. *Dammit.* She knew Granny was going to say that, and in all honesty, there was no way she could ever return to the twenty-first century without first saving Gray and Colum from that fate. But to stay here in this keep and act like nothing had gone off kilter with Gray? "Look —I didn't mean we weren't going to figure out what was about to happen and derail it. I don't want anything to happen to Gray or Colum. B-but I can't stay here. Not in Gray's keep." *Not in Gray's bed.* How had things gotten so complicated so fast?

Granny leaned forward and propped her elbows on her knees. The older woman shook her gray head as she stared down at the floor. "I never thought I would live to see the day when one of my own would allow her stupid pride to kill a good man."

"I said we were going to save them!" The sense of guilt already clawing at her unfurled and grew into a raging beast. How could Granny think she would abandon the two men and leave them to their fates? She would never do such a thing and Granny should know better.

Trulie blinked back angry tears as she stomped across the sitting room to the narrow doorway of her private chamber. Yanking open the door, she stopped and spoke without looking back. "You know I am going to make this right. Don't I always make everything right?"

She didn't wait for a response. Whatever they said didn't matter. She plowed into the room and slammed the heavy door so hard that the flames on all the candles flickered horizontally with the force.

"You and I are not finished." The deep voice echoed from the shadows.

Trulie squeaked and fell back against the door. "How in the hell did you get in here?" Her heart pounded so hard it took her breath away. She flattened her palms against the smooth wood at her back and silently cursed the sudden weakness in her knees.

Gray's voice rumbled steady and low. "A wise chieftain ensures some corridors of the keep are known only to him." His face was shadowed in the half-light of the room, but Trulie could still make out hard lines of sadness around his mouth.

"And that gives you the right to just show up in my room?" She flinched against the tremor in her voice. Damn him for putting her through this.

Gray shifted in place and sucked in a slow, deep breath. "What have I done to anger ye so? Tell me so I might set things right."

She dropped her head, closed her eyes, and covered her face with her hands. How could she tell him the thought of marrying a thirteenth-century Scot scared the living daylights out of her? An inner voice nagged at her conscience. *Really? Is that the real reason you keep making excuses to avoid his marriage proposal?* It wasn't a proposal. It was an edict, an order so he wouldn't be embarrassed in front of his clan. *You know better,* the voice shot back.

She had lost her mind. Now she was arguing with herself. Trulie lifted her head. He hadn't moved a muscle, just stood in a stiff, wide stance with his arms crossed, looking like a prisoner awaiting his sentence.

"I need time," she whispered.

"Time for what?" Other than frowning, he still didn't move.

She sidled along the tapestry-covered wall of the room toward the small cushioned bench in front of the hearth. She really needed to sit.

"I need time to adjust to this place. I need time to adjust to this time." She dropped onto the roughly woven cushions with a huff. "The past fifteen years of my life have been very different from what you know here. Things were . . ." She searched for the words. They were what? The flimsy excuse sounded lame even to her.

"Ye came from here. Ye had to have some idea of what ye would return to." He eased a step forward, like a great cat stalking its prey. "Why did ye come here?" He edged closer until he stood right in front of her. "Or mayhap the real question should be why did ye ever leave the time ye now seem so reluctant to set aside?"

And there it was. The ugly truth of it stripped bare between them. Trulie turned away from his unwavering stare. Maybe it wasn't the thirteenth century that scared her so. Maybe the immediate connection to Gray was what really frightened her.

"I need time," she whispered. The feeble excuse was all she could say. How could she explain something to Gray she didn't fully understand herself?

He jerked away with a tensed growl and stormed to the far side of the room. "I canna—" He bared his teeth against the words he couldn't seem to find. "Why can ye not—" He cut himself off again, cursed under his breath, and slammed a fist against the wall beside the room's only window. Yanking the bit of tapestry covering the window aside, he wrapped it over the black iron bar bolted above the opening. Leaning out across the wide stone sill, he lifted his face to the rising moon. "I must know the truth. Why the hell do ye refuse to wed me?"

Before she could answer, Gray whirled around and pointed a shaking finger at her. "And dinna say ye need more time. Ye are a time runner, for God's sake. Ye explained yer gifts to me. The wheel of time is at yer command."

"I can't explain it," she said. "I just know I don't want a wedding feast planned as a knee-jerk reaction to some bitch and her son stirring up a bunch of gossip." At least that was her pride's part of the confusion. The rest of her hesitancy was just a muddled-up mess of emotions she couldn't quite explain. She would know when the time was right to get married. Wouldn't she?

"Knee-jerk reaction," he repeated quietly. He moved forward, scrubbing his fingers in the dark stubble shadowing his jaw. After a long moment, he finally lifted his gaze and focused on her. A determined expression narrowed his eyes as he studied her.

This couldn't be good. Trulie braced herself.

He strode across the room, knelt at her feet, and cupped both her hands between his. He searched her face for what seemed like forever before he spoke. "I care about ye. Surely, ye ken what lies in my heart."

She remained silent. The ability to speak had left her.

Gray's head jerked down. He stared at their hands, lightly

stroking his fingers across hers before he spoke again. "As a lad, I witnessed my mother's pain." He lifted his face and held her captive with the emotions in his eyes. "Her life with my father came with great sacrifice." He rubbed a calloused thumb across the top of her hands and drew in a sharp breath. "I would rather die than have ye know such sorrow and loneliness. It would be my honor to share my name with ye—to call ye my wife." He slowly rose, braced his hands on either side of her, and leaned in until his mouth was a hair's breadth from hers. "Surely, ye ken ye own my heart and soul, *mo luaidh*. Whether ye agree to wed me or not."

His words made time stand still. Quite a feat for a man to accomplish with a time runner. She touched the roughness of his cheek and drew in a shaking breath. Heaven above, how could she resist such a man who made her feel so . . .

He edged closer. With the barest of touches, his warm lips brushed hers. "Say it, *mo chridhe*," he breathed across her mouth. "Say it will be so."

"It will be so," she finally whispered, fully surrendering her heart and succumbing to Gray's spell.

He brushed her lips with a chaste kiss, then scooped her up from the settee, crossed the room in three broad strides, and lowered her to the bed. Then he stretched out beside her, fully clothed, candlelight and so much more reflected in his eyes. With his head propped in his hand, he stared down at her while lightly tracing a fingertip across the curve of her lower lip. "What have ye done to me?" he finally whispered.

Before she could say a word, he cupped her cheek in his hand and kissed her. The kiss became a hungry claiming as his emotions flooded into her. She laced her fingers in his hair and pulled him down, opening up and welcoming him in, relishing the faint taste of whisky in his kisses.

Without breaking the connection, he pushed her skirts aside. The heat of his touch trailing up her leg and tickling her inner thigh made her ache for more. She arched into him and curled a leg around his hip as he brushed teasing fingers across her wetness.

Maneuvering through the folds of his plaid, she found his impressive length and wrapped her fingers around it. She pressed closer, guiding and teasing his hardness where she needed it most

"Nay, my love." Gray gently rolled her to her back and rose above her. "Tis going to be a long night. Ye best lie back and relax."

"Relax?" A gasp escaped her as he crouched between her legs and shoved her skirts up around her waist.

"Aye, dear one," he whispered, then blew across the curls at the vee of her thighs.

"You're not fighting fair." She clutched the bedsheets, trying not to writhe in anticipation of what was coming next.

"I will never fight fair when it comes to claiming ye, my own."

She held her breath as he slowly teased the tip of his tongue across her aching nub. A moan escaped her as he rumbled an appreciative groan against her mound and sucked her in with deliciously slow pulls.

As he cupped her buttocks in both hands and shifted her hips higher, she tightened her legs around him, bucking and digging her heels into his back. He dipped his tongue into her heat, all the while gyrating his thumb against her swollen button. She cried out as he slid two fingers deep inside and returned to sucking, pulling, and thrusting. A groan ripped from deep in her throat. She rocked hard against him, losing herself in the delicious delirium. Waves of bliss crashed across her. Body and soul hummed with the most ancient of pleasures.

With a smug, rumbling laugh, he stretched out beside her, nuzzling and nibbling her throat as she gasped for air.

"Proud of yourself?" she said once she was able to speak.

"Should I not be?" He smiled down at her while trailing a fingertip between her breasts.

"Just remember. All's fair," she warned as she slid downward and shoved his plaid to the side.

When he hissed in a sharp breath, she couldn't help but smile. Palming his bollocks in one hand, she licked the length of his swollen shaft. His groaning became louder when she swirled and sucked the head, then swallowed him as deeply as she could.

"Lore a'mighty, woman." The sound he made was something akin to a growl as he arched his back while she alternately sucked and stroked.

She moved against the ridge of his shin as she kissed and sucked until he begged for mercy. Aching and wet, impatience and aching need took over. She straddled him, and slowly slid down his hardness until well seated with a satisfying wiggle. "You know I am not a patient woman. I couldn't wait any longer," she said with another slow shifting of her hips.

Gray pulled her forward and caught one of her nipples in his mouth, nibbling and sucking until she straightened and rocked hard and fast.

He arched and bucked, yanking her harder against him. As he emptied, she rode faster and pumped ever harder. As he shuddered one last time, she reached the pinnacle. A raw shriek tore from her as blissful release exploded through her. She convulsed with the waves of pleasure, then collapsed in a gasping heap on top of his heaving chest. His arms tightened around her and held her close.

"Trulie."

Struggling to find the energy to lift her head, she pushed her damp curls out of her eyes. "What?"

"Ye are mine." His expression was hard and serious, his eyes narrow and stern. "For all eternity, ye ken? Ye belong to none but me."

Her already hammering heart skipped a beat and a delicious shiver having absolutely nothing to do with what had just transpired rippled across her.

"Say it, woman." He framed her face with his hands. "Say it to me now."

She stretched and kissed his chin, then offered a lazy smile. "I am yours for all eternity. I promise."

He gathered her to him once more, traced a finger down the center of her back, then settled the cheek of her ass in one hand. "Rest a bit now, woman. As I said, we have a long night ahead."

CHAPTER 15

"Rory swears he saw no one." Colum stood beside Gray on the outer gallery overlooking the remains of the stable. Charred posts poked up through piles of ash like scarred fingers reaching for the dismal, overcast sky. Scorched blocks of foundation stones marked the boundaries of what had once been one of the finest stables in all the Highlands. Colum gave a disgusted snort. "Perhaps one of the stable lads left a brazier unattended."

Gray leaned forward; his elbows propped on the damp stone railing. "Perhaps," he said. But doubtful. Especially after what Trulie had told him she sensed right before the fire.

He straightened and clasped his hands behind his back. His gaze followed two soot-covered lads raking debris into a pile. "So ye truly believe it was an accident?"

Colum's face darkened as he resettled his feet into a wider stance. "I do not."

"Neither do I." Gray rolled his shoulders, shrugging off the misting rain. "Two such fires in the same year is no accident."

"Lady Trulie couldna see the bastard who set either of them?"

Colum's question was forgotten as Gray spotted a new figure

joining the handful of youngsters sorting through the blackened mess.

At the far side of the rubble, pawing through ash and chunks of charred debris was a worker Gray didn't know. A man of average height and build, capped with nondescript mud-brown hair hanging in chopped-off, dripping hanks. The steady drizzle plastered the man's gray tunic to his bent body. His hands and knees were black from sorting through the remains. The only distinguishing feature Gray noticed about the stranger was that he hitched to his left whenever he took a step. Gray looked closer and discovered why the man walked with such a strange gait. His left foot looked like a large misshapen stone wrapped in wet leather.

Gray nodded at the man. "Who is he?"

Colum dismissed the mud-covered soul with a shrug. "One of Aileas's retinue when she first arrived at MacKenna keep. Part of her dowry, I believe."

"I dinna recall ever seeing him before." Gray paced the length of the balcony, watching as the man fished out bits and pieces of twisted metal and tossed the shards into a wooden bucket.

"He works with the smithy," Colum said. "See how he searches for scraps of iron?"

"Has he been questioned about the fire?" Gray pulled a fold of his plaid up over his head as the downpour became heavier and sleet joined the rain. The wet spring weather would delay cleanup and rebuilding. He squinted up into the sky. Foals would be coming soon. A temporary shelter for the horses would have to be made. He returned his attention to the unknown man limping through the debris. "Colum, has the man been questioned?"

When Colum still didn't respond, Gray turned, then rolled his eyes. No wonder the man at arms had failed to answer. His cock had taken control.

Colum stood at the far side of the balcony, motionless, eyes trained on a young woman as she scampered out into the gardens with a bit of cloth held over her head.

Gray walked over and nudged Colum out of his paralysis. "Ye best not let Granny see ye drooling over that one. She will think ye lied about having no interest in wedding." He nudged him again. "By the way, have ye stolen a kiss yet?"

Colum shifted his stance and adjusted his plaid as though he suddenly needed a bit more room from the waist down. "Aye, and the promise of more." He leaned out over the wall and watched the girl fill a basket with snips of herbs. "Her lips are sweet as honey wine and ye can lay odds she will warm my bed this verra night."

Gray shook his head and strolled alongside the railing. Colum's bed was never empty long, but what the poor maidens failed to realize was Colum enjoyed the chase almost more than the catch. Once they succumbed and warmed his chambers, his interest quickly waned. "Ye say that about all the maids. Have ye yet to find the one capable of warming yer heart?"

Colum made a face and adjusted his sword belt. "The only part of my body I care to warm is located a bit lower than my heart."

Gray understood completely. He had once felt the same—before he met Trulie. Colum would someday meet his match, especially if Granny Sinclair made up her mind the man should wed. "Aye. Well. Ye best take care and give Granny Sinclair a wide berth."

"By the way . . ." Colum's interest in the topic disappeared as the curvaceous girl disappeared back into the keep. "What date have ye set for yer wedding?"

Irritation grated against Gray's nerves, making the day even more unpleasant. "No date has been determined."

Colum cocked an eyebrow but said nary a word.

"The woman will not agree to a date until she has resolved what she calls our *issues*." Gray hissed out the word as though it were a curse. And it damn near was. What good was Trulie's promise to marry if she would not agree to a day?

"Set the date," Colum said. "Ye are the chieftain. Name the place and time."

"She said if I did that she would not attend," Gray said. "I already thought to try that."

"And I dinna suppose trussing her up and carrying her to the church would work?" Colum leaned forward as though ready to make it happen if Gray just gave the word.

"I would prefer she come to me of her own free will." Gray blew out a frustrated breath. He had to admit he rather liked the idea of a bound and gagged Trulie delivered to the church on a day of his choice, but lore a'mighty, there would be hell to pay once she was freed of her bonds.

Colum shrugged and nodded his agreement. "Well, what issue is she wanting to be resolved?"

Gray counted off the items on his fingers. "Two murders, two fires, and two attempted murders."

"Two attempted murders?" Colum asked. "Who?"

Gray grinned. "You and I, my friend." He clapped a hand on Colum's shoulder. "According to Mistress Trulie, it appears we are about to be poisoned."

Colum stared at Gray as though he had lost his mind. "For truth?"

"Aye."

"Speaking of poison." Colum's troubled expression shifted to one of anticipation. "Is this not the day of Lady Aileas's exodus?"

Gray chuckled. Just the thought of the keep without Aileas's annoying presence made the day suddenly brighter. "Aye. Today is the day. Her servants should be loading her trunks as we speak."

"Ye know Fearghal has gone missing?" Colum bobbed his head up and down as if to stress his words. "No one has seen neither hide nor hair of the dolt since the guard dragged him from the hall."

Gray tossed his plaid back over his shoulder. "What say ye?"

"No one has seen Fearghal," Colum repeated, slowly enunciating his words as though Gray were a child. "Pray tell me ye did not allow someone other than myself the pleasure of slitting the bastard's throat?"

Gray frowned and shook his head. "I gave no such order." He turned away and continued his pacing across the length of the gallery. That news did not set well at all. Fearghal missing was a great deal like discovering a diseased rat hiding in the walls of the keep. Fearghal never ventured far from his mother. Even as a grown man, he depended on his brute of a mother to protect him. Gray had no doubt the sniveling drunkard was capable of evil as long as the man could orchestrate it while cowering in the shadows of his mother's skirts.

He turned and gave Colum a stern nod. "I want him found. Immediately."

~

"You are positive this stuff really works?" Trulie peered down into the linen pouch at the tiny heart-shaped seeds. "I just grind some up, mix with water, and drink it?"

"Yes." Granny nodded as she shook a knobby finger at the small cache of seeds. "Just a dab in water is all you need but be certain the seeds are well crushed or they won't work." Granny turned back to the worktable and stacked several small wooden bowls. "Oh, and Trulie . . ." Granny turned back. "When you start running low, you will have to jump back to the beginning of the first century to gather more from the Mediterranean stash. The map is drawn out in my journal. You won't have a bit of trouble finding it."

"The first century? Seriously?" Trulie drew the string around the neck of the seed bag and secured it with a knot. "It would be just as easy for me to hop back to Kentucky and get birth control there. The last time I spoke with Kenna through the fire portal, she said she could make any appointments I needed. Why can't I get these seeds any closer than the first century? And in the Mediterranean?"

Granny wiped her hands on the front of her apron and shook her head. "Silphium is much more effective than wild carrot seeds or Queen Anne's Lace. But the plant became extinct by the end of the first century—greed and climate change." A hopeful grin brightened her face as she patted Trulie on the arm. "But with any luck, you and Gray won't decide to wait too long to start having babies. I am certain you won't need to make a trip back to Kentucky or the first century."

"Uhm . . ." Coira cleared her throat. "What else do ye recommend to make sure a bairn doesna take seed?" The maid's freckled cheeks flamed with scarlet patches of red. "Mam died when I was too young to learn of such things, and none of the serving maids can decide what works best."

"Don't have sex," Granny said with a stern look over the top of her glasses. "That is the surest way not to get babies." She turned from the table, squared off, and drew herself up as though she were about to make a speech.

Trulie tucked the pouch of seeds into a drawer and closed it with a loud bang. "It's okay, Granny. I'll talk to Coira about it later. I can't sit through that lecture again."

The chamber door rattled on its hinges as someone pounded on the other side.

"My goodness. Keep your britches on." Granny patted her sleek gray hair and grumbled under her breath as she toddled across the room at a fast clip, then yanked open the door.

Tamhas stood with both hands propped atop his staff, his eyes sparkling with the smile hidden in his beard. "I thought ye all would wish to come and give Aileas a proper farewell. After all, ye may never see the poor woman again."

Trulie winked at Coria. Tamhas was right. She wouldn't miss Aileas's going-away party for anything in the world. "So, she's all packed up and ready to go?"

He nodded as he held out his arm for Granny to take. "Aye. Her servants have placed the last of her trunks in the carriage. All that remains is the Lady Aileas herself."

Kismet and Karma bounded out the door ahead of everyone. Trulie couldn't help but laugh. Even the animals wanted to see Aileas gone. Trulie hurried to catch up with the group. Tamhas's stride was long and sure for a man his age. His staff gracefully thumped along beside him. Granny nearly skipped at his side. Trulie looped her arm through Coira's and giggled at a sudden vision of them all skipping down a yellow brick road. It was amazing how much Aileas's departure made the keep seem like a brighter place.

"But you know, I heard they can't find Fearghal." Granny's chuckling revelation floated back to Trulie.

"What do you mean they can't find him?" Trulie hurried to catch up with Granny and Tamhas.

Granny shrugged. "Ask Coira. All the serving girls are chattering about it. They said no one has seen him since he got booted out of the hall for being such an ass."

"Do ye think the chieftain had Fearghal gutted and hung out to dry?" Coira's eyes danced at the possibility.

"Coira!" Granny skidded to a stop and whirled around to face them. "Do you have to be so graphic? Crime-a-nitly, child! Where did you learn such a term? You sound like a twenty-first century redneck bragging about the deer he just shot."

"Mistress Trulie said . . ." Coira clamped her mouth shut and cast an apologetic look in Trulie's direction.

"Gray didn't say anything about having Fearghal punished." Trulie made a mental note to speak to Coira later about what should or should not be shared with Granny. "All I know is that Aileas is getting sent to some distant cousin in the lowlands. The place sounded like a convent or something."

Coira's grin widened. "Aileas would make a much better monk than a nun."

Even Granny snickered this time, before clearing her throat, grabbing Tamhas's arm, and proceeding down the hall.

Her interest piqued; Trulie attempted to bring the focus of the conversation back to Fearghal. "So, what do you think happened to him? I mean, really. Is there any gossip about where he might be?"

Coira frowned as she hooked her thumbs into the front placket of her apron. "Nay. 'Tis verra strange. Master Fearghal never strays far from his mother."

Trulie stretched to better see as they came to the end of the corridor and passed through the arch leading out into the bailey. Shimmying sideways, she kept close to the wall. Quite a crowd had gathered to see Aileas leave.

An enclosed carriage waited with its lacquered door propped open. A scrawny lad balanced on top of the pile of baggage secured with a rope. The worn leather trunks and lopsided bundles bulged at an ungainly angle on the iron platform attached to the back of the carriage.

Trulie studied one of the longer, linen-wrapped bundles lashed across the very back of the wagon. Maybe Fearghal was in there, rolled up like the cowardly slug that he was. She looked closer and reached out with her senses. No. That wasn't him. Whatever it was in that roll didn't emit an aura.

The murmuring of the crowd became louder as Aileas emerged from the keep and paused on the wide stone step. Trulie felt a confusing twinge of sympathy for the woman. It was more than obvious that Aileas had been weeping. Her red-rimmed eyes were even more bloodshot than usual, and her pockmarked nose was red and dripping.

Aileas pulled a crumpled wad of cloth from her sleeve, pinched it up against her nose, and blew so hard the sound echoed through the courtyard. As she shoved the handkerchief back into her sleeve, she looked around, stopping when her gaze fell on Trulie.

Trulie stared back, unblinking. She refused to be the first to look away.

Aileas lifted her double chin and her mouth pulled down into a deeper frown. Without taking her gaze from Trulie, she stomped down the steps. Her dark skirts bounced with a haughty jerk as she flounced to the open door of the carriage. Before she hefted her girth up into it, she paused and pointed a shaking finger at Trulie. After she threw herself up into the seat, she made a slashing sign across her throat before the servant slammed the door shut.

"Bring it, Aileas," Trulie said as the carriage pulled away.

CHAPTER 16

The warmth and bustle of the early-morning kitchen never ceased to amaze Trulie. She had never been a morning person. In her opinion, anyone starting their day with such vigor won her admiration. She stifled a yawn behind her hand and blinked hard against the last dredges of sleep.

"Do ye think Cook kens why we walk through the kitchen each morning?" Coira tugged on Trulie's sleeve as they paused in front of the widest hearth. Suspended from iron bars over the fire, several round-bellied pots bubbled and hissed.

Karma pushed his way between them, lifted his glistening black nose, and sniffed. His perked ears relaxed as he backed up a step and plopped down on his haunches. Apparently, whatever was in the pots didn't smell good enough to tempt the dog's voracious appetite.

Trulie leaned closer and inhaled. No wonder. The bland, sticky smell of boiling grains made her wrinkle her nose. The MacKenna clan loved their parritch.

She glanced at two scullery maids currently elbow deep in two tubs of steaming water, then turned back to Coira. "Have you heard anything?"

Coira glanced around the room, then leaned in close. "They

dinna confide in me anymore, mistress. They fear my closeness to ye."

"Well, I don't think any of the staff knows why we're wandering, through." Trulie hitched in a quick intake of breath with another uncontrollable yawn. "Honestly, I think they are all too busy to even notice we are here." Rubbing the corners of her eyes, she lowered her voice. "I don't sense anything different from yesterday. I think it's still not the right time."

As they entered the vacant herb-drying room, Coira stole a glance back over her shoulder at Trulie. She started to speak and then stopped, as though she had changed her mind.

"What?"

Coira stared down at her feet, then shook her head. Karma nudged his head up under the silent girl's hand and whined. His great black tail barely wagged as he leaned against her. Even the dog sensed Coira's uneasiness.

"What is it, Coira? You know you can ask me anything." Trulie wrapped an arm around the maid's shoulders and gave her an affectionate shake. "We're alone in here. Now tell me. What's wrong?"

"Granny says yer line can see troublesome things that will happen to those around ye, but ye canna see any ill that might befall those of yer own blood. Why, mistress? Do the Fates not care for ye enough to protect ye?" Coira's troubled gaze was filled with confusion. "I worry for ye, mistress."

Trulie had often pondered the very same thing, until the day she had finally asked Granny. "Granny says we can't see our blood kin's misfortunes because we wouldn't be able to bear it if we weren't able to change it. She says we should be thankful. Knowing one's own future is a curse, not a blessing. That's what Granny always told me."

Trulie hadn't quite agreed when Granny had shared that particular kernel of wisdom, but the more she saw of the world, the more she understood it to be true—especially if it was a vision of an unalterable event making itself known. Those were always the worst. She drew in a deep breath. A foretelling of a *possible* future could often be avoided entirely. But a person's final fate could never be changed.

"And sometimes, when Fate sends us visions, they're warning us about things we won't be able to change."

Coira's voice fell to a hoarse whisper and her face paled. "How long did it take ye to know the difference between a warning to change someone's path and an omen that canna be altered?"

"Not long," Trulie said as she hurried them through the archway leading out to the gardens.

Karma trotted ahead. A little way up the path, a scent caught his attention. Ears perked forward and his snuffling nose barely inches above the ground, the dog wove in and out between the clumps of weeds. As he analyzed each and every scent, he occasionally paused, lifted his head, and shook with a violent, snorting sneeze. Granny said Karma was clearing his nose for serious tracking whenever he had a snorting fit.

A disturbing weight settled on Trulie's heart as she watched the dog vacuum his way around the garden. She despised the visions she knew she could never change. A shudder shook through her at the memory of the last time Fate had revealed someone's unavoidable end.

Fate shouted whenever it shared the unavoidable. It grabbed your heart with icy fingers and squeezed until you cried out with the pain. They demanded your full and undivided attention. Fate refused to be ignored.

As the warming rays of the early-spring sun topped the wall, the light frost covering every surface sparkled as though lit from within. Trulie rolled her shoulders and forced the dark memories away. Thank heavens the vision of Gray and Colum dying from poison had not been accompanied by pain. She turned to Coira and offered a consoling smile. "At least Fate hasn't decided to whisper anymore lately. Maybe she will leave me alone for a while."

"I hope so," Coira agreed.

Suddenly, Trulie stiffened, halting in the middle of the path. Her senses vibrated like a metal detector closing in on buried treasure. Something at the farthest corner of the garden pulled at her, urging her to come closer. "There is a plant. Over there. It holds the poison that takes the men."

She forced herself to remain calm as she made her way to the corner. Squatting down closer to the tangled mess of leaves and stems, she scanned the scrubby clumps of new growth. This corner of the garden had been sadly neglected. Weeds lined the inside of the stone fence and the ground looked as though it hadn't been worked in a while. Trulie bent and pushed aside the tallest of the weeds, searching for plant types she could positively identify. There they were. Several long, narrow leaves pushed their way up through the soil.

She knelt and looked closer at the leaves. The plant was so young and the leaves so tiny, she couldn't tell for sure. "We need to get Granny. She's better at identifying plants than I am."

Coira's face brightened as Trulie stood. "The men willna be in danger until the plant grows large enough to bloom. I recall ye said ye saw pretty purple flowers that looked like wee sock caps."

"Wee sock caps," Trulie repeated under her breath as she tried to bring to mind all the lessons in herbal lore Granny had given her. Sock caps. Purple flowers. Trulie eyed the tiny plant just pushing through the dirt. *Dead man's bells.* It had to be foxglove. She shivered with the recognition. Digitalis poisoning was a terrible way to die. Nausea. Vomiting. Wild hallucinations and unbearable headaches. Then, if you survived all that, the beating of your heart gradually slowed until it stopped.

She patted Coira on the shoulder and nodded back toward the keep. "Come on. At least now we have a warning flag. We just need to watch for little purple flowers."

Coira beamed with their discovery. "Now the men will be safe. All will be well."

Karma pushed around them, hesitantly sniffed at the dangerous plant, then hiked his leg and peed on it. "Thank you, Karma. That should help immensely." Trulie ruffled the dog's velvety ears.

He smiled up at her, his long red tongue lolling out one side of his mouth.

Trulie headed them all back toward the keep. The knot of tension centered in her chest didn't seem quite so tight. If they could just figure out who wanted Gray dead, life in medieval Scotland might actually be enjoyable.

"AILEAS IS GONE and Fearghal canna be found. Why will ye not settle on a date?"

Trulie didn't turn to face him. She paused from sorting through colored threads on the table and shot a sideways glance back over her shoulder that left no doubt about her feelings. She was obviously not in the mood to discuss wedding plans.

Gray couldn't help it. He wanted the ceremony done and behind them. The more he mused about the role of husband and father, the more he yearned to embrace it. Summer was fast approaching. It would soon be time to head out across MacKenna lands and visit all his people. When he rode across his lands, he wanted his wife at his side. Not only did he look forward to introducing Trulie to the clan, but surely enjoying Trulie's charms beneath the star-filled summer nights would guarantee a strong son by next year.

Farther down the long wooden table, Granny thumped a crooked finger atop the square of linen spread in front of her. "I think the first of May would be a perfect date. What better time to marry than on the Feast of Beltane." Granny leaned forward, excitement brightening her face as she continued. "A very fertile time, I might add."

Beside the hearth, Tamhas chuckled as he chimed in. "Aye. A marriage feast on Beltane could ensure the welcoming of your first born by Brid's day."

Gray leaned forward and lightly traced his finger across Trulie's hand. "What say ye, *mo chridhe*? Shall we plan the joining for May first?"

Trulie still didn't speak.

His frustration grew stronger as her mouth pressed into a determined line. He knew that look. She was gearing up to list all the reasons why they should wait.

Trulie huffed a stray curl off her forehead, dampened her fingertips with the tip of her tongue, then pinched apart several tangled threads. A tense silence filled the room. Even the flames of the iron candelabra in the center of the table stilled as though awaiting Trulie's answer. Holding the threads up in front of the light, Trulie squinted at the knotted hanks as she spoke. "Until we nail down your little pyromaniac and potential poisoner, we don't need to get sidetracked with wedding plans." She lowered her hands and smoothed the separated colors across the table. "Who knows what they might do if we agitate him . . . or her with nuptial preparations."

Gray wasn't sure about some of those words, but he caught enough of the gist to know that he did not agree. He would dive headfirst into the pits of hell before he bowed to the whims of some gutless fool too cowardly to challenge him face-to-face. The more he thought about it the hotter he burned. Nay. He'd had enough. It was time to turn the tables.

"No more waiting. If it takes our joining to flush out the enemy, then so be it. May first, Trulie. What say ye?" He leaned forward and stilled both her hands with his own. She had to agree. Waiting for an attack made a warrior weak.

Granny eased away from the table and joined Tamhas at the hearth. Karma's nails clicked across the stone flooring as he walked over to Trulie's chair and plopped down beside it.

The low-burning fire in the hearth hissed and popped. Sparks sizzled as they rose into the darkness of the flue.

Gray glanced around the room. Time felt suspended, as though the cosmos wanted to hear Trulie's answer too. "What say ye, my love?" She had to agree. Surely, she would not delay their day any longer.

"You really think we can marry without someone getting torched, poisoned, or maimed?" she turned toward him, one brow arched.

He bit back a chuckle. Her expression reminded him of a mother interrogating her child. "I will make it so," he swore in a solemn voice. "I swear it."

She finally gifted him a slight nod. "Then May first it is."

Excitement surged through him like the burn of good whisky. Finally. They would be as one. He swept her up into his arms and kissed her soundly. *"Tha gaol agam ort, mo chridhe."*

She blinked up at him and waited, both her finely arched brows raised this time.

"I love ye, my heart," he translated as he pressed his forehead to hers.

Granny clapped her hands as her triumphant "Whoot!" rang across the rafters. Karma barked and Kismet surveyed the room with a bored flip of her tail.

"Now we are getting somewhere," Granny proclaimed with an excited bob of her head. She turned and patted Tamhas's shoulders, nudging him toward the door. "Come on. We have a lot to do."

"We?" Tamhas repeated with a horrified look. "What do I have to do?"

Granny shoved him harder until he shuffled sideways. "A lot. Now get moving. There is no time to waste."

The old sorcerer rolled his eyes, turned, and plodded toward the door. When he reached the arch, he paused and glanced back at Gray. "May the gods be with us both, nephew," he called out as Granny shoved him into the hallway.

"WERE YE NEAR THE TUNNELS TODAY?" Colum leaned in close, lowered his voice, and glanced around. "Near the passage that opens to the sea?"

Gray didn't answer as he pulled a scarred longbow free of the rack. "The *taifeid* is worn on this one." He held the weapon sideways in front of Colum and plucked the bowstring. "See that it is replaced, ye ken?"

"Aye." Colum took the weapon. "Did ye hear what I asked?"

"I heard." Gray selected a shorter bow and examined it closely. "I am not deaf. 'Tis the heart of yer question that troubles me—especially now that Trulie has settled on a date." The location of the escape tunnels leading from inside the keep to an elaborate network of hidden caves was known to very few within the clan. Keeping such knowledge to only the most trusted ensured the safety of the stronghold.

"The outer wall was ajar." Colum handed Gray another bow and took the short one from him. "Mere inches, but wide enough to allow a smaller body to squeeze through."

"Yer thoughts?" Gray turned and faced Colum. Colum never came to him asking questions without good reason. Knowing his trusted man-at-arms, Gray waited to hear whom Colum thought had trespassed through their tunnels.

"Fearghal," Colum said. "I ken in my gut that bastard hides in the darkness beneath our land."

Fearghal. Gray scrubbed his fingers through the stubble on his jaw. Admittedly, no one had seen the sniveling wimp since nearly a fortnight before his mother left. But how could the bumbling fool survive such an existence? The clumsy oaf had never mastered any basic survival skills. Fearghal could not hunt, was afraid to fish, and had a hard time sitting a horse long enough to ride across the paddock. The only thing Fearghal had ever perfected was draining tankards in one long swallow. The fool didn't even do that well. The ale usually ran down either side of his face and streamed into his oversized ears.

"Ye truly suspect Fearghal hides in the caves?" Gray struggled to believe it. "Besides the fact he probably fears the dark, how did he come upon them? Their location was never shared with the man."

Colum frowned and glared back at Gray. "Well, then who do ye think it is?"

Gray winked and clapped a hand hard atop Colum's shoulder. "I have no idea, but I trust my man-at-arms willna rest until the mystery is solved."

CHAPTER 17

Karma growled a low deep warning and blocked Trulie's path to the table. He lifted his head, ears perked to alert position, and his broad-chested body tensed and ready to spring.

"Karma. What is wrong with you? I just want to get a drink of water." She moved to one side to get around the dog.

He moved with her, growling louder this time. He butted his broad head so hard against her knees that she nearly lost her balance.

"Karma!" She squatted down to the dog's eye level and cradled his head in her hands. "There is no one here but Granny. We are perfectly safe. What's troubling you?"

The dog whined, twisted out of her hands, and looked up at the table.

Granny rose from the bench by the hearth and hurried across the room. "You best listen to him, Trulie. He is your guardian."

Trulie slowly stood, wondering what had set him off. She concentrated on the room, easing around in a clockwise circle as she scanned for anything unusual. Nothing seemed amiss. "He has been edgy all day. I wonder if he doesn't feel good or something."

She rubbed his head as she leaned over and looped her fingers through the cool handle of the smooth clay pitcher on the table.

Karma lunged with his teeth gnashing. A startling growl rumbled from deep in his throat as he sprang upward and knocked to the side. The crock of water spun out of her grasp, wobbled over the edge of the table, and shattered when it hit the floor. The dog straddled the splattered mess, placing himself between Trulie and the spreading puddle. He lowered his head and bared his teeth, making it perfectly clear that no one was getting near that spilled water.

"Who brought that water to this room?" Granny asked as she moved carefully toward the enraged dog.

"I don't know." Trulie picked herself up from the floor and brushed her skirts back into place. A sense of guilt filled her as she read the reprimand on Karma's face. "I am sorry, Karma." She held out her hand. "I didn't understand that you were warning me about the water."

Karma immediately relaxed, lowered his head, and ran to Trulie with an I-was-just-trying-to-protect-you whine.

"I know," she crooned as she hugged him to her chest. Thank goodness she had been gifted with a guardian—especially one like Karma. Not all time runners were so blessed. Only the eldest daughters received animal spirit guides. Thank goodness for birth order. The irony of the situation wasn't wasted. Always before, she had hated being the oldest. As she stared at the broken crockery, a plan unfolded in her mind. "You know..." She waggled a brow at Granny. "This could be a good thing."

Granny pursed her lips, then glanced from the mess back to Trulie. "We are the only ones who know you didn't taste that water."

"Exactly."

"Whoever brought the water here will be watching for results." Granny barely tapped her chin as she circled the puddle.

"Yep."

"We can make this work." Granny paced faster now, excitedly rubbing her hands together.

"That's what I'm thinking." Trulie circled the table and surveyed the room. "So, you think I need to be found on the floor beside the mess, or should I make a fuss and take to my bed because I feel sick?"

"That's the problem." Granny squatted down and scowled at the wet floor. "We don't know what kind of poison they used, so we have no idea of how it would affect you."

"Can you smell anything?" Trulie inhaled a deep breath. Nothing smelled suspicious to her.

Granny leaned forward and took a hesitant sniff. She waited a moment, sniffed again, and then shook her head. "No. I can't make out any kind of smell. It just smells like wet floor to me."

Trulie picked up a shard of the broken crockery and brought it close to her face. Karma grumbled his disapproval as she touched the tip of her tongue to the damp side of the fired clay.

The taste made her turn and spit. As she wiped the back of her hand across her mouth, she noticed her lips were already getting numb. "Yuck. The taste reminds me of old almonds. It's so bitter the unknowing drinker wouldn't swallow much and judging by the way my lips already feel, it wouldn't take much to be effective."

Granny's expression darkened into a thoughtful scowl. "Cyanide." She turned and glared back down at the puddle.

"Cyanide? In the thirteenth century?"

Granny dismissed Trulie's statement with a wave of her hand. "Organic cyanide has been around for centuries and is easily attainable."

Seriously? Trulie gingerly dropped the contaminated bit of pottery back to the floor. "How do you know so much about cyanide?"

"That is not important." Granny's tone implied Trulie really didn't want to know how Granny had come by such information. "And since they used that dad-blasted poison, our little charade is going to be a bit more difficult."

"Fast acting and deadly, huh?"

"I am afraid so," Granny said. "Especially if mixed strong enough to numb your lips with barely a drop."

Trulie motioned Karma to the opposite side of the room, snatched a cup from the table, and stretched out on the floor beside the puddle of poison. "Well, maybe we can make them think they didn't mix it right, so it wouldn't kill me right away."

Granny bent over Trulie, spit in her hand, and wiped her wet fingers across Trulie's cheek.

"Granny! That is just gross!" Trulie cringed, shying away as Granny spit in her hand again.

"You have to look like you were drinking the water when you collapsed. How else am I going to make your face look wet? I can't use that." Granny nodded at the poison and reached for Trulie's face again.

Trulie grabbed Granny's wrist and held it away from her face. "My face is wet enough. Now just go stir up a panic so we can see how everyone reacts."

"You know we are going to have to make Gray believe it too," Granny said as she wiped her hand on her skirt. "He is not going to be happy when he finds out we fooled him."

"He'll get over it." Trulie did her best to assume the most likely position of someone who collapsed from poison. She closed her eyes and motioned toward the door. "I'm ready. Let's rumble."

GRAY HIT the door at full force, barreling into the room as the door bounced against the wall with a resounding bang. He didn't give a damn. All he knew was Granny had sent word that Trulie had collapsed. A knot of fear choked off his air as he pounded into the room.

Karma lashed out like a rabid animal, lunging toward him as he moved closer. Teeth bared and hackles raised, the protective dog stood watch over his mistress. The animal's reaction fanned Gray's fear into deeper panic. *Lore, dinna let her be dead.* Any direction Gray moved, Karma mirrored it.

"Ye must let me pass," Gray said as he slid his dirk from its sheath in one slow, smooth movement. He would do his best not to hurt the dog, but he would be damned straight to hell before he allowed the animal to prevent him from reaching Trulie. She looked so pale, even the pink of her lips had taken on an odd hue. "Allow me to help her, Karma. Ye ken I willna harm her."

A softer warning growl clicked deeper in the dog's throat. Karma hunkered down, ready to pounce as he hesitantly eased back a mere body length away from Trulie.

Every muscle tensed for an attack; Gray slid over to Trulie without breaking eye contact with the dog. He passed the dagger to his left hand, keeping the tip pointed toward the dog as he reached for Trulie with his right.

So cold. Gray pressed his fingers harder against her throat, letting out a relieved breath as a strong, steady heartbeat met his touch. Her pale, clammy skin concerned him. The rise and fall of her chest was too rapid, too shallow to satisfy her need for air.

Gray glanced at the dog one last time as he slid the knife back into its sheath. "Stand down, lad. I mean to place her in her bed."

Karma relaxed back a step. The dog no longer bared his teeth, but his hackles were still raised. Gray felt the dog's gaze upon him as he scooped Trulie up into his arms.

As he stood, Trulie's head fell back, her mouth sagged open, and her limp arms swung free. Rage pounded through Gray. Vengeance burned through his veins with every beat of his heart. Be they god or be they human, whoever caused his woman such harm would rue this act if it took him an eternity to find them.

He lowered Trulie into the bed, holding his breath to keep from roaring out his pain as he straightened her head on the pillows. With a shaking hand, he smoothed a silky curl away from her damp forehead. He traced the backs of his fingers across her cheek. "What happened, *mo chridhe*?" he whispered. "Pray tell me who did this to ye?"

Trulie didn't move. Her breathing seemed shallower.

He looked up as Granny and Coira hurried into the room. "Tell me." He struggled to keep from shouting. "Tell me everything so I might seek revenge."

Granny barely shook her head as she clasped her hands in front of her waist. "I sent for you as soon as I found her lying on the floor."

Gray eased down on the bed beside Trulie. He kept one hand resting atop her motionless arm and nodded toward Granny. "My love said ye ken how to heal as she does. Come. Lay yer hands upon her. Ye must make her well."

Granny's eyes filled with tears. "I can't," she whispered with a trembling shake of her head. "It is a rare occasion when the Fates allow us to heal our own bloodline." She wheezed out a shaky sigh. "And I already tried."

"Ye lie!" he roared, springing toward Granny. He would force her to lay hands on Trulie. Force the power through her. By the gods, he would not allow his love to die.

Karma leaped forward and slammed into him. The dog's bared teeth snapped at the end of Gray's nose. The heat of the beast's lungs blasted Gray's face as Karma's guttural snarls shook through him.

Granny rushed forward, pushing her slight body between the enraged pair. "Enough. Both of you." She yanked on Karma's ear while she pounded a shaking fist against the center of Gray's chest. "This does not help Trulie."

Gray forced the hand he clenched about Karma's still-vibrating throat to slowly relax. Granny was right. Trulie loved Karma. He could not kill the beast, especially when it was the animal's love for his mistress ruling his actions. He pushed off from the dog and stepped back.

Granny nodded toward Coira. "Go find Tamhas and Colum. Alert them that the keep is no longer safe." Then she turned to the still-rumbling dog. "You go with her. Protect her, Karma. I will stay here with Trulie."

The dog shook, then growled a grudging acquiescence as he followed Coira out of the room.

Granny remained silent until the door clicked shut behind them. "All right, Trulie. Time to involve Gray before he goes on a bloody rampage and kills an innocent bystander—namely your dog or me."

Trulie's eyes opened and she pushed herself up to a sitting position.

Gray stumbled and sank back down on the bed to keep from falling to his knees. "What the . . ." A strange mixture of relief, confusion, and a sudden certainty he was about to get sorely vexed hit him dead center.

He snatched her up by the shoulders and gritted his teeth against the urge to shake her. "Are ye trying to kill me, woman? What the hell kind of game are ye playing at?"

"We discovered someone put poison in the water. We want them to think they almost succeeded in getting rid of me." Trulie gently pulled herself out of his grasp and sat cross-legged in the center of the bed. "That way we should be able to catch who did it just by watching how everyone reacts."

He didn't know if it was the plotting gleam in her eyes or her tone that fanned his rage even more. He yanked her up by the shoulders again and this time shook her hard. To hell with attempting to control his ire. "Ye scared damn near ten years off me. Did ye not even think how I might feel when I thought ye would surely die?"

She opened her mouth to speak—

He shook her again. "I've half a mind to redden yer arse with the flat of me hand until ye canna sit. What the hell were ye thinking?"

She dug her nails into his forearms and hissed an enraged whisper, "Shut. Up. The plan won't work if you bellow it across the Highlands."

Granny ran to the door, pulled it open, and checked the outer sitting room. After a few moments, she quietly eased it shut and lowered the crossbar into the latch. As she hastened back to the bedside, she patted her hands together. "It's all right. There is no one out there. But Trulie is right, Gray. You need to keep your voice down."

He stared first at Granny, then back at Trulie in disbelief. Had they both lost their minds? With an irritated growl, he tossed Trulie back against the pillows. "I should have ye both flogged."

"Would you swallow that hardheaded Highland pride of yours for about five seconds? Think about what I just said. It makes perfect sense." Trulie scooted to the center of the bed and yanked her clothes back in place. "Dammit, Gray. Don't you know the best way to catch a murderer is to use their target for bait?"

He stomped to the far side of the room. Better to put a bit of distance between himself and the sharp-tongued woman he had been foolish enough to love. He turned and stabbed the air with a shaking finger. "If ye ever put a scare into me like that again . . ." His voice trailed off. He didn't know what he would do but he would damn well make sure she would not like it.

Trulie slid off the bed and went to him with both hands held out. "I'm sorry. I didn't mean to scare you, but the fewer people who know the truth, the more effective the trap." She motioned for him to join her over on the bed. "Come back over and sit down. We will fill you in on the details."

Gray glared down at her small, upturned palm. So soft. So tiny. How could a mere slip of a woman cause such a stir? He shifted his focus to her eyes. The emotions shining in their depths pulled at his heart and answered that silent question.

With an exhausted groan, he scrubbed a hand across his face and slid the other into Trulie's grasp. She owned him—body and soul. He might as well accept that fact and admit defeat. "So, tell me of this grand plan devised by the Sinclair women."

TRULIE WANTED to move so badly she could barely stand it. Her nose itched. Her feet were cold and if she had to lie on top of that lump in the mattress much longer her tailbone would be sore for days. But the whooshing sound of rustling skirts and the occasional thump of moving furniture told her she best keep her eyes shut and remain motionless. Maidservant Beala was still in the room.

Karma grumbled a low warning from his post at the head of the bed. Trulie could tell from the closeness of his rumble that the dog was standing as close to her as he could get, with his head even with hers. *Thank you, Karma.* She would be lost without him. Actually, she would be dead.

"Dinna worry, my braw beastie. I mean the mistress no harm."

Beala's high-pitched voice sounded a few feet from the bed. Her accent was thicker than most of those in the keep. Trulie figured Beala must have come to the MacKenna clan from another region of Scotland. She visualized Beala rambling around the room with her odd rolling gait. For some strange reason, the spindly girl moved like a chimpanzee. It wouldn't have surprised Trulie if the girl took to dropping to all fours just so she could move faster. But whatever the reason she walked the way she did, Beala didn't let the infirmity slow her. Trulie had seen the girl on several occasions outdistance the other maids even with her arms filled with linens.

Trulie wished the maid would hurry and finish. An uncomfortable urge to pee had taken hold and she struggled to control it. She concentrated on breathing in slow, shallow breaths and opened her senses to the room. Maybe she could pick up a vision off the girl. Beala had the run of the keep. Maybe she had some residual energy clinging to her.

Resentment. Frustration. Anger. Trulie held the next shallow inhale and focused harder. *Excitement. Revenge. Worry.* Her lungs burned for want of more air. She pulled in the slightest breath and eased it out again. The emotions bouncing off Beala were not what she expected. This was no residual energy. Emotions projecting with such vibrancy could only come from Beala's core.

The soft click of the chamber door interrupted her study. Trulie held her breath again and listened hard. A weight sank the mattress down beside her, nearly rolling her off the bed. A large furry foot pawed repeatedly at her arm. She cracked an eyelid to a black wet nose just inches from her face.

"She's gone?"

Karma agreed with a soft *woof* and slathered his long tongue from Trulie's jawline all the way to her eyebrows.

"I love you too, Karma," she said while dodging more doggie kisses. She shoved him down off the edge of the bed.

"Yer scheme willna work if yer giggling is heard down the hallway."

Trulie pointed at the door as she scrambled out of the bed. "Watch the door. I need to pee."

Grinning, Gray folded his arms across his chest and leaned back against the now bolted entrance. "Do ye now? Pray what would ye have done if I had not come to sit with ye?"

She hurried to retrieve the chamber pot out from under the bed. "I would have improvised." She patted the floor and stretched for the handle. "Who shoved the thing so far back? I don't know if I can reach it or not." If she didn't get that bowl soon, there was going to be a puddle on the floor.

She peeped under the bed, gauged the exact distance of the curved handle, and stretched to reach it again. Finally. Her fingers curled around the smooth, glazed handle and she pulled the pot out from under the bed.

As she straightened, she noticed Gray's impish expression. "Turn around," she said while twirling a finger in the air. "I can't pee if you're watching."

He didn't move—his smile reached his eyes.

"Gray!" She stomped her foot. Big mistake. She clamped her thighs tighter together. "Turn. Around. Now," she ordered through clenched teeth.

"What will ye give me?" he asked with a pointed look up and down her body.

She knew exactly where this was going and it was not going to happen. Since her self-imposed comatose state had begun, all love play had stopped. She didn't like it either, but they couldn't risk it. All they needed was a wayward servant to pass by and overhear them shouting hallelujah to the orgasm gods.

"We could be quiet," he suggested in a seductive tone.

"We have never been quiet," she said as she short-stepped over to a massive oak wardrobe and yanked open the door. "If you're not going to turn around, I'll climb in here to pee."

"Fine." He faced the wall. "Do what ye must, but 'tis a truly sorry day when a man's betrothed willna grant him the divine pleasure only she can give."

She rolled her eyes as she hiked up her shift and squatted over the pot. Finally. Blessed relief. She propped her chin in her hands as she waited to finish. "You just need to think about how great it will be when all this is over."

"Och, I have," he said in a strained voice. "Trust me, *mo chridhe*, I have."

Poor Gray. She clamped her mouth shut against the urge to giggle. Her frustrated love stood facing the door, hands propped over his head and feet slightly spread, looking as though he was waiting to be patted down and searched for weapons.

The hang of his plaid temptingly outlined the muscular curve of his hip. The way he leaned forward gave her quite a nice view. The corded muscles of his arms flexed as he lightly drummed his fingers on the wood.

Damn. It had been a long few days of self-imposed celibacy. She wet her lips and squirmed in place. Mercy, she ached for him too.

"Are ye done yet, lass?" He shifted in place but remained spread-eagled She tiptoed across the room. A delicious shiver stole through her as she smoothed her hands up his back. "Do you swear on your favorite horse's life you will be quiet?"

Gray didn't turn, but she immediately felt his body tense and heat up beneath her hands. "Och, aye, lass. I swear on Cythraul's life. I shall be quiet as a tomb."

It took mere seconds to strip off her shift and toss it to the floor. She ran her hands up under his clothing, reveling in the hardness of his well-muscled thighs. His buttocks tightened as she pressed her nakedness against him.

He sucked in a sharp hiss. "Lore, woman. Ye feel good against me, but I would much rather have ye in front."

"Soon," she whispered as she reached around and tickled her fingers down his stomach. Stealth sex was pretty exciting. She shivered again and snuggled tighter against him.

A deep groan escaped him as she wrapped her fingers around his cock and pulled.

"Shhh. You said you would be quiet." She cupped his sack in the other hand, straddled one of his legs and rubbed her wetness against him as she stroked him again.

"Aye," he said in a strained whisper. "I . . . will." He shifted in place.

She ran the tip of her tongue up his backbone and treated him to another stroking pull.

Gray jerked. His ribcage expanded and his body tensed.

"Are you holding your breath?" She couldn't resist a soft giggle as she nibbled a trail of kisses along the salty sweetness of his skin.

He rolled out of her hold and stripped off every stitch of clothing in one yanking motion. Jaw clenched, he snatched her up, slammed her against his chest, and covered her mouth with his.

She wrapped her legs around him and hungrily welcomed the raw need of the kiss. It had been too long since he'd been inside her.

He slid her lower in his arms, successfully driving his hardness into her. He clenched her ass in both hands as she clamped her thighs tighter about him.

"Not a sound, love," he whispered against her mouth.

"Not a sound," she said while arching against him.

Gray lifted her up and down with slow deliberate thrusts. She moaned into his mouth, plunging her tongue deep to keep from crying out.

He lowered her across a heavy round table in the center of the room, lifted her hips, and drove himself deeper into her heat. His hands slid to her waist as he slowly eased his way out then slammed in hard again.

With both hands clamped on the edges of the table, she bit the inside of her cheek to keep quiet. If he didn't move faster, she was going to die. "Harder," she finally whispered. She dug her heels into the small of his back and pulled him forward. "Harder. Now."

His sly grin spread as he clamped his hands tighter about her waist. "As ye wish, m'lady." The grin disappeared as he hammered into her.

Yes. She arched her back, delighting in every thrust. The coppery taste of blood filled her mouth as she bit her cheek to keep from screaming. The room disappeared as he pounded her into blinding ectasy.

Gray froze, clutched her hard against him, and groaned. He tensed for a long moment, then slumped across her with a great exhale.

She wrapped her arms tight around him and trailed kisses across his shoulder. "Well done," she whispered as she snuggled her cheek against his.

"Aye," he whispered back. "Well done, indeed."

CHAPTER 18

Gray shifted from a shallow dozing to alert wakefulness. Without moving, he took care to scan the darkened room by opening his eyes to the barest of slits. Nothing moved in the shadows. Nor seemed amiss. He slowly repositioned his head, as though shifting in his sleep. The wooden chair creaked in protest with his moving weight. But other than Trulie's soft breathing and the sound of the quietly hissing fire, he heard nothing.

Sharp clicks, then the rhythmic pat-patting of toenails against the flooring not covered with pelts. Karma huffed a warning woof into the darkness. The dog waited but a second then rumbled a deep vibrating growl.

Gray rose from his chair and slid to the foot of Trulie's bed in one fluid movement. The dog sensed something too. Whatever had awakened him had not been a dream. He pulled his dirk from its sheath and palmed the worn haft with readiness.

A slow steady grind of stone against stone came from the shadows. Gray crouched behind the end of the bed and peered over the mound of blankets. The far wall was definitely moving, but how could it be? Only he knew about this particular stretch of tunnels running through the keep.

The grinding ceased. Karma growled louder, daring the intruder to enter the room. A dark mass flew through the air and landed with a wet splat on the floor beside the hearth. Gray crouched lower, straining to make out what had landed in front of the fire.

A great black shadow moved toward the object. Firelight glistened off Karma's rich-black coat as the dog eased up on whatever had hit the stones. He snuffled the object, raised his head, and looked back at Gray as though trying to tell the man what he had discovered.

Tension cramped Gray's muscles. Lore, he wished he knew what the dog was trying to tell him. Karma snuffled the wet-looking pile again and raked a paw across it. Then the dog shifted, kept his head low, and rolled over on his side.

Dread stabbed through Gray as he watched Karma go limp. Had the dog succumbed to some sort of poison? Shadow and light danced across the animal's still body. Gray couldn't tell if Karma breathed or not.

A rustling movement from the secret passage drew Gray's attention back across the room. He would have to tend to the dog later. It was now up to him to protect his lady love from whoever dared to enter the room.

A cloaked form shuffled into the half-light. Gray rolled the knife in his hand, gripping the handle tighter. He strained to recognize the intruder, but the darkness, paired with the hooded black cloak, hid the demon's identity.

The nose-burning scent of fresh pitch alerted Gray just as the hooded figure swung a wooden bucket out from under the cloak. He jumped from behind the bed just as Karma sprang to life and lunged across the room.

A shrill screech split the darkness. The wide-bottomed bucket of pitch hit the floor, wobbled, and splashed the noxious contents, but didn't tip over.

"Now!" Trulie cried as she popped upright in bed. She freed herself from the tangled sheets and hopped to the floor.

Karma attacked. The enraged dog's snarling sent chills through

Gray's bones. The animal sounded like a primal beast tearing into its prey.

The cloaked figured screamed again, kicking and flailing against the beast's gnashing teeth. "Leave me, demon," a voice cried out as Karma yanked away the cloak and several layers of wadded-up clothing.

Beala kicked and scrabbled away from the dog. She held her bloodied arm tight against her torso as she dragged herself through the closing crack of the moving wall.

Beala? Gray stared in disbelief as the maid disappeared into the inky darkness and the wall slid shut.

"Stay here," he ordered as Trulie came up behind him.

"I will not," she snapped while nudging him forward. "I promise to stay behind you but I'm not staying here."

A frustrated growl tore free of his throat. The stubborn woman would be the death of him. "If ye dinna stay out of harm's way, I swear I will flog yer bare arse in front of the entire clan. Do ye understand?"

She agreed with a solemn nod.

Gray triggered the hidden release for the passage and the panel of the stone wall slid open. He grabbed a torch from its bracket and held it high as he led Trulie and Karma into the damp tunnel. "She could take several paths," he said as they came to a narrow turn that split into three different passages.

"Karma can track her," Trulie whispered. She patted Gray's side in the narrow confines of the tunnel. "Scooch over and let him up front. We can follow him."

Gray squeezed to one side against the damp, slimy wall. "Aye. Motion the lad forward. His senses will serve here much better than ours."

Karma wiggled past, then paused in front of the three tunnels with his head lowered. His snuffling snorts echoed through the winding chambers. He exploded with a violent sneeze, then dropped his head again. Suddenly, he swung toward the passage farthest to the left, slowly tilted his head to one side, then dove into the corridor.

Gray held the torch high, hunching forward to keep his head

from hitting the dripping ceiling. His shoulders scraped the sides of the tunnel as they slid deeper into the bowels of the maze. He hated the narrow confines. A man could scarcely draw a breath. "I will snap that woman's neck with my bare hands whenever we find her."

"No," Trulie said. "If you kill her, how will we find out what her deal is?"

She had a tight hold on the back of his plaid and he took comfort in her tiny fists pressed against the small of his back. Their slight pressure somehow calmed him. "What the hell do ye mean what her *deal* is?"

She patted his back. "You know . . . her story. Why she is doing what she does."

Gray grunted. He didn't give a damn what the woman's story was. She could tell it to the Earl of Hell when she arrived at the fiery gate.

A panicked scream echoed up ahead, followed by Karma's deep, threatening bark.

The stench of stale urine and human excrement hit Gray full in the face as he pushed into the room. Bile rose to the back of his throat and burned. He shielded his face with his arm and turned to Trulie. "Stay back. The air reeks."

She coughed and gagged behind him; his warning came too late.

"Call yer demon off," Beala cried as she crouched beside a low-slung cot crafted out of knotted limbs and a stretched hide.

"Karma, that'll do," Gray said. He kept his crooked arm over his nose and mouth. 'Twas a wonder the dog had not turned tail and run for want of fresh air.

Karma eased back a few steps, a warning still clicking deep in his throat.

Gray raised the torch higher and shuddered at what it revealed.

Lashed to the cot with bindings of leather and strips of filthy rags, lay an emaciated Fearghal. Dark stains pooled around him and dripped to the floor. His lower jaw sagged open as his blindfolded head leaned against his bony arm that was chained to an iron grommet jammed into the wall.

"What the hell have ye done to the man?" Gray swung the torch toward Beala where she cowered at Fearghal's feet.

"Cared for him." Beala's face transformed with a tender expression as she pawed at the exposed flesh of Fearghal's twitching ankle. "As soon as my dear one sees reason, us two will travel the world as man and wife."

"She is insane," Trulie whispered. "But she had to have help. How could she get him down here by herself?"

Gray wondered the same thing. Fearghal was not strong by any means, but surely the man could overcome such a slight maid. "Who helped ye get him here?" He blinked against the stench burning his eyes.

"I needed no help bringing my dear, sweet love to my bed." Beala rose and sat on the edge of the makeshift cot. She rubbed a filthy hand in a circular motion over her slightly distended stomach. "My fine man put a babe in my belly. He loves me. He goes wherever I ask."

The fool walked into his own death trap. "Ye carry *his* child?" Gray said.

Beala's wild eyes rounded wider as her head bounced up and down. "Aye. The babe's been planted well over four moons gone now." She leaned forward and stroked Fearghal's slack jaw, smiling down into his face. "My lover will soon be a da. I ken it will be a fine braw laddie. I seen it in a dream, so it must be so." She cupped Fearghal's face between her hands and cooed over him in a spine-tingling singsong voice. "A son for my fine man. A son to make him love me all the more."

Fearghal shifted slightly and a faint moan escaped his cracked lips.

"Ye see?" Beala turned to Gray with a beaming smile. "My lover sings along."

Gray struggled against the rise of vomit churning to be released. He had to get all of them out of here. Now. He raised the torch and maintained eye contact with Beala as he nudged Trulie backward.

"Out. Now," he said. "We can do nothing here. I shall send men to move them both up into the keep."

"You know she is mad," Trulie whispered. "You know she doesn't know what she's doing."

"I know." Gray nodded as he urged Trulie backward. "But that does not mean she can do whatever she wishes." With a glance back at the deathly squalor and filth, he rasped out a promise more to himself than Trulie. "Justice will be done."

CHAPTER 19

"Open the window," Trulie suggested. "Maybe some fresh air will help him."

Coira moved across the room and tied the tapestry back with a rope of braided cloth. "Nothing will help him, mistress. He has the look of death about him."

Trulie looked at Fearghal's glassy-eyed stare and silently agreed. It was just a matter of time. The man's body was shutting down. She and Granny both had tried to heal him several times. But each time they surged the energy into his emaciated form, the power ricocheted right back out. His fate was set. He would soon reach the end of this life's path.

"Well, then." Trulie sighed as she pressed a damp cloth against the man's sallow cheek. "We can at least make sure what time he has left is as free of suffering as possible." She inhaled deeply of the fresh air wafting in through the window, filling her lungs against the memory of Fearghal's prison. If she had been imprisoned in that stinking dark hole, she would want all the fresh air she could get.

Coira stood at the end of the bed and frowned down at the wasted man. "It surely had to be terrible trapped down there with such a girl."

Trulie nodded. There were some things worse than death.

"He is reaping what he sowed," Granny said from her chair beside the hearth. She lowered her sewing to her lap and peered at the girls over the top of her wire-rimmed glasses. "Coira, didn't you say Beala was the girl Fearghal bullied into thinking if she didn't give him what he wanted, he would have her kicked out of the keep?"

Coira nodded and glanced back at the man. She moved to a small stool beside a table filled with dark vials and bundles of dried herbs. The color deepened in her cheeks with the memory. "Aye. Beala was the maid."

"Be that as it may," Trulie said. "I think Fearghal has been punished enough. If we treat him badly now, then we are no better than he is."

Granny scowled off into space for a moment before returning her attention to the embroidery in her lap. She licked the tips of her finger and thumb, then ran them the length of the dark thread. Squinting as she twisted the end into a tiny knot, she finally spoke. "Well said, granddaughter."

Trulie returned the rag to the bowl of lavender-scented water sitting beside the bed. She started as the chamber door slammed open and bounced against the wall.

"Tamhas! Must you explode into the room? Our nerves are already shot because of the past few days." She pressed a hand against her chest, willing her pounding heart to calm down.

Tamhas arched a bushy brow and waved away Trulie's reprimand. "Ready yerselves. Aileas has returned."

This wasn't going to be pleasant. Trulie dried her hands on her apron. Gray had sent for Aileas as soon as they had emerged from the tunnels. Who knew how much longer her son would last? A contented feeling of pride warmed Trulie and settled her nerves. Even though Gray despised Aileas, he would never deny her what would most likely be the last visit with her son. Gray was an honorable man.

"Did her carriage just get here or is she actually on her way up?" Trulie nervously glanced around the room. They had done their best to make Fearghal as comfortable as possible. Surely Aileas wouldn't find fault with the room and make a bad situation even worse.

"What have ye done with my son?" a nasal voice bellowed down the hallway.

Tamhas snorted a disgusted grunt and tipped his head toward the door. "I believe that's yer answer."

Lovely. Trulie took a deep breath and faced the entrance.

Aileas blew into the room like a huffing black storm cloud. Her dark skirts shushed as they swirled around her. In each of her fisted, masculine hands, she clutched fluttering squares of lace-covered linen. Her fiery cheeks paled to a lighter pink when her gaze settled on what was left of her son.

"My poor wee laddie." She stifled a sob with a bit of linen and rushed to his side.

Fearghal didn't respond. His slack-jawed stare remained fixed on the stone wall beside his bed.

With a shaking hand, Aileas smoothed a bent finger across his sunken cheek. "What the devil have they done to ye, laddie?" She wheezed in a shaking breath and tucked his hair to one side. "I never wouldha left without ye if I had known. I thought . . ." Aileas's voice quivered to a higher pitch as tears streamed down her face. "I thought ye had gone on ahead as we planned. I thought ye had already left this accursed place."

Trulie swallowed hard and sniffed against the tears burning her eyes. No matter what Aileas had done, she was still a mother whose child was about to die.

"How did this happen?" Aileas said without taking her gaze from her son. "Who did this to my wee laddie?"

Trulie looked over at Granny and Coira standing beside the hearth. They shrugged in unison and nodded for her to take the lead and explain.

Trulie stood taller, clasped her hands behind her back, and eased toward Aileas. How in the world was she going to explain to Aileas that her son had bitten off more than he could chew when he decided to bully a mentally imbalanced maid into giving him sex?

"Well?" Aileas swiped a hand across her cheeks. "Tell me. All of it."

"Do you recall a servant named Beala?" Trulie waited a moment for Aileas to respond. The snuffling woman ignored her, just kept her hand pressed to her son's cheek. Trulie cleared her throat and spoke louder. "I think she helped keep your rooms before she came to take care of ours." Trulie moved closer. Maybe if she circled around where she could see Aileas's face, the telling might be easier. Trulie wet her lips and cleared her throat. "She is a small woman and walks with a strange rolling gait. Kind of blondish—"

"I ken well enough who she is." Aileas spit the words with such hatred Trulie jumped back a step. "What about her?" Aileas yanked the bedclothes back from Fearghal's collapsed chest before Trulie could continue. "Surely, that worthless chit couldna do this to my son."

Where was Gray when she needed him? Trulie cast a quick glance back at the door, wishing he would appear.

"Well?" Aileas hoisted her girth up from the edge of the bed and faced Trulie.

Trulie took a deep breath. There was no easy way to tell this, so she might as well jump in with both feet. "It appears Fearghal threatened to have Beala turned out if she didn't sleep with him." Trulie paused a second then blurted out the rest. "But evidently, after she gave in, in some strange sort of way, Beala fell in love with Fearghal and wanted him to marry her because she was pregnant . . . or maybe she wanted them to get married before she got pregnant. I am not sure about that part, but Fearghal must have refused . . ." *Dammit.* Could she sound any more ridiculous?

The look of pure hatred on Aileas's face ended Trulie's babbling.

This was not going well at all. "Anyway," Trulie continued. "We don't know for sure how, but Beala must have lured Fearghal down to a hidden chamber." She glanced over at the dying man in the bed. "She succeeded in chaining him to the wall. And she kept him there with no food or water . . . for quite a while."

All the color drained from Aileas's face as tears rolled down her cheeks and dripped from her jowls. Spreading the squares of linen between her hands, she mopped the bits of cloth across her face. "Where is my son's tormentor now?" she finally choked out as she blew her nose hard into the rag.

"We have her locked in a room where she can't hurt herself . . . or anyone else." Trulie forced herself not to cringe at Aileas's sharp look.

"I would see her." Aileas huffed and muttered under her breath as she plowed across the room. "Tell the MacKenna I would see his prisoner immediately." She didn't wait for Trulie's response before flouncing from the room.

"WHO ARE ye and why are ye here?" Gray barred the man from passing through the archway. He recognized him as the smithy's helper—the man who had come to MacKenna Keep along with the rest of Lady Aileas's possessions. He wanted to hear what the man had to say. There were too damn many secrets in this keep and very few people he trusted anymore.

"I am Gaedric." The man respectfully tucked his chin and kept his gaze trained on the floor. "The Lady Aileas was and always will be the honored daughter of my clan. I would serve her again if she will allow it." The man shuffled uncomfortably and bobbed his head lower. "That is, if the MacKenna sees fit for me to do so since she has returned."

Gray studied the man. He seemed honest. Humble even. Gray admired loyalty, even to one as undeserving as Aileas. "The Lady Aileas will not be here long. And what of the smithy? Are ye not bound to him?" Gray was curious to hear how the man would explain leaving his current station.

The man shifted from side to side. His large hands nervously plucked at the tattered hem of his stained tunic. "I would serve the lady for as long as ye see fit. The smithy says I am free to do so. He says he no longer has use for a cripple with few skills."

Gray made a mental note to pay a visit to the smithy. Perhaps the coarse man of steel could use a lesson in compassion. He understood the smithy's perspective, but there was never a need to be cruel. "I have no problem with ye serving the Lady Aileas while she abides here. But I must warn ye that after her son dies, she returns to her confinement."

Gaedric flinched as though Gray had struck him. He glanced up with watery, bloodshot eyes filled with emotions Gray didn't understand. "Her son will not heal?"

"No." Gray turned and motioned for Gaedric to follow. "Come. Ye can join yer mistress once we have seen to her request to question her son's murderer.

Gray paused as he reached the first landing in the staircase. "Gaedric, come. Now, man." Gray waited until Gaedric hesitantly moved forward and hefted his way up the first few steps.

Gray dreaded the chore set before him. Aileas wanted to see Beala and by rights as Fearghal's mother, Gray could not deny her. He scrubbed a hand over his tired eyes. Lore, he would be glad when all this was over. He hoped Aileas wished to take Fearghal's body with her. In fact, he would suggest it. What better way to rid MacKenna keep of the wickedness Aileas and her son had stirred?

Trulie met him at the top of the stair. The love shining in her eyes was all that gave him strength. He held out a hand and felt the tension slip away as Trulie slid her hand into his. Blessed be Tamhas and Granny Sinclair for bringing this woman to him.

"Fearghal will be gone by sunset," she whispered. "Death rattles in his lungs."

"Aye." Gray sucked in a deep breath as he tucked her close to his side. What else could he say? No love or even basic respect had ever existed between himself and Fearghal. He regretted the coward had suffered such an end. But from what he had gathered, Fearghal had chosen his destiny by his actions. Gray believed in accountability for choices made and Fearghal's situation confirmed that conviction.

"Who is that?" Trulie whispered with a glance down the staircase.

"Aileas's most loyal servant." Gray actually felt sorry for the woman who had cursed him with so many unpleasant hours. "He will more than likely join her retinue when she returns to sanctuary."

"The chieftain has stated I may question the prisoner." Aileas's loud, unpleasant voice boomed down the corridor.

Gray sucked in another deep breath as they rounded the corner. Lore, he felt as though he walked toward his own end. Two burly warriors barred Aileas from the room where they had placed Beala. They stood broad shoulder to broad shoulder with arms crossed and eyes fixed straight ahead.

Aileas waited with her fists clutched just below her sagging bosom. Her expression soured even further when her gaze fell first on Trulie and then on Gaedric. She jerked her chin toward them. "Those two have no right here."

Gray halted and slid his other hand atop Trulie's where she held onto his arm. "My betrothed has every right because I say it is so." He glared at red-faced Aileas, daring her to argue.

Aileas motioned toward Gaedric with a flip of her hand. "And him? He has no duty here."

"On the contrary," Gray replied. "Gaedric has sworn fealty to ye and yer father's clan. Ye should be honored by his presence."

Aileas huffed a disgusted breath as she whirled back and faced the stoic guards. "I have no time for such. Now, do ye mean to allow me to pass or not?"

Gray motioned to the guard on the left. "Open the door."

As the door swung open, Beala hopped down from the wide stone seat located below the room's high, narrow window. Her thin hands fluttered nervously up and down the wrinkled folds of her plain linen shift.

When Gray bent and entered the room, Beala's sunken eyes rounded even wider in her pale, drawn face. Her bare feet slapped against the floor as she skittered to the farthest corner with her odd hitching run. "Ye must not touch me. Fearghal is my husband!"

"Lying bitch!" Aileas roared as she exploded into the room. Gray grabbed her arm and held her back as she strained to reach the girl.

"Get behind me," Gray hissed to Trulie.

Gaedric limped his way into the room after them. The agitated man looked around, then moved to stand beside Gray. "Yer woman will be safe behind us."

"Leave hold of my arm." Aileas twisted in Gray's grasp. "Leave hold of me now."

"I said ye could come and question the girl. I never gave ye permission to attack her." Gray yanked Aileas back and brought his face close to hers. "If ye try to harm her again I shall have the guards remove ye."

Aileas's bloodshot eyes narrowed as her gaze darted first to Gray, then toward the corner where Beala cowered. "Agreed," she finally said.

Gray forced himself not to recoil. For the thousandth time since he had known Aileas, he wondered how the hell his father had ever married such a vile woman. He released her arm and eased back a step. "Ye may question the woman. That is all."

Aileas jerked the wrinkles from her sleeve and smoothed her thick hands down her skirts. She straightened her broad, rounded shoulders and walked slowly toward Beala.

Beala crouched behind the upended cot she had pulled to the corner. The closer Aileas approached, the higher the young girl peeped from behind her barricade. A smile lit up her small, pinched face. "Mother Aileas." Beala clapped her hands with chilling excitement and tittered with a happy cackling. "Have ye finally come to praise me for helping ye and my lovely Fearghal?"

"Shut yer maw." Aileas swiped a shaking fist through the air. "Keep yer vile mouth closed. No one wishes to hear yer lies."

The smile faded from Beala's face. A worried frown replaced it. "But I set the fires just as ye asked. The evil woman in the tower died so she canna cast any more spells on the keep." Beala crept from behind the cot, her hands twisting in front of her rounded belly. "And now Fearghal can be chief. I made certain old MacKenna couldna escape the judgment of the flames either." Beala chilled the room with an eerie singsong chant. "Old MacKenna and his witch are dancing with the devil. Old MacKenna and his whore are gone to the fiery pits of hell."

Aileas lurched toward the girl, wrapped her pudgy hands around Beala's throat, and charged forward. Beala crumpled under the force of Aileas's weight. As the woman landed on top of the girl, she repeatedly bashed Beala's head against the hard floor. "Shut it, vile bitch. I told ye hold yer tongue!"

"The babe," Beala choked out while squirming beneath Aileas's weight. "Take care lest ye kill Fearghal's babe." She weakly flailed against Aileas' attack.

Gray charged forward, only to be yanked back by Gaedric's iron grasp. The man's face had turned blood red; his eyes glittered wild and crazed. Gray fell back to Trulie, spreading his arms to shield her from attack.

But Gaedric didn't turn on him. The man lumbered his way to Aileas. He sank one hand in her knotted hair and yanked her away from Beala's limp body.

Aileas screamed and clawed at Gaedric's arm as he threw her back against the opposite wall. He clutched her by the throat and pinned her to the stones beneath the window. "Ye kilt my only son. *Our* son. Ye kilt him with yer infernal plotting. Why could ye not be happy with yer lot in life?"

"Ye think I would have my clan know I gave birth to the son of a crippled simpleton?" Aileas sputtered and clawed at Gaedric's arm with both hands. "Ye should thank the gods my wicked father allowed ye to live. I told him ye raped me after he did."

"I loved ye." Gaedric sobbed out a groan as his left hand joined his right around Aileas's throat. "And now I am cursed with the blood of honorable people because I listened to ye and didna lift a hand to stop ye from yer evil ways."

"He is going to kill her," Trulie whispered in a horrified gasp.

"Let him," Gray growled in response. "He has earned the right."

Gaedric roared out another broken sob as he slammed Aileas back against the wall. She spat at him, her face blood red as she strained against the attack. She brought her boot up hard between his legs. As his grip loosened from around her throat, she dug her thumbs into his eyes.

Gaedric bellowed in pain as he staggered back, an arm clamped across his eyes and his hand clutching his crotch.

Aileas screamed and charged forward, both hands raised to attack him again.

Gray shoved Trulie back in the corner. "Stay," he ordered. A red haze filled his senses and bloodlust pounded in his ears. He grabbed Aileas by the hair and yanked her off Gaedric. Just as she rolled to attack Gray, he pressed the point of his dirk against the folds of her double chin. "Give me one reason why I should not slit yer throat for ye."

Aileas's beady-eyed gaze darted from side to side as she stilled in his hands. Her gasping wheezes echoed through the chamber as she lifted her hands into the air with her fingers outstretched. "Forgive," she finally sputtered with a heaving breath. "Forgive."

"I beg ye, Chieftain. I beg ye . . . dinna kill her." Gaedric fell to his knees beside Gray and raised his clasped hands upward. "I beg ye let her live."

"Knowing all she has done, ye still wish her to live?" Gray could not believe the man kneeling at his feet could be so blind.

"There are many punishments worse than death," Trulie said from the corner. The calm serenity of her tone held Gray's inner beast in check.

Gray yanked Aileas's head back further and pressed the knife to her flesh until a single crimson drop of blood beaded up and trickled down the length of his blade. Aileas sucked in a hitching breath and squinted her eyes shut.

"Please, great MacKenna." Gaedric pawed at Gray's elbow. "'Tis not her fault. Her cruel father made her what she is. I beg ye . . . I will take her to the Isle of Man. There are places there. Remote places. She will never do harm again. I swear it."

Gray stared at his blood-stained blade. It would be so easy to slit the hag's throat and silence her without question.

"Gray." Trulie's quiet plea reached him. "Listen to Gaedric. I don't want her blood on your hands."

Gray forced his gaze away from the knife and locked eyes with Trulie. How could she expect him to let the murderess go?

"Please," she whispered.

"Guard." Gray yanked Aileas around and held her at arm's length. When his men entered the room, he shoved her toward them. "Bind her and leave her locked in this room until I give the order. She will be leaving with Gaedric as soon as he is ready for his journey."

"Thank ye, m'lord." Gaedric kissed the hem of Gray's plaid before he rose and took hold of Aileas's wrists.

Gray pulled away from Gaedric's fawning with a single shake of his head. "I advise ye to kill the wicked harpy afore she kills ye first."

Then he held out a hand to Trulie and led her from the room.

TRULIE CLUTCHED the light arisaid closer around her as the wind moaned through the bailey. The blinding sun, high in the bright-blue sky brought no warmth today. Heart heavy, she watched as Gray oversaw the pair of shrouded bodies loaded into the back of the wagon. His face was cold. Expressionless. He looked years older than the first time she had set eyes on him just a few short months ago.

Gaedric sat on the wagon's seat, the slack reins wrapped around one hand. Aileas, puffed up and silent with her wrists still bound, sat beside him. The wagon creaked as the last of the supplies were loaded around Fearghal and Beala's remains.

Gray nodded once to Gaedric, then turned and plodded up the stone steps. Trulie's heart ached even more. She wished there had been a way to spare him all this pain.

Gaedric clucked to the horses and slapped the reins across their backs. The wagon groaned as it shifted forward and started its last journey from MacKenna keep.

"And so it ends." Gray sounded bone weary as they watched the wagon creak and sway across the courtyard and pass through the outer gate.

Trulie slid her arms through his and hugged her cheek against him. "I am sorry," she whispered. "I am so sorry all this happened."

He took her hand and lifted it to his lips. "Without ye here . . ." His voice broke and rasped lower as he closed his eyes and pressed her hand to his cheek. "I never would have survived it," he finished in a strained whisper.

"I wish you had never had to endure it." She wrapped her arms around him and snuggled her cheek against his chest, wishing she could erase his mind. She and Granny had discussed doing that very thing to relieve his pain. But they had both sensed the same eerie knowing, the knowing sent from the Fates. Gray's memories were to be kept intact. For some inexplicable reason, Gray needed this pain. Damn the Fates and their cruel rules. His pain made him who he was.

Gray held her tight and rested his chin atop her head. One of his hands idly caressed a path up and down her spine. "Ah . . . but if I had endured nothing, who knows if Fate would have seen fit to bring us together."

"Fate, or Granny and Tamhas?"

"Any of them." His chest shifted with a deep intake of air. "Are ye certain . . ." His soothing baritone rumbled against her cheek, then faded into a heavy sigh.

"Am I certain about what?"

"Are ye certain the Fates would punish ye if ye traveled back to the past to prevent such evil? How could the gods frown upon ye for stopping one such as Aileas?" He eased back and peered down at her. "Are ye certain it is forbidden? How could they punish ye for changing it all for the good? So many good folk would be saved."

Her heart fell at his question. She had expected the subject to surface again. The man was as unrelenting as the Highland wind, and it was just human nature to wonder how the world could be improved if you just went back and corrected the mistakes of the past.

"I'm sorry, Gray. Fate doesn't give any wiggle room on this." It killed her soul to refuse him. She had to make him understand the delicate balance of action and accountability. Fate chose what it allowed a time runner to change. Fate's order could not be disobeyed. "I can't do it. It's the surest way to destroy a time runner . . . and very possibly, all those around me." A chill stole across her as she slid an arm's length away.

"I dinna ken how stopping Aileas from killing my parents could possibly destroy ye."

Another heavy sigh escaped her, she had tried to explain this before. What else could she tell him? She pulled the MacKenna colors tighter around her.

"I told you about Granny's twin sister, Tia." She took his hand and tugged for him to follow. Maybe a walk through the private gardens would make the explanation easier. Fresh air and the sounds of early summer in the Highlands tended to soothe the soul. She stole a glance at his. The tension there wasn't reassuring. He knew what he wanted, but she had to convince him that it was better if he didn't get it. "Tia not only dabbled with history, but she also manipulated it. She fouled countless lives . . . and she paid for it. Now she is a reminder to all Sinclairs about what we must never do."

"Explain." He pushed open the carved wooden gate leading to the inner courtyard and steadied her as she picked her way across a small bridge. Water gurgled in a peaceful shallow stream around the perimeter of the garden. "Trulie?" he prompted again.

A worrisome uneasiness nagged her as she walked. Something deep inside told her this was not going to end well, no matter how she phrased it. It was difficult enough to accept Fate's rules even when you knew in your heart how dire the consequences could be if you broke them. She took a deep breath and continued. "Tia would stand in one era and study any timeline she pleased without fully jumping. She had a penchant for watching several possible futures, then backtracking through time to see what triggered the events."

She trailed her hand down through the soft catkins sprouting beside the path. A glance at Gray revealed his expression was even less reassuring than before. The look on his face clearly conveyed that he didn't see how Tia's gift was such a bad thing. Trulie took another deep breath. She was getting to that part, and hopefully, he would understand. Granny had compared Tia's gift to watching different channels on television and rewriting the scripts as an example. Trulie smiled to herself. That analogy wouldn't quite work with Gray.

Trulie finally pointed to the shallow waters of the reflecting pool built in the center of the garden. "What if you could stand right here, look down into the water, and see what was happening anywhere in the world during any time period you wanted?"

He arched a dark brow and thoughtfully stroked his chin. "That would be a fair gift indeed."

"And what if you could split those visions to see every possible option for a particular line of time depending on which choice was made? What if you could pick the future that you liked the best and step back through the water to alter it even more—tweak it to occur exactly as you wished?" Trulie sat down on the low stone wall and dipped her fingers in the water.

His eyes widened as he slowly voiced his thoughts. "I could make the world a better place. I could ensure no ill befell anyone." He sat down beside her and leaned forward, his face bright with interest. "Think of the people ye could save. Think of the evil ye could avert."

She frowned down into the water as she disturbed her reflection with her hand. "And what if after you changed things for what you thought was an even better version of the future, it triggered a different chain of events you hadn't foreseen? Worse events. What if those you tried to save ended up suffering an even more terrible fate? What if those you loved turned on you?"

The smile faded from Gray's face. His expression darkened into a troubled scowl. He tossed a hand in the air as though dismissing what Trulie said. "Then I would jump through time again and repair the damage I caused. Ye could always undo whatever had been done."

"And when you did that, even more things spiraled out of control, because no matter how careful you were, something unexpected always happened. Somehow, no matter how hard you tried, you couldn't foresee every possible reaction you might trigger." She folded her hands in her lap, her heart heavy at the frustrated disappointment in the slump of his shoulders.

"What happened to your grandmother's sister?" He leaned forward and stared down at the ground. The muscles of his jaw flexed beneath the dark dusting of his late-afternoon beard.

"Fate took away her ability to bear children. Tia became corrupted with jealousy and rage. When she lashed out and sought revenge, she was ordered destroyed by the only man she had ever loved." Trulie stared down at her hands. "He declared her an abomination to the natural world and watched while they executed her. Slowly."

Trulie could tell by the expression on Gray's that face he still didn't agree with the rule. "Tia needed to be destroyed, Gray. She had become a monster. People suffered because of the things she did. They are still suffering because of her actions. Just because we are allowed to travel across the web of time doesn't mean we're allowed to change it to suit our own desires. Every thread is part of the whole. Nothing can be manipulated without affecting everything else. We must trust the wisdom of Fate and what will and won't be allowed."

"What ye say makes no sense," he said with a sideways glance. "Ye change a time as soon as ye shift into existence in another era. If ye truly feared to make things worse, the lot of ye would never travel the web at all." He turned to her, jaw set, his eyes dark and unreadable. "How could it possibly make things worse to save my parents from suffering such a cruel end?"

She gazed across the quiet garden greening beneath the warm sun. She had no good answer for him. A time runner—a good one with a conscience—knew in her heart what was okay to mess with and what wasn't. His parents' death had to be left intact. Trulie felt it. The knowing wasn't something she could easily explain. The understanding had been planted in her heart at a young age and nurtured into being so.

She reached for him. Her heart sank when he stood and stepped back for her. "Granny instilled a great respect for time and its ways within us. She taught us everything happens for a reason. We have to avoid the temptation to *force* our own will into the web. We all know the damage we can cause. Tia's mistakes taught us to treat our gifts with the proper respect and be careful when we leap." She dropped her hand into her lap and stared down at it. "We don't run across the threads of time all willy-nilly, without reason. Each jump is thought through and studied before it's done . . . at least by one of us." She bent and trailed her hand across the top of the shimmering water. Surely Granny had thought through this very trip before finally getting her to jump. "The reason we jumped this time was because Granny first insisted it was time for her last leap." Trulie didn't mention the part about Granny hinting that Trulie was destined to choose a husband from the past.

"Last leap?" Gray glanced back at her. His sullen look darkened even further.

She hated this. The more she told him, the worse things got. It never failed. Anytime they allowed anyone into their complicated world, the individual just couldn't grasp why a time runner would not manipulate things for the betterment of all concerned. More often than not, explaining their beliefs to an outsider was a deal breaker. An uneasy shiver ran through her, twisted her heart. She didn't want this deal broken.

"The last leap is . . ." Trulie went silent, struggling to find the right words. This was just going to confuse him more. She stared off into space. "As a time runner ages, her ability to control a leap decreases. When she decides she has exhausted this lifeline . . ." Trulie paused again. The words just wouldn't come. She wished she could just touch his hand and Gray would somehow instantly know everything she was struggling to explain.

How could she tell him that when a time runner took the last leap, it wasn't as though she actually died? It was more like her soul broke free of this physical plane and ascended to a higher level—a better level, according to the tales passed down through the generations.

Trulie shrugged. "I guess you could say she leaves this life behind and jumps to the next adventure. She gets a new life—a new start."

Gray shook his head and turned away. He didn't look back as he spoke. "I have heard all the strange vagaries I can stomach for one day." He lowered his gaze to the ground and barely turned his head in her direction. "Ye say ye canna save my mother and father from their terrible end, but ye see no harm in disturbing time to give yer grandmother a new life. Yer reasoning makes no sense." With his fists clenched at his sides, he strode away and left the garden.

Sadness and regret filled her. She didn't blame him for his resentment. He loved his parents and, knowing how they died, how could he not resent her for refusing to save them from that pain? It wasn't fair and she knew it. But nobody ever said life was fair, and the gifts of her bloodline created a perplexing outlook on dos and don'ts.

She stared at her hands and traced her thumb along the lines of her palm. "I guess it's a good thing we got this out *before* the wedding," she said to a nearby finch. The tiny bird cocked its head, beady black eyes studying Trulie as if it completely understood what she said. Its breast swelled with a polite chirp and then it flew away. A sad smile tugged at her mouth. Maybe the little bird wondered the same thing she did. Would there even be a wedding now that Gray fully understood what she was capable of doing and the complicated rules she followed?

She dipped her fingers in the cool water of the reflecting pool, frowning down at her troubled reflection. If Gray didn't come around on his own, she would be forced to take drastic measures. She would turn him over to Granny.

CHAPTER 20

Infectious merriment sifted through the trees as freely as the wind. Trulie stopped walking and listened more closely. Soft rustling of green leaves shuffling in the breeze. The light, gurgling of water trickling somewhere in the distance. "Come on, Granny. Laugh again so I can find you." Where was she? Trulie had been searching for what seemed like hours.

Splashing water followed by a high-pitched squeal pierced the peacefulness of the woods. Trulie shook her head and turned to the right. Granny sounded like a schoolgirl on spring break. Last leap, indeed. Who was Granny kidding? The way she had been acting since they returned to the past—a good ten years younger at least—Granny wasn't going anywhere anytime soon.

Trulie gathered up her skirts and plodded through the trees. Her feet sank into the loamy softness of the forest floor. A thicket of brambles snatched at her sleeves as she shoved between a boulder and the silvery-gray trunks of young saplings. The higher she stomped up the wooded hillside, the madder she got. Granny should be at the keep. Sitting by the hearth. Sewing. Or sorting herbs. Or one of those other nice, calm sedate tasks that a woman Granny's age was supposed to do.

Trulie huffed an irritating strand of hair off her nose. Another excited shriek pealed out a bit closer. "Good." Trulie slapped at a midge buzzing around her face. She hoped Granny had enjoyed enough playtime today, because they needed to talk. Things were still uncomfortably tense with Gray. He just couldn't seem to get past the fact that she refused to change his parents' fate.

Trulie lifted her skirts up to her knees and moved faster. Granny would know what to do about Gray. Trulie smiled. Maybe Granny would grab him by the ear and twist it until he understood.

Water sloshed just beyond a fallen tree overtaken with sprouting vines. Trulie stopped and looked around. She recognized the outcroppings of limestone shooting up through the dark mulch of the forest floor. The pond where she had nearly drowned was just up ahead. Thank goodness she had chosen the lower path that was free of the deadly, shifting shale.

She wadded her skirts into a manageable bundle and draped them over one arm, sorely missing the ease and comfort of her blue jeans. Tromping through the woods with yards of cloth swaddled around her was more work than tromping through a field of dried cornstalks on the way to the barn. Trulie paused. Memories of the peace and quiet of the Kentucky woods filtered through her mind. Wonder if the girls were okay? She hadn't connected with them through the fire portal in over a month. There just hadn't been a good time.

A grim pang of homesickness mixed with the feeling of things lost and never to be seen again settled across her. Time traveling played hell with a girl's emotions. She shook free of the melancholy and yanked her skirts into a tighter wad. With her free hand, she pushed around the pile of brush.

"Come to me, ye wee minx." More splashing was accompanied by a deep rumbling chuckle. "Come within reach and I will show ye what happens when ye tease me with yer charms."

Trulie froze. That did not sound like Granny.

"Oh no ye don't, my fine man." Teasing giggles drowned out more splashing. "If ye want me, ye have to come and get me."

Trulie wrinkled her nose and backed up a step. *Eww.* That was Granny. And Tamhas. She had better hurry and let them know she was here before things got any more heated. "Granny!" she called out quickly. "Granny, I am right over here behind these bushes and I really need to talk to you."

A mumbled expletive accompanied the sound of bodies thrashing in water. "Trulie, I am . . . busy. Go away. We will talk later."

Bullshit. Trulie took a hesitant step forward, taking care to keep her gaze glued to the ground just in front of her toes. She really did not want to see her own grandmother skinny-dipping with her *boyfriend.* Tamhas was a little old for that title, but the thought of any more sensual of description made Trulie want to gag. "I do not qualify water polo with your boyfriend as busy," she snapped in response.

Granny's chuckle echoed Tamhas's amused snort. More water splashed. "This better be important," Granny called out. "Come on, Tamhas. We better see what mess the children have gotten themselves into this time."

"I am going to wait over in the clearing at the low side of the pond." Trulie waited for an answer. None came. All she heard was splashing accompanied by low murmuring. "Did you hear me?"

"We heard you!" Granny's tone clearly indicated she was not pleased with Trulie's timing. "We will be there in a minute."

Good. Trulie shoved back through the bushes. A narrow path of tramped-down leaves led off in the general direction of the clearing. Arrow-shaped indentations here and there in the soft ground hinted that deer followed the path as a regular route to water.

Pacing around the perimeter of the mossy clearing, she drummed her fingers atop her folded arms. What was taking them so long? She squinched her eyes shut and shook her head. No. She did not want to even imagine what was taking them so long.

Granny finally pushed through the bushes. Her eyes sparkled behind her wire-rimmed spectacles. Vibrant pink glowed across her cheeks. Her wet hair trailed down her back in a long silver stream. Trulie couldn't recall a single time when Granny had looked so . . . satisfied. She swallowed hard against an involuntary gag.

"Now what is so important it couldn't wait until the evening meal?" Granny peered over the tops of her glasses while she smoothed back her long, wet hair and twisted it into a knot at the nape of her neck.

"Where is Tamhas?" Trulie glanced toward a tangle of bushes.

Granny's cheeks flushed an even brighter shade as she gave her hair a final pat. "He will be along shortly."

Judging by the look on Granny's face, Trulie didn't want any details. "I need your help," she blurted out. Granny had to make Gray see reason.

Concern wiped all merriment from Granny's expression. She shook the wrinkles out of her skirts and took a step forward. "What's wrong?"

"It's Gray." Trulie quickened her impatient pacing to a frustrated stomp in a tight circle. "He's . . . he's . . ." she groaned. "He refuses to see reason."

Granny studied her with a confused scowl. "About?" When Trulie didn't speak, she rolled her eyes heavenward and lifted her hands. "I need a little more to go on than 'He refuses to see reason.'"

Trulie stopped pacing and stared down at the ground. "He can't understand why I won't go back in time and keep his parents from dying in that fire."

"I see," Granny said softly. She reached for Tamhas as he pushed through the brush with his wet hair slicked back into a tight queue. "Did you explain to him why you couldn't?" she asked while stroking his burly forearm and leaning against his shoulder.

"If the lad has set his mind on what he wants, she will not be able to turn him no matter what she says." Tamhas kissed Granny's hand and leaned against his staff against his shoulder.

"He's right," Trulie agreed. "I even told him about Tia and he still wants me to go back and save them."

"He blames himself for his mother's death," Tamhas explained. His face darkened with the memory of that night as he stared off into the distance. "Perhaps his guilt is what drives him to not see the reason of yer words."

"But I can't risk it." Trulie could tell by the look on Granny's face that the wise old woman had shifted into plotting mode. Good. That was exactly what this problem needed—a Granny plan of attack. "And since he asked me, and I said no, things aren't . . ." She flicked a hand. "Things just aren't right anymore." The uncomfortable weight of the situation crushed her in its grip. A dull ache throbbed through her like an ill-timed heartbeat.

Granny slid from Tamhas's embrace, easing her way around the circle as she thoughtfully tapped a bent finger against her mouth. After one slow lap around the clearing, she stopped and stared down at the ground. "Perhaps it is time to study that fateful night from a different angle." She slowly lifted her head and stared at Trulie.

Trulie slowly moved forward, barely shaking her head. "Are you talking about alternate timelines?" Now was not the time for Granny to be cryptic.

"No." Granny shook her head. She scrubbed both hands up and down her arms beneath the bell of her sleeves as though she had taken a sudden chill. "I am talking about showing Gray what really happened that night—from his parents' point of view."

A sense of foreboding shivered through Trulie. "What if what we show him is worse than what he already knows?"

Granny lifted her chin and smoothed her hands down the front of her soft-gray dress. "That is not the case. I knew Gray's mother well."

"And you were going to tell me this when?" Trulie did her best to keep her jaw from dropping. Why hadn't Granny told her this before?

"I am telling you now. That is all that matters." Granny fixed Trulie with a stern look and jerked her head toward the deer path. "Go get Gray. Meet me in the gardens. It is time he saw the night of the fire from a different perspective."

∼

H E H A D to let it go. Gray scrubbed his palms against the cold roughness of the stone wall. For sanity's sake, he had to let it go.

"I canna release it," he admitted in a defeated whisper. His head sagged forward and he closed his eyes. The night of the fire exploded inside his mind. His mother's cries. His father's roared curses. Cythraul's screams as the terrifying blaze set the fearless warhorse bucking against the choking, smoke-filled air.

And all of it could be prevented. Gray lifted his face to the gentle breeze and sucked in a deep lungful. If only Trulie would agree, all the pain and terror of that terrible night could be wiped away like blood washed from a shield.

Trulie. He fisted one hand and brought it down hard against the stone. He hated himself for allowing this obsession to drive a wedge between them. What the hell was wrong with him? Since her arrival, he had felt whole. Complete. Why the devil did he have to ruin it?

"Ye are wanted in the garden," Colum called from the carved stone steps leading down to the bailey. "Come, Gray. Ye brood over-much about that which canna be changed."

Damn, Colum. The man had no idea of what he spoke. All he knew was the Sinclair women had somehow traveled back from the future. The fool did not realize the extent of the women's powers.

"Who waits in the garden?" Gray had no intention of moving from the narrow footpath running atop the curtain wall. Looking out upon the wild beauty of his land was the only solace he found these days.

"Yer woman waits." Colum shifted on the narrow stairs and leaned against the wall. "A wise man never keeps his woman waiting."

"What do ye ken about my woman?" Gray spit over the wall. The taste of the situation curdled on his tongue. He almost flinched at the frustration he heard in his own tone. Lore, he sounded like a man who had just been booted from his lover's bed. "What does she want?" he said as he leaned with his forearms propped atop the wall. The day was nearly spent. It would soon be the time in the evening when both sun and moon shared the sky as they slowly swapped places, the in-between time when energy painted the horizon with cooling blues and heated crimsons. "What does she want, Colum?" Gray repeated as he turned away from the rugged hills spanning as far as he could see.

Colum turned and loped down a couple of steps. "Come to the garden and ask her yerself." The grating crunch of his boots thudding down the rest of the staircase shadowed his voice as he called out. "Ye best hurry. Granny is with her and ye ken how patient that old woman is."

Granny? Suspicion perked all Gray's senses to battle status. Both Granny and Trulie summoning him to the garden could only mean the two were up to something. He closed his eyes and rubbed his knuckles across his forehead. He had the distinct feeling that the pounding ache in his head was about to get a lot worse.

CHAPTER 21

The pegged hinges of the wooden garden gate groaned as it creaked open. The iron latch clattered back into place as it shut. Someone had just entered the garden. Trulie didn't have to turn to know it was Gray. Her body tensed as her senses shifted into high gear. No one else affected her that way, and up until their disagreement about the night of the fire, the ripple of energy had always been pleasant.

She wiped her damp palms across the folds of her dress and nervously shifted in place. Ever since the day of their disagreement, the flash of energy whenever Gray neared was more of a sting than an acknowledging caress. It was as though the energy slapped her, reprimanding her for not striving to make things right between them.

"Calm down, Trulie," Granny said. "Jitters don't solve anything."

"I can't exactly control the jitters." Trulie clenched her teeth. It wasn't like she had a switch she could flip to shut off her emotions.

A rush of yearning warmed her as Gray walked toward them. The set of his wide shoulders, the strength in his stride—a feast for her eyes and a balm for her soul. She wet her lips, hoping Granny's plan would clear the tension between them. By the determined set of

Gray's jaw, he was wound as tight as she was. This had to work. If it didn't, she didn't know what would.

"Ye called." Gray forced the words out as though the very act of showing up in the garden displeased him beyond measure.

Granny's eyes narrowed and her thin lips flattened into a determined line.

Not good. Trulie glanced uneasily between Granny's scowl and Gray's thinly masked insolence. Gray was about to get hit with both barrels of a Granny tongue-lashing, and he was too wound up in his own little world to know it.

"I knew your mother," Granny said as she slid her bent thumbs around the waist of her apron and spread her feet into battle stance. "If you took that tone with her, she would've thumped a knot on that hard head of yours."

"Ye are not my mother," Gray said before Granny finished speaking. His chin inched a bit higher and his narrowed eyes clearly showed what he felt about Granny's revelation.

"I may not be your mother"—Granny's *I have had enough of your attitude* tone shifted into warp drive—"but you are going to listen to what I have to say and you're going to listen good. I'm tired of Trulie moping around this place because you're so wrapped up in what you think you know and how you think things should be. The two of you should be planning your life together, but instead, you're damned and determined to drown yourself in your past. You're too thick-headed to realize what's for your own good. How can you be a good chieftain when you walk around with your head so far up your ass?"

Trulie covered her mouth and held her breath. If Gray's face turned any redder, he would burst a blood vessel.

"Out of respect for Trulie . . . and yerself," he said, in a growled warning, "I shall overlook yer insults."

"Hmpf." Granny blew out an unimpressed huff of air. "Don't do me any favors." She jabbed a bony finger at the reflecting pool centered in the garden. "If you think you can yank yourself away from wallowing in self-pity for five minutes, I have something I think you should see."

Again, Trulie glanced at Granny and then back to Gray. The man's stance said he was thoroughly infuriated. If he clenched his fists any tighter, the corded muscles in his arms were going to snap. Had Granny pushed him too far? Trulie hugged herself against the nauseating roll of her butterfly-filled stomach. *Please don't leave* echoed over and over in her mind.

"Ye go too far, old woman." His tone rang with cold deadly warning. He eased forward with the smooth, lethal ease of a predator about to lunge. "I could banish ye for such disrespect against the MacKenna."

"Then do it," Granny said. She threw out her chest and squared her narrow shoulders. "Or show me how wise your mother raised you to be by learning from what I am about to reveal."

The man's furious, unblinking stare slid back to Trulie.

"Please," she whispered, her clasped hands begging him to try.

The corner of his mouth twitched. His frosty glare seemed to thaw a degree or two. "Proceed," he finally barked.

It took every ounce of self-control Gray had ever known to keep from stomping out of the garden. Damn that old woman and her disrespectful tongue. If any of his clan had witnessed her behavior, he would have been forced to oust her from the keep permanently. he swallowed hard and allowed himself another glance at Trulie. The soft yearning in her eyes made them glisten wet with pleading. He would do it for her, go through whatever ridiculous ritual the old woman seemed hell-bent on doing. But he only did it for Trulie.

"Over here, Gray." Granny pointed to a moss-framed flagstone close to the low rock wall surrounding the reflecting pool. "Stand right there."

Aggravation pounded through him with every beat of his heart. The old woman spoke to him as though he were a mere lad. Thank the gods it was just the three of them within the privacy of the garden. With one long stride, he moved to the spot Granny indicated.

"And you stand here." Granny nodded to Trulie and motioned to a spot beside Gray.

Trulie's pallor concerned Gray. She looked decidedly unwell. A twinge of guilt twisted through him. The strain of the last several days had not been easy on his lady love either. He stared down at the water, wrestling with his conscience. It was not his fault, he silently argued. If only the lass had seen that terrible night, she would understand why he felt as he did.

Granny turned toward the outer gate. "Tamhas, you may enter now. They are both ready."

"What game is this?" Gray bared his teeth at Tamhas's aloof expression. Surely, the old demon didn't side with the women? Lore a'mighty, the man's own beloved sister had died in that fire.

Tamhas walked toward them with a surety reflected in his swaying stride. His polished staff marked each footfall, sliding easily through his gnarled hand. "There is no game this day, MacKenna." Tamhas took his place beside Granny with a sharp nod at Gray. "'Tis time ye saw the truth of the night that changed yer life."

Gray ripped his gaze from Tamhas and turned to Granny. The pale blue of the old woman's eyes had taken on an eerie golden glow. Her lips barely parted as she stared down at the waters of the small pond and slowly lifted her hands.

"Show us the truth," Granny commanded in an eerie whisper.

An unholy chill rippled up Gray's spine. The very air tingled across his flesh. A sense of uneasiness crackled in the wind.

"Wash away smoke and flame. Dust away time gone by. Connect us with those we seek. Show us the reason why." Granny pressed her hands against her chest, then shoved them away as though releasing a stream of energy out over the reflecting pool.

Gray glanced back and forth between Granny, Trulie, Tamhas, and the shimmering surface of water. All looked to be imbued with an unexplainable luminosity. Three sets of eyes and the gently rippling pool burned with inner fire.

A hissing sizzled around the water's edge. The wind picked up. High-pitched moans echoed through the garden.

Gray ducked as something brushed his shoulder. He unsheathed his sword as another force shoved him to one side. He squinted through the debris-filled wind whipping all around them, unable to see anything. The air was thick with . . . what? He couldn't make out what swirled all around. All he knew was that he couldn't see a damn thing.

Then everything went silent. Suffocating darkness crashed around him. He slashed his sword through the air, groping through the darkness with his other hand. There was nothing there. It was as though nothing he had ever known existed except darkness.

A flash of light jolted through his awareness. He made out the unmistakable crackle of flames somewhere in the distance.

"Alastair!" A frightened voice called out—a woman's voice.

Gray's heart nearly stopped. *Máthair.* That was *Máthair* crying out for *Athair.*

"Isabeau!" his father shouted back.

"*Máthair! Athair!*" Gray groped deeper into the darkness. The sickening stench of suffocating smoke forced his arm across his face. Terror surged through him. It was that night. The night of the fire. What unholy power had Trulie's grandmother unleashed to send him back to that terrible night?

As he fought against his rising panic, his parents appeared before him.

"Alastair." Gray's mother held out her arms to his father. "Come to me, *mo luaidh.* Take my hand afore it is too late."

"*Mo chridhe,*" his father said as he took her hand. "Are ye sure? Is there no other way?"

"'Tis time." Isabeau smiled while clutching his hand to her chest. "Gray is strong. He will be all right. Tamhas has promised to guide him."

"Then I am ready." Alastair nodded.

As one, they stepped out onto the narrow balcony jutting out from his mother's bedroom window high above the jagged stones of the moat surrounding the tower. A narrow banister, barely ankle high, surrounded the shelf meant only for housing pots of herbs and flowers when the weather was kind enough to grow them.

"Nay!" Gray shouted into the vision. Neither of his parents turned. "Halt!" Gray shouted again. He tried to rush forward, tried to reach out, but his arms and legs refused to move. Gray roared against the paralyzing darkness. "Release me! I must stop them!"

Alastair and Isabeau looked into each other's eyes, smiled, and stepped off the ledge into the arms of the darkness.

"Nay!" Gray roared, his scream catching in his throat.

Instead of plunging into the stone courtyard below, his father and mother slowly evaporated into shimmering clouds of golden dust soon scattered by the wind.

Gray's knees buckled. He collapsed into a huddled mound in the center of the velvety darkness. What had he just seen? What did it mean? He raged against the raw pain of renewed loss ripping through him.

A soft touch brushed the side of his face. *"An toir thu dhomh pòg?"*

Gray scrubbed the heels of his hands against his eyes. He had surely lost his mind.

"An toir thu dhomh pòg?" his mother's voice repeated.

"How can I give ye a kiss, *Máthair*?" Gray didn't bother opening his eyes. Why should he? All that surrounded him was darkness. "Ye are dead, *Máthair*. Ye left me. Or have ye forgotten?"

"Gray," his mother softly chided. "Ye ken better than to speak to me with such harshness."

"Ye best listen to yer mother, lad," his father said. "Ye may be grown, but I can still give ye a swift kick in yer arse."

Gray opened his eyes and nearly choked at the sight of his parents standing arm in arm in front of him. "What is this?" He stumbled to his feet and turned around, railing at the darkness. "What cruel trick have ye played, Nia Sinclair? Have ye not an ounce of compassion?"

"Gray," his mother called again. "Stop yer caterwauling and listen. Yer father and I are not dead. We both live and breathe just as surely as ye do."

"I saw ye die . . . the first time. And then . . . just now, I saw ye disappear. How can ye stand there and tell me ye both live? Is this some wicked cruelty that spirits do for amusement? What witchery is this?" He stumbled sideways, searching for an escape. He had to get free of this infernal darkness.

Alistair MacKenna clapped a broad hand atop Gray's shoulder and clamped down. Hard. He yanked his son back over to stand in front of Isabeau. "Ye always were a hardheaded lad. Ye get that from yer mother."

One of Isabeau's dark brows arched a notch higher than the other. "Ye err, my love. Yer son is just like yerself."

Gray sucked in a deep breath. Even as ghosts, his parents playfully bantered, as they had in life. He took little comfort in that realization. He pinched the bridge of his nose and rubbed the corners of his burning eyes. "If ye swear ye are not dead, then where are ye . . . living?" And why, by all the fires of hell, had they allowed him to believe they had suffered such a terrible death? Gray didn't voice that part. One question at a time.

Alistair rolled his eyes and looked toward where the heavens might be if they weren't floating in some strange field of darkness. "Talk to the boy, Isabeau. He always seemed to listen to ye better."

Isabeau stepped forward, took Gray's hand in hers, and smoothed it against her cheek. "Ye see, my son? Warm flesh. I am no ghostie."

"How?" It was the only word Gray could force out through the chaos churning through his mind and emotions.

"Yer father joined me in my last leap," she explained. "Most think the bodies are left behind, but it doesna have to be so. If we are content with our forms, we are permitted to take them with us."

She really lived? Gray reached out and barely touched the tip of his finger to his mother's smiling lips. Warm flesh. Aye. She lived. A sudden rush of resentment shoved aside the relief that his parents were truly alive. "Why would the two of ye put me through such suffering? Do ye have any idea or even give a damn about the sorrow ye both caused me?" He turned until he stood nose to nose with his father. "Ye might not give a rat's arse if yer son suffered, but did ye not give a thought to what all this would put yer clan through?" Gray shoved forward, bumping his father back a step with his chest. "What the hell were ye thinking, man?" Gray bumped his father again. "What the hell were ye thinking with?"

Alistair squared off like a bull about to charge.

"Now, Alistair," Isabeau said in a soothing tone as she barely touched his shoulder. "Mind yer temper. The boy has been through a great deal."

Alistair's face darkened to an enraged shade of purple as he knotted a fist tighter and slammed it with an upward thrust squarely under Gray's chin.

Gray flew backward through the darkness. He rolled, knees over head, and landed on his stomach. *Damn.* He rubbed his jaw and blinked hard against the pain. Dead or alive, the old bastard still gave one hell of a punch.

Alistair MacKenna stomped forward until he stood staring down at his son. "I willna have ye disrespecting myself or yer mother. Now, if ye are prepared to listen, we will explain as best we can." His father spared a quick glance back over his shoulder as he scratched his head. "I'm not so sure I understand it all myself. All I ken for certain is that I am a happier man than I have ever been."

Gray held up a hand to his father. "Help me stand, old man. This darkness throws me balance."

Gray's father chuckled. "Aye. And that punch to yer chin didna do verra much for it either, I'll wager."

"Aye," Gray agreed. His father made a valid point. Still rubbing his jaw, Gray threw the other arm around his father's shoulders. Alive. The strangling knot in the center of his chest finally loosened and disappeared with the acceptance that what had seemed impossible— wasn't.

"Ye live." Gray knelt before his mother.

"Aye, laddie," Isabeau laughed as she rumpled his hair. "I ken 'tis verra difficult to understand but trust me when I say yer father and I are alive and well. We have traveled to the next place." Her voice trailed off in a pleased sigh before she continued. "I canna describe the joy we now know. Life is only filled with happiness. There is no hatred or suffering. All we meet coexist with love and respect. Only kindness is known in our land."

"It sounds truly like heaven," Gray said. "But why did ye not tell me where ye had gone?"

"Fate must play out its destined course." Isabeau's smile faded and her eyes darkened. "If we had warned ye, told ye what truly was, we might have unknowingly altered things yet to take place."

"Ye are a time runner," he whispered as the realization hit him. "Why did ye not tell me?"

A sad smile returned to his mother's face as she leaned against his father. "I never traveled through time again after I met yer father. The gift only passes from mother to daughter, so I saw no point in troubling ye with that knowledge."

A distant moaning like a slow, steady wind began filling the darkness. Alistair and Isabeau met each other's gaze, then both turned toward Gray. "We must return now. Our time here grows short."

Gray grabbed both their arms and pulled himself into their joined embrace. "Will I ever see ye again? Will ye ever be allowed to return?"

"Aye, lad." Alistair grinned as he clapped Gray on the shoulder. "Dinna worry. Yer mother would not be the happy woman she is if she couldna watch over her son and ken him to be well."

Isabeau pressed a kiss to Gray's cheek and smiled up into his eyes. "I promise ye will see us again soon. I swear to ye, we watch over ye at all times."

Gray braced himself against the weight of sadness settling within him. "I miss ye both so verra much," he said as he closed his eyes.

"We love ye, son," his parents echoed in unison. "Ye do us proud."

He swallowed hard against the knot in his throat and opened his eyes to see them one last time, but it was too late. All he saw was his own reflection in the pool.

A soft, warm touch rested on his upper arm. "Are you all right?" Trulie whispered. "Gray, are you all right?"

He kept his eyes trained on the scowling face staring back up at him from the water's surface. Was he all right? No. He was damned confused. But now he vaguely understood what Trulie had been trying to tell him. If she had granted his request, traveled back, and changed his parents' fate, Alistair MacKenna and Isabeau de Coucy would not be enjoying the life they now knew. And Fearghal and Aileas would still be there, nettling everyone they met. And Beala— who knew what would have happened to that poor, confused maid?

"Gray?" Trulie's voice trembled.

He pulled her into his arms and pressed his cheek to her silky hair. "I understand now," he whispered. The words caught in his throat as his mother's smiling face focused in his mind. "Forgive me, *mo chridhe*. I swear I shall never doubt ye again."

He turned with Trulie still in his arms and nodded to Granny. "Vision or reality?" Everything had seemed so real, but how could it be so?

A faint smile pulled at Granny's mouth as her gaze lowered to the water glistening in the pool. "Both. I took your mind back to the night of the fire and walked you through what really happened. While ye relived it, I opened the bridge of this reality to your parents. Rarely are those who have taken the last leap interested in returning—but in this instance, your mother's desire to see you happy gave us both the strength for a short visit."

Gray bowed his head and hugged Trulie tighter. "Thank ye . . . more than ye know."

CHAPTER 22

"Since May first came and went during all the chaos of finding arsonists and murderers, what date are you and Gray going to choose now?" Granny settled the flat basket woven from thin strips of wood higher on her hip.

Trulie slid the handle of a deeper basket into the crook of her elbow. After a quick glance around the garden, she untied the neckline of her kirtle and fanned it open wide. Mercy, she was used to humid Kentucky summers. They were best survived by drinking tall glasses of iced tea and staying in the shade. But an overly warm day in Scotland, dressed in entirely too much wool and linen, was about to turn her into a steaming puddle of sweat. "I don't know exactly. It will have to be soon because Gray wants all the clan to be able to travel to the keep. If we wait too much longer, they'll be too busy tending to their crops and stocking their larders for winter. They wouldn't be able to risk losing a month of work for the wedding."

"A month?" Granny stopped walking and fixed Trulie with a duly impressed gaze. "So, it's to be a full clan gathering then?"

Trulie grinned at her grandmother's expression. The time frame of the wedding probably did need a little explaining, even though Granny came from this era. The Sinclair clan had been even more remote than Clan McKenna. Their few remaining members had rarely gathered in one spot for any celebrations.

"The ceremony itself will only last a few hours," Trulie said. "But Clan MacKenna considers the wedding of their chieftain an opportunity to party. Gray says they have waited a long time for things to improve here at the keep."

Granny cut a woody stalk of rosemary and tossed it into her basket. "Sounds a bit like that Highland gathering I forced you girls to attend one summer."

"From what I understand, a MacKenna wedding celebration is a lot like a Highland gathering that lasts two weeks." Trulie bent to snip off several velvety, gray-green leaves of sage. "The other two weeks will tie up the clan in traveling to and from the keep. The kin from the farthest borders would have quite a ride to get here.

She stopped short when she noticed the tall spikes of a deep-purplish-blue flower. "It's blooming, Granny." Her blood went cold as a vivid picture of Colum stretched out across a cold, stone slab flickered through her mind. Why didn't she see Gray too? Was he safe now?

Granny looked over at the corner of the garden. "That's the foxglove. The one from your vision. But the poisoning shouldn't happen now. They both should be safe. Beala is dead."

"I don't know," Trulie whispered. Worry tightened a band around her chest and squeezed. Was the vision still active? Or was she just remembering it from before? "Have you picked up on any negative energy lately? Coira hasn't mentioned anything, has she?"

"Not that I know of." Granny scowled down at the plant. "Why don't we just pull the thing up by the roots and burn it?"

Trulie sat her basket on the stone path and used a small dagger to snip the tops from several chamomile heads. Granny's suggestion to destroy the foxglove wasn't half-bad. But what if that wasn't the plant supplying the poison to be used on Gray and Colum? "No. I don't want to destroy it just yet. We don't even know if the vision is still credible. And even if it is, we don't know if that is the plant the culprit will use."

"What if it's not the plant?" Granny pointed her knife at the majestic purple blooms. "That is some powerful poison. It needs to go."

"There are also good uses for it. You know that." Trulie fanned her apron in her face to stir a cooling breeze. "Shall I call Tamhas so he can refresh your memory?"

"No thank you." Granny shot an insulted look her way. "I know more about herbs and such than that man could ever know."

Trulie hefted the fragrant basket of greens back onto her arm. "Come on. Let's go find Coira. Maybe between the three of us we can figure out if Gray and Colum are still in danger."

"And what good will Coira do when it comes to visions?" Granny bent and plucked some mint and added it to her basket.

"None," Trulie said. "But she's one of the few close friends I have ever had. There is no harm in keeping her in the loop."

GRAY SETTLED his pewter tankard back on the table with a thud. He felt more relaxed—nay more joyful—than he had in a very long time. Tapping his fingers against the cool metal of the cup, he nodded at everyone sitting at the long table. "There are none left who seek my death. The keep has finally been cleansed of those who would cause evil mischief."

"Are you sure?" Trulie leaned forward, unknowingly propping her bosoms atop her folded arms. The neckline of the dress she wore dipped low enough to give Gray a teasing glimpse of her creamy-white breasts.

He shifted in his seat. All he was certain of was that it was entirely too long before it would be time for them to retire to their chambers. The hall was full of summer travelers stopping by to catch up on the latest goings-on of the MacKenna clan. With a wedding on the horizon, decorum demanded he entertain his guests.

"Gray." Her tone yanked him back to the present.

"Aye?"

"I asked you if you were sure no one else would want you dead?" She lowered her voice, leaned forward, and revealed even more of her delectable bosom. "You haven't angered the king, have you?"

He wet his lips. Lore, he could almost taste the sweetness of her skin. Sucking in a hitching breath, he silently promised his cock blessed relief later on. For now, he best pay attention to his future wife's interrogation. "Alexander has no ill will toward me," he said. Then he couldn't resist a smile as he shot a pointed gaze at his lady love's chest. "Yer dress is verra fine."

Trulie's eyes widened. She quickly glanced down at her exposed cleavage, then straightened. Her cheeks flushed an embarrassed pink as she quickly glanced around the table.

"Dinna worry," he whispered while leaning close. "No one saw yer delightful bounty but me."

Her cheeks flamed redder. She tugged her neckline upward. "Behave yourself," she hissed between clenched teeth. "And pay attention. This is serious. Granny and I both think the vision I had of you and Colum might still be active."

Lore, he loved it when her skin glowed with her emotions. He scrubbed a hand across his face to keep from angering her even more by smiling. He best take care with his teasing or she would send him to his bed alone. "I understand yer worry. But we canna live each day in fear." He paused, took a long, deep draught of the yeasty ale, and returned his mug to his table. "We will be vigilant, but I refuse to walk through life as a coward."

He held out his hand. "Come, my love. Walk with me."

She took his hand, steadying herself as she rose from the bench running the length of the table. Gray rested a hand on the small of her back and steered her toward a table surrounded by a group of what looked like extremely weary men. "Yon sits the Earl of Dunbar —trusted friend to King Alexander himself."

Trulie froze. She squeezed his hand as she leaned close and whispered. "I don't think it would be wise for me to talk to him. He might get defensive if he realizes I'm not exactly from this time."

Gray gently tugged her forward. "I trust Patrick. After all, it was his father who arranged for the king to meet my mother's cousin, his current wife, Marie de Coucy."

Trulie still resisted. Worry furrowed her brow as she nervously glanced toward the earl and his men. The color rose higher on her cheeks the closer they came to the table.

"MacKenna." A burly, barrel-chested man with a coal-black beard rose from his seat.

"Lord Dunbar." Gray offered the man a polite nod. He was surprised the earl had wandered so far north. "Welcome. What news from yer travels?"

Lord Dunbar waved away the question and made a polite dip of his head at Trulie. "Traveling through Scotland never changes. Successful hunts and occasional sport with foolhardy thieves." He sidled his way out from behind the table and held out a hand to Trulie. "Now properly introduce me to this dark-haired beauty soon to be yer wife."

A twinge of jealousy rippled through Gray. Lord Dunbar had been known to dally with another man's woman just for the thrill of the risk. Gray lightly rested a claiming arm around Trulie's narrow waist. "Patrick III, seventh Earl of Dunbar, might I present to ye Lady Trulie Sinclair, my betrothed."

Lord Dunbar's deep-set eyes twinkled as though already plotting. "Chieftain MacKenna has chosen well. 'Tis my immense pleasure to meet such a lovely woman." He held Trulie's hand overly long while smiling into her eyes.

"The pleasure is mine," Trulie said, then eased her hand free and tucked it behind her back.

Lord Dunbar chuckled and turned back to Gray. "Word came to me of yer troubles. My condolences on the death of yer parents. Alistair MacKenna was a fine chief."

"I thank ye for yer kindness." Gray tightened his arm around Trulie as Lord Dunbar's gaze wandered to her cleavage. "MacKenna Keep has suffered much ill will the past several months, but things should improve now."

A look of distaste curled Lord Dunbar's lip as he nodded his agreement. "Aye. I also heard that the Lady Aileas has finally received all she deserves."

"Well said," Gray said. Womanizer or not, Lord Dunbar had a way with words.

"Excuse me, gentlemen," Trulie interrupted. "I need to get back to Granny."

Lord Dunbar bowed, then rumbled with an appreciative chuckle as Trulie spun away before he could snag her hand again. "Ye are a damn lucky man," he said out the side of his mouth.

"Aye," Gray agreed. A sense of pride swelled within him as he indulged his gaze with the delightful sway of Trulie's hips as she walked back across the room. "And how fares the Lady Dunbar and your children?" Time to turn Lord Dunbar's mind back to his own wife.

"All are well." Lord Dunbar smiled. "And another child will join our family before Yule."

"Congratulations." Gray glanced back at Trulie. "I hope to enjoy such a welcoming in my own clan once Lady Trulie and I are wed."

Lord Dunbar's face took on a thoughtful frown as he smoothed his hand across his beard. "Have ye settled on a day for the wedding, or do ye intend to wait until Donell shows his hand?"

Dunbar's question unsettled Gray. What had the man heard? "Donell has not been to MacKenna land since he signed the marriage contract and saddled my father with Aileas."

"The man knows of his daughter's treatment. Word has it he has Alexander's ear and demands justice." Lord Dunbar clasped his hands behind his back. "If ye ask me, 'tis ludicrous. All ken how much he loathed his daughter, Aileas."

Gray studied Lord Dunbar. What did the earl have to gain by posing as messenger for a now penniless lowland laird? Gray had heard of Donell's penchant for drink and romps with as many bawdy women as he could pay for at a time. The man ruled his clan with his thirst and his cock rather than his mind. "Pray tell, what price has Donell placed on this justice?"

Lord Dunbar shrugged as he turned and looked around the hall.

"Land, more than likely. The drunken fool seems to have learned that coinage slips too easily through his fingers."

"If Donell wants land…" Gray stood taller and flexed his fists. "Let the fool come and try to take it."

Dunbar's rotund body shook as he rumbled with amusement. "Ye know the coward will do no such thing. 'Tis the verra reason that brings me to yer keep." The lord's face grew serious as he turned, scooped up his tankard, and sucked down a long swallow. "I respect ye, MacKenna, as my father respected yours. Ye are an honorable man. A good man who should not meet his end at the hands of a coward." Dunbar stared down at the floor as he swirled the last dredges of liquid in his glass. His face tightened into a grim scowl as he lifted his head and locked eyes with Gray. "Watch yerself, MacKenna. Watch all within yer keep. If Donnell's drunken rants hold an ounce of truth, evil still lurks within these walls."

CHAPTER 23

"**A**nything yet?" Trulie slid her hand along the cool, damp wall at her back until she found Granny's arm. Karma's tail thumped against her leg as the dog pressed closer.

"Nothing," Granny whispered.

Trulie had been afraid that would be Granny's answer, because if she didn't pick up the slightest vision, then chances were that Granny wouldn't sense any energy either. Trulie squinted across the night-shrouded garden. The partial sliver of moon hanging low over the horizon cast a ghostly pall across the gray-white slabs of stepping-stones and rows of gently swaying plants. Maybe this wasn't the best idea, she decided, a bit too late. Maybe it was the wrong night to catch the would-be assassin. She snorted with frustration. There were many maybes whirling through the air.

"Are you sure it was this garden?" Granny moved closer, visibly flinching as her shoe crunched in the dry soil piled against the wall.

"Shh," Trulie hissed. Without looking back, she rested her hand on top of Karma's head, trying to quiet the dog's soft, impatient growl. "You finally received the same premonition. Didn't it look like this garden to you?"

Granny's pale skin glowed in the darkness as she leaned forward and looked from east to west. Her lips puckered, as she wrinkled her nose and adjusted the position of her glasses. "Yep. This was it. But a lot has happened since then. Things could change. That was before we found out about Fearghal and Beala. My vision hasn't recurred since then. Has yours?"

"Just the part about Colum." Trulie scanned the perimeter of the garden, then pressed back against the wall. "I told you what the earl said. From the sound of his warning, the premonition must still be valid."

The slightest movement in the shadows beside the far wall caught Trulie's attention. Karma murmured another low warning growl. Trulie squeezed Granny's arm, then pointed at the dark figure moving slowly toward the corner where the foxglove grew. Karma crouched into attack stance; his ears perked toward the figure.

The sliding crunch of metal sinking into wet soil echoed through the night. Trulie stared at the darkened corner until her eyes watered from the strain. Whoever was after the poisonous plant had decided to dig it up after the summer rain, rather than be satisfied with snipping off a few of its leaves.

Trulie tugged on Granny's sleeve and settled her other hand on Karma's head. "Stay here. Both of you," she whispered, then gathered up her skirts and eased away from the wall.

Granny nodded and pressed flatter against the wall. Karma softly whined his disagreement, but rolled back on his haunches and sat beside Granny.

With her gaze locked on the cloaked figure wrestling with the plant, Trulie crouched low and skittered to the far wall adjacent to the foxglove. The mysterious person wasn't accustomed to manual labor. Every time the shovel bit into the dirt, Trulie distinctly heard a huffing grunt.

She sized up the figure cloaked all in black. They weren't very tall. In fact, she could tackle them to the ground. The more she thought about it, the better she felt about that plan. Yep. That was exactly what she was going to do. Tackle the scum and sit on their chest while Granny went for help.

Trulie prepared for the perfect moment to spring. As the shadowy form bent to yank the plant out of the ground, she launched across the last few feet between them. Her solid hit knocked them both to the ground. The fiend emitted a surprised squeak as Trulie landed on top of them.

Karma growled, leaped across the garden, and joined Trulie. The dog couldn't stand idle any longer. But as Trulie and her prey rolled to a stop, he took a step closer, snuffled the heavy cloak, then woofed a happy greeting and wagged his tail.

"Coira!" Trulie fell back on her heels as the maid flailed her way out of her hooded garment.

"By the fires of hell, Mistress Trulie. Ye damn near broke my neck." Coira rolled to a sitting position. "Lore a'mercy. I thought ye were with the MacKenna."

"What are you doing here digging up the foxglove?" Trulie yanked Coira back down as she tried to scramble to her feet. What a way to spend a night, mud wrestling with Coira.

"Can ye not believe what yer own eyes tell ye? If I get rid of the herb, there will be no more murders." Coira yanked the hem of her shift up to her face and wiped at the splashes of mud.

"Trulie." Granny's urgent whisper called across the garden.

"Why didn't you tell me you were coming out here?" Trulie huffed an expletive under her breath as she held up a finger to Granny. "In a minute, Granny. I am busy stalking Coira."

"A quick temper is a verra ugly trait in a woman," Coira said as she stood and shook out her skirts.

Karma whined as he stared back at Granny, his tail wagging in a slow rhythm.

"Trulie." Granny called out again, her voice stronger this time.

"What is it?" Trulie turned, exasperation fanning her temper. Tonight had been a total waste of time. Why hadn't that stupid vision shown her it was Coira messing with the poisonous plant?

"I have seen who our prospective murderer is." Granny scurried across the garden like a rabbit seeking shelter.

"What?" Trulie couldn't believe what Granny had just said. How could Granny know who the assassin was? Trulie hadn't received any new premonitions. All she had gotten was a shortened version of the first one. "What did you just say?"

Granny pressed a hand to her chest as she glanced back across the shadowy expanse of the garden. She swallowed hard and licked her lips while gasping for breath. "Dammit to hell. I am too old for a night run through the garden."

"Calm down." Trulie rubbed a hand up and down Granny's narrow back. "Take a deep breath and tell us what you saw as soon as you catch your breath. You can't die on me now." Trulie slipped Granny's hand into hers and lightly patted it. "Are you sure you really had the vision or were you just rehashing the one I told you I had?"

Granny shot her a withering look that clearly said *Do not even go there.*

Kicking the quickly wilting plant to one side, Trulie bent, scooped up the spade, and jammed it into the ground. "I am not saying I doubt you. But I haven't picked up anything new since the last one. I've only seen the part about Colum since Beala and Fearghal died. I just keep going over the same details to try to catch our suspect. Are you sure that's not what you're doing?"

Granny folded her arms across her chest and jerked her chin down in a decisive nod. "I am positive. The killer is a woman and she looks a lot like Aileas."

Trulie tried to wrap her mind around the fact that Granny had gotten a warning and she hadn't. And someone who looked like Aileas? Trulie shivered. She hadn't noticed anyone around the keep fitting that description. "Coira, have you seen anyone who looks just like Aileas working in the kitchens?"

"Nay." Coira shivered with such a look of disgust; Trulie didn't doubt she had seen no one fitting that description.

Granny's eyes narrowed as she wrinkled her nose and stared down at the foxglove. "I am certain of it. And she works in the kitchens." Granny paused and tilted her head as though watching something crawl among the plant's leaves. "But it seems as though she is hidden from the others. It is all very strange. And she brought her own poisoned leaves . . . or maybe it's just she always keeps them with her." Granny scowled harder, her face puckering with the effort. "The herbs are tucked in a drawstring bag. She wears it looped around her neck and tucked way down in her shirt." Granny tilted her head to one side as though trying to improve her view. "She fears someone is going to find the poison. Afraid that if she doesn't do the job right . . ." Granny squinted her eyes tighter, slowly moving her head as though following the assassin's movements. "She can never go back to wherever she came from. Her hands shake every time she rubs some kind of braided chain of hair hanging around her neck. It's looped through a hole in the bag of poison."

Granny's hands knotted into shaking fists. "She is back there in the shadows. With a strange look on her face. Maybe even be laughing. It's . . . it's hard to say. What is she watching?" Granny stomped her foot and her eyes popped open. "You and I were standing in front of a stone mausoleum. We were holding each other, crying. You had one of those brooches with the MacKenna insignia in your hand. That woman must be stopped."

A gnawing uneasiness nagged at the back of Trulie's mind. Why hadn't she seen what this mysterious woman had done? Why had the newest version of the vision only come to Granny?

GRAY CRADLED his head in his hands, digging his thumbs into his temples in slow, tight circles. "Explain again how ye choose which things ye will attempt to change and which ye willna bother?" Trulie's logic made his head hurt. He would never understand it.

"Premonitions haven't happened yet." Trulie paced around the small confines of the underground chamber used for storing root vegetables through the winter. She turned and faced him as she reached the farthest earth wall of the dugout chamber opposite the heavy oak door. "When Fate sends me a premonition, depending on the feel of it, it's kind of like an invitation to change it before the bad thing happens. A blessing from Destiny." She shrugged as if she couldn't fathom why he didn't understand.

"And Granny can identify the woman who wishes me dead?" He stood in the open doorway of the hole. He had never liked this room, and since the stench of Fearghal's prison chamber, close spaces disturbed him even more. The damp chill of the place made his skin crawl. He shifted his weight from one foot to other. Lore, he hoped they finished soon.

Trulie nodded as she lifted the lid of a wooden barrel and peered inside. "Yes. Granny said she got a good look at the woman's face. She said she looks a lot like Aileas."

"Like Aileas?" Gray stifled a shudder. Had nature been so cruel as to have used that same mold twice?

"I know. That was my reaction too." Trulie eased the lid back down on the barrel and dusted the dirt from her hands. "So, can you think of anyone who meets that description?"

He sorted through all the servants he could think of. Try as he might, no Aileas maidservant came to mind. "Nay." He shook his head. "But if Cook just put her to work in the kitchens, I may not have seen her."

He motioned Trulie forward out of the depths of the cellar. "Come. Get Granny and I shall send for Colum. We will walk through the kitchens and see if we can oust Donall's hired assassin."

Trulie sneezed, scrubbed her arms, and nodded her agreement. "There's something else I need to ask Granny. Something really bothers me about her vision."

"What bothers ye?" He took the braided rope of onions from her and supported her arm while she climbed up the narrow stone steps. He hadn't understood why she had chosen to feign an errand to the root cellar to share the news of Granny's discovery, but the longer he was around this precious woman, the more he learned it was no use questioning her motives. His complicated lady love usually had good reason.

"I should have gotten the vision too," she said as she emerged from the narrow hallway and stepped out into the wide, airy space of the kitchen's full larder.

He didn't see the problem, but apparently, she was quite troubled that Granny was the sole receiver of the vision. "Mayhap ye have been too distracted to properly receive another vision."

She gave a doubtful shake of her head. "Maybe. I am hoping Granny can explain it."

~

"Do ye not think the woman will attempt to flee when she sees the lot of us entering the kitchens?" Tamhas counted them off with a bent finger. "The five of ye and Gray? Lore, how big is this woman to warrant such an army?"

"Colum is guarding the door leading out to the gardens in case she makes a break for it." Trulie pulled Granny to the front of the group and pointed her toward the archway leading to the kitchen. "We are all going to walk into the kitchen. As soon as you see her, let me know. Gray and I will do the rest."

Granny folded her spindly arms across her small frame and gave Trulie a strange up-and-down look. "You still don't know what the girl looks like?"

"I was going to ask you about that. Why would you receive the new vision but I didn't? I saw the last one about Gray and Colum, but that was before a lot happened that apparently changed the outcome of that particular vision. This time, you said you saw so much more, and I didn't get the vision at all. Am I losing my touch, Granny?"

A thoughtful scowl narrowed Granny's eyes. She bowed her head.

Trulie held her breath. She knew what Granny was doing. She was replaying the premonition in her head. Uneasiness rolled Trulie's stomach into a nauseated knot. If she got through this ordeal without puking, it would be a miracle.

Granny finally lifted her head, looked at Gray, and frowned even more. "Now, I remember seeing Colum stretched out on the stone, but I did not see Gray." She pressed both hands to her cheeks, scowling as if straining to bring the vision into focus. "Even though I don't see Gray, I know his body is in that mausoleum. I felt Trulie's heart breaking."

Trulie put a reassuring arm around Granny. "It's okay if you can't tell for sure." With a nod toward the kitchen, she continued. "But that still doesn't explain why I didn't get the vision too. Am I losing my touch?"

"No." Granny smiled. "It just means you are pregnant."

Trulie's knees nearly buckled as Granny's words sunk in. "I can't be pregnant." A tiny voice inside her head counted off exactly how many days had passed since her least favorite time of the month. The realization hit. "But I've been drinking those nasty seeds. You said they would work."

Granny just chuckled in response.

Gray made a strangled coughing sound as though someone had just knocked the wind out of him.

She has to be wrong, Trulie silently prayed. *You know she is right*, a nagging inner voice insisted.

Gray cleared his throat as he lightly settled both hands on Trulie's shoulders. "A child? Are ye sure?" he asked Granny.

"Positive," Granny affirmed. "Your bloodline is now blended with ours. That also explains why I no longer saw you in the vision. We cannot portend the future for our own."

"I drank all those freakin' seeds," Trulie repeated. Why wasn't anyone listening to her? "I can't be pregnant. I have been careful— very careful."

Granny shook a bent finger just inches from Trulie's nose. "What did I tell you was the only way to guarantee you never got pregnant?"

"Don't have sex," Trulie said.

"You got it," Granny agreed. "Congratulations," she added with a wink.

Gray turned Trulie in his arms and cradled her to his chest. "A child. We are already blessed with our first bairn." He brushed a tender kiss to her forehead, then touched his nose to hers. "Now a firm wedding date must be set. All yer stalling must cease."

"I have not been stalling." Trulie clenched her teeth against a wave of nausea. Her stomach rolled again as if now that the news was out, it had free rein to churn at will. She pushed Gray away, glared at Granny, and turned toward the archway leading into the kitchen. "We will firm up our plans later. Right now we have an assassin to catch."

CHAPTER 24

Gray struggled to put the excitement of Granny's revelation to the back of his mind. *A child.* He wanted to roar it to the world. Trulie carried his child.

"Gray!" The irritation in Trulie's voice broke through his reverie.

"Aye?" He stepped forward and pulled Trulie behind him.

"What are you doing?" She thumped him on the back, then elbowed her way back around in front of him.

"Keep yourself behind me. Ye have no idea if the woman will fight or flee when she realizes she has been found out." He firmly set her back behind him.

"I am going to kill you myself if you don't stop this nonsense." She nudged him hard with her hip and wormed her way back in front of him. "You watch and make sure Granny is safe. I can protect myself."

"You might as well let her be," Granny said, chuckling, as she patted Gray's arm from the other side. "Life will be a lot easier if you figure out early on which battles are worth fighting."

Gray noted the tense determination in the set of Trulie's jaw. Ah, but such battles make life worth living.

"I shall wait with Colum in the gardens," Tamhas announced. "I still fail to see the need for a small army to confront a single female."

"I shall come too, Master Tamhas." Coira gave Trulie an excited hug as she squeezed past her in the hallway. "I canna wait to help ye care for the new bairn."

"Now that we have reduced our ranks, shall we finish this?" Trulie looped her arm through Granny's, lifted her chin, and marched them both into the kitchen.

Gray hurried to catch up with the women. The distinct clicking of toenails against stone told him that Karma followed close on their heels. The great dog huffed a low-throated growl with each step as though keeping time with their pace.

A heavyset woman with graying hair pulled back in a disheveled bun ambled forward and met them. She wiped her muscular hands across the flour-covered apron lashed around her waist. "So many in my kitchen and lore, the MacKenna himself. Can I be a helping ye, my chief? Is anything wrong?"

Ignoring Trulie's grumbling, Gray pushed around Trulie and Granny, effectively placing himself between the two women and the worried-looking Cook. Trulie could growl all she wanted. He would not have his woman placed in front of him as though she were a shield. He cast a stern glance back over one shoulder before turning back to Cook. "We have a wedding feast to plan. Lady Trulie and I have set a date. We wed at the end of summer. What better time to celebrate a joining than during the time of plenty?"

A sharp intake of breath sounded behind him. Gray forced himself not to laugh. There would be hell to pay with Trulie later, and he looked forward to the battle.

Cook's eyes bulged and her mouth fell open. "That's less than three months' time." She threw both hands in the air and looked toward the ceiling as though searching for divine guidance. "Lore a'mighty, just three short cycles of the moon to prepare for a great feasting. For the entire clan? Three months' time?" Cook's tone bordered on hysteria as she pressed both hands to her pudgy jowls. Her gaze darted about the kitchen in rapid glances that lit here and there on every shelf in the kitchen.

Poor woman. Gray supposed three months was barely enough

time for Cook to plan a proper fortnight of feasting for the entire clan and even more visitors. But what better excuse for them all to be in the kitchen? "Aye. Barely three months. Of course, ye have my complete approval to take on more servants if need be." Gray paused and glanced around the kitchen as though counting heads. "How many do ye have right now? Are there any new servants that might not be properly trained for such preparations?"

Cook looked at Gray as though he had lost his mind. Perspiration dotted her brow as it furrowed with a frown. "New servants?" she repeated as she tapped a pudgy finger to her double chin. Her eyes went wide with recollection as she turned and wagged a finger toward an open doorway leading to the separate room where all the herbs and spices were prepared and dried. "There is Dullas." Her voice took on a strained, uncomfortable ring. She leaned forward and lowered her voice. "She is an odd one, that one is."

Aye. No doubt. Gray looked across the room with interest. After all, the strange woman intended to commit murder and then return to her home unscathed. Gray nodded toward the door Cook had indicated. "I would see this, Dullas."

"Aye, my chief." Cook bobbed her head, then turned and waddled a few steps across the massive kitchen. "Dullas!" she bellowed, loud enough to shake the massive smoke-stained beams that stretched across the ceiling.

The door slowly creaked open and a good-sized woman shuffled forward. Her worn overdress strained across her rounded shoulders and an apron stained with patches of green hung loosely around her neck. She kept her head bent and the brim of the white cap tied on her head flopped well over her face. Her hands fluttered in front of her waist as though she carried on an animated conversation with someone only she could see. "Aye, Cook?" she mumbled, loud enough to be heard above the clatter of pots and pans.

"Dullas, come forward. The MacKenna would have a look at ye." Cook hurried the reluctant woman forward with a quick wave of her hand. "Come now. Make haste. There is much to be done and no time to be wasted."

The wide, limp brim of Dullas's cap bobbed up and down with the woman's odd jerking movements as she trundled forward.

Gray studied her closer. The woman moved as though already condemned to the gallows. His gaze lit upon the braided chain of hair barely visible just inside her collar. It looked to be the braided chain Trulie had described from Granny's vision.

Dullas didn't lift her head as she halted a few feet in front of Gray. She twisted one of her apron ties so tight around her short, stubby fingers they puffed red and looked ready to burst.

Gray didn't say a word. Sometimes the best way to get a person to admit guilt was by giving them enough rope to tie their own noose. He folded his arms across his chest and walked a slow circle around the still-murmuring woman.

"Stand up straight, Dullas," Cook said with a clap of her hands. "I beg yer forgiveness, my chief. I had no doings in the choice of this one for the kitchen, and she has been with us a verra short time."

"In truth?" Gray circled even closer around the eerily animated maid. It didn't escape him that each time he leaned in to see her face, Dullas shied the other way. The bits of her whispered conversation he did catch reminded him of Tamhas's ramblings as he read aloud from one of his journals. Snatches of phrases referring to exact amounts of measure, weight, and color. What the devil was the woman reciting? "Ye have run these kitchens for many a year, Cook. Who would dare usurp yer authority and force a servant upon ye?"

Cook's already-flushed cheeks reddened to an even deeper shade. "Yer stepmother," she said with disgust, while hurriedly crossing herself and glancing upward. "During her last . . . visit . . . she bade us take this one in."

So Aileas herself had brought Dullas to his kitchens? That revelation confirmed what Gray already suspected. Disturbed Beala had not acted alone out of some twisted attempt to win Fearghal and Aileas's favor. Aileas had used Beala as a pawn in her game to win complete power. And it appeared one of her other game pieces continued playing well after her mistress had gone.

An impatient huff and a cleared throat prodded Gray forward. Trulie's patience was wearing thin. Time to end the game.

"What sort of charm do ye wear around yer neck, Dullas?" Gray ignored Cook's sharp intake of breath as he yanked back Dullas's cap and revealed her face. Lore ha' mercy. Gray forced himself not to recoil. Dullas was the mirror image of Aileas, except the poor woman had an angry scar puckering down the side of her face, then crossing her throat.

The maid kept her gaze trained on the floor, her lips moving rapidly with barely whispered conversation. She bowed over her gesturing hands, ducking her chin to her chest like a turtle retreating into its shell. "No charm, great one. Bit of a keepsake from sister. Would never mean to displease ye. Will burn it if I must." When Dullas spoke louder, her voice rasped and broke like the croaking of a bullfrog.

A keepsake indeed. Gray turned to Cook. "Did it not occur to ye to question why the sister to the old chieftain's widow would be told to work in the kitchens?"

Cook avoided looking Gray in the eye as she spoke. "The Lady Aileas said it was better for her sister to work in the kitchens than be sent back to be raped by their father and his men."

Gray's sense of honor wanted to believe that reason, but his good sense knew better. Aileas had never given a damn about anyone but herself. He had no doubt she would use her sister to clear the path to ultimate power.

"I would see the keepsake yer sister left ye." Gray held out his hand and waited. It was Dullas's move. If the maid could see through the evil Aileas had planted in her mind and choose the right path, she could remain a servant in MacKenna keep for as long as she wished. But if she could not break free of Aileas's grip, her tenure in the kitchen was over.

Dullas stared at Gray's open hand as though she just realized her chieftain stood before her. Her thin brows arched higher and her hands gestured faster. "Ye must be careful, great one. The measure must be true or will cause ye great harm." Her thick hands opened and closed with an excited frenzy. "Aileas telled me of the weak heart in yer great chest. Ye best allow me to mix the herb lest it cause ye harm." Dullas tugged at the drawstring bag around her neck and nodded to herself. "I telled Aileas I would speak to the chief. I telled Aileas I would make ye whole." Dullas sadly shook her head. "Aileas never believe a thing I say about me lovely plants."

From the way Dullas squinted up at him, Gray wondered if the poor woman could see at all. A mixture of pity and anger rushed through him. He hoped Aileas was currently toasting in the hottest part of hell. He could not fathom how Dullas could possibly undertake something as complicated or wicked as poisoning. He frowned over at Cook. "What tasks have ye this woman doing?"

Cook made a face as though she understood exactly what Gray was wondering. "Dullas knows every herb there is, my chieftain. She knows their every use. None here have ever found an herb or plant in existence that she canna identify and nurture into growing. I swear I never seen anything like it. The woman can barely figure out how to tie her apron but put her in an herb garden and ye will find none better."

That wasn't exactly what he wished to hear. Gray turned back to Dullas. "Are ye loyal to yer chief, or are ye bound to the wishes of yer sister and yer father?" Dullas's future depended on the answer she gave and what Trulie discovered when she studied Dullas's intentions.

As if she already knew Gray's plan, Trulie eased up beside Gray and looped her arm through his. He smoothed his hand over hers and hugged her against his side. Her touch steadied him, soothed him, and assured him he was on the right path.

"Dullas." Gray waited until the woman finally turned her head toward him. "I would ken where yer loyalties lie. MacKenna Keep can be yer home forever or ye can be sent back to yer father."

Dullas frowned and tilted her shaking head to one side like a dog listening to its master. The tip of her tongue darted across her lower lip as her gaze shifted to Trulie's face. Without a word, she fumbled around her neck until her stubby fingers closed around the hair necklace. She yanked it off over her head in a series of awkward, jerking movements. "Here," she croaked as she held out the stained drawstring bag to Trulie. "Take care and measure well or will do chieftain harm." Then she pointed a shaking finger at Trulie's stomach. "I ken the herbals ye need to help the bairn grow strong and healthy. If Herself will tarry just a bit, Dullas will gather the best leaves for a fine tea."

Dullas turned to Gray and shook her head as she ran a shaking finger along the scar across her face. "Father hurt Dullas." Her gravelly voice trembled as two big tears squeezed out and rolled down her face. "Beg ye, my chieftain. Beg yer leave to stay here and serve ye."

Gray closed his hand around the bag Trulie held and nodded his approval. A glance down at Trulie's face told him without a doubt that Dullas had passed the scan of her intentions. Dullas had never been a true threat.

"What did she say?" Cook waddled closer, straining to see Dullas's face as the shaking woman shied away.

"She fears I will send her away because Aileas was her sister," Gray lied.

Dullas ducked back into her cap and pulled the brim well over her face.

Cook's mouth pressed into a frowning line. "Shall I have her packed up and sent back to her father?"

"No," Trulie chimed in at the same time as Gray.

Gray patted Trulie's hand as he repeated, "No. Dullas is welcome to stay in the MacKenna kitchens as long as she likes. This is now her home."

"Ye best be thanking yer chieftain," Cook urged with a jerking nod in Gray's direction.

Dullas's limp bonnet flopped as her head bobbed up and down. "Verra grateful, my fine chief. I thank ye kindly," she croaked out strong and loud as she turned and shuffled back to her room filled with racks of drying herbs.

CHAPTER 25

A pleading whine escaped Karma as he propped his wet muzzle atop Trulie's shoulder. Trulie rolled back on her heels and swallowed hard. The combined aroma of wet dog and whatever rotted thing Karma had rolled in pushed her stomach dangerously close to reversing gears and tossing up her breakfast.

She pressed her lips tighter together and rubbed her mouth against her shoulder. Maybe she would feel better if she did puke. Nausea was torture. She pushed herself to her feet and rubbed her fists against the small of her back. What a way to feel on her wedding day—an ever-present urge to gag and a dull throbbing ache in her lower back, as though her body was about to snap in two. What a lovely day this was going to be.

Karma looked up at her with sad, brown eyes. His tail swished back and forth in the tub with a *please don't be mad at me* wag. Trulie clamped her mouth shut tight as she poured another bucket of water over the dog's back. Her lungs burned for want of air as she tried to speak without inhaling his aroma. "You know you're going to get a bath whenever you roll in something dead. If you don't want a bath, stop rolling in stuff that stinks." Trulie held onto the side of the wooden tub as a violent gag nearly knocked her off balance.

This was ridiculous. Wedding or no wedding, she was done. She felt terrible and would be better off if she just went back to bed. She pointed toward the far side of the garden. "Go lay down under those shade trees. You're just going to have to stay in the garden until some of your *eau de stink* wears off. No wedding feast for you."

Karma immediately leaped out of the tub and shook what appeared to be gallons of water out of his fur.

"Karma!" Trulie shied away from the curtain of water a second too late.

"Trulie Elizabeth Sinclair, I cannot believe you're out here washing the dog on the morning of your wedding day." Granny appeared in the doorway, one fist on her hip while she pointed at the inside of the keep. "Get in here right now. Your own bath is ready and time's a wasting."

Trulie silently wished she could just stretch out in the shade with Karma and take a nap. Karma might stink, but he was a lot quieter than Granny. That patch of cushiony moss beneath the oak looked extremely inviting.

"Trulie—now."

Trulie massaged the back of her neck as she obediently turned and followed Granny. Maybe a nice, long bath would make her feel better. She rolled her shoulders and stretched her neck from side to side. She must've slept crooked or something. Every muscle was stiff. Visions of porcelain tubs and pulsating showerheads with steaming-hot jets of water flitted through her mind. A wistful sigh escaped her as she rounded the corner and faced an oversized wooden tub. For some odd reason, the niceties of the future had been foremost in her mind the past few days. "Not exactly a spa with jet sprays is it?"

"What has gotten into you today?" Granny scowled at her as she added another bucket of steaming water to the tub. "You have been in a foul mood ever since you lifted your head off your pillow. This is your wedding day. You should be happy."

Trulie wasn't about to complain to Granny about not feeling well.

Heaven forbid the woman brew up another nasty remedy from ingre-
dients Trulie probably didn't want to know about. She best blame her
mood on the latest gossip from the keep. At least that reason wouldn't
trigger some sort of noxious tea. "Colum told Coira the priest doesn't
approve of us." There. That should give Granny something to chew
on. Unfortunately, Trulie had no doubt it was true. The old familiar
weight of being the odd one out blackened her mood even further.
She thought she had escaped that when she decided to leave the
future.

She shrugged her shift off her shoulders and shucked it into a pile
on the floor. She smoothed her hands across the barely noticeable
bump of her belly. A baby. A shiver of excitement tingled through her.
The newest MacKenna hadn't been planned, but Trulie had to admit,
life now seemed much brighter with Gray at her side and a baby on
the way. She would never let on to Granny but coming back to the
past was the best thing they had ever done.

Trulie dipped a toe in the steaming water. Perfect. The tempera-
ture was just below scalding. She eased into the tub, leaned back
against the towel padding one side of the elongated barrel, and
exhaled as she closed her eyes. "Coira also told me she doesn't like
the priest. Called him a beady-eyed little hypocrite . . . or something
to that effect. I think she said part of it in Gaelic."

"About that . . ." Granny uncorked a dark bottle on the stool
beside the tub and poured a thin stream of fragrant oil into the bath-
water. Lavender-scented steam rose from the iridescent shimmers of
the perfumed liquid spreading across the surface.

"Spit it out, Granny." Trulie cracked open an eyelid. She didn't
like the look on Granny's face. Unpleasant news was logjammed
behind Granny's tight-lipped expression. Trulie would bet her
favorite pair of jeans on it.

"There will be no priest," Granny said with an exasperated flip of
her hands. She trailed her fingers atop the water and shook her head.
"Gray wasn't comfortable with all the questions the pompous little
man was asking, so . . ." Her voice trailed off and she turned back to
the stool and grabbed a chunk of rose-colored soap and a folded rag.

"So . . . what?" Trulie straightened in the tub. No priest meant no wedding. Now, what were they going to do?

"So . . . Gray told him to leave." Granny soused the rag and soap in the water, then rubbed the two together until a sweet-smelling lather flowed over her hands and dripped down into the tub.

"Gray couldn't just put up with the man for one more day? He couldn't wait until after the ceremony to tell the man to leave?" Trulie slid back down in the tub, held her breath, then completely submerged beneath the surface. It really wasn't necessary for Granny to answer those questions. Trulie knew the answers well enough without even talking to Gray. Once the man set his mind to something, the devil himself couldn't force him to change. But that didn't change the fact that they now had no one to perform the marriage ceremony. It could take forever to get another priest this far up into the Highlands—especially this late in the summer. What about all the food? What about all those people who had come from miles away? What were they going to do now?

Trulie broke up through the surface with a sputtering breath. "So, what are we going to do now? Just have a big party?" If it was up to her, she would sneak out the back gate, find a place to hide, and once everyone left, she and Gray could just live together. They had already signed the marriage contract. Who needed a wedding? An involuntary twitch shook her. Lordy, she hated crowds.

"Tamhas is going to perform the ceremony." Pride brightened Granny's face like a ray of sunshine. "The dais has already been prepared at the front of the hall. The maids and I covered it with heather and ivy. It looks lovely, if I do say so myself."

"Tamhas is not a priest." Trulie plucked the soapy rag from Granny's extended hand and scrubbed it down one arm. Her stomach did a nervous somersault at the very notion of standing up in front of the largest number of people she had seen since coming to Scotland. Great hall with Gray had been nothing compared to the teeming mass of curious villagers who had descended upon the keep.

"Tamhas doesn't have to be a priest." Granny shook her head, leaned both elbows against the edge of the barrel, and folded her hands. "According to the laws of the land and this time, as long as you and Gray state you are man and wife to each other, you have a marriage—whether you have a priest or not. If you make your oath in front of Gray's clan, the marriage will be cemented by all the witnesses."

Trulie slid down until her chin rested just above the fragrant surface of the water. She pulled in a deep breath, savoring the calming scent of lavender infusing the steam. She studied her bright-red toes peeping out of the water at the other end of the tub. Her black mood shifted at least three shades lighter as a plan unfolded in her mind.

"Trulie Elizabeth." Granny's voice took on a stern *what the devil are you up to now* tone.

"What?" Trulie raised a leg above the surface of the water and watched the steam rise from her skin.

"Don't *what* me, gal. I don't like that look in your eye. What are you plotting?"

Trulie took the soap and lathered a foaming path of creamy bubbles down her leg. Drawing a finger through the suds, she smiled at the faint layer of hair coating her shin. That was one good thing about the past; she no longer had to shave her legs.

"Trulie!" Granny thumped the side of the tub. "Out with it. What are you plotting?"

"I want to marry Gray in private." There. She had said it out loud. Trulie rose from the water and held out a hand for the folded linen piled on another stool. Suddenly, the overly warm water was making her stomach roll. "You know how I hate crowds. I can't stand the idea of standing up in front of half of Scotland like a sheep about to be slaughtered."

Granny's mouth pulled down into a disapproving frown. She shook out the cloth and scrubbed it across Trulie's shoulders as she stepped from the tub. "You can't do that. Gray is the MacKenna chief. He has responsibilities to his people."

Trulie gathered the linen under her arms and clutched it to her chest. Her mood shifted back to darkness as she padded barefoot across the stones, then plopped down on the cushioned bench beside the hearth. "What about Gray's responsibilities to me?"

"Ye will always be first in my heart and mind, *mo chridhe.* Why would ye doubt that?"

"Get out of here, Gray!" Granny moved in front of Gray and tried in vain to push him back out the door. "It is bad luck for you to see Trulie before the wedding. Get out of here. Go find someplace else to be."

Gray settled his feet wider apart and smiled down at Granny as though she were a yapping puppy. "I will not be going anywhere until I find what is troubling my love."

Trulie's stomach shifted with a sickening flop. She swallowed hard against the urge to gag. The dried crust of bread she had forced down earlier was getting dangerously close to coming back out. She closed her eyes, pressed both hands against her temples, and eased in a deep breath. If she got through this day without heaving, it would be a miracle. And wouldn't that be a fine way to impress Gray's clan? Trulie clamped her mouth shut tighter at the mental image of blowing chunks all over Gray as they stood together saying their vows. Lordy, she just couldn't do this.

Gray moved quickly across the room and knelt in front of her. "What is it? Are ye unwell?" He squeezed her hands while his worried gaze searched her face.

She shot Granny a warning glare over the top of his head. She wet her lips and took in another shaking breath. "I think it's just a combination of hormones and phobias." She swallowed hard and forced a smile. "I'll be fine."

"Hormones and pho-bee-uz?" Gray sounded out the strange word as though it felt odd on his tongue. An enlightened look brightened his face. "The child? I have heard tell how women are often ill when they get with child."

She couldn't help but smile at Gray's concern. In an instant, he had forgotten about the celebration he had been excited about for days. All that mattered was her. Guilt butted in and stirred her conscience. She couldn't be selfish and dodge the crowd. This ceremony meant a lot to Gray. Hormones and phobias be damned. She would get through this day one way or another—for him.

GRAY RUBBED his thumbs across his damp palms, refusing to give in to the urge to wipe his hands across the backside of his plaid. He stood taller and sucked in a deep breath. A contented sense of completeness buoyed him. Life was good. He forced himself to clasp his hands in front of his sporran. *A chief never exhibits anything but strength and surety.* His father's words echoed through his mind, causing Gray to lift his chin and stop fidgeting.

The largest room of the keep hummed with the excited conversations of his people and guests from even as far away as Ireland. Servants scurried in and out among the clusters of chatting folk, passing out small, folded linens soaked in cool, fragrant water.

A trickle of sweat started between Gray's shoulder blades and rolled down his back. The belted waist of his léine felt as though someone had doused him with a bucket of water. Lore a'mighty, perhaps they should have had the ceremony outside.

The crowd went silent and heads turned as the droning sound of bagpipes rang out from the arch of entwined ivy festooned across the entrance of the hall. Two barrel-chested pipers, faces red and cheeks rounded as they puffed into their chanters, flanked Trulie as she stood smiling in the doorway.

Pride and love burned through Gray with every hammer of his heart. There she was. His woman. The mother of his unborn child. Gray drew in a deep breath. Thank the gods she took that jump back in time.

Trulie wore a simple dress of the whitest linen. The tempting mounds of her full bosoms rounded pink above a scooped neckline embroidered with a design of trailing ivy. The high waistline flowed out into graceful folds that barely stirred as she moved slowly toward him. The long bell-shaped sleeves hemmed with more carefully stitched leaves of green gently swayed with every step.

Lore a'mighty, he couldn't help it. He shifted his weight from side to side. Surely even father would have fidgeted if mother had ever come to him in such a way. He swallowed hard against the sudden dryness of his mouth. He was blessed beyond measure and was about to wed an angel.

The throng parted, smiling and nodding as the pipers filled the hall with the soulful wail of their song and led Trulie to the front of the room.

As his precious lady reached the dais, Gray stepped forward and held out his hand. "I have never seen such loveliness." Unspeakable emotion shattered his words into a broken whisper.

Trulie slid her damp palm into his. The lass was as nervous as he was. Her cheeks flushed pale pink as her gaze fell shyly to the unusual bough of herbs and flowers in her hands. The cluster of yarrow and dill trembled between them. Yarrow for everlasting love, myrtle for the emblem of marriage, and dill for protection against evil. Dullas had thrust the bundle into Gray's hands just before he had entered the hall. The silent woman had pointed to the alcove where Trulie waited, then turned and shuffled away. A young serving girl who had befriended Dullas had whispered the meanings of the bundle before scurrying back to the kitchen.

Gray gently eased Trulie up beside him, crooked his finger under her chin, and brushed a chaste kiss across her mouth. "*Tha gaol agam ort,*" he whispered across her lips.

Trulie smiled. "I love you too," she whispered back.

A clearing throat directly beside them broke into the moment. Gray straightened and turned to a very smug-looking Tamhas.

"Shall we begin?" Tamhas's eyes sparkled with happiness as he lightly bounced in place.

Gray couldn't remember the last time he had seen the old demon so happy. And that was just fine. Happiness was in abundance this day. Finally. MacKenna keep had found peace. Gray nodded once. "Aye. Proceed."

Tamhas took Trulie's bouquet and nodded toward their hands.

"Join yer hands," he instructed as he turned and handed the flowers to Granny.

Gray smiled his reassurance as Trulie's hands trembled in his. He stroked a thumb across her cool, damp skin. She swayed a bit off balance, then jerked back into place, blinking hard and running her tongue across her bottom lip.

"Are ye unwell?" Concern piqued his senses as he freed her hands and steadied her by her shoulders. The flushed color across her cheeks had heightened to an alarming shade. "Is it the heat, lass? We shall stop right now and finish this in the gardens." Gray could kick himself. What the devil had he been thinking? A formal wedding, inside the keep, in the heat of late summer?

She shuddered with a deep intake of breath. A sheen of perspiration shimmered across her pale forehead and the area around her mouth took on a sickly-yellow shade. "I will be fine," she promised in a weak whisper. "We just need to hurry."

Uneasiness stirred through him. From her increasing pallor, he verra much doubted if they could hurry fast enough. "Nay." He crooked an arm around her waist. "Ye will never last. We must find ye some relief."

She looked up at him and opened her mouth. But before any words came out, her eyes rolled back and she crumpled.

He caught her up in his arms as concerned gasps and exclamations rippled through the crowd. Trulie's head sagged to one side, her arms dangling limp and lifeless in the air.

"No! Not the baby." Granny rushed up to the dais. "Blood, Gray." Granny's horrified expression fixed on a dark-crimson stain slowly soaking through the folds of Trulie's white gown.

He hefted her higher against his chest. *Dinna take her from me*, he prayed over and over as he strode from the dais to the winding staircase leading to their private rooms. "Get the midwife. Now." A nauseating mixture of fear and rage pounded through him as warm wetness dripped down his arm. "Granny, come! Yer healing touch, Granny—now!" *Dinna take her or the child* hammered through his thoughts as he vaulted up the steps.

The sickening plop of blood against stone spurred him to move faster. He kicked through the final door to their private chamber and eased his precious love down on the bed. Gray choked back a groan and a bitter curse. All color had drained from Trulie. She already looked as though her soul had left them.

He traced a trembling finger across her clammy cheek. "Dinna leave me," he rasped out past the knot in his throat. "I beg ye, my love. Please dinna leave me."

Trulie's eyelids fluttered open as she slowly turned her face toward him. Her eyes filled with tears as she rested a finger on his lips. "Please forgive me," she whispered, then her hand dropped back onto the bed.

THIRTEEN. That was how many slabs of stone made up the floor of the room. Why the hell had the stone masons settled on thirteen? Gray stared down at the muted grays and blacks striated with lighter veins of white. The stones were cold. Unfeeling. Who knew how many tragedies the blocks had witnessed?

He raked both his hands through his hair, tempted to yank it out by the roots. The day had plummeted from joyous brightness to the suffocating darkness of sorrow. He lifted his head and stared at the closed door, refusing to lose her. Trulie's rules of time runners and not dabbling with the past could just be damned. If the Fates took his beloved from him, he would send one of the other Sinclair women back in time and have them do whatever it took to warn Trulie of this day. He shifted his glare upward; defiance clenched his jaw. The laws of time meant nothing. He would never let her go.

Hesitant footsteps sounded behind him. He didn't look around—just returned to the mindless chore of pacing. It had to be Colum. Like the brother he had never had, Colum would be the only one brave enough to sit with him during this time.

"The midwife—" Colum cleared his throat with an uncomfortable cough. "Has she come out and said how Lady Trulie fares?"

"Nay." Gray kept his gaze locked on the floor.

The iron latch of the door clicked. He halted, sucked in a deep breath, and tensed for the worst. Colum moved to his side and rested a reassuring hand on his shoulder.

The door slowly opened. A red-faced woman emerged. Her left arm clutched a wooden bowl piled high with blood-soaked rags. Ringlets of damp hair clung to her face as she wiped a forearm across her forehead. She glanced at Gray and then quickly looked away.

"Tell me," Gray hissed. "Tell me. I must know."

"The babe, a son, has returned to heaven, my chieftain." The midwife's mouth tightened as she avoided looking Gray in the face and stared back at the door. "Thanks be to the Fates' permission and the Lady Nia's healing touch. Yer wife lives. She is resting." The midwife's voice softened as she added, "For now."

A son. Gray closed his eyes and bowed his head, holding his breath against the pain. His firstborn son was dead. The midwife's assessment of Trulie's condition echoed through the blanket of sorrow settling over him. *For now.* The midwife had added *For now.* Gray stiffened, then jerked toward the woman. "What the hell do ye mean *For now?*"

Colum latched onto Gray's arm with an iron grip. "'Tis not her doing, Gray. Control yerself, man." Colum yanked him back. He pulled hard against Gray's shoulder until Gray finally straightened and stood rooted to the spot.

A cruel mix of painful emotions threatened to double him over. Gray clenched his shaking hands and forced himself not to roar at the terrified midwife. "My wife. She must live. Ye must tell me it will be so."

The wide-eyed woman bit her lower lip and barely shook her head. "I canna say. Yer wife must find the will to live. 'Tis up to a greater power than I."

"That greater power best realize that Gray MacKenna will not allow his love to be taken. They already robbed me of my son. I'll be damned straight to the fiery pits afore I allow them to take my wife as well." He collapsed onto the bench beside the closed door and dropped his head into his hands.

"Gray!" Colum waved the midwife toward the outer hall as he rushed over to the bench beside Gray. "Ye must not speak so. 'Tis blasphemy . . . and mayhap a foolhardy challenge to the gods."

Gray raised his head and looked Colum dead in the eye. "Then let the challenge begin, for I will never allow them to take her from me."

CHAPTER 26

A cool, wet nose snuffled into her palm and a soft whine vibrated into her hand. Trulie slid her fingers along the velvet of Karma's muzzle without opening her eyes. "I love you too, old friend," she whispered.

The mattress sank with the weight of the dog as he returned to his place against her side. His warmth sank into her like a soothing tonic. *Bless him. He doesn't know what to do to make me better.*

A calloused hand pressed against her forehead. She didn't open her eyes. It took too much effort. The rough hand moved to her cheek, then nudged firmly against the side of her throat. She wished whomever it was would go away and leave her alone. Even breathing made her body hurt. The hand shoved beneath her shoulders, lifted her up, then gently lowered her back down to a cool dry pillow.

A frail groan escaped her as she settled back into place. The movement hurt. But the dry pillow beneath her head did feel much better so maybe it was worth the pain. She held her breath against another sob threatening to shake free. She needed to go back to the darkness. At least when she was unconscious her heart didn't hurt so badly.

"Trulie," Granny called softly just to the right of her head.

Trulie didn't answer. She didn't feel like talking. If she kept her eyes shut and remained still, maybe Granny would just go away. A drowning sense of loss and sadness pushed her deeper into the safe darkness of her mind.

"Don't you dare give up, Trulie Elizabeth." The silky back of Granny's hand pressed gently against Trulie's cheek.

Granny always did have the softest skin—kind of like crinkly satin. Trulie drew in a deeper breath as a burning teardrop squeezed out from under one eyelid and rolled a hot trail of wetness down the side of her face.

"It will get better, gal," Granny whispered as she pressed a kiss to Trulie's forehead and wiped the tear away. "The hurt will become easier to bear in time. I promise it will. I have been where you are."

Trulie turned her head away from the impossible-to-believe advice. Maybe Granny had known pain and loss, but that didn't lessen the empty ache that made it nearly impossible to breathe. She swallowed the throbbing pain of unshed tears and nestled deeper into the softness of the fresh pillow. *Go away, Granny. Just go away.*

A door creaked, then closed with a soft thud.

Even in her weakened state, Trulie sensed Gray had entered the room. "I would see my wife." Hesitant footsteps scraped against the stone floor.

Trulie almost sobbed aloud. *No. Make him go away. I can't see him right now.*

The footsteps shuffled closer. Holding her breath against the pain, she forced her pain-racked body to roll away from the man she had so terribly failed. The coolness of the stone wall radiated against her face. She couldn't face Gray. Not this soon.

"Trulie." His deep whisper rolled across her as his fingers barely touched her hair.

She closed her eyes tighter and pressed a clenched fist against her mouth. He needed to leave. She needed time to figure out what the devil had gone wrong and where she had messed up. What had she done to cause the loss of their baby?

Tears burned and gut-wrenching sobs threatened to explode free of her control every time his hand stroked across her hair. Their son. He had been so perfect, down to his tiny toes. What the hell had she done wrong? Why has she lost him?

She squeezed her eyes tighter shut and buried her face deeper into the pillow. She couldn't allow Gray to see her collapse. Hadn't she failed him enough? The last thing he needed right now was a hysterical woman. In fact, maybe he didn't need her at all. Maybe he would be better off without her.

"My love," he whispered again, raw pain echoing in his voice.

Trulie hiccupped back a sob as her darkest fears spiraled out of control. First, they had lied and said Granny had to come back to complete her last leap. Then they had lied and said they came back to this godforsaken century just to help Gray solve his parents' murder. That wasn't the only reason those two had pushed Gray in her path. And now look what a mess. Why the devil couldn't they have just left her alone?

She buried her face in her hands and clamped her jaws shut. Well, fine. The murders were solved and the keep had been purged of any residual evil. As for the other . . . she clenched her teeth until she trembled. The chair beside the bed creaked as Gray stood. Good. He was finally leaving.

She held her breath against another sob. Granny's meddling had resulted in a heartbreaking failure. But it could be remedied. Trulie shivered with the finality of the decision. It was time. Time to return to the emotionless safety of the future and let Gray get on with his life in the past.

∼

"No." Gray tested the tautness of the bowstring with his thumb, then handed the weapon back to Colum. "I will not be going on any hunts until Lady Trulie returns to her place at my side." *And in my bed*, he silently added. "There is much work to be done here."

Colum frowned at the nock throat, then ran a hand down the red heartwood of the belly of the bow. "She seemed . . ." The man's voice trailed off as he mindlessly tapped his fingers along the delicate curves of the weapon. "She seemed . . ." He waved the tip of the bow through the air as though marking time for music. "She seemed a bit thin, but she looked to be well," he finally said.

She was not well. His beloved Trulie had not been the same since that dreadful day. Gray selected another bow from the rack and tested the strength of the wood. "Lady Trulie needs more time to heal. I will not leave her side until the sadness leaves her eyes." The hunt could be damned, along with any other duty that might pull him from the keep. Granny had asked him to be patient. He had mastered patience early on in life. He would wait an eternity if that's what it took to win Trulie's smile.

"Coira—" Colum abruptly stopped speaking. He settled the bow across the battered table running the length of the weapons room.

"Coira what?" Gray said. Colum had the worst time when it came to sharing anything involving emotions. It was almost as though the Sinclair women had cast a spell that tied his tongue to punish him for the way he went through women. Gray waited, watching a myriad of emotions flash across Colum's face.

"She fears Lady Trulie plans to return to the future." Colum took a step back as though he feared the words he had just unleashed would explode in his face. "Coira is quite certain Lady Trulie plans to leave with the rise of the next full moon.

Gray closed the distance between them. "What the hell has she told ye? All of it. Tell me all that has been said and tell me now." If Colum held back any knowledge that would cause Gray to lose Trulie —rage tightened his hands into fists—he would break the man in two.

"Lady Trulie blames herself for losing the child. Feels she failed ye." Colum stepped back, increasing the floor space between them. "Coira said yer wife thinks ye will be better off if she returns to the future and ye go on without her. Find another to marry and give ye bairns."

"Go on without her?" Gray threw back his head and roared his anguish to the winds. "There will be no going on without her."

Colum white-knuckled the narrow arm of the bow he clutched against his chest. He started to speak several times, then finally flattened his lips into a frown and shook his head. It was obvious the man was not comfortable speaking about such things.

Gray's rage cooled a bit, but the urgency didn't. Apparently, no number of soft words could convince Trulie she was not at fault. Lore a'mighty. He turned away from Colum and walked to the long, narrow slit of a window. The opening was just wide enough to allow a man to effectively rain down a volley of arrows on any who dared threaten MacKenna Keep.

The bit of sky showing through the slit looked dark and ominous. Gray reached through the window and felt the air. Cold. Damp. The wind promised a bone-chilling rain, perhaps even ice or snow. He felt an odd sense of unity with the weather. It currently mirrored his troubled soul.

"I will speak to Granny and Coira. This verra day, even." He turned and looked back at Colum. "It is time for Lady Trulie to realize she is my wife and her place is at my side."

TRULIE SNUGGLED DEEPER into the hooded cloak and turned her back to the frigid wind. Maybe a walk through the dormant garden hadn't been such a great idea after all. Karma trotted up ahead. The great black dog lifted his nose higher, closed his eyes, and seemed to smile. In spite of herself, Trulie's heart lightened the barest notch. Karma helped her survive the darkness.

The final visit to the tiny grave had been almost more than she could bear. But Karma's comforting weight leaning against her had pulled her through. When he had pointed his nose toward the sky and softly howled, she had thought she would surely break down. But in the end, the lonely cry echoing across the valley had seemed the perfect farewell to her precious little boy.

Karma looked back and softly woofed as though urging Trulie to hurry. When she quickened her pace, he pranced forward, crunching through the frost-covered leaves. Words couldn't describe the bliss on the dog's face as he lapped at the scents swirling through the air.

Maybe she should try it? She closed her eyes and faced the biting rush of cold. Inhaling deeply, she waited for whatever it was that made Karma so happy. Nothing came.

She ducked back around and pulled the hood closer around her face. "I don't know what you smelled that made you so happy. All I picked up was seawater and pine trees."

Karma responded with a playful yip and a slow wag of his tail. Then he took off at a run and loped deeper into the maze of shrubbery winding through the end of the garden.

Trulie sighed and trudged on. Apparently, Karma had given up on completely pulling her from her dark mood. She guessed she really couldn't blame him. She had been this way for weeks.

But everything was about to change. She quickened her pace and followed the dog along the stepping-stones winding through the garden. Soon, there would be no more yards and yards of heavy clothes. No more freezing her tail off in the garderobe or balancing acts on the chamber pot. The luxuries and conveniences of simple indoor plumbing were one of the many reasons to hurry back to the future. And blue jeans. And deodorant—real deodorant. Not just a bunch of herbs rubbed against your armpits.

She mentally ticked off all the wonders awaiting her in the future. Maybe if she kept her mind busy with all of the *things* that would make life easier, she could find a way to ignore the sick weight of *what abouts* squeezing the life out of her soul. What about Granny? What about Coira? And the two biggest: What about Gray? And what about their love?

The emotions nearly choked her. Not again. She refused to give them any more power. Not after shedding three lifetimes of tears. She curled tighter into the cloak, pulled the hood low over her eyes, and charged ahead.

Watching her boot tips flash in and out from under her skirt, she suddenly collided with the solid mass attached to the worn pair of boots pointed at her. She bounced off the broad chest and would've landed on her bottom if not for the strong hands catching hold of her arms.

"Take care, my love. What causes ye to hurry so?" Gray tipped back her hood and smiled down into her eyes.

Every basic instinct urged her to melt into his embrace. She could just close her eyes and lose herself in the safety of his arms. It could be all right again. She blinked hard, regained her footing, and pushed herself an arm's length away. No. She couldn't bear it if she failed him again. Gray deserved better.

She didn't miss the shadow that immediately darkened his expression. Hurt and disappointment burned in his eyes, and his smile faded into a flat, determined line. She couldn't help it. Once she was gone, he could set about the business of getting on with his life. He would forget her in no time.

"I will not allow ye to leave me," he said in a tone that shook her to the core. He closed the distance between them and cupped her face in his hand. "Ye belong here. With me. For heaven's sake, forgive yerself, woman. Ye canna control what Fate deems shall be."

"Have you forgiven me?" she said as she retreated from his touch. No matter how much he denied it, she would never believe him. She had watched his excitement about the baby get stronger with every passing day. Now he expected her to believe that he wasn't disappointed in her? That she hadn't failed him? Sake's alive, she had lost his firstborn son.

"There is nothing to forgive," he said, his voice strained. "Why can ye not believe me when I say it was not yer fault?" He stomped forward, grabbed her by the shoulders, and shoved his face only inches from hers. "Our child died. Our son. I hate it as much as yerself but I have never—not for the barest instant—blamed ye for the loss of the babe. It happens, Trulie. Why can ye not understand that some things are just meant to be? Are ye not the one who swears ye canna make changes to the past to make a better future? Did ye not tell me all things happen for a reason?"

"What could possibly be the reason for stealing our baby?" she sobbed more to the gods than to Gray as she pounded her fists against his chest. A keening wail escaped her as she hit him again and again. "What did we do to deserve this pain? Why did it have to happen?"

Gray stood silent. His red-rimmed eyes shone wet with unshed tears as she unleashed her rage against his chest. She railed against him. Damn him for making her lose control. Damn him for cracking open the unceasing ache that plagued her every waking hour. She collapsed into his arms as all her sorrow and pain finally broke free.

"I am going back to the future." She hiccuped a sob into the rough wool plaid covering his chest. The warm spice of him surrounded her, coaxed her into voicing all her secrets. "I cannot do this kind of pain ever again. I can't survive this."

He gathered her closer, tightened his arms around her. Nestling her head under the crook of his chin, he stroked her hair with a shaking hand and gently rocked as her heart-wrenching sobs broke free and echoed her despair across the winds.

CHAPTER 27

"I refuse to lose her to the future." Gray walked a slow circle around the cushioned bench where a grim-faced Granny and a frowning Coira sat. "Tell me what it will take to make her stay—other than placing her in irons." He did not add that he would also not hesitate to lock Trulie in her chambers. He would do whatever it took until she came to her senses.

Granny worried the strings of her apron as she stared off into space. "I don't know how we can convince her the future really isn't any safer from heartache than the past."

"Ye best come up with a pretty good example or Mistress Trulie is gonna call ye a grand hypocrite." Coira hopped up from the bench, backed up to the hearth, and smoothed her backside toward the heat.

"Coira," Granny said. "Is that ladylike with a man in the room?"

"Me arse is cold and I am a servant. I dinna have to worry with acting the lady."

Gray took in a deep breath and dug his fingers hard into his throbbing temples. For some reason, it greatly disturbed him that his wife's independent attitude appeared to be rubbing off on the servants. Heaven help him if they all adopted her ways. "Why did ye say Granny would risk looking a hypocrite?"

"If Granny had not taken Mistress Trulie and her sisters to the future, the youngest girls would have died when they were naught but a few weeks old." Coira turned and extended both hands toward the cheerful flames licking across the logs. "Mistress Trulie would surely have died too. She spoke of a weakness with her heart when she was just a wee one."

Gray turned back to Granny. "Is this true? Did ye jump to the future to escape the danger of the past?"

"That was different." Granny snorted out her disgust as she slowly rose from the bench. "I did what I had to do to keep my babies alive— I was not running away from what I feared. There is a big difference between what I did and what Trulie is about to do." The old woman toddled across the room and lit the candles of the black candelabra on the table. "Trulie is running from her feelings. She thinks she can outrun her pain. Somehow, she has gotten the misguided notion that if she returns to the future, life won't be so hard to bear." With a tired intake of breath, Granny leaned both hands on the table. "We have to find a way to make her realize heartache finds you anytime it wishes. A particular century won't protect you from its touch."

A plotting look knotted Granny's brow. A small grin sprouted at the corners of her pursed lips as she began pacing around the room.

Good. Gray breathed easier with the realization that Granny had shifted into the calculating frame of mind that usually ended up being a very large pain in the arse. Hopefully, this time would be more successful. He was willing to risk it. "What are ye planning?"

"What if . . ." Granny paused, her eyes narrowing. "Why couldn't . . ." She started again as her face brightened with whatever was blossoming in her mind. She clapped her hands, a full-blown plan sparkling in her eyes. "I need to look into Trulie's future—the one that would take place if she stayed here. There has got to be something we could show her that would convince her she needs to stay in this time. I have to find something so awesome Trulie would never want to miss it."

Granny's logic made Gray's head hurt worse. What the hell did she mean by looking into a particular future? The very idea of what

Granny might discover twisted his gut. He scrubbed a hand across his weary eyes and pinched the bridge of his nose. Lore, he felt to be a hundred years old. "Are ye certain it can be done? Without any danger?"

"Absolutely." Granny snapped her fingers and smiled. "Futures are created by our choices. Every choice in life has its own particular future. The multiple possibilities from each choice are the strands that create the web of time. You know this, Gray. We showed you this with your parents."

He chose to ignore her lecturing tone. "Ye are certain ye can find the future Trulie needs to see? The one that will make her stay?" He wasn't sure if he liked the risk or not. What if Granny picked the wrong one and showed Trulie a possibility that she couldn't stomach?

"Let me see what I can find." Granny rubbed both hands together in anticipation. "I haven't played with the strands of time in weeks, but I feel sure I can find the perfect choice to convince Trulie to stay."

Gray swallowed hard. This had to work.

TRULIE PULLED the last kirtle from the wardrobe and held it up. Coira might be able to wear it if Granny took an inch or two off the length and added an inch or two to the bust. Her friend might be shorter but she was exceedingly better endowed. Trulie added the gown of deep green to the pile on the end of the bed. There. That should do it. All the things she had acquired since arriving in this century had been fairly divvied up.

She swallowed hard and shoved her hands deep into the pockets of her jeans. A glance at the folded bits of parchment neatly lined up on the table made her swallow hard. Her written goodbyes would be found in the morning, long after she was gone.

Guilt wrung out her heart as she backed up to the fire. She supposed writing her farewells was the coward's way, but it was all she could emotionally handle right now. Her nerves were raw from the last few weeks. She couldn't take much more.

A light knock from the inner door of her sitting room pulled her from her thoughts. She stared at it. Who the devil could that be? It was nearly midnight. With a frustrated glance at her twenty-first-century outfit, she crossed the room, then pressed her back against the door. "Who is there this late?"

"It is me, mistress," Coira called out with another rap on the door. "Let me in, aye?"

Trulie wedged her body harder against the wood at her back. She wasn't about to let Coira in. That would be like sounding a warning alarm across the entire northern tip of Scotland. Coira was more efficient at spreading news than the internet.

"Go away, Coira. It's late and I'm tired." Trulie leaned her head back against the door and waited.

A hard thud bounced against the lower half of the door. That had to be a solid kick. "Let me in, Mistress Trulie. Now!"

Trulie turned and stared at the door. Coira was uncharacteristically bossy tonight. "You can kick the door all you want. I am not letting you in."

"I ken what ye are about. If ye dinna let me in, I shall wake everyone in the keep and tell them."

Trulie glared at the latch. How did Coira know what she was up to? She had to be bluffing. "I don't know what you're talking about. Go away. I am trying to get some sleep."

"So be it," Coira snapped from the other side. "I shall run to the chieftain and tell him ye are about to time jump again."

Well, dammit. Coira wasn't bluffing. Trulie lifted the iron latch and yanked the door open.

"See? I knew ye were about to leave!" Coira pointed at Trulie's jeans. "I knew tonight would be the night ye picked to leave us all behind."

"What do you want?" Trulie chose her words carefully. If she didn't play this just right, Coira would still sound the alarm in a heartbeat.

The maid lifted her hands and shrugged. Karma sat beside her with his ears perked and his tongue lolling out one side of his mouth in a toothy, doggy grin.

"Well? What do you want?" Trulie didn't like the look on either of their faces. It was that smug *I have you right where I want you* expression that always meant they had the advantage. She made a mental note to scold Karma later. The dog needed to realize where his loyalties belonged.

"Come to the outer sitting room. There is a visitor ye need to meet afore ye go." Coira tipped her head at the door behind her and offered a smug smile.

This could not be good, but what choice did she have? Trulie yanked her denim jacket firmly in place and closed the door tightly behind her. Kismet was probably lurking somewhere in the shadows and she wouldn't put it past the sneaky cat to take off with her carefully written notes of farewell.

"We won't keep ye overly long," Coira said with a curt toss of her red curls.

An eerie shiver raced across Trulie's flesh as the maid led her into the main sitting room shared by the Sinclair women. A young woman sat on the edge of the high-backed bench on the far side of the hearth. A wild mass of out-of-control ringlets dark as coal tumbled across her shoulders and spilled down her back. But it was the girl's eyes that stole Trulie's breath and made her heart thump harder. She had only seen such an icy-blue, lightning-filled shade in one other set of eyes. And it was those unusual blue eyes that had started the undoing of her life. They had taken hold of her heart and soul and refused to let go.

Gray sat in a broad-backed chair opposite the smiling young lass. His hands trembled on the chair's wide armrests, and he sagged slightly to one side, as though remaining upright was a chore.

The dark haired girl giggled behind her hand. Mischief glinted in her eyes as she hopped up from the bench and bounced toward Trulie. "I am so verra glad ye agreed to see me. I feared ye wouldna come."

Trulie slid her attention from the sweet girl's beaming face to Granny's smug grin. "I don't know how long you have known these people, but there are times when they are pretty stubborn. Did they bring you here?" Trulie returned her attention to the animated girl fidgeting in front of her. It wasn't the child's fault Granny was up to no good. Trulie didn't know how Granny had managed to come up with a child—one who looked to be in her early teens and had Gray's eyes, but she had to admit, Granny was playing her little game very well.

The girl winked a dark-fringed eye at Coira as she bubbled, "Oh, I have known Coira and dear sweet Granny all my life." Merriment fairly glowed from the girl as she patted a hand over her mouth and ducked her chin. "Sorry. I wasna supposed to say that."

That was impossible. Trulie looked from Granny to the girl and then over at Gray's intense stare. "Who are you?" Trulie asked. She couldn't be who they wanted her to believe the girl really was. How in the world had Granny managed to find a girl that looked so much like Gray?

"My name is Chloe," the girl said with a perfect curtsy.

Chloe. Trulie lost her footing as her heart leapt into her throat. She had always loved that name. One day . . . if she had ever had a daughter . . . Trulie shook away the thought and cleared the knot of emotions from her throat. *You know who she is. You have never told anyone how much you love that name.* She shook her head at her taunting inner voice.

"Are ye all right?" Chloe asked. "Do ye need me to fetch ye some water?"

"I am fine, thank you." Trulie swallowed hard. She shoved her hands into her jacket pockets to hide their trembling. She nodded at the full moon shining a path of white light through the far window. "Won't your parents be worried about you being out so late?"

Chloe's grin widened into a sparkling smile. "Nah. Da kens for sure where I am and Mother will soon ken it as well."

Gray pushed himself up from the chair. An excited shiver coursed through Trulie. Did Gray's shoulders somehow seem wider? His chest broader? Was the man actually strutting with pride? She took a step back and knotted her hands in her pockets. She hadn't seen him so relaxed, so happy, since . . . She closed her eyes against the thought.

"Ye ken who she is," he whispered as he pulled her into his arms. His warm breath tickled against the sensitive skin just beneath her ear. His arms tightened around her as he pressed a kiss against her temple.

"She can't be," Trulie said in a strained whisper. Yet how could she deny the proof right before her eyes. Trulie turned and opened her eyes to Chloe's knowing smile. "Why are you here, Chloe?" It felt so strange to say the name, and yet so natural.

"Ye ken why I am here," the girl said as she tugged on Trulie's sleeve until Trulie pulled her hand from her pocket. She slipped her small hand into Trulie's and glanced toward the window. "But I canna stay verra much longer. They said I mustn't tarry overly long beyond the path of the moon."

Chloe smiled up at Gray before she leaned in closer to Trulie. "I had to come. Ye had to know what ye would miss if ye chose to leave Da and go back to yer modern future."

The young one's face became serious as she squeezed Trulie's hand harder. "But I will warn ye that the world would most likely be a much better place if ye rethought bringing Ian into it." Chloe's mouth puckered with an irritated scowl. "My own lot in life would be a great deal easier without that numpty always poking his nose into things that dinna concern him."

Trulie's mood lightened in spite of the ever-weakening voice of conviction whispering in her head that opportunity was slipping away. If she was going to return to modern-day Kentucky, she needed to leave—now.

"Who is Ian?" She couldn't resist asking. Chloe's bubbling personality chased away the darkness plaguing her soul. How could she not feel happier knowing that at some point in the future, if she chose to stay in the past with Gray, Chloe would join their lives?

The girl rolled her eyes and blew out a disgusted huff. "Ian is the youngest and by far the biggest pain in the arse of all my brothers."

"All yer brothers?" Gray repeated as he pulled Trulie into a tighter embrace.

"Aye," Chloe said. "Would the two of ye please bear in mind that after bringing four worrisome boys into the world, the chances of gifting me with a little sister are fair slim and ye should set aside the trying." Chloe glanced toward the window, then edged into the beam of moonlight. She held up both hands and patted the air as though bidding Trulie and Gray to take care. "Just leave it be, will ye? I canna stomach another brother who thinks he can tell me what to do."

Trulie pressed a hand to her mouth and blew Chloe a kiss. "Thank you, Chloe." Warm happy tears streamed down her face as she held a shaking hand up in farewell to her daughter.

Chloe smiled and waved as her image faded into the moonlight. "Bye, Mother! Bye, Da! All my love to ye both."

GRAY STEADIED Trulie as they crunched through the sparkling crust of untouched snow. "'Tis just a bit farther." His breath fogged an eerie blue-white cloud into the air. The shallow drifts of the crystal blanket rolled across the hillside, colored an even icier blue by the in-between time just before dawn.

"Is anyone else going to be there?" Trulie gathered her skirts higher and forged up the hillside.

"Only us," he said as he brought her gloved hand to his mouth and pressed a kiss to it. All was finally as it should be. At dawn, just as the sun crested the frozen horizon, he and Trulie would voice their union. The vast wildness of the rugged Highlands would serve as their only witness. His soul sang with long-awaited contentment. Finally. He and Trulie would be as one.

"There." Gray pointed to the crest of the peak. Majestic pines towered against the ever-lightening blue of the sky. A small clearing glistened amid the dark circle of the trees. A waist-high stone, its edges worn and rounded by centuries of Highland weather, reached toward the sky from the center of the ring of snow.

"It's perfect," Trulie said as she pushed her furred hood to her back.

Even in the low light of pending dawn, his heart warmed at the happiness on her face. "The old ones claimed this place to be holy. A place to speak to the gods. What better place to say our vows and become one?"

"I agree," she said softly as she took his hand and walked with him to the clearing.

The top of the stone was bleached white with age, but the unending whorls of the goddess could still be seen across the surface. He positioned himself on one side of the pillar and Trulie took her place opposite him. He nodded toward the horizon, squinting against the cold bite of the wind. "The sun comes to us," he said as he scooped her hands into his.

"It's time," she said, smiling as the golden glow struck the crystals of snow and kissed the world with the first fire of its color.

"Tha gaol agam ort." Gray centered their clasped hands above the stone and repeated in English, "I love ye."

"I love you too." She squeezed his hands and repeated in Gaelic, *"Tha gaol agam ort-fhèin."*

"I pledge ye my life. I pledge ye my heart. I pledge ye nothing less than my soul." He took a deep breath and swallowed hard against the wave of emotions crashing through him as the fiery rays of the morning light illuminated the clearing.

As the sunlight flooded full against the east side of the stone monument beneath their clasped hands, the rays shot up through a well-placed channel bored through the center of the stone. The blinding white beam of light exploded up through their clasped fingers. Their hands glowed. Their flesh appeared illuminated and melded into one.

Trulie gasped as she stared down at the glowing mass between them. She lifted a tear-streaked face to him, blinking back the threat of more tears as she spoke. "I give you my life. My heart is yours. Our souls are joined as one. I shall walk with you through eternity and beyond."

"So let it be spoken," he whispered as he leaned forward and sought the softness of her mouth.

"So let it be done," she said as she sealed their joining with a kiss.

EPILOGUE

Two Years Later (approximately)

The soft weight of her head beneath his chin lured him into wakefulness. Gray drew in a deep, satisfied breath. Was there any better way to awaken then with the feel of yer woman in yer arms? Without opening his eyes, he slid an arm around her. The loose weave of soft linen rippled beneath his fingertips. He nuzzled a kiss to her forehead, reveling in the delicious, sweet scent of her. "Why have ye donned yer shift? Ye know I love the feel of ye bare against me."

Trulie nestled more snugly into the dip of his shoulder and tickled a finger down through the hair curling toward his stomach. "I am the size of a beached whale and putting off enough heat to melt the polar ice cap. You should thank me for sparing you."

He chuckled and shifted higher in the pillows, pulling her more comfortably across him. His love always had a way with words. He wondered if he would ever completely understand her. "Ye are my fine beauty and I shall never get my fill of ye."

His heart swelled near to bursting as he gently caressed a hand over her swollen belly. His poor precious lass. So large with his child she must surely be miserable. Aye, she had grown large, but she was also the most beautiful sight he had ever beheld in all his days. He pressed another kiss atop her head. "And how is our fine, strong bairn today?"

As if to answer, the babe rolled, shifting Trulie's stomach beneath his palm, then bumped a strong thump against his hand. Trulie arched her back and pressed firmly against her side. "Trying to find more room. He seems to enjoy hooking his toes on my ribcage and stretching."

A surge of pride flashed through Gray. A chuckle rumbled from him as he pulled free the laces of her shift and slid his hand inside it to rub slow circles around her silky belly. "Aye. He will be a braw laddie and need a good strong name. A name befitting a future chieftain."

A sense of awe silenced him as he enjoyed the magic of life slowly shifting beneath his hand. What a wondrous gift they had been given. A fine, precious gift. Thank the gods Trulie had chosen to stay with him. Remembering the exact moment she had decided to stay in the past, he gently traced a fingertip around what seemed to be the outline of a small foot, or maybe part of a wee arm stretching Trulie's belly. "Do ye reckon this one is our Chloe?"

Trulie propped herself higher in the bed and shoved more pillows behind the small of her back. She settled her hand atop his and peered down at her middle, frowning as she studied her belly. "I am not sure. She mentioned four brothers but didn't say if all of them were older or younger." Her gaze shifted up to him. Something in the depths of her green eyes warned him her mood had just changed.

Lore a'mercy. May the gods be with him and not let him say the wrong thing. Ofttimes of late, retreat was the better part of valor. He draped an arm over his eyes and burrowed back into the depths of the plump bed. As the birthing day drew nearer, his love's moods shifted faster than a storm at sea and could oft be as deadly. "Colum is seeing to the hunt today." He patted the spot beside him. "Come, my dearest. Let me hold ye while we both rest a bit longer."

"About Colum."

A huffing groan escaped him before he could stop it. He kept his arm over his eyes and prayed he could avoid another *discussion*, as his wife so dearly loved to call them, about Colum and his penchant for dallying with the maids. He knew that tone. He had best tread lightly. "I have spoken to him about his ways, just as ye asked." *Dammit, Colum, ye wanderin' bastard. I will wring yer wenchin' neck the next I see ye.* Gray shifted his arm slightly and stole a peek at Trulie.

She quietly folded her hands on top of her enormous midriff. "Your lectures have not been effective. Just last night, I caught him behind the tapestries with not one, but two of Cook's kitchen maids." She glared off into space, slowly tapping a finger on her belly. "Granny and I have seen good things regarding Colum. It's time he settled down." Her lips curled into the dangerously beautiful plotting smile Gray had learned meant trouble. She awkwardly moved to the edge of the bed and wobbled to her feet. "Could you please let Coira know I am ready to get dressed?"

"Aye." Gray rolled from the bed, snatched his plaid off the hook, and wrapped it around his waist. He would gladly fetch the maid if it meant he could avoid what looked to be a treacherous morning in the bedchamber.

"And don't go far," she warned, as though she had read his thoughts.

Gray paused, his hand on the latch and his breath held as he waited. *Lore a'mighty. What mischief is she about to stir?*

Trulie smiled as she draped a light arisaid about her shoulders. "Once I am dressed, we will all meet in the solar."

"We?"

Trulie nodded. "You, me, Granny, and Colum."

He blew out a heavy sigh and asked, "And we are meeting because?"

"Because Colum is perfect for Kenna."

READ ON FOR AN EXCITING EXCERPT FROM:

My Highland Bride
Highland Hearts - Book 2

CHAPTER ONE

Scotland
The Highlands
Thirteenth Century

"Have ye ever seen such a lovely set of bosoms?"

Colum Garrison lowered his cup enough to peer over its metal rim. *Aye.* Diarmuid had the right of it there. The man had a keen eye when it came to the lasses. The newest serving girl was indeed a comely maid blessed with a bounty of curves.

He drained the tankard, licking the last of the tangy ale from his lips, then slid the empty mug to the table. "An untapped MacKenna keg against that fine ale ye bring all the way from Ireland. What say ye? I give ye fair odds. Whoever leaves the hall with her on his arm claims the spoils, aye?"

Diarmuid squinted one eye shut while scrubbing his fingers through the short black curls covering his jaw. "Fair odds, my arse. If I win the gift of that lass's charms, ye'll give me yer best bow along with that keg of fine MacKenna whisky."

Colum tapped his thumb against the handle of his empty

tankard. Yon sweetling would easily choose him over Diarmuid, but wager his best bow? Over something as flighty as a woman's druthers? Instinct and past experience with Diarmuid's less-than-scrupulous wagers gave him pause. The man's terms reeked with the stench of a carefully laid trap. Colum drummed his fingers on the rough table. "That bow was a gift from the chieftain. There is none like it in all the Highlands."

Diarmuid grinned, held up his index finger, then slowly allowed it to droop at the knuckle. He gave a sly wink and flipped the sagging appendage, making it appear boneless. "What ails ye, my friend? Are ye not feeling *up* for the wee challenge?"

Colum banged his empty mug on the long trestle table and waved the girl toward them. "I will show ye *up*, ye bastard. After the lass has been with me, she willna give yer wee sausage a second glance."

Diarmuid rubbed his hands together, his impish grin widening into a devilish smile. "We shall see, man-at-arms. We shall see."

The teasing look in the young woman's eyes, paired with the coy tilt of her head, settled the matter nicely. Aye, the lass was as good as his, and so was another keg of Diarmuid's fine ale. Colum slowly traced a fingertip around the curve of his mug. Soon his fingers would trace along much finer curves.

The girl tucked her broad wooden platter under her arm and sashayed toward them. When she reached their table, the red-haired vixen leaned across the bench and propped a hand on it. Her smile widened as she not so subtly arched her back, providing an even better view of the creamy cleavage about to spill free of her tightly laced kirtle. "Aye, master. Can I be a fetching anything for ye?"

Colum unleashed his most beguiling smile, leaned forward, and ever so gently slid a finger under her silky chin. Diarmuid never stood a chance. This wee filly was already his. The truth of it shone in her clear blue eyes and her barely parted lips, already begging for his kisses.

A deep voice boomed across the crowded hall. "Colum! Here. Now. The MacKenna bids ye to his solar at once. Best be about it, man."

Colum let his hand drop, clenching his teeth to keep from cursing aloud. Damn Galen and his ill-timed interruptions. What the hell was wrong with the man? Could he not see there was serious business at hand?

Diarmuid chuckled and scooted Colum farther down the bench, bumping his way in front of the still smiling maid. "Dinna worry, friend. I will make sure this fine young lass doesna feel neglected by yer absence." Diarmuid tickled a finger up and down her lightly freckled forearm as a beguiling smile lit up his face. "Do ye happen to fancy sausages, m'dear one?"

A low-throated growl escaped him as Colum swung out from the bench and stood. He searched the far wall of stone archways for Galen. 'Twas a sorry day indeed when he had been fool enough to make that clot head his second in command. Aye, Galen was a fine warrior, but the stubborn bastard had a talent for being a verra large pain in the arse.

Barrel-chested Galen grinned and waved from the widest of the arches leading up to the private rooms of the keep. He nodded and winked, rolling up on his toes to bounce a bit higher than his stumpy height, which barely brought him to Colum's shoulder. His smirking grin widened to a toothy smile as Colum closed in on him. "Now, lad, dinna fret. I feel sure ye can win the lass back from Diarmuid as soon the chief is done with ye."

"Ye just cost me my best bow and a keg of whisky." Colum shoved Galen aside as he shouldered through the doorway.

Galen lowered his broad shoulder and effectively bounced Colum a few steps sideways into the opposing wall. The man might be short of stature but he was nearly as wide as he was tall and stood as solid as *Beinn Nibheis*. He jabbed a short stubby finger into the center of Colum's chest. "I saved ye from yer chieftain's wrath, ye ungrateful bastard. Were ye not just telling me how the MacKenna warned ye to leave the maids alone for a bit? Did he not tell ye he grows weary of getting his arse chewed by both his wife and her grandmother for how ye run through the women in the keep? Good Lord, man. Ye should be thanking me. I saw Mother Sinclair herself heading toward ye from the kitchens."

Damn the squat bastard. Colum rolled his shoulder, still stinging from scraping the rough stone of the wall. He glanced back behind them. Sure enough, Granny Sinclair was currently blessing out Diarmuid. She had one bony hand clamped around the serving girl's elbow while she shaking a bent finger just inches from the tip of Diarmuid's nose. The old woman didn't even pause for breath as she whipped around and shook the same finger in the face of the wide-eyed maid.

It appeared a debt of gratitude was owed rather than a swift kick in the arse. Colum clapped a hand to Galen's meaty shoulder and hurried them both farther down the hall. "I owe ye greatly, my fine friend. I swear to do the sword dance at yer next wedding."

Galen shook his head and held up a hand. "I've seen yer great gawking from hopping about to the pipes. Spare me the favor, ye oversized son of a *Lochlanach*."

Colum gave Galen a friendly shove and widened his stride. Galen wasn't the first man to accuse him of Viking ancestry. And what of it? Colum found no fault in being compared to some of the most fearless warriors on land or sea. "So, tell me, friend. Does our chief truly wish to see me or were ye merely saving my hide?"

Galen's bushy brows arched higher on his balding head, greatly resembling a pair of oversized wooly worms. "Oh no, lad. The MacKenna did summon yer arse."

"For?"

"I dinna ken." Galen shook his head and scratched a hairy shoulder before yanking the neck of his tunic back in place. "But I did hear him say 'twas really for Mother Sinclair—her and the Lady Trulie. What the hell have ye done now, and do ye even remember her name?"

Colum halted. An uncomfortable sense of foreboding settled in his gut, then took to churning like a great serpent stirring the bowels of the sea. "Mother Sinclair, ye say?"

"Aye." Galen added a solemn nod.

"*And* the Lady Trulie?"

"Aye." Galen pulled up short and eased back a step as they reached the arch leading to the stairwell up to the chieftain's private rooms. The man eyed the narrow doorway as though it were the gateway to hell.

"And yer certain ye have no idea of what it might be?" Colum glanced toward the winding stone steps leading up to the MacKenna's solar and swallowed hard. With the Sinclair women plotting against him, he would feel more at ease going to the gallows.

Galen thumped Colum's shoulder, then hurriedly motioned the sign of the cross over his chest. "I dinna ken. But I will say a prayer for ye and make a sacrifice to the old gods as well. Here's to the hopes that all the entities watch over ye. I feel ye will be a needing the lot of them." Galen jerked his chin toward his chest, squeezed Colum's arm one last time, then turned and barreled back down the hallway.

Colum watched Galen disappear through the arch. A deep-seated sense of survival strongly advised him to follow the man. Colum shook free of the urge. He had saved the MacKenna's life several times; surely his chief would protect him from whatever the women plotted.

He traced his fingertips along the cold rough stones of the tower wall as he slowly climbed the winding stairs. Aye, the MacKenna would protect him. A delayed flash of pride surged through him. What the hell was wrong with him? Afraid of two women?

He sucked in a deep breath and took the remaining steps two at a time. He was not a coward As soon as the words crossed his mind, he felt a bit sheepish. It sounded as though he was trying to convince himself of his own courage.

The tension in the room hit him as soon as he walked into the chieftain's private solar. He paused a moment, wiping his damp palms on the coarse wool of his plaid. Well, mayhap not tension—'twas more like the gut-tightening feel a man got the night before a battle. There was damn sure something ill a stirring, and he did not care for the feel of it at all.

Gray MacKenna, chieftain of Clan MacKenna and Colum's best

friend since they were both snot-nosed lads, lounged comfortably on one end of a pillowed bench with a look on his face that could only mean trouble. His wife, Lady Trulie, sat at his side, one hand slowly stroking her great rounded belly as though comforting the child within.

"My chief." Colum nodded as he studied Gray's expression closer. What the hell was the man thinking? More oft than not he knew Gray's thoughts before the man even spoke them; they had fought side by side that long. But he had no idea what his liege was thinking this time. Sucking in a deep breath, Colum turned and politely bowed to Lady Trulie. "M'lady."

Lady Trulie didn't say a word, just lowered her chin in a polite nod and continued rubbing the wool-covered mound of her belly.

Colum got the uncomfortable feeling he was being sized up as prey. He widened his stance, sent up a prayer for divine protection, and hoped like hell Galen was making that promised sacrifice to the old gods.

Gray blew out a noisy exhale and shifted among the pillows. He still didn't speak, just appeared to be struggling against some inner turmoil. Whatever it was had to be serious. The man looked as though he was about to explode. Had the clan been attacked? Was the king on the rampage again? If that were the case, why would the Sinclair women intervene? Had the Fates sent them one of their visions?

Colum caught a subtle movement out of the corner of his eye. Senses on edge, he jerked and faced it. Nothing moved but the slight shifting of the MacKenna colors hanging beside the great stone fireplace. Lady Trulie's huge beast of a dog, Karma, rolled to his side on the hide stretched before the hearth and groaned in his sleep. Colum swallowed hard. Damn them all. What the hell was afoot? He turned back and faced his chieftain.

Lady Trulie resettled herself in the corner of the settee. The devilry flashing in her smile worried Colum more than anything else. Her thoughtful expression sent a chill through his bones. Lady Trulie was a great deal like her grandmother. She demanded a heavy dose of respect, and any who underestimated the woman quickly rued their stupidity. Her dangerous smile shifted to a look of intense concentration as she wriggled uncomfortably in the seat. Leaning forward as far as her rounded belly would allow, she shoved another colorful pillow down behind her lower back. "Lordy, I wish this baby would come soon. I feel like a bloated cow."

Colum bit the inside of his cheek. Lady Trulie had never behaved like any other woman he had ever known. But he supposed that stood to reason since she came from some strange place called Kentucky in the even stranger-sounding future.

"Are ye not well then, m'lady?" Colum ignored Gray's barking laugh. And damned, if his chieftain didn't sit there and shake his head as if he couldn't believe Colum had asked that question. What the hell was he supposed to say to the woman? 'Twas obvious she was miserable. He was merely attempting to show proper respect to his chief's wife.

Lady Trulie smiled as she swatted Gray's arm. "I am quite well, thank you." She motioned toward a cushioned chair beside a low table containing a metal pitcher and several cups. "Please—pour yourself a drink and have a seat while we wait for Granny."

"While we wait for Mother Sinclair?" Every muscle tensed several notches tighter. He felt like someone had just doused him with a bucket of water from the coldest part of the loch. Why the hell were they waiting for Mother Sinclair? Damn Galen and his faulty eaves-dropping. When he had heard Gray mention Mother Sinclair, why had the man not found out what in blue blazes was about to befall?

"Aye." Gray grinned and slid out of swatting reach of his wife. "Mother Sinclair wishes to have a word with ye."

"I see." Colum resettled his stance and clasped his hands to the small of his back.

Gray's grin widened to a knowing smile and a wicked chuckle escaped him. "Do ye not wish to sit, man?"

"Nay." Colum rolled his shoulders. "I prefer to meet Mother Sinclair standing."

Gray barked out a laugh and rose from his seat. "I know ye need a drink before she arrives."

Colum verra much doubted there was enough whisky in all of Scotland to prepare a man to face Mother Sinclair. "Will the two of ye give me no hint as to what the woman wants with me?"

"Nothing bad." Lady Trulie fidgeted in the seat, arching her back while pressing a hand to the bottom of her ribs and pushing against the subtly moving swell of her stomach. "I promise it's nothing bad."

Colum very much doubted the accuracy of her statement.

The door creaked, then softly bumped closed behind him. Colum did not have to turn to know Mother Sinclair had entered the room. The hairs prickling up the back of his neck announced her presence like a blaring battle horn.

The slight old woman hurried past him. Her twisted staff with the odd crystal embedded in the top tangle of roots lightly thumped out her every step. "Sorry to be late, everyone. I had a small situation to sort out in the hall." Mother Sinclair shot Colum a disapproving look as she lowered herself into a chair.

Colum straightened his shoulders and stood taller. He would be damned if he cowered over something as normal as charming a pretty maid. Hell's fire—he was a man. What the devil did the woman expect?

"I have a very important task for you, Colum Garrison." Granny straightened her tiny frame in the high-backed chair like a Fae queen holding court. Her eyes narrowed as she fixed him with a piercing glare over the tops of her wire-rimmed spectacles. "But you will have to change your ways."

"My ways?" Colum shifted in place but kept his hands clenched at the small of his back. Damned, if he didn't feel like a prisoner waiting for the king's choice of gallows or the axe. "And what *ways* might those be?"

"I believe you know exactly what *ways* I refer to." Mother Sinclair took a deep breath and glanced over at Lady Trulie. "You still agree, even considering the man's past behavior?"

What the hell did she mean by that? Colum stole a glance at Gray, but his fine Highland chieftain refused to look him in the eye. Verra well. He had battled alone before and won. Aye. But never against Mother Sinclair. Colum sucked in a deep breath and stuck out his chest.

"I think he will be just fine, Granny." Lady Trulie beamed at Colum as though he were a prized horse being selected for breeding with a favored mare. "Besides, you said you received the same vision I did."

Oh, holy hell. Colum stiffened. Both the Lady Trulie and Mother Sinclair had seen him in another of their damn visions? The last time he had appeared in one of their visions, they had seen him poisoned and left for dead.

"Very well." Mother Sinclair's mouth tightened into a flat, determined line. "In one week's time, another of my granddaughters"— she motioned toward Lady Trulie— "Trulie's middle sister closest to her in age will arrive."

Colum waited, all the while wondering from where or maybe from *when* the next Sinclair sister would come. He would speak to Gray later about the disloyalty of the man toward him. Hell's fire, he had fought at the man's side for years. Did that not account for anything? 'Twas damn shameful the way his own chieftain had allowed a pair of women to reign over him in such a way. If all they needed were additional guards to protect such an important visitor, why the blazes had Gray not given the order himself? "I shall see to it that additional guards are set in place. Have no fear for the lady's safety. I will personally see to it."

"That is exactly what we want," Granny said. Her tight-lipped frown softened into a sly smile. "We want you to *personally* see to Kenna."

Gray leaned against the fur-covered arm of the settee and scrubbed his hand across his mouth. With his gaze locked on the floor, his shoulders trembled as he coughed with a strange snorting.

Was the MacKenna laughing? Colum took a step closer and glared at him. "My chieftain?"

Gray straightened and let his hand drop. He sucked in a deep breath, then cleared his throat. "Aye, Colum. See to it the guards are doubled around the keep. But I do charge ye personally with the seeing after of Lady Kenna at all times. As soon as she arrives, she is yer responsibility. See that ye stay at her side, ye ken?"

Stay at her side? Colum smelled a very large rat. What the devil did these three play at? "Is there anything more I should know about the Lady Kenna?"

"Nay. Not a thing."

Colum studied Gray. The man's face grew ruddier by the minute. Instinct warned Colum to run like hell. He cleared his throat and edged closer to the door.

Granny strolled behind the couch and set a staying hand on Gray's shoulder as he leaned forward to speak again. "I am sure you will figure it all out when the time arrives," she said. "But know this . . . ." She pointed the crystal of her staff at the center of Colum's chest. "Trulie and I chose you for a reason. You would be wise not to disappoint us."

Disappoint them? When had he ever failed to protect a charge? When had he ever failed his chieftain? "I swear to ye, I will keep the Lady Kenna safe."

Again, Gray scrubbed a hand across his mouth and muttered something toward his lap. Colum peered closer. Wariness set off more inner alarms as he picked up on the unspoken byplay going on between Lady Trulie's pointed glare and his chieftain's apologetic shrug.

Colum swallowed hard and eased closer to the door. Had Gray just said it wasn't the Lady Kenna's safety that concerned him? Colum studied Gray closer. Aye and for sure, the man had said just that—he felt certain of it. Lore a'mighty, may the gods have mercy on his soul.

CHAPTER TWO

Kentucky
Twenty-first Century

The fire popped and crackled in the cast-iron stove, but Granny's voice came through the red-hot coals loud and clear. "It's time, Kenna—time for you to join us here in the thirteenth century."

Kenna balanced the bowl of popcorn on the arm of the couch and leaned toward the open grating of the stove. The handful of popcorn she had just shoved into her mouth at the exact moment of Granny's announcement threatened to strangle her. She coughed, swallowed hard, and thumped her fist against her chest.

"Come again, Granny?" She wheezed in a deep breath, then gulped down a sip of iced tea to wash away the popcorn caught in her throat. "You want all of us to come see you and Trulie? For a short visit—right?" She prayed Granny would say it was time for a *short visit*. She would love to see Granny and Trulie . . . for a *short visit*.

"No. Not all of you. Just you. And permanently. It's time you came back and seized your destiny." Granny paused. The only sound coming from the woodstove was the lively crackling of the fire. Granny's firm tone silenced the sound as she continued, "The twins will be staying in the twenty-first century for a bit longer."

Kenna unfolded from her cross-legged position on the couch. What if she didn't want to grab her destiny in thirteenth century Scotland? What if she liked it right here in twenty-first century Kentucky just fine? Yes, seeing Granny and Trulie would be wonderful, but there was just too much going on to leave right now. Life was finally starting to settle down and run smoothly. It was kind of nice living like *normal* people for a change—or as close to normal as a girl born to a long line of women able to jump back and forth across time ever got.

"The twins are graduating this month. Tell Trulie the terrible twosome turned into a pair of intelligent eighteen-year-old beauties," Kenna said, hoping that if she changed the subject Granny might back off. But that was another thing. Even though her baby sisters were eighteen years old, how could Granny suggest leaving them alone to fend for themselves? Granted, Mairi and Lilia were mature for their age, but they still weren't ready to get booted from the nest and fly solo.

Kenna scooted to the edge of the couch and propped her elbows on her knees. She had to buy them all some time. "Lilia's creating her own line of natural cosmetics for the shop. She already has every teenage girl in town clamoring for the lip gloss she developed."

The flames lengthened and danced faster across the chunks of wood. The coals fanned a hotter orange red as Granny's tone took on a decided edge. "Tell the girls I am very proud of them and it will be their time to join us soon. I'm sending an old friend to look after them, since you're coming to join us. Eliza will help them sort through whatever they might need until their time to come to us arrives. They have a bit longer to hone their skills in the twenty-first century before I call them back to the past."

Kenna glared at the fire, frantic to change Granny's mind. She wasn't ready to sacrifice indoor plumbing, internet, and take-out pizza to name a few. Why did she have to leave *now*? "But Granny, I need—"

"Enough, Kenna. You knew this time was coming, and you know better than to argue with me once I have made up my mind."

Kenna huffed out her frustration. Wasn't that the freaking truth? Arguing with Granny was a lot like arguing with the weather. Both did as they damn well pleased no matter what anyone said. But maybe she could at least bargain for a little reprieve.

"Just give me a month." Kenna held up a finger closer to the fire. She couldn't see Granny, so she wasn't certain if her elder had opened the fire portal enough to create a viewing window. With Granny, you never knew for sure. "Give me one solid month to get everything ready before I jump back." Surely Granny would grant her some time to get things settled . . . and maybe during that time, if she thought about it really hard, she could figure out an excuse Granny wouldn't be able to deny that would allow her to stay comfortably ensconced in modern times for a few more years—at least.

"One week."

"A week?" Kenna scooted off the couch and knelt in front of the woodstove. "I can't be ready to jump the web in just a week. That's impossible."

"Make it possible, Kenna. One week is all you get."

Gray-white ash crept up the chunks of glowing embers as the heat of the fire abated. Granny's voice took on a metallic, hollow sound, fading in and out as the connection through the portal weakened. "Don't waste your time pouting or plotting to stay in the future. You knew this day was coming. Accept your destiny and embrace it."

Kenna held her breath to keep from shouting *it isn't fair* into the dying flames. She couldn't do that. Granny deserved respect. No matter how much her elder irritated her, she couldn't defy the woman who had given up so much to ensure that her four grand-daughters not only survived their rough beginnings in the thirteenth century but thrived in whatever time Granny chose to place them. "Fine. I guess I'll see you and Trulie in a week." Fighting against the thundering frustration cutting off her air, Kenna stirred the coals one last time and forced out a strained "I love you, Granny."

"I love you too, gal." Granny's pleased chuckle fanned the coals a hotter orange for a brief instant. "You will thank me, gal. I promise. You will thank me."

Kenna slammed the cast-iron door to the stove shut and closed all the dampers. She very much doubted she would thank Granny when she was balancing on a chamber pot or washing in icy water dipped out of a loch. The thirteenth century. Dammit. Kenna shuddered, flopped back on the couch, and dropped her head into her hands.

Keys rattled in the front door right before it swung open and banged against the wall. Giggles and frantic shushing echoed down the hallway. Kenna straightened and glanced at the ancient mantel clock squatting in the center of the bookshelf. Lovely. The twins were home, and they were late. Again.

"Would it kill you two to be on time? Just once?" Kenna snatched up the bowl of popcorn and headed to the kitchen. She was in no mood to deal with bubbly sisters who were currently lucky enough to not have a freaking care in the world.

"We're not that late. It's only five after," Lilia said with a glance at the clock.

Both grinning girls—twins who looked nothing alike—plopped down on stools in front of the bar that separated the den from the kitchen.

"And sounds like you're in a real snit. Are you really that torqued over five measly minutes?" Mairi helped herself to the bowl of popcorn, then eyed Kenna with a look that irritated her even more.

Kenna clenched her teeth and tapped a finger against the countertop to a silent count of ten. She didn't need to take it out on them. It wasn't her sisters' fault that Granny had decided her visa to the twenty-first century had expired. She turned to Lilia. "Five minutes is five minutes. We agreed you would both be home by seven so we could go over next week's schedule at the shop—since, if you recall, we are introducing *your* new seasonal line of bath oils."

A flash of irrational sisterly irritation heated Kenna even further.

"And how many times have I asked you not to wear my tops? You stretch them out so much I can't wear them after you're done with them."

Petite but well-endowed Lilia glanced down at the snug T-shirt straining across her full breasts. "Oh. Sorry. I thought you said you didn't want this one anymore."

"What is going on with you?" Tall, willowy Mairi reached across the counter and gently patted Kenna's hand. "Spill it, Kenna. You never get like this unless someone has crossed you. What's rubbed your fur the wrong way?"

Kenna gripped the edge of the counter so tightly, her knuckles popped. How could she tell her baby sisters that their comfortable life was about to get put through the time-travel grinder again? Her heart sank even lower. How could she tell them she was about to leave them too?

"You've been talking to Granny, haven't you?"

Kenna nodded without lifting her gaze from the yellowed countertop. "Yes, Mairi. I spoke to Granny. The two of you just missed her." A heavy sigh escaped her as she sagged against the cabinet. "She sends her love and said to tell you both she is very proud of you."

"If that's what she said, then why do you look like you're about to throw up?" Mairi's eyes went wide and she suddenly sat ramrod straight. "Oh, no—is Trulie all right? Please say she didn't lose this baby too." Mairi hopped off the stool and rushed around the counter to Kenna's side.

"Not again." Lilia rounded the other end of the kitchen island.

Kenna waved them both a step back. "No. No. Nothing like that. Trulie is fine and due to deliver our little niece or nephew into the world any day now."

"Then what?" Lilia bumped Kenna with a curvaceous hip and grinned. "Did Granny tell you it was your turn to go back to the past and hook up with a sexy Highlander?"

Kenna didn't say a word, just turned and glared at Lilia. Baby sister already knew the truth of it, and she hadn't even needed any of her damn foretelling visions that happened to be her dominant talent as a Sinclair time runner.

"Holy shit, she did, didn't she?" Lilia's mouth dropped open.

"Holy shit," Mairi echoed.

Her sisters' profound statements pretty much summed up exactly how she felt about the situation. Kenna yanked open the overhead cabinet door, blindly patted her hand to the back of the shelf, and snaked out a bottle of brandy coated in a thick layer of dust. "Granny didn't exactly put it that way, but she might as well have. You know she's always had plans on seeing us settled, and not in this time. In Granny's mind, thirteenth-century Scotland is the only era fit to claim as home base." Kenna plunked the round-bellied bottle down onto the counter and nodded to Mairi. "Get some glasses. I need a drink, and you both will too after you hear Granny's plan."

"Wow. It really must be bad if you're going to let us drink too." Lilia circled back around and perched on the stool. "Especially Granny's brandy."

"Here." Mairi slid the glasses into a line beside the bottle. "But are you sure you really want a drink? You know alcohol always makes you feel awful no matter how little you drink."

Kenna nodded, pulled the stopper free of the bottle, and poured a generous splash of the dark-colored liquid into each of the glasses. They had gotten this bottle when they missed their targeted era on a practice jump and landed in fourteenth-century Italy. Granny had taken a liking to the sweet brandy and brought a bottle of it back when they returned home. What a jump that had been. They all loved Italy.

A strained rumble gurgled up from her queasy middle. "I already feel awful." And she did. The thought of jumping back to the past had her stomach churning. She often wondered if something was wrong with her. She was a time runner, for cripes' sake. A Sinclair. Born to a long generation of females able to skate back and forth across time whenever they pleased. Kenna downed the swallow of brandy and cringed against the burn. She was a time runner all right. Every time she jumped the web, she vomited everything but her socks. She swallowed hard against the nausea, already roiling with a sickly burn. Even thinking about jumping back in time was making her ready to throw up.

"So, when do we leave?" Lilia asked. She sniffed the contents of her glass, wrinkled her nose, and pushed it away. "That smells like cough syrup."

"*We* don't leave." Kenna licked her lips and refilled her glass with an even more generous splash of Italy's best. She stared down at the rich ruby liquid for a long moment, then forced out the words. "I am going. Alone."

Mairi intercepted the glass just as Kenna lifted it to her mouth. "No more. Not until you have shared what's going on. After that, you can drink all you want and sleep beside the toilet."

The idea of retching the night away stayed Kenna's hand. Mairi had a point: making matters worse by self-induced misery was not the solution. "Granny says it is time for me to jump back. By myself."

"She wants you to leave us? Here? In this century?" Mairi gathered up the three glasses and set them in the sink.

"I can't believe Granny would have you leave us." Lilia leaned forward, propping her chin on her fists. "What are we supposed to do without an *older adult* to make sure we don't do anything stupid? I know we're not considered minors anymore but until we turn twenty-one, we are still kind of limited when it comes to business dealings. Nobody wants to deal with a couple of kids. What if we need a loan or something to expand the shop? How are we supposed to support ourselves?"

Kenna shoved the ancient brandy bottle back to its place on the high shelf. So much for fueling herself with liquid courage. "She says she's sending a friend to look after the two of you until it's your turn to jump back. Someone named Eliza. Do either of you remember Granny ever mentioning her?"

"A friend named Eliza." Lilia sat straighter on the stool. Her dubious look said it all. Lilia didn't like this sudden upheaval any more than Kenna. "I don't remember Granny *ever* talking about some woman named Eliza."

"Is she a time runner too?" Mairi leaned against the counter beside Kenna. Her dark brows puckered with a worried look and she caught her bottom lip between her teeth. Mairi struggled when it came to meeting new people. All the Sinclair siblings had learned at a very young age that their survival depended on knowing whom they could and couldn't trust with their family's secrets.

"I don't know." Kenna closed her eyes and bowed her head. She suddenly felt a great deal older than her twenty-three years.

"How much time do we have left with you?" Lilia slid off the stool and scooped up the sweater she had tossed across the back of the couch. She hugged the fuzzy gray garment and stared down at the floor. "I don't want you to go. I'm tired of our family being split up across centuries. It was bad enough when Trulie and Granny jumped back."

Kenna's heart ached. She felt exactly the same way. "I don't want to go either." She rounded the counter and hugged an arm around Lilia's shoulders. "But Granny sacrificed so much for us. How can I refuse? I owe it to her to at least give whatever she's cooked up a chance. Look how happy Trulie is. Granny's grand plan worked out great for her." Kenna struggled to keep her tone upbeat and convincing. Quite a feat, since her spirits were currently sagging so low, they could wipe out her footprints.

"We will be fine." Mairi's voice cracked and she turned away.

Kenna blinked hard against the threat of tears as Mairi ripped a paper towel from the roll and dabbed at the corners of her eyes.

"You're right. We have to do this for Granny." Lilia brushed her fingers across her cheeks and sniffed.

Kenna blinked faster and swallowed hard against the unshed tears making her throat ache. When had her two little tomboy sisters grown into such mature young women? Kenna coughed and turned away. "Well . . . we have a week to get me ready to meet my sexy Highlander. So, we best stop all these tears and get busy."

Lilia's smile trembled. "So, I guess this means I get to keep this shirt?"

Kenna bit her lip and busied herself with gathering up the paperwork from the shop that was scattered across the kitchen countertop. She silently cursed the quiver in her voice as she jerked her chin down in a quick nod. "After we figure out a plan of attack for the shop, you and Mairi can go through my things and take whatever you like." They might as well. She sure as hell couldn't traipse around thirteenth-century Scotland in jeans and T-shirts.

GET your copy of MY HIGHLAND BRIDE and see how the story ends!

If you enjoyed this book, please consider leaving a review on the site where you purchased your copy, or a reader site such as Goodreads, or BookBub.

Sign up here to receive my newsletter:

Author Maeve Greyson Newsletter

Many thanks and may your life always be filled with good books!

Maeve

ALSO BY MAEVE GREYSON

HIGHLAND HEROES SERIES

The Guardian

The Warrior

The Judge

The Dreamer

The Bard

The Ghost

A Yuletide Yearning

Love's Charity

TIME TO LOVE A HIGHLANDER SERIES

Loving Her Highland Thief

Taming Her Highland Legend

Winning Her Highland Warrior

Capturing Her Highland Keeper

Saving Her Highland Traitor

Loving Her Lonely Highlander

Delighting Her Highland Devil

ONCE UPON A SCOT SERIES

A Scot of Her Own

A Scot to Have and to Hold

A Scot to Love and Protect

HIGHLAND PROTECTOR SERIES

Sadie's Highlander

Joanna's Highlander

Katie's Highlander

HIGHLAND HEARTS SERIES

My Highland Lover

My Highland Bride

My Tempting Highlander

My Seductive Highlander

THE MACKAY CLAN

Beyond A Highland Whisper

The Highlander's Fury

A Highlander In Her Past

OTHER BOOKS BY MAEVE GREYSON

Stone Guardian

Eternity's Mark

Guardian of Midnight Manor

ABOUT THE AUTHOR

maevegreyson.com

USA Today Bestselling Author. Two-time RONE Award Winner. Holt Medallion Finalist.

Maeve Greyson's mantra is this: No one has the power to shatter your dreams unless you give it to them.

She and her husband of over forty years traveled around the world while in the U.S. Air Force. Now they're settled in rural Kentucky where Maeve writes about her courageous Highlanders and the fearless women who tame them. When she's not plotting the perfect snare, she can be found herding cats, grandchildren, and her husband—not necessarily in that order.

Made in United States
North Haven, CT
01 March 2023

33344864R10174